BEYOND THE BLUFFS

Kimberly Atwood Balser

Thank you to Myrna D'Ambrosio for all the support and your editing expertise! I couldn't do this without you! Many thanks to the readers that have given me such positive feedback about this series. Writing this series has definitely been one of the most challenging tasks, but I have learned so much and enjoyed the journey along the way.

KAB

Prologue

The shrill sound of a child's scream pierced the air as Krista ran frantically down the dark hallway looking for her daughter. She checked her room where she'd put Mara to bed only a few hours ago, but the twin-sized bed was with the green and black comforter was untouched as if no one had lain in it. Not even a wrinkle, or an outline of a small child. "Mara! Are you hiding? Where are you?" Krista's heart began pounding as she waited to hear her daughter's voice, but there was nothing but silence.

Krista called out to her husband in a panic. "Chad! I can't find Mara!" but there was no answer. She went back to their room frantically searching for her husband. The bedspread appeared the same as Mara's bed; completely made with the decorative pillows pulled up, waiting for someone to sleep in it. It was as if everyone had just disappeared, and left her behind. She tiptoed down the winding staircase, toward the front door when it suddenly opened on its own, as if inviting her outside.

"Where are you?" Krista cried out, as she stepped cautiously outside, expecting gusts of wind that had blown the door open. Instead, there was silence, except for the calming sound of ocean waves in the distance. 'That's strange. We don't live near the ocean; why can I hear it?' she questioned. Maybe she'd imagined hearing the screams. Maybe she would go back inside and find Mara back in her bed. She was terrified as she scanned the lawn unable to see anyone except darkness. "Mommy, where are you?" She knew it was her daughter's voice!

1

"Mara! Tell me where you are!" She looked behind her to see the looming mansion with lights on in the windows that made them appear as if they were eyes watching her. "Where am I?" Krista said out loud. She was looking at an old ivy covered mansion, but Mara and her bedrooms were the same.

"Mommy! Help me!" She could hear her tiny voice clearly as she ran across the well-manicured landscape. As if on cue, the skies opened up and rain started pouring down out of nowhere. Mara's voice seemed to be all around her now. "Where are you, baby? I can't see you!" Krista was sobbing, as she reached the lawn's edge to a steep cliff. She was afraid to look down as the white-capped waves rose closer to the top of the cliff, threatening to sweep her away. There was a presence of someone behind her. Krista could almost feel their breath on her neck and began to run away from the cliff, toward a stone structure in hopes of hiding from whoever was chasing her. As she came closer, Krista ran directly into a gravestone, hitting her knee so hard that she fell down, gripping her leg in pain.

The wind and the huge raindrops falling drowned out any sound of footsteps, but she could feel them closer as though they resonated through the muddy slick grass. Managing to get up, she limped toward the moss-covered stones that turned out to be a cave. "Mara? Are you in there?" She yelled over the wind, as she proceeded into the dank dark hollow. Suddenly she could feel breathing on her neck and spun around. No one was there, but she could still feel their presence and ran back out without a sense of where she would go. But she knew being trapped inside the cavern wasn't safe either.

"Don't think you got away with anything, princess. She is mine, and soon you will realize just how much." A woman's voice whispered with malice intent. Krista recognized the voice; she'd heard it before, but where? Krista was frozen in fear, telling herself she was just dreaming. "I will wake up now! I'm waking up now! This isn't real!" Her bare feet were slipping in the mud as she struggled to keep her footing until she'd reached the cliff that left her nowhere to go except down.

"Or maybe it's what's coming to you, princess!" The voice hissed in her ear again. Krista turned around, just in time to look her aggressor in the eyes, as she felt a push on her back and she was suddenly flying in the air toward the churning waves. It was the face of Jane Ahearn. The woman who had tried to kill her before and now she was back! Krista screamed as she felt the water all around her, swallowing her into the depths. Just as she struggled to breathe, she felt someone grabbing her arms, shaking her.

"Krista! Wake up!" Chad's voice pulled her out of the depths of the churning water and back into reality. She opened her eyes, and saw that her husband was right next to her. "Breathe, Kris. Remember, you talked to Dr. Mayfield about this last month. You told me she gave you deep breathing exercises if you needed them. You need them now." He put his strong arms around her as she began to realize it had been a nightmare. She just nodded her head and took several deep breaths and tried to relax. At least she knew what to do now.

"Feeling better now?" Chad asked quietly. It was 3 am and he needed to get up at 5:30. Krista was finally able to calm down.

3

"I'm a little better. "Krista lied to her husband as she crawled out of bed still tired. It *was* helpful to have him near being supportive but he'd never really understand the terror. "Where're you going, Kris? It's 3:00 in the morning!" Chad tried to coax her back into bed.

"I just want to check on Mara. I'll be right back." Krista waited for him to say she was being ridiculous, but he let her go.

"Okay. She's fine, but I understand." Chad knew she'd never get back to sleep if she didn't check on their daughter. Krista quietly walked down the hall and poked her head into Mara's room. She was fast asleep, hugging her stuffed doggie with floppy ears that she'd had since she was born. Grateful that it had really just been a dream, Krista went back to bed. It was when she was sliding her legs under the covers that she felt a pain on her right knee. 'That's strange, maybe it hit my knee on something while I was moving around in my sleep.'

* * *

Krista remembered how far she'd come from almost 7 years ago, when she began having nightmares about a girl who was identical to her. She'd seen a psychic who'd informed her that she had a sister that she couldn't remember. Along the way, the receptionist at her school had been planting messages and creating drama in the hopes of making her look crazy. Jane Ahearn turned out to be the daughter of Stanley Ahearn, a well-known director in Hollywood, who had married her mother years after she disappeared from Krista's life. Her sister, Amanda, had also been in on the charade and had seduced her husband after being hired as a secretary at her father's realty office.

Yet some of the messages did come from her twin sister, Karen, who died when they were only 3-years-old. Krista had very little recollection about Karen. But when she decided to have a psychic reading done revealing that she had a sister, she became intrigued. Her father William finally revealed what had happened so long ago; that Karen had died in a car accident, and how her mother had left without a trace. Little did any of them know that the Ahearn girls knew that Krista was in their father's will and wanted to kill her in order to inherit the entire Ahearn fortune that he'd made as a successful Hollywood director. Luckily, William was able to convince the police and Stanley to come to their rescue just in time. But during the stand-off where Jane was pointing a shot-gun at Krista, the police had fatally shot Jane in order to save Krista.

It was a bittersweet moment when Krista finally met her mother face-to-face after an accident that landed her in the hospital. Although her mother eventually died from complications, Krista was able to talk with her about the past years, her sister and the love that her mother had for them all this time. After Karen's death, her mother was unable to cope and after an unsuccessful suicide attempt, had amnesia and was unable to recall anyone from her past.

It had been a traumatizing experience for everyone, but a few months later, there was a happy announcement that Krista and Chad were having a baby. It was completely unexpected, but they were financially ready, and there was some time to emotionally recover from all that had happened. It was when Krista wished her mother was there to give her advice during the pregnancy. Luckily, her Aunt Barb and grandmother, Sara Carson, had renewed a relationship with her, and her father, William. It was as if the family had finally come together to welcome a new baby. Chad had been ecstatic with the news and was very supportive to her with what turned out to be a difficult pregnancy for Krista. She'd spent several days in the hospital with hyperemesis gravidarum which was a medical term for excessive nausea and vomiting during pregnancy and given IV fluids along with a diet and anti-nausea medication to help combat the symptoms. Because Krista was a twin, the doctors checked several times to find out if she was having twins. But there was never any indication.

"Remember, Kris, there wasn't any indication that your mother was either." Her father reminded her many times. It had been in the back of their minds during her entire pregnancy. But unlike her mother, Krista's labor went smoothly and without any problems. She also didn't have any 'surprise' of twins; she had a healthy baby girl. She had Krista's blue eyes and wisps of blonde hair. "It's like seeing you as a baby all over again," William whispered. His eyes filled with happy tears, as he held his granddaughter shortly after she was born. It had been a moment that Krista would remember forever.

Chad and Krista had discussed names and decided to call her "Mara" to combine her mother's original name "Maria" and her grandmother and great-grandmother's 'Sara and Laura'. After the Burton family became three, life would never be the same, in more ways than just the usual adjustment to their new addition.

Mara was an easy infant to care for: she only cried when she was hungry or needed her diaper changed, and reached her crawling and walking milestones far ahead of most children her age. She was able to speak in sentences by the time she was a year old and Chad had been so proud, he went out and bought Mara a 'computer' that was meant for kids 5 and up. Krista laughed, "Are you expecting Harvard next month? She's a year old!" Chad just laughed as Mara started playing around with it soon after. Even her pediatrician, Dr. Williams, said that Mara was in the highest percentage for her age group.

Yet, Krista felt as though Mara wasn't connecting with her. She'd felt that way since Mara was born but she was afraid to admit this to anyone, including her husband. Mara didn't cry and hug her when it was time for her to leave for preschool at age 3; she'd simply said, 'bye, mama,' and walked away, which even the teacher found surprising. Krista had been in tears for the entire day, calling the teacher several times only for her to report that she was 'just fine.' Chad joked with her that she 'couldn't let go', but he knew that Mara seemed to seek out his attention more than Krista's. As much as he loved his daughter, he wanted to protect Krista from being hurt.

In Williams' eyes, Mara was perfect. After she was born, he took Tuesday and Thursday off every week to take care of her, while Chad began taking over more responsibilities at the office. William was cutting down his hours at Carson Realty now and planning to retire soon. William would spend hours playing with Mara, reading to her and taking her to the park, and Mara loved spending time with him. "Gam'pa!" She would say when she saw him. Krista couldn't help feel excluded when Mara seemed to prefer her husband or her father's company. When she talked to Chad about her feelings, he insisted that

7

she start seeing Dr. Mayfield, a psychiatrist who'd helped her recover after she'd been kidnapped.

"I don't need to see her every time I'm upset, Chad!" Krista had snapped at him. She felt as though Chad and her father had been using Dr. Mayfield as a way to 'shut her up' about anything. She'd placated them and seen her a few times. Dr. Mayfield had taught her some breathing exercises, which were helpful when she was anxious, but she couldn't take away what was in her head. Because the dream worried her. After all, the nightmares in the past were what initiated the truth about her sister and her family. She'd learned what really happened, and the secrets, because there were more than she'd ever thought possible. Krista never felt as though she could convey the lack of connection she had with Mara to anyone, but what she knew was that something was really wrong, and she had nothing to go on except instinct.

Krista

"Mara! Time to get up!" Krista was tired from lack of sleep, but when her alarm went off she was up and on autopilot with the usual Monday morning routine. Mara's blonde curls were sticking out of her green comforter decorated with swirls of black and yellow. Mara had never liked the color pink and made it known so they redecorated her very pink room as she transitioned from a toddler bed to a twin-sized bed.

"Momma, don't like pink! I like green and black!" Krista and Chad didn't think anything of it, as they redecorated the room according to her requested color scheme. Mara had her own ideas about everything. "She's such an individual," Chad kept saying. But Krista knew there was something more than individuality about Mara's behavior. She always showed Krista her worst, and then turned on the waterworks when her husband or father was around.

Mara groaned as Krista poked at the covers playfully. "C'mon sleepy-head! Time to get up for school!"

"Mommy, stop!" Mara said angrily as she pulled the covers back over her head. Krista reached down and pulled the comforter completely off of her. Krista barely had time to shower and pull herself together for work. She didn't even have time to wash her hair and hated the way it felt if it wasn't clean, settling for pulling her long blonde hair up in a clip. It wasn't the look she was going for this morning, but it would have to do. She'd found one of her favorite dresses that was fitted to

9

show off her slim figure, yet comfortable and a coral color that she hoped would brighten her mood.

"Mara, let's go sweetheart. You've got 30 minutes to get dressed and eat before you go to school." Krista tried not to sound as annoyed as she felt. "NO! I don't want to!" Mara yelled at her and tried to snatch the blanket out of Krista's hands. Krista wasn't in the mood for Mara's attitude and grabbed the blanket back. "You're going to school this morning! Let's go!" She tried to control her increasing aggravation, as she grabbed a pair of jeans and a t-shirt from Mara's dresser. Mara still refused to move. "Chad!" Krista called to her husband. He'd just gotten out of the shower and was getting dressed.

"What's up? I'm getting ready for work!" He sounded as irritated as she felt. She went from Mara's room to the hallway to talk to him privately. "I'm late! Mara won't get up and I need to get ready for work myself." This had been their usual routine every day since Mara had started first grade a few weeks ago, and it was getting old.

"Alright! Let me get dressed and I'll be right there! Why don't you just get a backbone, Kris? She's six years old, for Christ's sake! What are you going to do when she's a teenager?" Chad went back in the bedroom to get dressed as Krista followed him. "I suppose you think I have a choice? She doesn't listen to me! She only listens to you, because you give her what she wants!" Krista raised her voice, forgetting for a moment that Mara could hear her. "If you would back me up, maybe this wouldn't be happening!" She hated the sound of her voice as the words came out but lack of sleep was adding to her frustration.

"Back you up how exactly? She's just getting up for school." Chad asked as he got dressed quickly, and headed towards Mara's bedroom. Krista wasn't surprised to hear that she was up and was getting dressed as her father entered the room. "Hi daddy. I'm up and getting ready!" Mara greeted him with a smile, as she pulled a pair of black sneakers from the closet.

"Hi sweetheart! You look cute this morning!" Chad gave her a hug as she ran to him. He looked completely put together in his navy blue suit and matching tie. His dark hair was becoming streaked with some grey, but Krista told him it made him look even more handsome.

"What's this about giving your mother a hard time?" Mara glanced at Krista for a moment, as her expression changed quickly. "No, I didn't," she pouted. "Mommy was yelling at me," Mara insisted and hugged Chad. Krista shook her head, as Chad looked at her. 'Back me up,' Krista mouthed the words to him, hoping he wouldn't buy into Mara's crocodile tears in his usual fashion. Chad nodded as he withdrew from Mara's embrace. "Mara, you need to listen to mommy from now on." He told her as he kneeled down to get on her level. Mara nodded dutifully, with a smug smile that startled Krista.

It was then that Krista realized that seeing Dr. Mayfield might be a good idea. Was it just her anxiety about Mara's well-being or was it that she was scared of Mara? She was starting to realize that as time went by, she was realizing that she might be afraid of her own child.

Krista looked at the time. It was 8:15; she had an 8:30 meeting and was obviously going to be late. "Chad, you're going to have to drop Mara off, I'm already late." She grabbed her purse and keys, as Chad was saying something, but she was already out the door. As the director of counseling services at Johnston High School, it didn't look good for her to be late for a meeting! This had been the scenario for the past several weeks and it needed to change. She had just started driving to the school when her phone was already ringing. It was the principal, Edward Childers. She took some deep breaths as she hit answer on her Bluetooth. "Good morning, Edward!" She tried her best to mask her anxiety due to the stress of the morning and being late. Krista hated being late for anything, and she was usually early. That is, until Mara had started school. Now, she was late several times a week and knew that she was close to getting formally reprimanded.

"Where are you, Krista? We've been waiting on you for 15 minutes!!" Edward sounded annoyed, which was not his usual tone. She'd been a key part to this meeting about a discussion of how to implement more behavioral services at the school. "I'm so sorry I'm late. My daughter wasn't feeling well this morning so I had to rearrange daycare for her." She hated to lie about Mara and the real reason why she was late, but it was better than trying to explain the reality of her situation.

When she arrived 15 minutes later, Edward, the other counselors and several teachers were in a discussion of current policies. She knew her boss was more than irritated with her as she sat down and tried to collect her thoughts. "Hello, Krista, glad you could join us." Edward commented during a break in the discussion. Krista gave him a wry smile, "I apologize for being late. I'd like to discuss a plan for students that have behavioral needs that I've outlined here." She wasted no time handing out her outline and jumped into her proposal for students to utilize counseling services at school on an emergency basis as needed. After she finished her presentation, she could tell the other counselors and teacher were on board with her ideas, nodding their heads and giving positive comments. The principal agreed with her ideas, but she could tell by his icy stare that he wasn't happy. She braced herself for some repercussions, taking some deep breaths. It was right now that she understood why people took Xanax like aspirin these days.

As she returned to her office, Edward stood at the door with a frown on his face. "You know we need to talk about your ongoing tardiness."

Krista sighed. She'd always had a rocky relationship with her boss and she knew that her tardiness had been a pet-peeve with him. "I know. I'm really sorry. Mara had a rough morning and my husband-"

"I don't want to hear excuses anymore, Krista!" Edward cut her off, clearly really upset, referring to her so formally. Krista braced herself, half-expecting him to fire her.

"If you're late again like this, I'm sorry but I'm going to have to give you a written warning." Krista breathed a sigh of relief. Not that the threat of getting written up was good, but at least she had a chance to redeem herself.

"Like I said, it won't happen again, Edward." Krista replied, trying to keep herself from crying. She was exhausted from lack of sleep and now she was on the verge of losing her job.

"On a positive note, I like your ideas. They're very creative and I think they'll be helpful," Edward softened the blow. "Krista, you're very good at your job. Just try to be on time from now on." His tone was more sympathetic. Rather than try to explain her world at home, she agreed. "I will do that." As soon as he left, she rolled her eyes and tried to focus on her work. She was just working on budgets and productivity within the department when the phone interrupted her thought process. "Shit, now what?" She said out loud, then realized her door was open and quickly went to close it before she answered the phone. "Krista Burton." She made an effort to keep from sounding as irritated as she was.

"Mrs. Burton, this is Mrs. Palmers, principal from Thornton Elementary School. I'm calling about your daughter, Mara."

Krista's irritation turned to fear. "What's going on?" The nightmare from last night came to mind and she felt her anxiety kick in.

"Mara's just fine, Mrs. Burton. But I'm afraid one of the other students in class isn't. Mara and a few other children were on the playground during recess. One of the boys fell from the top of the jungle gym outside and has a serious concussion as a result." Mrs. Palmers began.

"I'm sorry to hear that, but what does that have to do with Mara?" Krista was confused.

"Because according to the other children that were outside, it wasn't an accident. Mara pushed him." Mrs. Palmers explained. Before Krista could ask any more questions, she continued. "One of the teachers outside also witnessed the incident. She said that the boy pushed ahead of Mara in line. Mara got upset and pushed him from behind before he could get situated to go down the slide. He ended up going off the edge and landed on his head."

Krista was horrified! Surely, there was a mistake! "Mrs. Palmers, I'm sure there's another explanation for this, but I understand that you needed to contact me."

"I need you to come and pick up Mara right away. Until we can get to the bottom of this, Mara won't be allowed back for the rest of this week." Mrs. Palmers was calm but firm in her decision. Krista was silent for a moment as she wracked her brain for a way to tell Mr. Samuels that she'd need to leave. Maybe Chad could or her father could help out. "Mrs. Burton, are you still there?"

"Yes, I'm sorry. Someone will be over to pick up Mara. I'll get in touch with my husband right away. My father is also on the list to pick her up, William Carson. Is that correct?" She needed to verify. She really couldn't leave work right now if at all possible.

"Yes, Mr. Carson and Mr. Burton are both on the pick -up list for Mara. Whoever picks her up can just go to the main office. She will be waiting in there." Mrs. Palmers informed her. "We can set up a meeting sometime this week with you and your husband to discuss the incident and what steps need to be taken if she's to continue attending this school."

Krista took a swig of her lukewarm coffee, wishing it were a shot of tequila right now. "I understand. Someone will pick her up shortly." Krista managed to say before she became choked up with tears of frustration.

"Thank you. I appreciate your cooperation with this." Mrs. Palmers replied curtly. Krista hung up, as she tried not to cry or scream. She wasn't sure which she wanted to do, probably both! She quickly called

Chad's cell, praying he'd pick up. When it went to voicemail, she hung up and dialed the office phone. 'He'd better pick up now!' Krista thought as the flashback of her husband's fling with his secretary who turned out to be her psychotic step-sister crossed her mind. Three rings. Krista was getting ready to slam down the phone when he finally picked up. "Chad Burton," he answered in his best professional-sounding voice.

"Chad, I just got a call from the school. They're claiming that Mara pushed some kid off the jungle gym and someone needs to pick her up from school right away!" Krista felt the lump in her throat give way to tears. "Before you ask, a teacher as well as students saw her. I'm not agreeing with them, but I'm in trouble for being late all the time for the past few weeks. Can you pick her up?" Krista pleaded, wishing that she had mental telepathy to let him know she was at the breaking point today. She could hear his annoyance as he sighed on the other end.

"Kris, honey, I can't! I've got a client in 10 minutes. There's no one else to cover this and it's a VIP client. Have you tried your dad?" It was always Chad's answer. As if her father didn't have his own life. He loved spending time with Mara, of course, but he'd recently started seeing a woman, Joanna, that he'd met after he joined a bowling league of all things. "I need to get out, Kris," William explained when she tried not to laugh. Krista was happy for him, especially after all the heartbreak they'd gone through in the past 6 years. "No, but I guess I need to." She sounded bitchier than she meant to, but it was too early and her tolerance for drama was minimal. Especially after Edward's warning about being written up!

"I'm sorry, honey. We'll figure it out. Call your dad first, okay?" Chad did sound sympathetic, but rushed. "Okay." Krista said and hung up without another word. There was no time and she was out of patience. She dialed her father's landline number, since he still rarely answered his cell phone. When his answering machine picked up, she groaned and slammed the phone down, then dialed his cell. "Hi, sweetheart, what's going on?" Her father answered. She could tell he was outside and could hear a woman's voice in the background.

"Dad, I'm sorry to bother you, but I need a favor. Mara's being suspended from school as of now and I can't get away to pick her up. Would you be able to pick her up and keep her until Chad or I get out of work later?" Krista crossed her fingers. The only other option would be her grandmother Sara, who in her opinion, shouldn't really be driving because she was starting to lose her memory.

"Of course I can, Kris, but suspended? What? She's in first grade!" William sounded just as shocked as she did a few minutes ago.

"I know, dad. I'll explain later, but they're expecting someone to pick her up sooner rather than later. Thank you so much for understanding. Both of us are tied up at work, so one of us will come pick her up from your house." Krista felt relieved as she called Chad back to let him know.

"Thank god! Okay, I'll pick her up after this client, Kris." Chad promised. "We'll talk more when we're home. In the meantime, just

17

try to relax. I know Mara has been a handful lately, but we'll figure it out." Chad tried to reassure her.

"Thanks. I've gotta go. I'm seconds from getting written up if I'm ever late, or even move the wrong way around here!" Krista told him. She called Mrs. Palmers back to tell her that William would be picking Mara up. "So I need to ask, is Mara going to be allowed to come back this week?" Krista needed to know now, since it was only Tuesday.

"I'll speak with the superintendent today. She definitely won't be able to attend tomorrow and likely Thursday as well. I'll be in touch with you later today to discuss a time for you and your husband to meet with us with a plan by the end of the week." Mrs. Palmers told her. Basically, she was saying her daughter wouldn't be allowed to attend the rest of the week. Krista bit back the urge to ask her what they were supposed to do the rest of the week as it would fall on deaf ears. "I'm sorry about this. We will be talking to Mara about what happened." She told the principal.

Krista realized after she hung up that she'd never once defended Mara's actions or questioned the principal's description of what happened. She knew that Chad would have reacted differently, because he never saw the Mara that she knew. She was struggling with her instincts; that something wasn't right with Mara, and she wasn't sure there was anything they could do to change that.

Chad

Chad tried not to let his wife's call about Mara interfere with his meeting with new prospective clients that were friends of Stanley Ahearn. Stanley's clout as a director in Hollywood helped make Carson Realty a success after making a deal with William because of an accident that had led to the death of Krista's twin sister when they were three years old. He had also been married to Krista's mother after Stanley had funded Williams' agency in return for his silence about the fact that Stanley had been drinking and caused the accident.

The history between William and Stanley was tumultuous. Yet after the passing of Krista's mother, and the attempted murder of himself and Krista, William and Stanley had a mutual respect for one another. So when Chad was given the heads up about one of Stanley's acquaintances from Hollywood that were looking to buy property in the Middletown/Newport area, he knew to pull out the best properties with their preferences.

Patrick Sampson was a young 30-something with recent success as an actor and was looking for a get-away from the Hollywood drama when he wasn't filming. Chad had been expecting Patrick to be demanding and eccentric, but he was actually very down –to- earth and didn't once mention anything about his career. His wife, Rachel was with him and she was just as casual. She did comment that she 'wasn't in the business' and preferred to stay out of the spotlight.

The property he found for them in Wickford turned out to be a success. It was the perfect location for them; close to Newport and

Narragansett, but a small community that would give them the privacy that they wanted. After giving them a tour of the three-bedroom raised ranch that had a covered boathouse as well as a dock and pier with a ladder, they gave an offer that was close to the asking price. They left the offer open and were staying in a nearby hotel for a week or so in order to be available to negotiate. He called William to let him know what was going on.

"Great job, Chad! I knew I was leaving these clients in good hands." William sounded happy with him, as he'd started taking steps towards retirement. William still came in a few times a week and took on a few clients, but he was preparing Chad to take over. William had some health issues recently including high blood pressure and an irregular heart rhythm which led him to his decision to cut back on his hours. He'd shared some of his medical issues with Chad and asked him not to worry Krista after he had starting to put Chad in charge about 6 months ago.

"Thank you so much for picking up Mara from school, Bill. I'm about finished up and I can come by in about half an hour." "I'm not sure what happened at school, Kris gave me the short version, but I can't believe that Mara would deliberately push someone to hurt them."

"She's been fine. She didn't say a word about the incident. I picked her up and she's teaching old grandpa how to play her crossword puzzles on-line." William laughed. Chad could hear Mara in the background. "Is that daddy?"

"It's your daddy. Do you want to talk to him?" Chad could hear William ask. "Daddy!" Mara sounded excited and immediately got on the phone. "Hi, daddy!" Mara greeted him. Chad resisted the urge to mention the incident that sent her home from school, but he wasn't going to reprimand her on the phone. "Hi, sweetheart. Are you being a good girl for grandpa?"

"Yes, I'm showing him how to play crossword puzzles on the computer. Grandpa needed a teacher." Mara giggled.

"Mara, what happened today at school?" Chad couldn't help himself. He wanted something to go on to prove this was completely blown out of proportion before Kris got home with her concerns about their daughter's behaviors.

"Nothing, daddy. This mean boy pushed me out of the way when I was in line at the slide, so I pushed him back." She said calmly. "He was mean, daddy. He pushed me first." Her voice was so innocent and yet she admitted to pushing him. Chad was stunned for a moment. He cleared his throat, "Okay, I'll see you soon. Can you put grandpa back on the phone?" His hands were shaking as he gripped his cell phone and was heading towards his car. "Hey, Chad, we're fine." William acknowledged.

"Great, Bill, I'll see you soon." Chad hung up, his hands still shaking as he tried to rationalize what his 6-year-old daughter had just told him. 'Maybe she didn't realize what happened to him,' he thought as he drove towards William's. He braced himself for his wife's reaction when she got home. He hoped that this was only a misunderstanding on the school's part. Kris would often say that Mara would misbehave around her and when he was in the room, she was fine.

Chad pulled into William's driveway 15 minutes later to find Mara and William sitting at his computer in a crossword puzzle game. "Daddy!" Mara ran to him as soon as he came in the door, her blond curls and blue eyes so like her mother's always melted his heart.

"Hi, sweetheart!" Chad swept her up in a hug, and set her down. "William, thanks again for picking her up. I think the Sampson's are going to buy that property. They're staying in town, so I think that's a good sign!" He greeted his father-in-law. After his affair with his former secretary almost 7 years ago, he'd gone out of his way to make things right with Krista and William. Kris was more forgiving, especially because of the deception and ulterior motives with the affair, but William had been tough on him through those years. It was only after Mara was born that he really began to trust Chad again.

"That's great news! Mara's teaching old grandpa here a thing or two about on-line games." William tousled Mara's curls as they headed into the kitchen. "Mara, can you let grandpa and I talk while you finish the game?" Chad wanted Williams' thoughts and any advice about her getting kicked out of school today.

"Daddy….." Mara started to whine, but Chad was quick to reprimand her this time. He remembered what Krista had been drilling into his head now for months 'back me up.' "Mara, go finish the game, I need to talk to grandpa for a few minutes," Chad was firm with his daughter. Her face changed from a smile to a pout in seconds, as she sulked but returned to the living room.

"So what happened when you picked her up, Bill?" Chad got right to the point. He knew that Mara was probably listening in and kept his voice down. She was exceptionally smart for her age and knew that despite his warm reception, she was going to have consequences.

"Mara was in the front office, sitting at a small desk across from the receptionist. She saw me and ran to me as the principal came out of her office and I told her I was here to pick up my granddaughter. She just asked that you or Kris call later to talk further about the incident. Really, there wasn't any discussion. When I asked Mara about it, she said that a little boy had cut in front of her and made her upset. She told me that 'it was no fair' and to get back in line. He turned around and stuck his tongue out at her, then fell off the slide. I can't understand how they can get away with suspending a first-grader, Chad. Maybe you should think about a private school for Mara," William suggested, obviously frustrated with Mara's school.

It was something he and Krista had never talked about, but it sounded worth considering. "She told me something that was completely different on the phone, Bill. She told me that he pushed her and so she pushed him back. She told me 'he was mean to me'," Chad still felt the chill of the words as he said them. It wasn't necessarily the words, but the way she said them.

"Chad, she's six-years old! If she did push him, it doesn't mean it caused him to fall off the slide. She could have just pushed him out of her way. It was just an accident. These schools lately; they're so quick to place blame on other kids! I remember when I was kid, even if someone was actually being a bully and you got hurt, and we moved on!" William shook his head, as if he was reliving his old school days.

Chad nodded in agreement. He could remember many days when other kids gave him a hard time and he'd just dealt with it.

"I know that Krista's going to be upset about this, needing to meet with the principal before she can go back to school. You're right about a private school, Bill. It's a good idea that I'm going to look into and mention to Kris." Chad felt better after talking to William about other options. He'd never been crazy about the public schools, especially since there seemed to be less concern about the education and overreacting when it came to simple accidents.

Krista

After a grueling day at work, Krista was finally leaving at 5:30. She'd stayed late to work on some projects that Mr. Samuels wanted finished by the end of the week. She was tired as hell, but knew that she was lucky to get by with a verbal warning today. Chad had texted her that he had picked Mara up and they were home. Krista tried to ignore the negative thoughts that she felt about her daughter's behaviors. It didn't help that Chad would always defend Mara. She tried to plan out how she was going to approach this school incident with her husband. Mara needed consequences, and although her husband agreed with her, he never followed through.

She was greeted by the smell of pizza as she walked through the door. "Smells like someone decided to order pizza instead of making dinner!" Krista walked in the spacious kitchen. They'd updated it right before Mara was born and she had to admit, it made cooking a much more pleasant experience. The custom granite countertops and open cabinet concept, along with the pale yellow paint made the kitchen a cheery place for making meals and often eating at the breakfast nook that Krista had insisted on. Mara and Chad were both working on their slices of pepperoni pizza from This Guy's Pizza at the kitchen island seated on the high pub-style stools. Mara looked adorable with her legs swinging, unable to reach the bottom rung on the chair.

"Hi, sweetheart, how was your day?" Chad got up and gave her a quick hug and kiss on the cheek. Krista groaned. "I'll tell you later.

Let's just say that I can't be late again when I've got an important meeting."

"I know, Kris, we'll talk later. Your dad actually had an idea that might work." Chad told her, as Mara ran up to Krista and gave her a hug. "Hi, mommy!" Krista hugged her back, knowing that her daughter was trying to give her extra attention in the hopes that she wouldn't be punished. Mara rarely showed much affection toward her mother, and when she did, it was usually because she had misbehaved.

"Mara, please go finish your dinner." Krista instructed her.

"I'm full, mommy. I wanna go play Paw Puppies games." Mara was using her best 'good girl' voice that she used to get her way. Paw Puppies was her favorite video game that she was normally allowed to play for an hour after dinner.

"No, Mara. You won't be playing any games tonight. I want you to go upstairs and get ready to take a bath. I'll be up in a minute to help." Krista told her firmly. Mara began whining and throwing a tantrum, as Krista looked to Chad to intervene. "Um, Chad, do you want to help out with this?" Krista's already frazzled nerves were at their breaking point and Chad noticed.

"Mara, you heard your mother! Get upstairs!" Chad said in a firm voice.

"But, daddy…." Mara protested.

"Get upstairs, now!" Chad insisted, his voice getting louder. Mara knew that he meant business and as if on cue, crocodile tears streamed down her face as she slowly walked up the stairs. Krista rolled her eyes at her daughter's drama routine. She could tell that her husband was

26

almost ready to go up the stairs after her to give her a hug. "Don't do it, Chad!" She warned him.

"Do what?" Chad asked, but he knew and nodded. "I'm a sucker when it comes to my crying daughter," he admitted. He went to the counter and pointed to the pizza. "Want it heated up?" He asked her.

"You know I do. Thanks. But put it in the oven. I hate the microwave; it makes the crust turn into a rock!" Krista advised. He was one step ahead of her and had set the oven to preheat, set two of the slices on a sheet pan and slid it into the oven. He came over to give her a hug and kiss. "I'm sorry you had a hard day, Kris."

Krista sighed. Hard was an understatement. Not only was she close to being written up, they needed to figure out where Mara would go the rest of the week since she wasn't allowed back at school for at least the next two days. She returned his affections, but knew they needed to talk about Mara now.

"I'm sorry too. Especially since Mara isn't allowed back in school for at least the next two days until we 'have a meeting' with Mrs. Palmers. I'm sure she'll schedule it when it's most inconvenient for us." Krista was being sarcastic. She was feeling extremely bitchy and she wasn't fond of Mrs. Palmers. She thought of her as dramatic and reacted to everything in order to get out of disciplining students. She would rather just send them home. Out of sight, and not her problem.

"Great. Now what? I've got back to back clients tomorrow. I'm assuming after today, Mr. Samuels isn't going to let you take time off." Chad agreed. It was a situation that needed a solution soon. He decided to introduce Williams' suggestion about a private school.

27

"Your father suggested sending Mara to a private school this afternoon." He looked to see his wife's expression as he tossed out the idea.

Krista immediately jerked her head around to look at him as she was pouring herself a glass of wine. "Are you kidding me? Do you have any idea how expensive those schools are, despite the fact that I don't agree with the religious component of those schools." Krista scoffed at the idea. "I know my dad means well, but he's been a little more than preoccupied with Joanna. Does he have any idea how much a private school costs?" Krista was more upset now that this idea was put up for grabs.

"Ok, ok, I get it. You're right, they *are* expensive. But we need to have some kind of plan." Chad agreed. Krista nodded. He was right. She knew that this wouldn't be the last time Mara was in trouble. It was probably the beginning of it. Krista sighed as she took a few gulps of her wine. "I know we do. Maybe it wouldn't hurt to have her see a therapist." She threw the idea out there. It was sure less expensive than a private school.

"That's actually a good idea," Chad nodded in agreement. "Do you know anyone that works with children?"

"No, but I could ask Dr. Mayfield. Maybe she has a recommendation." Krista was already pulling up Dr. Mayfield's contact number and called her. It was after hours so she left her a message to call her back in the morning. "She's good about getting back to me. Maybe in the meantime, I can let Mrs. Palmers know what our plan is going forward. Hopefully, they'll let her back into that school this week." Krista said hopefully. "In the meantime, what are we going to do with her being out? I hate to ask my dad, but I'm not sure we have any other options right now."

"I think that's our *only* option right now." Chad agreed. Krista made a call to her father, who picked up right away. "Hi sweetheart. How's Mara?" He sounded as though he were in a good mood. His new relationship with Joanna had really helped him transition into retirement and seemed happier.

"She's fine, except that she can't return to school for a few days. I was calling to see if you would be willing to watch her until the end of the week. Our plan is to try and get her in to see a child therapist. I have a call in to Dr. Mayfield for suggestions." Krista explained, hoping he wouldn't launch into his private school idea that he'd shared with Chad.

"Well, I was telling Chad that maybe she needs to be in a private school. Maybe she's not getting enough attention, or that she's bored. She's exceptionally bright, Kris." Krista rolled her eyes, at her father's suggestion and remembered to not fly off the handle and tell him absolutely not!

"I *know* she is, dad. She's bright enough to know that she shouldn't be pushing kids down the slide!" Krista couldn't help it. "I'm not sure how you think her going to a private school is going to change her behavior. Besides, it's really expensive; more expensive than fits in our budget." She added, because it really wasn't realistic for them. Chad was making a good commission when he made a sale and she made an adequate salary. But they both liked to put away enough in savings for Mara's college as well as their retirement.

"I could help with that, Kris. There's nothing I want more than to help out with my granddaughter's education." William offered, as Krista knew he would. His devotion to Mara was unconditional from the day she was born. He was the first one to defend her behavior, which was why Krista would have preferred someone else to take care of her the next few days, but it was too short notice.

"I know, dad. I appreciate that. For right now, I'm going to try the therapist route with Mara. So back to my original question; could you watch her for at least the next few days while we get this sorted out with the school?" Krista asked.

"Oh, of course I will." William sounded happy about it. "Joanna had fun with her today. It'll be great to have her around to keep us old folks on our toes!" He joked.

"Thanks dad. I really appreciate it, it's a huge help!" Krista was relieved. She knew that she'd have to try and rein her father in as far as letting Mara get her way, but at least they had a plan. "Either Chad or I will drop her off tomorrow around 8am, okay?" The wine was suddenly making her sleepy and she was ready to wrap up this call, eat dinner and get ready for bed.

"No problem. See you in the morning, sweetheart." William said and hung up. Krista sighed with relief as she put the phone down. "Ok, we're all set. I'm exhausted, and I'm starving. Is my pizza done yet?"

"Right here, just pulling it out," Chad told her as he pulled the hot sheet pan out with the pizza slices. He put them on a plate for her and she grabbed what was left of her wine and sat down to eat. Pizza never tasted so good especially since she hadn't eaten a thing all day.

"Thanks honey. Would you mind checking on Mara? She needs to get ready for bed soon, so maybe you could get her started on that." Krista asked him. She hadn't heard water running yet, which meant that Mara had no intention of taking a bath on her own.

"No problem. Eat and relax." Chad advised as he went over to give her a kiss and then headed upstairs to deal with Mara. "She needs a bath and don't forget to have her brush her teeth!" Krista called to his disappearing figure as he walked upstairs. She waited for the inevitable argument that would soon take place, but she was hoping that her husband was also growing tired of the nightly games. She ate her pizza in silence, remembering how close she and Chad had come to ending their marriage seven years ago, thanks to Stanley Ahearn's horrible daughters; especially Jane. Jane had no mercy. Krista hated to admit it, but she was glad that Jane's death meant that she no longer needed to look over her shoulder. But that dream last night, hearing her voice had lingered. 'She's gone,' Krista had to remind herself, as she had done in the past.

Krista's quiet dinner was interrupted with Mara yelling that she didn't want to take a bath. Mara hated baths and Krista made a note to herself of what to tell whomever Dr. Mayfield referred her to about this problem. She sighed and polished off the last sip of wine left in the glass.

"I'm coming up there, so I'd better start hearing water running by the time I get to the bathroom!" She announced loudly as she made her way up the stairs. As she entered the bathroom, Mara was sitting in the tub, screaming that she didn't need a bath. Chad was trying to keep his cool and Krista had to give him credit for making sure she actually stayed in the tub instead of taking off to her room. He gave her a look of gratitude. "She's taking a bath, Kris." He threw up his hands. Krista gritted her teeth and forced herself to deal with this nightly ritual again. She managed to get Mara washed up, rinsed off and toweled off while Chad got her pajamas ready. A half-hour later, Mara was finally ready for bed. Chad gave her a hug and kiss, then left to go watch his baseball game on TV.

Krista was finally ready to talk to Mara about today. She sat down next to Mara's head of tousled blond curls. "Mara, I know you've said that you didn't push anyone today, but I want you to promise me that no matter what, you need to wait your turn." Krista attempted to get an idea of what happened.

"Mommy, he was mean to me. I don't like people that are mean, he stuck his tongue out at me." Mara began telling her side.

"No matter what, Mara, it's not okay to do something that might hurt someone else. You need to tell the teacher and they can talk to that person, okay?" Krista hoped that some of what she was saying was getting through.

"Okay, mommy, I'll try. But I don't like a lot of the kids at school." Mara's response startled Krista.

"Well, you won't be going back tomorrow. For at least a few days, you'll be going to Grandpa Carson's house." Krista began and she could see her daughter's eyes light up. "But, you'll still need to do schoolwork and follow rules. If I hear that you aren't, you won't be getting back your video games for the rest of the week." She finished her sentence. Mara was quiet for a moment. "Okay mommy. I'll try to be good." She nestled her head under Krista's arm and it was impossible for her to be upset with her daughter any longer. "Alright, sweetheart. Get some sleep. I love you." Krista kissed her on the forehead and pulled her covers up.

"Love you too, mommy." Mara's high-pitched little girl voice always clutched at her maternal instincts to hold and nurture, no matter how bad the day had been. Krista turned the light off and as she was beginning to shut the door, she heard a quiet whisper 'see you soon princess'. She whirled around to ask Mara about what she'd just heard, but Mara's eyes were closed, and she appeared to be falling asleep.

'No more wine tonight,' she thought to herself, remembering the dream from last night. She was hoping for a sound sleep tonight.

William

It had been so long since he'd ever considered meeting another woman. Maria, (also known as Caroline) coming back into his life after decades of being gone seven years ago was hard enough. But finding out that she had been married to Stanley Ahearn, the famous Hollywood extraordinaire, it broke his heart all over again. Somehow, her death shortly after finding her had actually been easier than her missing without a word in decades. There was finality, a closure to her life and he was grateful that he'd gotten to at least talk to her once again before she was gone forever. After all, the second time around, she went by 'Caroline' and he knew that if she'd lived, she probably would've continued on with her marriage to Stanley.

He'd met Joanna Larsen after joining a bowling league about a year ago. Bowling hadn't been of huge interest to him, but a few clients that he'd met talked about it and invited him. William was always up for keeping his new clients happy and decided to join the team they were on, just to get out of the house. After Maria's death, he was more isolative than ever with the exception of going to work, so he agreed to go. He'd felt out of place there and was sitting by himself when a lovely blonde woman with striking blue eyes sat down next to him. "God, I hate bowling. I'm not sure why I'm here!" She commented. "The shoes are ugly and they smell!" She wrinkled her nose up, while pointing at the rented blue and red shoes.

William laughed. He loved her sense of humor. "Really? I was just thinking the same thing!" They struck up a conversation and discovered they had more in common than their dislike for bowling. She had just turned 59 and had been widowed about 2 years ago after her husband of 25 years had died of pancreatic cancer. She had a daughter and a son that were 28 and 25. Her son still lived in Rhode Island, but her daughter moved to North Carolina after she got married a few years ago. She had one granddaughter that was 5 years old that she often took care of several times a week. They talked until the bowling was over and people were leaving. "I guess we should go", William looked around and chuckled. "We seem to be the only ones left!"

Joanna laughed, "I guess so! My daughter told me I needed to get out more, so I went out with some people from work." Joanna was a nurse manager at Kent Hospital on the Med/Surgical floor. "I still don't like bowling. Do you?" Her spunk and attitude was endearing and William knew he wanted to see her again.

"Uh no, not really! But, I am glad I came tonight. I've really enjoyed getting to know you." William hadn't been this relaxed in the company of a woman since Maria. "I've had a good time Bill," Joanna said as she pulled her cell phone out of her purse. "I'd love to meet up with you sometime if you want to give me your number."

William was glad that she offered her number. His knowledge of the current dating 'rules' was zilch, so the fact that Joanna took the initiative was a green light for him. He pulled out his phone and typed in her number. He was glad that Krista had schooled him on how to add contacts to his phone. William agreed to call her later on in the week, which turned out to be the following day. As the time went by,

William found himself finally letting go of the past and open to letting Joanna in.

Now, they were inseparable. William had introduced his family to her. It bothered him that she seemed guarded about him meeting her children and grandchildren, but she explained that her son had some difficulties and her daughter lived out of state so she didn't see her very often. "Let's just enjoy each other's company." Joanna said when he asked to meet them. He'd agreed, although it made him wonder if she was hiding something.

Despite the small apprehension about her family, William knew he was in love with her after a few months and they'd discussed moving in together, but Joanna wasn't quite ready. "I love you, Bill, but I still need some time." William understood and knew it would be an adjustment for him as well. Joanna stayed overnight several times a week, but that was far different than actually moving in together. Neither one of them were ready for that level of commitment.

William had started cutting his hours at Carson Realty in the past two years. Chad had proved himself a worthy candidate to take over and he was glad that he had more time to spend with Mara and Joanna. When Krista called to ask him to pick Mara up from school, he'd been more than happy to do so. Seeing Mara grow from an infant to toddler to a first-grader was like watching Krista grow up all over again and he loved the time he spent with her. He still didn't understand why the school would suspend a 6-year-old. According to Mara, the boy had been mean to her so she was just holding her own. It was probably what Krista would have done at Mara's age.

Joanna and Mara seemed to get along really well, so he was surprised when Joanna came to him later after Mara left. "Bill, I just wanted to talk to you about Mara. We were playing a board game earlier and I was winning. Out of nowhere, she started getting upset and when I tried to talk to her, she said 'stop talking to me! You're not my real grandma! I do what I want!' I tried to talk to her about winning and losing; how it's part of life, but she refused to listen and then got upset, and dumped the game pieces off the board and stomped off." Joanna looked upset as she was telling him.

"Really? I've played many games with her and she's never behaved that way with me." William was shocked. Joanna nodded. "I've played before too, and she's never acted this way." Joanna seemed irritated with her more than upset. It was something that he didn't expect from this woman he'd known for a year. But he told himself that Joanna just wanted her to accept her.

"Maybe it was just because of what happened at school today. I'm sure it's fine, Jo." William reassured her. "She's told me how much she likes you." Joanna seemed relieved at that and he was glad. He loved both his granddaughter and his girlfriend. The last thing he wanted was to have to choose between them.

"I hope so." Joanna told him, yet he could tell that she had doubts. He gave her a hug before she left to go back to her condo in Warwick and babysit her granddaughter that evening. "I'm sure its fine. I'll see you tomorrow." Joanna had seemed relaxed when she left. He'd suggested private school to Chad as an idea, although he knew Krista would need some prodding about it. Krista didn't agree with the

Catholic influence of private schooling and it was expensive. The expense wasn't the problem; William was planning to pay for it himself, if his daughter would agree to try it.

Just as he had poured his nightly whiskey and ginger ale, Krista called to ask him to take care of Mara for the next few days. He agreed, glad to spend more time and perhaps, work on the private school idea. He hoped that Joanna and Mara would get along better than today.

Chad

It had been a long day and Chad was glad that his wife was finally able to relax. Work had been exhausting for him and Mara's school suspension added to the stress. Sometimes, he believed that Krista didn't realize that. He had known since Mara was a newborn that there was something off with her and Krista's connection and how it made Krista feel as though she wasn't a good mother. Krista had been an excellent mother since the day Mara was born, yet it became obvious to him, even before she had admitted to it, that something was off. Krista had been through so much the year before, with Stanley's daughter's scheming and using the death of her twin sister as a weapon, eventually holding her captive. Luckily, she'd been able to meet her mother before her unfortunate death. His insistence on seeing her psychiatrist, Dr. Mayfield initially made her resentful of him, but after a few months of taking prescribed anti-depressants, she agreed that it had been good for her.

She'd taken a break from Dr. Mayfield for a couple of months now and Chad noticed a difference. She seemed more on edge. He wasn't sure if Krista was taking her medication and he didn't want to ask. Between her nightmare last night and Mara's incident at school today, he felt as though he were tiptoeing through a minefield. He was glad that she'd contacted Dr. Mayfield about Mara, because hopefully, she would also schedule an appointment for herself.

Chad's thoughts drifted back to his new client, Patrick Sampson and how to reel him into the property. He really wanted to show his father-in-law that he was up to the task of taking over Carson Realty. Krista came down the stairs, as he was brushing up on his on-line research of Patrick and his lifestyle, just to hone in on his likes and dislikes in terms of types of homes that he'd lived in before.

"Chad, are you coming to bed soon?" Krista called down to him, which jerked him out of work-mode. He looked at the clock; it was only 9:30 and the baseball game that was on went into overtime. He knew that his wife was upset about her needed interaction with Mara's bath, so he gulped down the rest of his bottle of Sam Adams beer. "I'll be right up." He'd been thinking too much about work to really pay attention to the game anyway, as he turned the TV off and headed upstairs. He stopped outside Mara's bedroom door to listen for a moment, and heard whispering. He opened the door quietly, thinking that maybe he was just hearing the TV from the master bedroom as Krista sometimes watched a show while she was falling asleep.

Mara was sitting halfway up in bed, her nightlight near her bed illuminating her face. She was whispering out loud to herself. "Mommy doesn't know, she doesn't know." Her eyes were fixed on her rocking chair across from her bed. Chad crept closer to her bed. "Mara, who are you talking to sweetheart?"

She looked startled. "Daddy, you scared me! I'm just talking to my friend." She averted her eyes from the rocking chair as Chad sat down on her bed. "What's your friend's name?" He was feeling a little uneasy after everything Krista had been through with her sister. "I don't see your friend here," Chad observed.

"Oh, you can't see her. I'm the only one that can see her." Mara told him. Chad smiled and nodded, 'an imaginary friend. She's creative at least,' he thought to himself. "Does your friend have a name?"

"Her name is Jamie. She lives on an island." Mara didn't seem to mind talking about her 'friend.' Chad smiled. "That must be nice! Is it nice and warm on the island?"

"It's nice in the summer. Winter is cold. Jamie doesn't like it there in the winter." Mara was frowning as if it was upsetting to her as well.

"Well, maybe Jamie should go to a different island," Chad played along, intrigued with her creativity.

"She can't." Mara told him. "She's stuck on this one right now." Her facial expression changed from a frown to anger. "She's not happy." She said in an annoyed voice.

Chad suddenly felt uneasy. Mara had never mentioned an 'imaginary friend' in the past and there was something eerie about her mannerisms and her speech. As if she were reciting a script that someone had given her. "I'm sorry she's not happy. But it's time for you to go to sleep now, Mara." Chad told his daughter. He bent down to give her a hug and kiss. She hugged him back and laid down, pulling the covers up to her chin. "Night, daddy."

"Good night, sweetheart. See you in the morning." Chad glanced back at her as he shut the door quietly. He quietly waited outside the door for a few seconds to listen. Just as he began to walk away, he heard Mara's voice again and moved closer. He could hear her talking, but couldn't make out what she was saying. He chuckled to himself about his daughter's 'imaginary friend' as he went down the hall to bed where Krista was already sound asleep. He had been hoping she'd be still awake to talk to her about Mara. He turned the TV off from the reruns of Three's Company that Krista had been watching and went to bed. As he was drifting off, he thought he could hear someone giggling from far away.

Krista

The alarm that sounded at 6:00 in the morning jarred her out of a deep sleep. Krista was tempted to hit the snooze button, but shut it off and got up instead. There would be hell to pay if she was late. She looked over at her husband and gently shook him. "Hey, it's 6:00. It's time to get up."

Chad pulled the covers over his head, so she decided to get up, reset the alarm for 6:15 for her husband and make coffee. She stopped by Mara's room to start the waking process. And it was a process. Krista sat on the bed near her pillow and touched her hair. Mara moved slightly and made a noise. "It's time to get up," she whispered near her ear. Mara moved again and her eyelids were fluttering slightly. Krista could tell that she could hear her voice, hoping that this waking routine might work with her, because trying to get her up at the last minute wasn't the answer. It was trial and error at this point. She'd be going to her father's house this morning, so at least that wouldn't be a fight to get her there. Mara thoroughly enjoyed time with William. Her father catered to her and unfortunately, let his granddaughter get away with too much, which was why Mara wanted to be there in the first place!

Krista loved this time of day when she could revel in the quiet of the morning. It was a beautiful fall day, warmer than usual for mid-September in Rhode Island and she sat outside on their deck overlooking their small but well landscaped lawn enjoying her coffee. The blue hydrangeas were still vibrant for the season and she was glad that she'd talked Chad into planting them last year. They'd been thinking about putting in an in-ground pool, but in the end, it was a huge expense. Especially since Chad had talked to some of his co-workers. They'd complained about the cost and maintenance of a pool for only a few short months of summer in Rhode Island. In the end, they'd decided on planting some hydrangeas and perennials that would brighten up the space. Krista was the first to admit she was clueless to any kind of planting, so they hired a landscaping company instead of spending money on a pool.

"Hey, Kris," Her husband's voice startled her as she was taking a sip from her cup, causing her to almost drop the cup on the table.

"Chad, you scared me!" She recovered her cup by grasping it with both hands.

"I'm sorry, babe. I thought you heard me coming through the kitchen." Chad apologized and kissed the top of her head. "I wanted to talk to you before Mara gets up." His voice was quiet as he sat down next to her. "I agree with you that something is going on with her. I went by her room to check on her before I went to sleep last night and she was talking out loud. She was saying, 'Mommy doesn't know.'"

Krista was confused. "'Mommy, doesn't know about' what?"

"I have no idea! When I came into the room, I asked her about it and she said she was talking to her friend, 'Jamie' who lived on an island and wasn't happy."

Krista felt a chill come over her suddenly. "Jamie? Mara's never mentioned anyone by that name before, and she's never talked about imaginary friends. I hope Dr. Mayfield gets back to me today." She had a sudden flashback to her dream from the previous night about the voice that had been so familiar. The evil voice that reminded her of Jane Ahearn. But she refused to start her day out thinking about the past. 'Positive images, positive thoughts, let everything else go', she remembered Dr. Mayfield's mantra.

"It's just Mara using her imagination. I wonder where she gets it from!" He grabbed Krista's hand and squeezed it, winking at her. She playfully slapped at his hand and stood up.

"Gee, thanks. I think." She was glad that her marriage was one part of her life that she felt good about. It had taken a lot of counseling and work but they'd made it through after Chad's affair. She was finally able to trust him again and it made all the difference. "I need to go shower and get ready. Can you please assist with getting our sleepy-head daughter out of bed?"

"Sure babe. I just need a few swigs of caffeine first." He got up and poured himself a coffee, while Krista headed upstairs to get ready for work. She couldn't be late another day. She looked in on Mara as she headed to the bathroom. Mara was still asleep. 'Hopefully Chad has better luck getting her up than I do,' she thought grimly. She wasn't looking forward to the meeting with Mara's school principal this afternoon.

She was just stepping out of the shower, when she heard her phone ringing from the bedroom. She grabbed a towel, wrapped it around herself and ran towards her phone. It was Dr. Mayfield's office calling her back. "Hi, Dr. Mayfield, thanks so much for getting back to me. I was wondering if you could recommend a child therapist for my daughter. She's been having some behavioral issues at school and I think it wouldn't be a bad idea to have her see someone." Krista kept her eye on the clock as she stood there trying to dry off and talk at the same time.

Dr. Mayfield had helped her through so much. She was an older woman with a gentle, but firm approach. Krista could imagine her being a wonderful mother; Dr. Mayfield had a calming, nurturing effect that had changed her own opinion about therapy. "One of my colleagues who owns a practice in my building is experienced with children. Her name is Marcy Perrell. I think she'd be a good fit with Mara." She rattled off a number as Krista quickly put her on speaker phone and grabbed a pen to write it down.

"So, while I have you on the phone, I think we should schedule an appointment, Krista. It's been awhile. I won't be able to prescribe your medications if you're not coming regularly." Dr. Mayfield gently reminded her.

"I know, I've just been busy." Krista told her. She hurriedly scheduled an appointment on the fly for next week, not even sure if she was available, but trying to get off the phone. "See you then!" Krista hung up quickly and grabbed an old leopard print dress and a pair of black kitten heel sandals. She could overhear Chad in Mara's room.

"How's it going in there?" She yelled from the bathroom while putting on some make-up. She was glad she didn't bother washing her hair.

"Fine, she's up and getting dressed." Chad assured her. Krista was just thankful that her daughter listened to one of them! She looked through her jewelry box to grab a few bracelets and glanced over the black velvet case that held her sister's half-heart necklace. 'Help me get through this day, Karen!' she thought, hoping that her sister could hear her. Krista waited for a few seconds for a sign, as her sister usually did send one; usually a light flickering on and off again. But there was nothing this time. Krista tried to shake off the stress and went downstairs. "Are you ready to go yet?" She stopped at Mara's bedroom to check on the progress. Mara was dressed and had her backpack all ready. "See, mommy, I'm ready!" She had a precocious grin on her face, with Chad looking less than thrilled.

"Yes, you are, finally!" He said with a sarcastic tone to his comment, more to Krista than his daughter. Krista was pleasantly surprised then looked at the clock. "I need to leave. Can you drop her off at my dad's? I can't be late again." She hated being late, and there was no room for error right now with Mr. Samuels. "Good news though, Dr. Mayfield called me back with a referral! That'll help us out later on." She said, giving her husband a thumbs up.

Chad smiled, "That's great news." He looked just as relieved as she felt.

"I'm hungry!" Mara piped up, just as they were all headed down the stairs and Krista was going out the door. Chad groaned. "Sweetheart, Mommy needs to go to work and daddy will drop you at grandpa's house. You can eat there." He said this firmly, as he could tell Mara was getting ready to pout.

Krista gave them both a hug before heading out. "Bye, see you tonight! Be good for grandpa, Mara," as she got into her new-to-her black BMW that Chad had bought for her birthday in June. She just hoped that Mara would behave for her father, but she wasn't looking forward to scheduling a meeting with Mrs. Palmers today. As if on cue, Mrs. Palmers called her as she was pulling into the parking lot at Johnston High School. "Hello, Mrs. Burton, I'd like to schedule a meeting for this afternoon at 4pm. Would you and your husband be able to attend?"

Krista rolled her eyes as she put the car in park. She wasn't sure of Chad's schedule today, but she agreed to the meeting. She usually was able to leave work around 3:30, so she would have time to make it. "I'll be there. I'm unsure of my husband's schedule today, but I can be there."

"Great. I'll see you then." Mrs. Palmers agreed in a clipped tone. Krista immediately called Chad who said he would be there. Krista felt the relief wash over her and was finally able to focus. The rest of the day went by so quickly that Krista was shocked to look at the clock and see that it was 3:30 and she needed to go to her meeting at Mara's school. She ran out the door at 3:45 and called Chad on the way to Mara's school. It went straight to voicemail which usually happened when he was on the phone. Mrs. Palmers was a stoic, elderly woman who frowned on tardiness. She knew this because she'd met her when Mara was late on her first day of school, and felt as though she were the one being scolded. Krista was just glad her husband could be there to help her deal with this intimidating woman that held the key to getting Mara back in school where she belonged.

Chad

It had been a morning to remember. Chad never realized what a chore it was for his wife to deal with Mara in the morning, and now he had a whole new respect for her. Mara's resistance to getting up and getting dressed dragged the process on for 20 minutes longer than necessary. He'd dropped Mara off at William's which Mara was thrilled about. 'Of course she is, William spoils her', Chad thought even though he'd asked William to make sure that she didn't stay on her I pad or watch TV all day long. "Of course, I won't!" William assured him. But Chad knew better.

What was bothering him the most was Mara's conversation with 'Jamie' last night at bed time. He'd mentioned it to Kris this morning and luckily, she didn't get too upset. When he asked her about Jamie on the way to drop her off at Williams' Mara didn't say anything, except. "She's around sometimes. She's not here now." When Chad asked her where Jamie was, Mara just shrugged. "I don't know, daddy. She's off on her island somewhere. She hasn't talked to me today." Chad had arrived at William's house then and dropped her off and Krista called. "Mrs. Palmers wants to meet with us at 4:00 today. Please try to be there. I really want to get this over with." Her voice sounded frantic and tired at the same time. He agreed to make it work, knowing it was stressing her out.

As he drove to his office at Carson Realty, he tried to figure out how to rework his schedule in of how he could make the meeting at Mara's school. He had a 3:00 showing with another high-profile client that he couldn't reschedule because it could mean blowing millions of dollars in commission for the business. Yet, he wanted to be there for his family. Now he understood why William was ready to leave him the reins. Sometimes, success came with a price. Carson Realty was a success because William had worked 16 hour days for years after the death of Krista's sister and the loss of his wife.

He sighed as he reached the office and began to rearrange his schedule. There were two other realtors that he'd hired in the past two years; Greg Smithton and Michelle Ashworth that were both excellent realtors and they'd proven their track record. He'd just need to check with their schedules today and make it work.

Michelle luckily had an opening at 3:00 today, although she had a 4:30 scheduled later. He approached her immediately upon arriving. She was her early 50s, but looked as though she was 40. She was originally from Brazil and had beautiful tan skin that seemed to glow. Her 5 '8" figure was flawless and Chad was surprised that she never tried to model. She had thick dark curly hair that she usually wore up in a bun, but on the occasion that she wore it down, she turned heads everywhere she went. When Krista had met her, she immediately had been apprehensive about Chad's loyalty because of his previous indiscretions with his former secretary. But, despite her good looks, she was all business. And she was married as well with three children. Besides he and Krista were in a good place now. He would never jeopardize their marriage again.

"Good morning, Michelle. I've had something come up this afternoon with my daughter. Could you cover this VIP client at 3:00

in Jamestown today? It's a socialite couple that's looking for a getaway from NYC a few times a year. I was going to show a new property that's been listed on Beavertail Road, right near the water." He asked her as she was looking at her schedule.

Michelle smiled as she stood up, nearly at his height. "Not a problem, Chad. My 2:00 rescheduled today, so I'll be more than happy to take over." She patted his arm, as he thanked her. Sometimes he swore she was flirting with him, but he refused to think about that further than in the moment. Chad's phone rang and he gladly took the call, thankful to get away from any awkward moments.

It was William. Chad walked to his office and shut the door. "What's going on Bill? She was fine when I dropped her off!" Chad was feeling frustrated. What now? Had she brought up Jamie? Had she hurt someone? He realized suddenly that the possibilities were endless. "Mara's been acting really strange this morning. I'm not sure what to do, Chad." William sounded upset, which was unlike his father-in-law. William was the first one to stick up for Mara whenever anything happened.

"What do you mean by 'really strange?" Chad questioned.

"She's just been really mean to Joanna today. Joanna was trying to help her with her schoolwork and she told her to 'back off, bitch.' I couldn't even believe it myself, but I overheard the conversation. Five minutes later, Mara acted as though nothing had happened. Did Kris get hold of Dr. Mayfield? " William sounded stressed and upset.

"I know that she heard back this morning. I'm not sure if she got an appointment, but Kris and I are meeting with Mara's principal this afternoon at 4:00. By, the way, we'll be picking her up after the meeting, probably around 5:00." Chad added, hating that his father-in-law was stressed out and not being able to pick his daughter up now.

"That's fine, but we need to talk later when you pick her up." William sounded suddenly disenchanted with his granddaughter at the moment, which worried Chad even further. What were they going to do for childcare if the meeting with Mrs. Palmers didn't end up with Mara coming back to school tomorrow?

"I'm sorry about that Bill. We'll talk later." Chad promised him. With Michelle covering his client showing at 3:00, he dove into his work, and finally remembered to send his wife a text that he would be at the meeting.

"Thank you! See you soon!" Krista responded. He dove back into his work and when he glanced at the clock it was 3:45 and he was probably going to be late for the meeting, especially with traffic.

* * *

Krista pulled into the Thornton Elementary parking lot at exactly 3:56. She was glad to know that Chad would be there; she was starting to wonder until his text to her. Now, she felt somewhat relieved as she walked into the school and down the hall to Mrs. Palmer's office. She'd put in a call to Marcy Perrell, the child therapist whom Dr. Mayfield had recommended. She hadn't heard back from her yet, but at least she could tell Mrs. Palmers that she was in touch with a therapist, which might work in Mara's favor. She gave her name to the receptionist in the office, who immediately called Mrs. Palmers. She sat down. The clock ticked by 10 minutes and now she was irritated. Trying to fill her time, she called Chad to find out if he was on his way. Thankfully, he picked up.

"Hey, babe, I'm on my way. There's some traffic, but I'll be there in 5 minutes." He told her. "Has the meeting started yet?"

"No, I've been sitting here for a few minutes. I like how this woman likes *us* to be on time, but *she* can be late." Krista was already fuming about the hypocrisy of Mrs. Palmer's regime of 'being on time.' Apparently, that was only for others!

"Calm down, Kris, take some deep breaths. We don't need to walk in there angry, right? I'm pulling into the parking lot now." Chad tried to get his wife to calm down before he hung up. As she put her phone back in her purse, Mrs. Palmers walked out to greet her.

"Hello, Mrs. Burton, how are you today?" The woman looked the part of a principal for all the wrong reasons. Krista couldn't really guess how old she was, because she had the look of someone that was born at her age; she looked and acted as if she'd never been a young child. She'd always existed as a grouchy 60- something- year old woman that had a chip on her shoulder. Her short blond hair was cut perfectly and she wore a gray skirt/suit jacket combination that Krista was sure had to come from Nordstrom's. She wore minimal make-up, except for the foundation that seemed to seek out her years of overly tanned-skin with a dollop of bright-pink lipstick. 'Does she think this looks good?' Krista couldn't help but laugh to herself. She wasn't a fan of this woman from the start so she couldn't help but feel nit-picky about a woman that immediately suspended Mara without any explanation and then kept her waiting.

She stood up and was shaking her hand, just as Chad walked in the door. Krista had never been so glad to see him. "Mrs. Palmers, this is Chad, my husband." She introduced them quickly. Chad smiled and extended his hand as he glanced at her, while giving Krista a wink. She knew that he was thinking the same thing as she was about Mrs. Palmers. Mrs. Palmers seemed impressed with her husband as she led them into her office.

"Mr. and Mrs. Burton," Mrs. Palmers began. Chad stopped her right away. "Please, it's Chad and Krista." Krista was happy with the way he took charge and immediately personalized them with first names.

"Very well, then, Chad and Krista. We need to talk about Mara and her continuing her education here. From what we've seen over the past month, she's been aggressive toward other students and I'm not just speaking about the little boy that she allegedly pushed off the slide yesterday. In the month that she's been here there have been complaints from other parents that she's been telling them that she has special powers, and that they better listen to her. She's bullying them." Mrs. Palmers was direct. Krista was astounded at what she was hearing.

"Mrs. Palmers, Mara is 6 years old! How is it possible that you're labeling her as a bully at this age?" Krista's voice rose to another level and Chad patted her leg, which meant 'let me deal with this.' Before Mrs. Palmers could answer, Chad chimed in. "What my wife means is that Mara is young and sensitive. Is it possible that the other students might have upset her and she felt the need to defend herself?"

Mrs. Palmers looked confused for a moment. Krista could tell that she was trying to weigh out the comments. Chad was the go-to guy when it came to meetings and he'd just stopped the train-wreck of what she had said.

"Chad, you seem to make a valid point. The problem is that the parent of the little boy, Lucas, is very upset about what happened. We need to have a plan in place so that this doesn't happen again." Mrs. Palmers wasn't accustomed to someone challenging her. Krista noticed that she seemed increasingly nervous.

Krista decided to speak up again, despite Chad nudging her. "Mrs. Palmers, we understand that there are certain behaviors that need to be addressed and we're working on getting Mara in to see a child psychologist to be evaluated." Chad nodded in agreement, giving her leg a squeeze again as a reminder to stop talking.

"Well, that's definitely a step in the right direction. Given the circumstances, I'd prefer that you provide a letter from the doctor seeing Mara prior to her returning to school here." Krista's mouth dropped open. What if this woman didn't have an opening for a month?

Chad spoke up. "Mrs. Palmers, we are really concerned about the behaviors and hope to have her seen soon. We're hoping by the end of the week." Krista kicked him under the table at that point but he continued on. "If she's seen and they can provide documentation, then I hope that will take care of Mara being able to return on Monday. " He had the ability of conveying confidence, despite the lack of current evidence. Krista had renewed appreciation for her husband's gift of gab because he did it with conviction! But now she needed to scramble and try to deliver. Something he didn't consider. He was the voice of the operation, not the deliverer of action when it came to doctor appointments. The only reason he went to his own primary care doctor was because *she* scheduled them.

"Well, I'm glad that you understand our position here. Of course if Mara is going to be seeing a counselor and we have documentation, she'll be welcomed back." Mrs. Palmers seemed contented with Chad's statement. She stood up then and said, "As soon as you can give us a letter from a professional, Mara will be able to attend school again. I really hope that she can work through whatever is troubling her." Krista bristled at the last comment. She was acting as though *they* as parents were the problem! She wished that Mrs. Palmers had just a few hours with Mara at home to see what was really happening! Still she smiled and thanked her for the meeting. Chad, of course was on his 'realtor special' behavior as she sometimes referred to it.

As soon as they were outside the school, Krista couldn't help but talk about how Mrs. Palmers seemed to blame them and keep Mara out of the school. "Kris, she's doing what she has to do. You need to remember that the little boy she pushed went to the hospital and now the parents are upset. Wouldn't you be upset if someone did that to Mara?" Chad asked.

Krista had to admit, he made a good point. She knew she was in defense mode, but deep down, she also knew that it was coming from her own skepticism about Mara. She'd barely talked to Dr. Mayfield about her feelings, worried about what she would think. Chad knew that things weren't right, but she never really let him know how truly scared she was. Because if her feelings about her daughter were accurate, it meant that she couldn't be helped. If her daughter was really just struggling, then it would still be hard, but manageable.

As they arrived at their cars, Chad asked if they could go for a coffee or a drink. "Oh no! What now?" Krista knew this wasn't going to be good news. "Just tell me now. There's no sense sugar-coating this!" She threw up her hands.

"Your dad called me this morning. I guess Mara was being nasty to Joanna today, even calling her a bitch. Bill was really upset about it. I let him know that we're getting her into therapy. I just wanted to tell you before we pick her up today." Chad looked suddenly afraid of what she might say or do.

Krista took a deep breath as Dr. Mayfield and Chad were always reminding her about. "That's really bad timing, considering we don't have another option for Mara the rest of this week. I'll be lucky to get her in to see Marcy Perrell this week!"

"We'll just have to see how the rest of the day went when we pick her up. I'll meet you there." Chad said as he got into his black BMW X5 SUV. It had been a splurge for him after selling a multi-million dollar property in Newport on Ocean Drive to a former child celebrity that had left the entertainment business long ago, but still managed to be successful with a career outside of Hollywood.

Krista followed him, hoping that things had improved. She knew why her husband had warned her. She just wished that she had the magic wand to connect with her daughter who didn't appear to have any empathy. She knew professionally that it was a huge red flag. Lack of empathy meant that the child didn't care if someone else was hurt. It was a scary thought, and she hoped that she was wrong.

William

He'd never imagined that he'd feel as frustrated as he did today with his granddaughter. She seemed fine and happy to be at his house. But when Joanna gently tried to help Mara with her homework, she turned on her. William had allowed Mara to sit and watch TV with him for an hour, which she loved as they watched a rerun of "America's Got Talent". Mara was perfectly content watching the dancers and singers until it was over. "Ok, Mara, it's time to do some of your schoolwork." William insisted.

"No! I don't want to!" Mara resisted and began pouting. William tried to bribe her at first. "Hey, Mara, if you do a little schoolwork for an hour, then we can watch the next episode." Mara began to pout and complain, "I don't want to. I don't have any schoolwork!" She told him.

But William insisted and turned off the TV. Joanna had been in the kitchen at the time and offered to help her with her homework. Mara's eyes suddenly narrowed in anger, her cheeks were turning pink as she turned to Joanna. "You're not my mom! Don't tell me what to do, you bitch!" The sound and tone of her voice was like a mature woman. William and Joanna both froze in shock at what his six-year-old granddaughter had just said.

William found his voice first. "Excuse me, young lady! You will not speak to anyone in this house this way! Where did you learn that language?" He came closer to Mara who was still standing defiantly in front of him. All 4 feet of her, but his granddaughter stood as though she were 8 feet tall.

"Kids in school talk like that all the time! I don't like this school! They hate me! You must hate me too!" Mara's face changed from fury to full-on tears in a second. William tried to feel some empathy for his granddaughter's tears, but the tone of her voice made him angry and scared at the same time. He took a deep breath and kneeled down to her small stature. "Mara, no one hates you. But you can't use that language or call people names. Do you understand that?" William knew his granddaughter was exceptionally smart, but for the first time he noticed that she didn't seem to really care unless she was getting her way.

Mara nodded, as a few more tears filled her blue eyes. Those eyes reminded him so much of his Maria and of her mother. "I'm sorry, grandpa." She threw her small arms around him and for the moment he was convinced that she was just upset about not being able to return to school and believed that everyone was against her. Still, Joanna was standing in the background, horrified and almost afraid of Mara.

"Okay, Mara. But the person you should be apologizing to is Joanna. She loves you too. You were very mean to her just now." William told her in a gentle voice. He pulled back from Mara's hug, expecting her to immediately apologize. But he noticed a hint of bitterness behind her blue eyes that hadn't been there a minute before. It was a look of hostility made him fearful for a moment. The flash of anger left as soon as it had appeared. Mara nodded her head and turned to Joanna who had been sitting silently at the kitchen table.

"I'm sorry, Joanna. I didn't mean what I said to you." She said the words, yet to William there was no sincerity behind the words. Joanna nodded, "Okay, Mara. If you want to do your schoolwork on your own, I understand. You just need to tell me that instead of getting angry."

"I will." Mara said quietly. "Are you still mad at me?" She asked. It was hard to tell if she was sincere or just feeling sorry for herself.

Joanna got up from the table to face Mara. "No, of course not! Let's forget it about it." She told her quietly. Mara smiled, showing off one of her front missing teeth that had fallen out last week. "I'm glad we're friends again." She went and went to hug Joanna as if nothing had ever happened.

"Mara, let's get back to your schoolwork so that you can finish it and we can watch the next episode of our show!" William clapped his hands, hoping that this unexpected drama had come to a close. Mara agreed and sat down in William's den to finish her math problems. Joanna watched for a moment, while William decided to call Chad and let him know what happened. Something wasn't right; he could feel it.

*   *   *

As Chad pulled up to the house at around 5:00, William was waiting for him. Mara had just had dinner and Joanna had left to go to her yoga class. Chad had a serious look on his face as he walked in the door. "Hi, Bill. How're things going?" He kept his voice down, knowing that Mara was in the vicinity.

"Things were okay today." William told him, but his facial expressions spoke differently as he motioned for him to come into his den for some privacy.

"Daddy!" Mara came running from the living room to give him a hug. Chad scooped her up into a bear hug and gave a kiss on her head.

"Hi sweetheart! I hope you've been good for grandpa today!" Chad looked at William who kept quiet.

"Of course I was. Wasn't I grandpa?" Mara lied and looked coyly at William, although she seemed as though she were being truthful. She probably didn't understand yet that he already knew about what happened today.

"Mara, you need to tell the truth." William warned her. Mara frowned and began to pout and cry. "Daddy, can I go back to school tomorrow? Joanna was mean to me today."

"Mara, that's not true. You need to tell your daddy what happened today." William said sternly. Mara's tears continued. "I don't want to. You said everything was okay now."

Chad bent down to his daughter. "Were you rude to Joanna today, Mara? Look at me!" He insisted. She looked at him and then down at her toes. "I wasn't nice, but I said I was sorry." She admitted in a quiet voice. William nodded in agreement.

"Thank you for being honest, Mara." Chad told her. "I need to talk to grandpa for a few minutes, so go in the living room and finish watching your show." Mara was glad to be out of the hot seat and skipped back over to her spot on the couch.

When William was able to meet with him alone in his den, he told Chad in detail what had happened. "It's like she was someone I didn't know, Chad. I don't know how to explain it! One moment she was fine, the next she had this …I hate to say it……but a look of evil….it was in her eyes. Then it disappeared and she was back to being a sweet kid again! Did Kris get in touch with that therapist today?"

Chad was remembering how he felt last night when he'd checked in on his daughter. He'd had the same feeling, the same strange hatred look in her eyes when she turned to him. "She called, but had to leave a message. Maybe this is just a passing thing for her? I mean, wasn't Kris a little stubborn when she was Mara's age?" He wanted to believe that this was nothing more than a little girl being obstinate and pushing her limits.

"Of course she was, but this was different. The voice she used didn't even sound like her; it was as if …someone was speaking for her." William told him. Chad shook his head.

"Bill, I'll make sure that Mara gets an appointment this week. She needs to or else she can't return to school." Chad had his game-face on and William knew that he was going to do his best to make it happen. "So in the meantime, can you take her the rest of the week?"

"I will of course. But I have a bad feeling, Chad. Something's not right with Mara." William shook his head.

"I know, Bill. Trust me. We'll get her to a therapist and figure this out." Chad agreed with him. He knew his wife would agree. He was beginning to understand what Krista had been talking about now. As they opened the door to leave the den, William noticed that Mara was hovering nearby the door, as if she were trying to listen to their conversation. He thought about calling her out on eavesdropping, but at this point he didn't feel like getting into a power-struggle. After Chad left with Mara, Joanna called him on her way back to house from her class. "Bill, I think it's best if I'm not here tomorrow while Mara is here."

William was grabbing a beer out of the fridge and stopped in his tracks. "What? Why, Joanna?" He flipped the cap off the bottle and took a swig. He didn't drink often anymore but after today, he felt a beer was in order.

"She doesn't like me. It's not just what she said to me, Bill. There's something else that I couldn't tell you while she was here. When she was in the other room doing her homework finally, I walked by and overheard her talking to someone. There wasn't anyone there, but what she said was frightening. She said 'I'll get all of you one of these days. You won't even know what happened, but you'll all be getting what's coming to you!' Something's really wrong and I'm scared, Bill."

Krista

Krista drove home, hoping to get a call from the therapist that Dr. Mayfield had recommended. It was if suddenly everything that had happened 7 years ago had just resurfaced. She hadn't had a nightmare since then, but now they were back. She wouldn't tell Chad now, but she had little hope that the therapist would be of help to what was going on with her daughter. She suddenly had another idea.

Making it home before Chad and Mara, she took the opportunity to run upstairs and rummage through her jewelry box. The card was tucked away in the back from so many years ago, but she finally found it; Nadine –Spiritual Advisor and Medium. She just hoped that Nadine was still in town or at least in the area. Krista knew that she'd probably have more answers in 5 minutes than any psychiatrist around.

Krista still remembered the day she met Nadine; she'd walked into a tarot-reading shop, when Nadine had sensed something wrong and insisted that she do a reading. It was then that she'd been told about her sister Karen's existence, although she had been skeptical. But in the end, Nadine had been right. She needed her now and she quickly called as she looked out the window to see Chad pulling up into the driveway. She didn't want to tell him about this, and Nadine didn't pick up, so she left a quick message to call or text her back.

The rest of the evening was spent ordering take-out Chinese and getting Mara ready for bed. Mara was actually easier to deal with this evening, but Krista had a feeling it was knew that because William had set limits with her today. "Did you hear back from that therapist yet,

Kris?" Chad asked for what seemed the millionth time in 24 hours to which she shook her head. She wasn't going to tell him about her call to Nadine. Maybe Nadine had moved, or just didn't do psychic work any longer. But she hoped not.

They were both exhausted and were in bed around 9:30. Chad was so tired, he didn't complain about the TV being on, as Krista liked to have it on as she was falling asleep. It was habit that she'd always had, but especially after everything that happened with her sister, meeting her mother and being held hostage by the Ahearn sisters.

There was a sudden crash that sounded as if glass was breaking that jerked her out of a dead sleep. She wondered for a moment if she was dreaming, but Chad's eyes were open. "Babe, did you hear that?" Krista gripped his arm. "I sure did!" Chad said, suddenly alert.

" I'm just glad you did too, so I know I'm not dreaming!" Krista was glad that he'd heard it too.

"You're not! Stay here, I'm gonna check it out." Chad got out of bed, crept to the closet and found a golf putter that he used to practice once in a while. He knew he had some kind of advantage at 6'3", but it never hurt to have a back -up weapon. He went towards the door.

"Chad, please don't go out there! You don't know who's here! Maybe someone is breaking in!" Krista insisted.

"Kris, we have a security system for a reason. The alarm hasn't been set off, but I need to check on Mara! Do you have your phone?" He asked and she grabbed it off the nightstand.

"Of course! Do you want me to call the cops?" Krista still felt disoriented being jerked out of a deep sleep. Chad shook his head and motioned her to be quiet as he opened the door and headed into the hallway toward Mara's room. Mara was sound asleep and there were no windows broken. He sighed in relief to know that she was safe. He went through the rest of the house with the putter above his head ready to swing at anything that moved but there was no sign of an intruder anywhere. The sound of breaking glass had been clear as day, so where had it come from?

Chad checked the downstairs living and kitchen area, then headed for the unfinished basement. It was his plan to eventually finish it and make into a recreation room/den but so far, it was holding place for old stuff they hadn't had time to get rid of yet. He flicked on the light and looked around amongst the boxes. There were two small windows that only a small child could get through but both were intact. He turned off the light and headed back to bed. "Kris, there's no one here," he advised her as he came back to bed.

"Are you sure?" Krista was still gripping her phone. She'd been terrified the whole time Chad had been searching the house. Chad crawled back into bed and gave her a reassuring hug. "Kris, its fine. Go back to sleep."

Krista glanced at her phone and noticed she'd gotten a text notification. Curious, she looked at it. It was from Nadine, sent 20 minutes ago at 1:40am. It read, 'Call me as soon as you can. It's very important.' Krista looked at her husband who was settled back in bed now. "Kris, go back to bed! Why are you on your phone now? It's 2:00 in the morning!"

She knew he was right, as she put the phone down. It could wait until it was time to get up: after all it was only four more hours. As she glanced over at the dresser, she noticed with the picture of her, Karen and her mother at Block Island had fallen over. 'That's really strange' Krista thought as she drifted off to sleep.

When the alarm went off at 6am, Krista wrestled with it, trying to hit snooze but she missed and it continued to go off. She sighed as she rolled over to shut it off. She was awake, so she decided to get up. Chad was still sleeping soundly and Krista hated to wake him but at the same time she knew he'd be upset if he overslept. She pulled the covers off of him and whispered 'wake up' in his ear. He mumbled something and rolled over. Krista yawned and got up to make coffee, when she saw the picture on the dresser had fallen over. She picked it up and there was broken glass all around it. Then she saw the large crack in the mirror above the dresser. It was as if someone had taken a razor blade and run it across the mirror. "I knew I saw it!" Krista said out loud.

"Huh? What are you talking about, Kris?" Chad rubbed his eyes and sat up when he saw Krista cleaning up the glass from the dresser and then the crack in the mirror. "That must have been that sound we heard last night. How the hell did that happen?" Chad immediately jumped up and went to inspect it up close. "Maybe the wind just knocked the picture frame over." Krista tried to focus on the picture instead of the huge crack in the mirror.

"Of course, but I didn't see this! Kris, what's going on?" Krista shook her head. "I have no idea. Oh my god! Mara!" They both ran to her room to find her sleeping peacefully. They both sighed with relief. "Let's let her sleep", Krista whispered as she closed Mara's door and went back to their bedroom to retrieve her phone. She looked through her text messages to find the one from Nadine at 1:40 am. She didn't want to tell Chad about contacting her. "I'll go make us some coffee. Why don't you take your shower?" She offered so she could text Nadine back without him questioning her.

She went downstairs and started the coffee brewing and quickly texted Nadine back. "I just got this. I will call you in an hour." She took some deep breaths, knowing that she couldn't tell Chad about speaking to Nadine, at least for now. Despite all they'd been through with the Ahearn sisters, he still was doubtful about anything that related to the paranormal. "I just don't want to talk about it anymore, Kris! Let's just focus on our future." Her phone signaled that she had a text. It was Nadine. "I will be waiting for your call. Important."

"Is that work texting you already?" Chad asked as she jumped at the sound of his voice as he went to the coffee pot and poured himself a cup. She instinctively closed down her phone to the home screen. "Yeah, just Mr. Samuels making sure I'm prepared for today's meeting." It wasn't far from a lie. Since she was late to a meeting earlier this week, Mr. Samuels had been checking up on her with various emails and texts about projects and meetings.

Once they both showered and got ready for work, Krista went to wake Mara up and take her over to her father's house for the day. Mara didn't give her a hard time for once which was surprising. "Mara did you hear any noises last night?" She asked her as she assisted her with brushing her long blonde hair into a ponytail.

Mara was quiet for a moment. "No, mommy. But Jamie was in my dream." Krista was stunned. This 'Jamie' that Chad had mentioned yesterday.

"What was Jamie doing in your dream?" Krista questioned, trying to appear casual.

"She was getting mad because she's still stuck on the island and she wants to be here." Mara told her. "I like her dreams when she's nice, but she wasn't nice last night."

"What does she do when she's not being nice?" Krista's heart jumped into her throat and she tried to stop her hands from shaking as she finished brushing Mara's hair. Mara was silent and shook her head. "I don't want to talk about it, Mommy. It's scary. She breaks things." Mara admitted.

Krista managed to finish her hair and turned Mara around to face her. "Sweetheart, she's just in a dream. She can't hurt you, okay?" She tried to reassure her daughter, although she was knew there was no logical explanation for the mirror being basically slice in half or the picture frame broken when there was no wind to blow it over. She gave her a hug, "Let's get going! I'm taking you to grandpa's house today.

"I'm ready." Mara picked up her little green and black backpack that was sitting in the corner of her room. She hoped that Mara wouldn't get too used to going to her father's house. She had clearly mastered the art of manipulation there.

Chad had already left, so Krista was bringing Mara to her father's house. During the 10-minute drive, Mara was quiet until they turned onto Williams' street. "Can we go to that island sometime?" She asked suddenly.

Krista was taken by surprise. "What island?"

"The island where grandma used to live." Mara said candidly. Krista was floored that her daughter would know anything about where her grandmother lived. She hadn't really talked about her mother, what happened to her or where her ashes were spread with Mara. She had only told her about her grandmother from her own memories growing up, and very vague details about where she was buried.

"Well, we can talk about going there. Is there a reason you want to go there, Mara?" She asked.

Mara looked as if she were going to say something then shook her head. "No. I just wanted to see it." Krista was thankful that she was pulling into her father's driveway. "We will sometime soon, sweetheart. In the meantime, you need to follow your grandpa's rules. That includes being respectful to Joanna too." Krista reminded her.

"I will, mommy. I promise." Mara said as Krista dropped her off with her father. "Did you hear anything back from that therapist yet?" Her father asked as soon as he opened the door.

"No dad. I'll call again today. In the meantime, please don't give in and reward her when she doesn't do her schoolwork." Krista said calmly. Inside, she wanted to let him know that he hadn't helped with his continuing to spoil Mara.

William nodded. "I know and understand. It's tough on a grandpa though." He joked.

"I know dad, but she needs it.   Dad, will you let me know if she talks about any dreams or someone named 'Jamie'? She said something this morning about a dream she had last night." Krista asked her father as soon as Mara was out of earshot. She left out the mirror being broken in the middle of the night. There was no point getting her father all worked up right now.

"Sure, Kris. Is she okay?" His brow furrowed in concern.

"Oh, of course. I just wanted to mention it to you in case she says anything about it." Krista was quick to reassure him. "Hopefully, I'll have an appointment scheduled with that therapist soon. Thanks for watching her this week." Krista hugged her dad. He really was a great father and grandfather. "One of us will pick her up probably around 4:30."

As she left, she glanced at Nadine's last text. "I'll be waiting for your call. Important." She was trying to decide to wait until she had arrived at work, but the suspense was too much for her. With shaking hands, she dialed the number. It went straight to voicemail and Krista felt almost frantic, especially after Mara's recollection of her dream last night. She left her a message and tried to focus on the day ahead. She made a mental note to call Marcy Perrell, the therapist again this morning. Despite her lack of confidence that she would help Mara, she knew it was the only way to get her back into school.

Just as she arrived at school, her phone rang and thankfully, it was Marcy. "I received your voicemail and also got a call from Dr.

Mayfield. I understand Mara needs to be seen as soon as possible?" Marcy asked. Krista was relieved that Dr. Mayfield had expressed the urgency and went on to fill Marcy in on Mara's behaviors and the most recent incident that led to her suspension. Marcy told her that she could fit her in on Friday at 2:00. "Thank you so much! I appreciate you getting her in so quickly." Krista was impressed with her already.

"No problem. I just hope that the school isn't expecting 'overnight' changes,'" Marcy warned. Krista hoped so as well. "We're just trying to take it one step at a time, Marcy." Krista told her. "See you on Friday." She sent a quick text to Chad to let him know that Mara had an appointment, then called her father to let him know that his everyday babysitting duties would be coming to an end. William sounded relieved, and she knew there was probably more going on with Mara during the day than he would admit. "How's she doing today?" Krista couldn't help herself.

"She's been fine, Kris. Right now she's eating some breakfast and she's going to work on her vocabulary words with Joanna afterwards." William sounded optimistic. "Don't worry, Kris, she'll be fine! Go back to work!" He insisted.

"Thanks dad, I really appreciate your help this week." Krista knew they would've been in a huge bind if he hadn't stepped in to babysit this week. "You know I'll always be here to help." William promised her. Mr. Samuels texted her suddenly asking where she was. "I've gotta go, dad. My boss is looking for me!" Krista quickly hung up, shut off her car and quickly walked into the school, hoping that she hadn't just ruined her career for being late yet again.

Chad

He tried to keep his mind on work this morning, but he couldn't shake off the uneasiness from the nighttime drama. He was still trying to rationalize the broken mirror in the bedroom. Mirrors didn't just break by themselves, there had to be another explanation; but what? He got a text from Krista telling him that she'd gotten an appointment with the therapist on Friday. 'Thank god', Chad thought to himself. He knew that William thought the world of his granddaughter, but after yesterday's behaviors and his father-in-law's health issues, he didn't want to burden him with babysitting Mara for an extended period of time.

Michelle knocked at his open door just then. "Chad, I'm sorry to bother you, but I wanted to talk to you about that client and the Jamestown property that I showed yesterday." He could tell she was looking him over anytime he was around her. It was flattering, yet made him uncomfortable at the same time.

"Sure, come on in Michelle." Chad said, hoping that they were interested and putting out an offer. He couldn't help but notice Michelle's tight blue short skirt that fit nicely around her hips and her low-cut baby pink blouse that exposed her cleavage. 'No, not going there,' he thought to himself, although the visual made it difficult to focus. She sat down in the chair facing him, but her slender muscular legs were still in view. He cleared his throat and forced himself to keep his eyes on something else besides her body.

"They weren't really interested, I'm sorry to say. I'm surprised! I thought they would love it." Michelle began. The client was another one of Stanley's connections, David Ackwell. David was an up and coming director in Hollywood and Stanley seemed to have taken him under his wing. Despite the history that William and Stanley had, Chad had grown to have some respect for Stanley. He'd been kind to Krista after her mother had died and stayed in touch. He'd gone out of his way to use his connections to help make Carson Realty more successful and compete with the best.

"So what *is* David looking for?" Chad questioned. He could tell that this was going to be an interesting conversation by the worried look on Michelle's face.

"He wants to talk to Stanley about selling his Block Island property." Michelle told him. "And he wants *you* to 'grease the wheels'. Not my words, these were his, just to clarify." She rolled her eyes.

Chad just laughed. "I don't think so! Nobody talks Stanley into anything, I'm pretty sure he knows that."

Michelle nodded in agreement. "I know, but David has already approached Stanley with an interest and seems to think that he might be considering selling. After all, he really isn't there very often and after all that happened there. I'm surprised he didn't put it on the market years ago." Michelle put in her two cents. She wasn't working for Carson Realty when everything had happened with the kidnapping and Stanley's daughters, but she'd seen the news and heard the gossip.

"Well, that's different then if it's not coming out of left field. I definitely don't want to approach Stanley about this out of the blue."

Chad was talking more out loud than to Michelle as he was trying to figure out his plan. It would take some planning and an initial conversation with Stanley to make sure that David wasn't bluffing about mentioning selling the property in the first place.

"But from now on, let me work with David. Seems like he's trying to be sneaky. No offense to you, but I'd rather deal with him myself. He's a high-profile client and could cause some problems that I don't wish on anyone." Chad knew David used his wealth to get what he wanted from women and wouldn't put it past him to put the moves on Michelle for the Ahearn property. Michelle could make her own choices, but he didn't want Carson Realty's reputation to be marred by coercion.

"Of course. I'd rather you take over anyway." Michelle agreed. "I just wanted you to know." She gave him a sly smile, looking him over as she stood up. Chad could tell that she was flirting with him, but he wouldn't go there. He'd learned his lesson the first time around.

"Thanks for telling me about this, Michelle." Chad focused his eyes on the computer screen in front of him to avoid looking at her in her short skirt as she was leaving his office. He thought for a few moments before he picked up the phone to call Stanley. He wasn't sure if he was at the Block Island property this week, although he did like to visit in the fall. He went to pick up the phone when it rang. It was Stanley. Chad was shocked by the irony of it as he picked up. "Chad Burton," he said, purposefully not acknowledging that he knew it was Stanley.

"Chad, Stan Ahearn here," he said in his usual VIP voice that screamed out 'narcissistic asshole' (as Krista had coined it), yet Chad was used to him by now so it didn't irritate him anymore. Stanley became more involved after what he started to refer to as 'the incident' with his daughters kidnapping his wife. Initially, Chad had been ready to leave his father-in-laws' business because of Stanley's arrogance, but he'd toned it down. The loss of Krista's mom had really changed him into a person with some empathy, a quality that Chad had never thought Stanley Ahearn possessed.

"Mr. Ahearn, how are you doing? Good to hear from you!" Chad addressed him formally, as he knew that Stanley preferred it when doing business.

"Chad I'm calling because I've heard David Ackwell has been gossiping that I want to sell my Mohegan Bluffs property. I'm telling you now that it's not the case, I'm not selling!" Stanley sounded irritated. "I guess your associate has already told you this." It was if the man had a camera recording everything that just occurred. Chad was starting to feel paranoid. He debated about lying to him, but then knew that he'd find out anyway. It was always better to be honest; he'd learned his lesson about that. Somehow, someday, the truth would come out.

"I had heard that, Mr. Ahearn. I'm glad that you called to let me know that isn't your intention." Chad said calmly. Yet he was anxious, tapping his pen and his right foot as he always did when he was nervous. William owned Carson Realty, but Stanley still had the power. It was the unspoken rule.

"Thank you, Chad. I appreciate that." He said. "There was another reason I was calling; I wanted to invite you and the rest of the family to visit on Block Island in a couple of weeks. Say the weekend after next?"

Chad was taken by surprise. "Really? We'd love that!" He actually wasn't sure how much Kris or William would, but he wasn't going to say otherwise. He wasn't sure if Kris had anything planned. "Let me check with Kris, just to be sure."

"I'd love to meet your little one. What's her name?" Stanley hadn't met Mara before.

"Her name is Mara. I'm sure she'd love it there. She recently said something about going…on a ferry ride." Chad caught himself. He left out the context of what Mara had said about going to the island.

"Well, let me know in the next few days. I'm in LA this week, but I'm headed to Block Island in a couple of weeks. Please make sure Bill knows he's invited and any other guests he'd like to bring." He said, with a hint that he knew about Joanna. Chad wasn't sure about what Stanley knew about her or the relationship between Stanley and William and preferred it that way.

"I will, Mr. Ahearn. I'll talk to Kris tonight about it. Thank you for the invitation." Chad was sure that Kris wouldn't want to go, but this seemed more like a request than an invitation. He was sure that there was something more to them coming to the Block Island estate. They hadn't been there for 7 years since her mother's death and life-celebration. They'd spread her ashes out on the bluffs, but there was a headstone in her memory. Since they'd never returned after the ceremony, Krista had never seen the headstone. He was hoping that she and William would be up to going back there. He felt as though Stanley had asked them to come for a reason.

But now he need to tackle David Ackwell's push to buy, and Stanley's firm 'no' about selling the Block Island property. When Stanley said 'no' he meant it! Especially when it came to his real estate. He sighed as he got back to work, checking out properties that might fit the bill for David. He and his wife were both picky, so he started searching for areas such as Portsmouth. It wasn't a well-known area for the buyer's market, but he knew several gems there. He was doing the research on some homes there when the phone rang again. The number was listed, it only said 'unknown'. He picked up, "Chad Burton, can I help you?" He was suddenly wondering why this call hadn't gone through the main line. Only a few people had his direct number.

"Hello, Chad. It's been a long time." The female voice had a husky tone that he knew he'd heard before, but couldn't recall from where.

"Whom am I speaking with?" Chad tried to remain professional. They sometimes got scam calls from other businesses, but it might also be a former contact he'd had.

"I'm sad that you don't remember the sound of my voice, especially since we've been together in the past. I'll be seeing you soon." The phone hung up and Chad was stunned. "What just happened?" He said out loud. He called the receptionist, Kathy, to ask if she'd put a call through.

"No, Mr. Burton. Any calls you received went directly to your extension." Kathy advised. Chad tried to forget about it. 'It was probably just a prank, or a wrong number,' he thought to himself, trying to avoid thinking about it further. There was enough going on with Mara; they didn't need any added drama. He dove into his work to find David Ackwell's 'perfect' home and put it out of his mind.

William

It had been an exhausting morning with Mara. When Kris had called, Joanna *had* been working with her on her vocabulary words, but not without a lot of resistance from his granddaughter. Joanna even tried to make it fun and play a game, but Mara was more interested in playing a game on her mini-Ipad he'd bought her for Christmas. Now, he was regretting it and remembered Krista telling him that she was too young and it would keep her away from interacting socially. Krista had been right.

After Joanna managed to get Mara through her homework an hour later, she came and sat next to him on the couch. "Now, I know why you have kids when you're young! I just don't have the energy anymore." She laughed.

"She's full of energy. Thank you for spending time with her." He put his arm around Joanna. He felt grateful that she'd come into his life and accepted his family as if they were hers. Joanna gave him a hug. "There's something I need to mention; she was talking about visiting Block Island. She was talking about some person named 'Jamie' and how she had a dream that she would be going there soon." Joanna told him.

"What? She's never been there. I know Kris has told her about her grandmother that was buried there, but she's never brought it up before." William said. Then he remembered Kris telling him about Mara having dreams last night and mentioned the island and 'Jamie.'

"Kris told me this morning that Mara had a dream about some person named 'Jamie'. It's probably just her recalling her dream." William tried to reassure Joanna.

"I hope that's all it is, Bill, I really do. But she seems to be fixated on this island. She talks about it as if she's been there before." Joanna insisted.

"Grandpa! Look what I made for you!" Mara came into the living room to show him a drawing. It was picture of a house on a cliff with the ocean below. She'd done a remarkable job with the perspective for a 6-year-old. Then he spotted a gray spot near the cliff and pointed to it. "What's that Mara?"

"That's grandma's headstone." Mara told him without hesitation. William was silent for a moment. None of them had been back out to Block Island since the death of Krista's mother. That headstone was put up afterward. Stanley had sent him a photo and told him about the headstone that was erected there a few months later. He swallowed hard and tried to find the right words, but his heart was racing.

"It's a lovely picture, Mara. How did you know to put that headstone there?" William asked her.

"Jamie showed me. She told me where it was." Mara said. William was stunned. Now what Kris had said to him this morning made sense. "It's very nice," he told her, as he stood up with the picture and put it on the counter with shaking hands.

"Oh, good. Jamie told me you might not like it." Mara said as she went to hug him. William scooped her up and gave her a hug, but the picture was haunting. How could she have known about that headstone? He wasn't sure what to say or if he should tell Kris and Chad about it.

"Of course I do, sweetheart." William smiled. "Now, how about you take a break from schoolwork and we'll go for a swim?" William had put in an in-ground pool several years ago that proved to be a project, especially when he could only use it four months out of the year, but he liked to swim and Mara had learned to swim when she was only three.

"Yay! Let's go swimming!" Mara was excited and went to change into her swimsuit, while Joanna gave him a look of disgust.

"Are you kidding me? She was suspended from school and supposed to finish her schoolwork, which by the way, isn't even close to being done. Now you're rewarding her!" Joanna shook her head and stormed out of the room.

William went after her. "Now wait a minute, Joanna. Come back, let's talk about this!" He was suddenly worried that Joanna might decide that she was done with the relationship and followed her. "Joanna, let's talk," He insisted while she grabbed her purse and keys.

"We'll talk later, Bill. I need some time away right now." Joanna told him, still sounding upset. "We are fine, don', t worry. I just need to get away for the afternoon. I'll call you tonight, ok?" She gave him a hug. William felt relieved as he hugged her back. "I'm sorry. You're right, I am spoiling her. Please call me later." He kissed her before she walked out the door, and hoped it wouldn't be the last time. Yet it was in the back of his mind that it almost seemed that she was making excuses to leave, getting upset about Mara swimming? It seemed unreasonable to him.

"Grampa! I'm getting in!" Mara announced from outside as she jumped into the pool. William immediately ran outside to the pool to make sure that she was okay. She was beneath the surface for what seemed a long time. William knew that she could swim very well, so what was taking her so long to come back up?

"Mara!" William was shouting and waving his hands. When she remained underwater, he took off his shoes and was getting ready to jump in when she suddenly surfaced. She was laughing and splashing water at him as she swam to the ladder. "I fooled you, grandpa!" She giggled.

William was still trying to catch his breath as she climbed out of the pool before he could speak. "Mara, that wasn't funny! What were you doing?" He found himself yelling at her now. "You know that an adult should be out here watching you! Those are the rules!" He sat down on a nearby woven lounge chair to collect himself. Mara grabbed a towel and wrapped it around her little body, shivering now.

"Grandpa, I was just playing!" She pouted as she sat next to him on the chair. Joanna's words came back to him; 'you're rewarding her?' He knew it was time to step in and stop being 'grandpa' for a moment.

"Mara, I'm very disappointed. What you did at school is something that is dangerous. That little boy could've been seriously hurt! You know the rules here; no swimming unless there's a grown-up outside. No more swimming today. You need to go inside, dry off and get back to your schoolwork." His voice came out more stern than he'd mean it, but she'd scared him.

Mara was quiet for a moment, as two small tears trickled down her small face. "I told you I was sorry, grandpa." She sniffled and buried her head in her lap with the towel over her wet blond curls.

William wanted to give in to her tears, but he knew it wasn't helping her. "I know, Mara. But it's time to go get changed, have some lunch and get back to your schoolwork." He said firmly. She looked surprised but when she saw that he meant business, she nodded and went inside to dry off and change into her clothes. He went to the counter and picked up the picture of the cliff with the headstone, intending to hang it on the fridge, but he couldn't bring himself to. The visual of Maria's headstone that he'd never seen in person was too much for him, even after all these years.

William kept an ear out for her upstairs while he was making lunch. He could hear her whispering, but couldn't make out the words. Who was she talking to? He walked up the short flight of stairs to the guest room and peeked around the corner. Mara was standing at the mirror, whispering. "I did what you said, but he's mad at me now." She kept nodding as if she were hearing someone talking. "I want to go. I want to." She whispered and giggled as if she'd just heard a private joke. She suddenly turned around as if she were aware of someone watching. William quietly crept back down the stairs, trying to figure out what he'd just witnessed. He went back to making grilled-cheese sandwiches as he called for Mara to come down for lunch.

"Mara, lunch is ready!" He called up to her, keeping his voice calm, but he felt uneasy, almost afraid of what he'd seen. Between the mirror conversation, the pool and the picture of the headstone, he wasn't sure how to interact with his granddaughter right now. She appeared around the corner, as if she'd been waiting there. William was startled for a moment but recovered quickly. "Hi, sweetheart, come have some lunch." He put down a grilled cheese sandwich with some chips for her, as she sat down. Her silence made William feel more uneasy; Mara was usually talking non-stop. She was probably angry with him, although when he'd overheard her upstairs talking, she'd sounded happy, almost giddy.

"How's your sandwich?" William asked her as she gobbled down her meal within a few minutes. Usually she picked at her food and it took her at least 30 minutes to finish half of what was on her plate. She took a long drink of water and nodded. "It was yummy!" She smiled for the first time since he'd scolded her. "Are you still mad at me?" She asked him in an innocent voice.

"No, Mara. I wasn't angry, I was worried when you jumped into the pool." William told her as his eyes went to the picture that she'd drawn of the cliff and the headstone. "Where did you get the idea for your picture?" He asked her a second time.

"I told you already! Jamie showed me the island and the headstone. So I drew what she showed me." Mara said simply, as if that should be enough explanation. William had been curious if she would have the same explanation. She did. Whatever Mara was seeing seemed to be real to her at least.

"Well, we will go out there sometime so you can see it, Mara." William told her. "Now, back to your schoolwork!" He changed the subject and went over to her workbooks at his desk in the den where Joanna had been helping her. His den was small, but had character. Framed pictures of Krista growing up were hung around the room and there was a few of Krista and Karen. Mara only knew that she had an aunt that died very young; Chad and Krista never went into an explanation. Today, she seemed to hone in on a small framed picture set in the built-in curio cabinet. "Who are these girls with this lady, grandpa?"

William came closer to look. It was the picture that he'd taken of Kris, Karen and Maria when they'd been on Block Island. Kris had the same picture, but he knew she kept it hidden away. He took a deep breath. Just the sight of it brought back the memories of that day; the smell of the ocean, the girls had been playing in the waves as they came in and went back out. He could still hear their laughter and watching Maria loving their daughters. He felt the tears form and swallowed hard. "That's your mom and your aunt Karen when they were little with their mom; your grandma." He said softly.

Mara opened up the glass door and picked up the picture to look closely. "Mommy and Aunt Karen look exactly the same, grandpa." She remarked. William wasn't sure how much Kris had told Mara about Karen, so he was careful to be vague. "Your mommy and her sister were identical twins, Mara." William told her.

"Mommy told me that Karen died a long time ago." Mara said as William nodded. It was helpful information for him to know what to say next; he was starting to feel like he was walking through a landmine field with his 6-year-old granddaughter. "She did, but that was a long time ago, Mara. Let's get back to your schoolwork now!" William wanted to move her away from the photo. He wasn't sure what else she knew and he didn't want to talk about it further. Mara continued to study the picture for a few more seconds, then put it back. "Okay, grandpa." She was surprisingly agreeable, and seemed to pay attention as she went through here reading and comprehension exercises. "Grandpa, those were taken on the island, weren't they?"

"Why, yes, they were, Mara? How could you tell?" He knew that she'd never been there. "I've told you; Jamie showed me!" Mara told him. "Grandpa, you don't believe me, do you?" She turned to him with such anger that it frightened him.

"Of course I do, Mara." William said. He knew that it was out of fear that he was agreeing. Maybe this was the real reason for Joanna's sudden departure? He was thankful that Mara agreed and dropped the subject. It was something he'd mention to Chad and Kris later.

Krista

Her hopes of having a better morning were gone as she saw Mr. Samuels was waiting for her at her office when she arrived. "Krista, you're late for another meeting! I thought we'd talked about this!" He was normally patient and she'd never had a problem with him. In the past week, he'd become that overbearing supervisor that was making her life more difficult. They used to have a good working relationship, and she accepted her responsibility for tardiness, but he'd known her during the kidnapping incident; he'd been supportive then. Not so much now.

"Mr. Samuels, I wasn't aware of a meeting this morning!" Krista told him. It was the truth. She didn't recall any morning meeting that had been set up as of yesterday.

"I sent out an email yesterday afternoon. Didn't you get it?" Mr. Samuels asked. His tone softened slightly.

"I really didn't, Mr. Samuels. I would have been here for a meeting if I had known about it. You can check my email if you want." Krista offered. She knew that there had been no email yesterday afternoon, and she'd stayed the entire day. At least not an email about a meeting with her supervisor!

"I'm positive that email was sent out to everyone, including you. But I'm willing to give you the benefit of the doubt, Krista. Would you mind if I look at your email?" Mr. Samuels asked. Krista was shocked that he didn't believe her, but more than willing to show him. She opened her office and booted up her desktop. Her hands were shaking

90

because she was infuriated that her boss would accuse her of lying and have to prove it, but he'd see that there was no email! She waited the uncomfortable few minutes while her computer loaded and found herself trying to talk to him to fill the awkward silence while they waited.

"What was the meeting about?" Krista asked, hoping it would further let him know she hadn't gotten the email.

Mr. Samuels just shook his head. "We'll discuss the subject after I look at your email," he told her coldly. It was then that she realized her job might be on the line, but she knew there was no email when she'd logged off her computer yesterday.

She logged onto her computer as soon as it came up and brought up her email. She waited impatiently as it loaded. It came up and she looked it over. She was shocked to see that there was an email there that had been sent yesterday at 2:30pm in regards to the meeting. The subject was 'Discussion with Parents About Counseling Students'. "What is this? I know I didn't get it, I was here at that time and checked my email!" She was beside herself.

"But its right here! Its even is marked as 'read'." The principal shook his head. "I'm sorry, Krista, but we need to discuss your employment here." Mr. Samuels told her. Krista felt as if her legs were going to give out on her, but managed to steady herself by grabbing onto the side of the desk.

"But, Mr. Samuels, I swear it wasn't there yesterday! I never saw it!" Krista insisted, but she could tell it was falling on deaf ears. He'd never treated her in this manner in her almost 12 years she'd been employed at this school, and it was clear he didn't believe her.

"Krista, you've been a wonderful employee here for so many years, but the past few months you've been late most days, missing meetings and it's become a problem. In fact, the last time you were late and missed an important meeting was only a few days ago. Now, you're telling me you didn't see this email, but it's clearly here and marked as it's been read. That tells me you forgot or it wasn't important or maybe both. I hate to do this, but I'm going to have to formally write you up." He looked at her with regret as he said the words.

Tears were forming in Krista's eyes as she brushed them away. It was a slap in the face and she knew that that email wasn't there yesterday. 'Someone must have gotten into my email when I wasn't looking and deleted it, then went back and made it reappear, marking it as read,' she thought to herself. Maybe it was being paranoid, but given her past experiences, anything was possible! The name that came to mind was Amanda Ahearn. She'd been part of the scheming with her sister who ended up being killed by police. But Amanda was in prison, so there was no way she could be doing this.

Krista managed to get her emotions in check as went to meet her first student of the day. It would take several days for Mr. Samuels to formally write her up and in the meantime, she vowed to herself to focus on her students now. She was also going to find out who was trying to get her fired! Her cell was ringing, and she prayed it wasn't her father calling to complain about something Mara had done. She looked at the number which was vaguely familiar. Nadine! She picked up quickly.

"Hello, this is Krista," she answered, hoping that she was right.

"Hi, Krista, my name is Sadie Mercotte, Nadine's aunt. I know we haven't met, but I know that Nadine had seen you before and was trying to get in touch with you last night." The woman sounded upset and Krista shuddered as a chill went through her.

"She did text me in the early morning and I tried her back later, Ms. Mercotte. Is everything okay?" Krista asked, concerned.

"No, I'm afraid not. Nadine was hit by a car this morning. She was doing her usual walking and was crossing the road on Atwood Avenue near the school. The car was speeding and didn't even stop. She's in the ICU at Merriam Hospital." Her aunt was tearful as she spoke. "She's been in and out of consciousness, but she mentioned calling you and how important it was that she speak to you."

Krista felt her anxiety kick in as her hands started to shake. "I...I'm so sorry about your niece, Ms. Mercotte. I do hope that she'll pull through. I only met her twice, but she's a kind young lady and been so helpful." Krista felt her eyes tear up at the thought of this young girl in a hospital bed fighting for her life.

"Can you come here? Today? Nadine insisted this morning before she lost consciousness again." Sadie Mercotte asked her. Krista was shocked that Nadine or anyone in her family would want her to visit! She was a stranger!

"Ms. Mercotte-" Krista began.

"Please call me Sadie," her aunt insisted. "I know this may seem strange to you, but Nadine has asked you to come. I want to honor what she wants at this critical time." She added. Krista knew what that meant. Nadine's condition wasn't promising; she was in the ICU after all.

"I can come after 3:30. Is that soon enough?" Krista hoped that it was. There was no way she'd be able to leave earlier today after missing another meeting!

"That should be fine. Visiting is usually only for family, but if you call me when you get here, I'll make sure that you get to see her. Thank you, Krista. It's been bothering her today." Sadie sounded as sad as Krista had felt when her mother had passed away only hours before she'd been reunited with her.

"I'll be there." Krista promised. She called Chad to ask him to pick Mara up. "What's going on, Kris?" Chad questioned, surprised that she wasn't picking her up. Krista remembered she hadn't told her husband about contacting Nadine, so she told him she was working late. She hated to lie to him, but telling him about visiting a psychic girl in the hospital wouldn't go over well. "I'll be home around 6 at the latest," Krista promised. Chad agreed to pick Mara up, "I'll pick up dinner on the way home." Chad asked, sounding uncharacteristically suspicious.

"Of course!" Krista reassured him. She knew he could tell something was wrong, but she couldn't tell him about Nadine. Not now.

Thankfully, the rest of the day went by without any drama so Krista was headed to the hospital by 3:30. She called Nadine's number to let

Sadie know that she was there when she was in the waiting room at the hospital. Sadie came down and immediately brought her upstairs to the ICU wing. She looked like an older version of Nadine; long dark hair, brown eyes. Sadie's petite figure was apparent even underneath the baggy pair of jeans and oversized sweatshirt she was wearing. Her eyes were swollen and red from crying. "She's been struggling since I talked to you this morning." Sadie said in a broken voice. "Thank you so much for coming."

"Of course." Krista said softly. She brought her to Nadine's room and as Krista looked through the small glass window in the door, she could barely make out a person with all the machines. She suddenly felt terrified. The last time she'd been in a hospital was to see her mother who died. Sadie reached out and held her hand. "I know this is hard for you, but I know that she needs this." Tears were running down Sadie's face as she opened the door. "Nadine, sweetheart, there's someone here to see you." Sadie approached the bed. Krista was glad that Sadie had told her the extent of her injuries-there was a reason for all the machines that were attached. As she crept closer to Nadine's bedside, she could feel her anxiety kick in, as she was reminded of her mother in her final hours. She swallowed back tears that threatened to spill out, creating a giant lump in her throat.

Nadine's face had cuts and bruises, including road-rash from where her face had probably hit the pavement. She had internal injuries, including a ruptured spleen which they'd already operated on and were monitoring. Her left leg was broken and suspended in a cast. There was a huge amount of gauze covering her head as she'd also suffered a concussion. They'd done an initial brain scan but didn't have the results back yet.

Krista choked back the tears and reached for her small pale hand that was lying off the side of the bed. "Nadine, its Krista. Krista Burton. You tried to call me last night after I texted you. I'm sorry I was asleep." She felt the tears rising as she spoke. Nadine's eyes fluttered slightly and she made a moaning sound. Krista turned to Sadie, concerned. "Are you sure this is a good idea? I don't want to make her upset, it seems….like she's in so much pain…" Krista was searching for better adjectives to describe the situation, but none would come to mind. Except that Nadine appeared to be dying.

Sadie shook her head. "Don't worry about bothering her Krista, she asked for you." She motioned for Krista to move and away, as she sat near Nadine's head. "Naddy, it's auntie. Krista is here for you. Please let her know what you need to tell her, sweetheart."

Nadine blinked her eyes, letting them know that she was conscious. "Krista is right here and holding your hand now." Krista grasped the pale frail hand again. "I'm right here, Nadine. What did you need to tell me?" She couldn't help the tears from falling as she watched the young girl try to talk. "Maybe get closer", Sadie suggested and Krista dropped her ear as close as possible to her mouth so that she could hear.

"Evil…back…wants….her…." Nadine managed to say.

"Do you mean Mara? Evil wants Mara?" Krista asked, trying to make sure she understood. Nadine shook her head slightly.

"Evil…back…wants…to hurt…you," Nadine managed to whisper. "It's with her…." She closed her eyes. Krista felt Nadine's slight grip let go. Krista was confused as she turned to Sadie. "What does she mean, Sadie? Evil wants me, it's with her?" Nadine's eyes remained closed and Sadie motioned for her to follow her out of the room. "Is she alright? Should we call the nurse?' Krista was more concerned about Nadine's current state than what she told her as she followed Sadie back outside the ICU room.

"She's just tired. The doctors have told me that this will happen. If there was a concern about anything, those machines would be making noises." Sadie advised. Krista knew that was true from her own experience with her mother. "But what she told me, 'Evil wants to hurt me, it's with her.' What does that mean? She said that the evil wasn't after my daughter, Mara." Krista wanted to clarify.

"The evil is after you, not your daughter. Yes, that's right, Krista." Sadie said quietly, "But she meant that the evil *is with* Mara."

Chad

The rest of his day flew by and when he took a quick break to get coffee from Brewed Awakenings coffee house down the street, he realized that he needed to pick up Mara. 'Damn! Why did Kris pick today of all days to work late?' He was annoyed. It was after 4:00 and William was probably ready to be done with his babysitting duties, especially with what had been happening lately. Friday couldn't come fast enough to get Mara into that therapist so they could have some sort of normalcy. Getting Mara back to school for starters! He got back to his office, finished up a few things and headed out to pick up his daughter.

On the way, he called William to let him know. He picked up almost immediately. "Chad, what's going on? I thought you or Kris were going to pick Mara up by 3:30?" Chad was confused, thinking that Krista had told her father that he would be picking her up.

"Didn't Kris call you? She called me to tell me she was working late and I was going to pick her up. Sorry, Bill. I'll be there in a few minutes."

"No, she didn't. But it's fine. I'll see you in a few." William hung up, although he sounded a little irritated. Chad knew that babysitting Mara this week was creating some conflict with his new relationship with Joanna. The phone rang through his Bluetooth in the car and he answered it on instinct, despite the amount of spam calls he received.

"Chad Burton," he answered in his professional voice in case it was a potential client.

"Hello, again, Chad. I spoke with you earlier today. So nice to know that you answer all your calls, even when you're not in the office." It was the same voice that had called earlier today and hung up. "Who is this?" Chad demanded. "How did you get this number?" He suddenly swerved in traffic to avoid hitting someone and decided to pull over.

"Good idea to pull over, Chad. No talking and driving for you." The female voice giggled, as he tried to remember where he'd heard the voice before. Yet, it was muffled and sounded hoarse, as though she'd smoked her way through a pack of Marlboros on a daily basis.

"Who are you and why are you calling me?" Chad demanded. He found himself looking around as he continued his conversation, feeling paranoid now that whoever was calling might be watching.

"Let's just say that I'm very interested in buying a property on Block Island and the word on the street is you're the one to deliver." She suddenly got to the point.

"I guess that depend on which property you're thinking about." Chad suddenly knew where this call was coming from; David Ackwell and his team of sketchy lawyers trying to bully him into getting Ahearn to sell his property.

"I think you know exactly which property I'm talking about; the Ahearn estate on the bluffs." The woman said in a mocking tone.

"Tell whoever paid you to give you a refund for your services. Don't call me again or I'll be forced to take legal action." Chad told the woman.

"I don't know what you're talking about, but I do know you'll be sorry, *Chad.*" The woman emphasized his name before she hung up. Chad brushed his hand through as his hair as he tried to piece together the conversation. Why would David Ackwell go to such lengths? He pulled himself together before he headed back out to pick up Mara. He thought about telling William about this, but he didn't want to worry him, so for now it was a non-issue.

He knew he needed to let Stan Ahearn know about the conversation despite his qualms about calling him two days in a row. It was surprising that Stanley picked up on the first ring. "Hello, Mr. Ahearn, I'm sorry to bother you. I just wanted to let you know I think David Ackwell has hired someone to try and scare you into selling." He went on to describe the conversation with the woman that still hadn't given her name.

"Thank you for telling me, Chad." Stan didn't seem overly concerned about the situation. "I'm sorry that there are David's people out there blowing up your phone. My advice is don't answer, let it go to voicemail. If they don't leave one, it's not important. Think of it as being those constant Spam calls you get from time to time." Stan advised him.

"Thanks, Stanley, I mean Mr. Ahearn," Chad caught himself with the formalities. Stanley laughed, "Please Chad, call me Stan. I hope you'll think about coming out to the property in a few weeks. Talk to your wife and to Bill too." He brought the subject up again.

"I will. I'll let you know in the next few days." Chad told him as they hung up as he arrived to pick Mara up from William's house. When he arrived, William looked exhausted and Mara seemed ready to go for once instead of playing one of her games.

"Daddy!" Mara was happy and almost bouncing with excitement, standing right behind her grandfather as he opened the door. "Daddy, Grandpa says we can go to Block Island sometime and see grandma's headstone!" William had a look of shock on his face, as Chad said "What?" He immediately came inside as William made a motion around his neck to stop talking about it. 'I'll explain when Mara isn't here,' he mouthed his response to Chad.

Chad nodded. "Ok, Mara. How about you go watch some TV while I talk to grandpa."

"Ok, daddy!" She giggled and tossed her blond curls as she headed to the living room. Chad threw up his hands as soon as she was out of sight. "What the hell happened today, Bill?" He ran his hands through his dark hair, trying to keep his frustration in check. After all, he'd been doing them a favor, and Mara….well, she was just Mara.

William showed Chad the picture of the headstone near the cliffs that Mara had drawn and told him everything that had happened that afternoon, including Joanna getting upset and leaving as well as Mara insisting that she wanted to visit Block Island. Chad listened without chiming in although he wanted to, given the events that occurred for *him* today.

Chad was surprised at Mara's drawing but refused to believe that she somehow hadn't seen pictures of it before. William was insistent. "Chad, we've never been there since the headstone was placed there, unless you and Kris went by yourselves!" Chad shook his head. "No,

Kris has talked about it with me, but we never have mentioned it to Mara."

Chad launched into his day with the conversations with the random woman that had called him twice and the conversations that he'd had with Stanley Ahearn, along with the invitation to go to his Block Island property in a couple of weeks. "I know it's a lot to take in, Bill, but I think it's a good idea. I was going to talk to Kris about it tonight, among the other things that happened today." He laughed, as it was his way of dealing with so much in a short period of time.

"I don't know, Chad. I'll have to think about it. I appreciate Stan's offer to include me, but right now I need to talk to Joanna and get things straightened out with her." William seemed overwhelmed with the drama today.

"I'm sorry that you and Joanna are having trouble. We'll have a talk with Mara again tonight, there's only one more day to get through until she sees the therapist. I'll do my best to get off work early tomorrow, Bill." Chad felt a huge sense of responsibility for what was happening with William and his relationship with Joanna. Krista had been right. He did need to start backing her up and being firm with his daughter.

"Thanks, Chad, it'll work out with Joanna hopefully. No matter what happens, Mara is my only granddaughter and she's my priority. If Joanna doesn't understand, maybe it's just not meant to be." He meant the words, but Chad could detect a wistful look in his eyes that told him that he really loved Joanna and was hoping to have a future with her.

"Mara! C'mon, let's go home. It's getting late and your mom's probably waiting on us for dinner!" Chad called to her. She appeared seconds later from around the corner which told him she was probably eavesdropping. She didn't say anything about what they were talking about though as she picked up her backpack and went to give William a hug. He picked her up and hugged her back. "See you tomorrow, sweetheart."

"I'll be a good girl tomorrow, grandpa. I promise." Mara said quietly. She was smart enough to know that she'd be getting a lecture from her father on the way home. She would be right. The minute they got in the car, Chad was firm, but fair. "Mara, you need to listen to Grandpa and Joanna from now on. They both love you, and want you to do well in school. Grandpa is used to you coming over and having fun, but because you were suspended, you need to do your work." Chad advised, as she was silent, looking out the window and nodding. "Mara, are you listening to me?"

She glanced over at him. "Yes, daddy," Mara replied dutifully. They were pulling into their driveway and he put the car in park. "We're home. It looks like mommy's home too." He saw Krista's SUV in the driveway.

"Ok, daddy." Mara said still looking out the window.

"What are you looking at?" Chad was getting annoyed that she seemed focused on something that he was clueless about. Was there a person that he hadn't seen when he was driving lurking around the house?

"It's Jamie. She told me I would like it on that island." Mara said quietly. Chad was shocked into silence, unsure what to say at this point. Hopefully the therapist could find out what was really going on. He quickly changed the subject.

"We'll talk to your mom about it. Let's go, it's getting late. I'm sure she's got dinner ready." Chad opened the childproof door to let Mara out. "Daddy, don't be mad at me. Jamie follows me and sometimes I don't want to talk to her." Mara told him as she got out of the car and grabbed her backpack. Chad gave her a hug as they walked into the house. "No one is mad at you, Mara. We just want to get you back in school and have fun."

She nodded, following several feet behind him into the house. "I wish I could, daddy." She whispered, but he was already inside and didn't hear her.

***

As Chad walked in the door with Mara trailing behind, he could smell something burning and streams of smoke began to curl up from the oven. He ran to open the oven door and found a now-burnt pizza that was that obviously was supposed to be dinner. He quickly shut the oven off and grabbed the oven mitts to retrieve the inedible pizza. "KRIS! Where are you?" Chad yelled up the stairs, then glanced around for his daughter. Mara was inside behind him, and he realized the front door was still wide open. "Mara, close that door please. Your mom must be upstairs." For once, Mara didn't give him a hard time and shut the door, as he ran up the stairs two at a time, still calling her name.

"KRIS!" He immediately went to their bedroom and found her. She was face-down across their bed asleep. 'She must have been really tired," Chad thought initially. But on closer inspection, he noticed a pill bottle on the nightstand. It was the lorazepam that her Dr. Mayfield had prescribed for her to use 'as needed.' It had been a long time since she'd taken them, but now apparently, she'd felt the need to. But how many? Chad's heart began to pound as he reached for her pulse and relieved that she had one. "Kris, honey, it's Chad. Wake up. We're home!" Chad whispered in her ear with no response. "Kris! Wake up!" Chad felt himself panicking as he began shaking his wife. How many had she taken? What if she'd overdosed? He was looked for his phone as Krista finally moved, and opened her eyes. "Chad? What time is it?"

Chad felt a rush of relief as she seemed to be fine. "Kris, its 6:30! Mara and I just got home and there was a pizza burning up in the oven! What were you thinking? How many of these did you take?" He showed her the bottle of pills.

"Only one, really!" Krista insisted. "I haven't taken one in at least 6 months. I usually took only half of one, and this time I took a full one. I guess it knocked me out." She sat up and tried to get off the bed, but stumbled as she stood up. Chad's relief quickly turned to anger as he realized how awful this situation could have been.

"Kris, you could've burned down the house, with you in it! Do you realize that?" He hated how he sounded, but she'd scared him and he was reacting on instinct now.

"Mommy, daddy?" Mara's voice made him stop his tirade as she appeared at the open bedroom door.

"Hi, sweetheart. How was your day at grandpas?" Krista managed to walk over to Mara without stumbling. Chad was glad that she was telling him the truth about the amount of medication she'd taken. There was a time after her mother died that she'd been taking too many and Dr. Mayfield had taken her off of them. Luckily, she'd never gotten to the point of addiction, but Chad was still leery and wanted to make sure she didn't take them regularly.

"Joanna got mad and left, then me and grandpa had a good day. I drew a picture. Can we go visit Block Island, mommy?" Mara told Krista, as Chad wished for an invention for a 6-year-old filter. She'd managed to evoke more stress in her few sentences than she'd even realized for Krista. And for him because now he needed to explain.

Krista looked to Chad. "What's going on here?" She shook her head, her eyes filling with tears as she headed for the master bathroom and shut the door. Chad ushered Mara downstairs and instructed her to stay there. Mara was upset now and started to cry. "Mommy's mad at me now!"

"No, she's not. She just had a stressful day. Why don't you go watch one of your shows, and I'll be down in a few minutes?" Chad said soothingly. Mara nodded and went downstairs. He went back up and knocked on the door. "Kris, honey, everything's fine. I'll explain, just open the door."

Krista opened the door and finished washing her face. "Let me start by explaining *my* day first!" She told him about the email that someone had confiscated and made it look as though she was blowing off a meeting. She left out the part about Nadine's accident because she knew he'd be upset about her trying to contact Nadine again. "I was just upset when I got home, so I took a whole pill instead of a half, then put the pizza in the oven. I didn't know it would affect me like this. I won't do that again, honey, I promise. I'm sorry." Krista apologized, horrified that she could've burnt down their home that they loved so much.

"I'm just glad we got home when we did. I'll go order some take-out from Pat's Restaurant and get Mara situated. Go take a quick shower and we can talk after dinner about today's events." Chad knew that his wife needed some time to wake up. He wasn't sure how he was going to tell her about Mara's day about the headstone, his strange phone calls or the invite from Stanley to Block Island, but he definitely wasn't bringing it up tonight!

An hour later, Chad had picked up some chicken parmesan and pasta from Pat's. Krista had shaken off the effects of her anxiety meds and ate some dinner together. They kept the topics off all of the day's several dramas that had unfolded. Mara was fairly quiet during dinner. Surprisingly, she took her bath and went to bed without the usual arguments so that Chad and Krista could finally discuss their day.

Chad explained the phone calls about trying to get Stanley to sell the property and David Ackwell, then the drawing that Mara had done of the headstone of her mother's grave at Stanley's property on Block Island. "She's never seen it Kris, yet she knows. She keeps talking about this 'Jamie' person that she sees and talks to. Do you really think the therapist can help with this?" He'd assumed everything would be resolved with therapy. After today, he was starting to wonder if this was something else that couldn't be explained away as an imaginary friend.

Krista shook her head. It was tempting to tell him about Nadine, but she was still worried that he'd question why she'd contacted her. "I don't know, Chad. Honestly, I'm not sure it's a therapist that can help, but it's necessary to get her back in school." The TV was on in the background and neither of them had been paying attention. Krista suddenly looked over as a headline came across the screen; **"Local Providence Woman in Critical Condition after Hit and Run Accident."**

She stopped talking and went into the living room, grabbing the remote to raise the volume in time to hear the news anchor talking. "A young woman was struck down this morning as she was crossing road near Hope Street in Providence. The vehicle was described as an older model black Dodge Ram truck with tinted windows. Nadine Shaffer, age 25, is a local reiki/medium at Healing Solutions owned by her aunt, Ms. Sadie Mercotte. Any information about the accident including witnesses or persons that can identify the vehicle involved are urged to call Providence police. Ms. Shaffer is in critical condition at Merriam

Hospital." A photo of Nadine flashed on the screen along with the video of the vehicle as it struck her. Krista felt the tears sliding down her face as Chad came into the room.

"Kris, isn't that Nadine? That psychic girl that told you about Karen?" Chad recognized the name. Krista nodded. She knew she had to tell Chad about the part of her day she'd left out earlier.

"Yes, it is." She took a deep breath. " I need to tell you about what else happened today that led me to taking those meds again." Krista admitted to her husband. No better time than the present.

Krista

She'd never planned to tell Chad about contacting Nadine again. That is, until the news mentioned the accident. It didn't occur to her until now that the media would be involved as she'd visited Nadine. But she understood why it would be; a hit and run with serious injuries was newsworthy. She couldn't help but think that it wasn't an accident at all; it was just too coincidental to her reaching out to Krista after her call to Nadine the previous night. "So what happened other than what you told me? Do I need another beer for this one?" Chad asked, jokingly.

"Probably." Krista said with a straight face. She told him about contacting Nadine last evening and getting the text in the middle of the night. She mentioned the glass breaking the same time as the text.

"Do you really believe what you're saying, Kris? That some ghost broke the picture frame, and cracked the mirror because you texted that psychic girl?"

"No, let me finish. When I called her back at work today, her aunt informed me that she'd been hit by the car." Krista went into detail about going to see Nadine and what she had said to her. "She said that the evil isn't after Mara; that the evil is with Mara."

Chad was quiet for a moment, then got up to grab another beer out of the fridge. Krista could tell he thought it was bullshit and was ready to just stop the conversation. She was too tired from the day's events, plus what was left of the lorazepam that she was going to flush down

110

the toilet tonight. It was useless and didn't do anything except make her feel worse.

"Mara has said and drawn things today that I saw for myself. I don't know where they're coming from." Chad said, looking confused, almost afraid. "Then she was looking at the window in the car tonight. I asked her what she was doing and she told me that Jamie was following her and she was getting tired of it. What do you think we should do?"

Krista was glad that Chad didn't think she was going crazy. There really was something going on with Mara that couldn't be explained away that she had 'behavioral problems' or that this was an 'imaginary friend.' "I'm not sure. She's got that appointment the day after tomorrow with Marcy, the therapist. I'm wondering what that will accomplish except get her back into school though. I'm pretty sure Marcy isn't trained in working with children that seem to be interacting with ghosts." She joked and then began laughing, because what else could they do?

Chad laughed along with her, "I know, right? Next time, Kris, make sure that the therapist has exorcism certification in her repertoire." Krista giggled. There was nothing funny about the situation, but they needed to laugh to remain sane. They were both so stressed and unsure of what to do now. "I'm going to stay in contact with her aunt and maybe she can make some suggestions. Nadine learned from her, so I'm sure she could help or at least point us in the right direction." She waited for Chad to tell her all the 'psychic stuff' was nonsense and make fun of her, but he shocked her by being more open to what she was telling him.

"I can't say that I believe that ghosts are infiltrating our house, but after what we went through with your mom and sister, I definitely think some things defy explanation. Besides, something isn't right with Mara. I saw it today. Tonight when she was looking out the window in the car, she seemed to be in a trance. It couldn't hurt to talk to her." Chad said with a serious look on his face, so she knew he wasn't just placating her.

Krista curled up next to her husband and relaxed against his arm, grateful that he was understanding. "Thanks, babe. I think it might help, and at this point, I don't think it'll hurt. She felt closer to Chad now that he seemed to understand that it wasn't just 'all in her head'; that something was really going on with Mara. Something that might not be solved by going to a therapist.

They headed up to bed around 10:00 and checked on Mara, who was fast asleep. They shut the door quietly. "Looks like we could have some quick fun, if you're in the mood, Kris." He pulled her into his arms and gave her a long kiss that made her realize how much she'd missed their intimacy because of their busy schedules.

"I am definitely in the mood. Let's go!" Krista pulled him into their bedroom, surprising herself with the passion that she had for spur-of-the-moment sex. It wasn't that they never did. It was just very sporadic, and usually planned around Mara's schedule. This time was different; spontaneous and as if they were finally shedding some of the final scars of the past years. It was actually better than it'd been on their honeymoon. She'd never felt closer to him and it was after 11:00 when they were resting, and Chad was setting the alarm for the next day. "We need to do this more often," Krista laid her head on her husband's bare chest. "I agree. More often as in every night!" Chad told her as he gave her a long kiss. They both drifted off into sleep.

Krista woke up to the sound of footsteps in the hallway. Her heart was pounding as she sat up in bed and nudged Chad. "Honey, wake up! I hear someone in the hallway!" Chad mumbled and turned over, but she heard them again: the creaking noise seemed to be going downstairs. "Chad! Wake up!" She wasn't whispering now, as he finally woke up. "What? He was irritated.

"I heard footsteps. Can you please go check on Mara?" Her whole body was immobilized by fear, heart felt as though it was jumping out of her chest. She couldn't explain why, but she was afraid to go into the hallway. Chad groaned as he got out of bed and put on his pajama bottoms. "It's probably just Mara going to the bathroom." He told her as he opened the bedroom door and went down the hall. It was silent for a few moments when he called out, "Mara! What are you doing?"

Krista flung the covers off herself and threw on a long shirt, her maternal instinct took over her fear. "Chad? Mara? What's going on?" Her adrenaline kicked in as she rushed down the stairs, but she couldn't see them. "Chad? Mara? Where are you?" She was frantic now, and uncertain if she was dreaming, but as she stubbed her toe on a dining room chair, she knew that she was awake. The back deck light was on and the sliding glass door was open. She saw Mara and Chad sitting on chairs on the deck. Mara was staring straight ahead, while Chad was saying her name over and over; "Mara, it's daddy, Mara can you hear me?" But she wasn't responding.

Krista rushed over to them, "What's going on? What's wrong with her?" Krista hugged Mara to her, but Mara didn't respond. She was staring straight ahead as if she could see something in the distance.

"She's sleepwalking, Kris." Chad whispered to her. "She was walking down the stairs when I came out and I followed her. You know they say not to wake someone that's sleepwalking. Here we are." He waved a hand in front of her face. "Mara, its daddy. Wake up!"

"She's here." Mara said in a low voice that was completely unlike her usual high-pitched childish tone. Chad held her hands and looked directly in her open, yet unseeing eyes. "Mara, sweetheart, who's here?"

Mara seemed to be waking up as she turned toward Chad and Krista. She was finally blinking and looking confused. "Daddy, mommy? Why am I outside? I'm cold." She was shivering, as the night temperatures had dropped into the low 50s that night. "You were walking in your sleep, sweetheart, let's get you inside and warmed up!" Chad scooped her up in his arms, while Krista ran upstairs to run a warm bath. Mara was shaking and Chad grabbed a thick green throw blanket to wrap her in while the water was filling. "Daddy, I had a scary dream. It was Jamie, but she was real and telling me scary things."

"What scary things?" Chad asked.

"She told me that she hates you and mommy; that something's going to happen to you." Mara began to cry. "I used to like her, but now she scares me."

Chad hugged Mara close, comforting her. "Sweetheart that was just a dream. Dreams aren't real, just like Jamie isn't real. Nothing is going to happen to me or your mommy." Chad reassured her, although he had to admit, he had been a little alarmed with the sleepwalking.

"She's real, daddy." Mara insisted. Krista came downstairs just then, "Mara, let's get you into the tub for a few minutes to warm up and then into bed." Mara was quiet during the quick bath, and Krista made an effort not to ask about her dream so that she would be able to go back to sleep. "Mommy, can I sleep with you and daddy?" Her daughter surprised her with that request. She hadn't asked to sleep in their bed since she was three years old and sick with the flu. Krista suddenly felt closer to her just then. "Of course you can. Get dressed and then come on in, okay?" Krista gave her a quick kiss on the forehead.

Krista found herself unable to sleep afterwards, while Mara who was between her and Chad, slept soundly. There had been too much drama in too short a time period. She remembered her own 'bad dreams' especially the most recent one and with the events that had happened in the past week, it was enough to keep her mind racing until she finally fell asleep an hour before the alarm went off at 6:00. Krista groaned as she hit snooze several times. She was dozing in and out as she heard Chad getting up and showering, then waking Mara up to get her started. "Kris, honey, you're gonna be late if you don't get up." Chad gave her a gentle hug.

"So tired. What time is it?" She asked groggily.

"It's 6:45." Chad told her and she immediately jumped out of bed. "Why didn't you wake me up before? I've got less than 30 minutes to get out the door!" She said, frustrated. He knew she hated to rush around in the morning.

"I'm sorry, Kris, but you were tired. Don't worry, Mara is all ready to go. I put some coffee on for you, so get in the shower and get ready. I'll take Mara to your dads this morning." Chad told her calmly. Krista nodded and quickly showered, dressing quickly and headed downstairs where Chad had a cup of coffee with her favorite vanilla creamer waiting for her. "I'm sorry if I was upset with you, babe. I'm just stressed about being late! Pretty sure I'll be getting written up today for the past couple of weeks." Krista was in panic mode now.

"Don't worry about what hasn't happened, yet Kris. Just get to work and take it one step at a time. Remember?" Chad reminded her of one of Dr. Mayfield's recurring 'adages' that she told her over and over. She kissed him and gave Mara a hug. She looked cute in her little jeans and sky-blue sweatshirt. At least Chad had made sure she matched! Mara had a habit of picking mismatched outfits that looked as though she'd dressed for a walking yard sale.

"Be good for grandpa today, okay kiddo? I'll pick you up tonight." Mara nodded. "Bye, mommy." She seemed less like her usual obstinate self in the past 24 hours. Krista was skeptical, but she was going to take it for what it was. Maybe this 'Jamie' person had scared her enough to stop antagonizing everyone around her.

Krista made it with a few minutes to spare, knowing that Mr. Samuels would be watching. Sure enough, as soon as she walked through the reception area toward her office, he 'happened' to be walking through the area. "Good morning, Krista." He greeted her on a first name basis which she thought was an improvement of the Ms. Burton nonsense from a few days ago.

"Good morning!" She forced herself to sound cheerful despite her anxiety about Mara and last evening. She was looking forward to a few minutes to catch up on her voicemails and emails when Mr. Samuels followed her into her office and shut the door behind him. "Something has been brought to my attention that is very disturbing, Krista." His voice was serious and her heart started pounding. What now? She noticed he had a piece of paper in his hand which was noticeably shaking.

"I received a forwarded email last night that was received from one of your student's parents. He placed the piece of paper down on her desk in front of her. "This was an email that was sent by you, from your email address here at the school. "Now, I understand that sometimes parents get upset and carried away when suggestions are made to them by professionals, but I have to tell you, I'm shocked at what was written in this email! I have to address this with you." He sounded apologetic, but not enough to make her feel confident that this was going to go well.

"Edward, I haven't written an email to a parent in at least a month. You know that I would never be unprofessional, especially when it comes to an email!" Krista was already in defense mode. She very rarely communicated with parents via email for the very reason that information could be taken out of context.

She picked up the printed email that Edward handed to her to read. At the top was from her own email address at the school and she knew immediately that someone ws after her. The message sent in the forwarding was blunt and to the point;

Fwd: From: ban.summers@gstone.com to
Edward.Samuels.johnston.edu
"Mr. Samuels, I'm very disappointed to have this appear in my inbox this evening about my son. I sincerely hope that this woman will not continue to work for the school. She is unprofessional, a bully and should not be working anywhere in any school district!"
Beverly Summers
From: kristaburton@johnston.edu
"Mrs. Summers

Your son, Devin Summers had an appointment with me yesterday. He really needs some motivation from home, as he is lacking in that area. He has goals to go to college, yet at this point, he'll be lucky to graduate. I'm hoping that you can work with him on focusing on his schoolwork, so that he doesn't fall behind. Please contact me if you have any questions about this and how we can work together to help him realize he needs to maybe rethink his future plans of college choices. Perhaps a vocational college would be more appropriate.
Sincerely,
Krista Burton

Krista was stunned after reading the email that had her name attached it, and that it had her email address. The only accurate statement in the email was meeting with Devin, but she'd given him support as she did all of her students. "This isn't true, Edward. You know that I would never say those things to a student or a parent! I did not write this! You know me Edward, I would never say such things to anyone in person, email or over the phone!"

"It came from your email from the top of the page. I'm just telling you about it because I want you to follow up with her immediately this morning." He said in a serious tone. "I know you've had nothing but respect for your students, but this needs to be addressed immediately." He was nervously fumbling with his tie. "Mrs. Summers called me this morning, demanding an explanation!"

Krista tried not to let her anger about this email ruin her morning, or let her boss know that she was upset. "I'm demanding an explanation for how an email got sent from my computer that I didn't write! Edward, you've worked with me for years, you know I would never say to this to a student or a parent! Someone hacked into my computer and sent this to make it look like it was me!" She knew she was repeating herself, but he had to know something was wrong; that someone was out to sabotage her!

"I understand that, Krista. I'm going to have security go over the footage from the cameras in the office to figure this out. In the meantime, we need to respond to Mrs. Summers as soon as possible." Edward advised her. Krista felt a little relieved that he believed her enough to check the cameras, but what if whoever was doing this managed to dodge them? She hadn't forgotten about the meeting message that someone had marked as read.

"I appreciate it. I'll call her in a few minutes. I just have a 9:00 student and then I'll follow up with her." Krista promised. Her phone rang just then, announcing the student's arrival. "My student is here. I'll let you know as soon as I speak to Mrs. Summers." Krista assured him.

*   *   *

After many apologies and promising Mrs. Summers that she didn't write the email, Krista was hopeful that she could salvage her job with the understanding that the student would be transferred to another counselor.

Mrs. Summers agreed to the transfer and was less angry at the end of the call. Krista was relieved. "Thank you, Edward. I appreciate you giving me the benefit of the doubt. But I really hope that you'll check with security, because I didn't write that email. There's someone here that's out to get me in trouble for whatever reason and it's not only detrimental to myself, but to the students as well."

Edward agreed with her. "I will be checking with security today and let you know if they found anything. Make sure that you change your password to your computer and also that it is shut down before you leave for the day."

"I will." Krista knew that she always shut down her computer, but she was definitely changing the password and being more careful. She was sure that if whoever got away with this twice was going to try it again.

William

He'd tried calling Joanna several times last night after Kris and Chad picked Mara up, but it went straight to voicemail. 'She must really be upset,' William found it difficult not to get her lack of contact. He'd finally given up and tried to watch some old Andy Griffith reruns on TV when she finally called him back at 8:30. He had mixed emotions as he picked up the phone.   "Hi, Bill. I'm sorry, I was busy out in the garden this afternoon. Then I took a nap and just had some dinner, and saw that you called." Joanna's tone didn't indicate any anger from this afternoon, much to his relief.

"I'm just glad you got back to me. I thought you might still be angry at me." William was a bundle of nerves, but he really was just being honest with this woman that he hoped would be part of his future.

"Bill, I'm really sorry that I left things like I did. It wasn't fair to you. You're only doing the best you can. I guess it just brought me back to my own struggles with my kids and my granddaughter. Anna can be a handful, just like Mara sometimes! I was babysitting for her yesterday, and I guess what was going on with Mara hit a nerve. It's really fine, Bill. I overreacted." Joanna admitted. "Sometimes being grandparents can be just as tough, even though I've heard it's supposed to be easy; spoil them and send them home!" She laughed. Bill loved her laugh, it was light and giggly.

"I'm really glad, Jo. I've got one more day with Mara tomorrow, but I'd love for you to come visit. Maybe we could start over?" William suggested, wishing that he'd asked her to come tonight, not tomorrow.

"Could I come over tonight, Bill? I feel like we should talk in person." Joanna just answered his prayers.

"I'd love that, I really missed you after you left today." He threw caution to the wind, glad that she seemed to feel the same as he did. She was there an hour later and they were able to talk, straighten things out, which made William more confident than ever that he wanted Joanna in his life permanently. He wasn't ready to propose marriage, and he was certain that she wasn't either. He brought up Joanna moving in with him again, but she shook her head. "I'm still not ready to make that step yet. But I am glad that we worked things out."

William talked to her about the rest of the day with Mara and the strange picture of the headstone she'd drawn as well as the invitation to visit the Ahearn property on Block Island in a few weeks. "I haven't been back in 7 years." He admitted, "But I think it would be good for Mara if I went too, since I think that Kris and Chad are planning to go."

"I'll think about it." Joanna said conservatively. "I've just got a lot going on with my son at home. Besides, I've got a heavy work schedule this next week. But we'll see." She changed the subject to some movie that she wanted to see and the discussion ended there. William tried not to ask more questions as it was clear she didn't want to give details about her son, but it bothered him that they'd been together for about 9 months. Yet, she had never introduced him anyone in her family, including her son.

"Ok, no pressure here" William joked. He was just happy that she was there with him. He felt a connection with her, and if there was a rift with her family, it wouldn't bother him; he was no one to judge considering his upbringing. Joanna did spend the night that made him feel more confident about their relationship. But something felt off; she was secretive and it was starting to bother him more than he'd like to admit.

***

The doorbell rang, jerking him out of a deep sleep. He woke up disoriented. William had never slept this late, but he'd had a dream about Maria last night. It wasn't like the dreams in the past where it was experiences he'd had when he was younger It was fresh in his mind that he could recall was hanging over him, like a low-lying cloud that he couldn't shake.

He could see Maria standing near the headstone that Mara had drawn and kept saying something that he couldn't hear, but she looked afraid. As he came closer, and closer so that he was next to her, her eyes looked frightened, "Look out! Behind you!" She warned as she moved closer to the cliff. As he looked behind him, there was a black shadow. He couldn't make out a face, the shadow of a woman seemed to be coming from the ground, hovering over him. "Be careful, Bill! You need to help Mara. Don't let her go!" He could feel Maria's presence as she went to hug him and then without warning, she disappeared over the cliff. "No! Don't go!" He'd shouted to her, just as the noise at the door had woken him. Joanna was still sound asleep as he got up to answer the door.

The doorbell rang again and William quickly put on his robe and ran downstairs. Chad was there with Mara who looked as tired as William felt. "It's been a long night, Bill. She's probably going to take a nap today."

"Really, what's going on?" William asked, hoping that he wasn't in for another day of feisty Mara. Especially since Joanna was here.

"Mara, why don't you go lie down on the couch and grandpa will be right with you?" Chad told Mara as she was just standing in the hallway, likely overhearing their conversation. She didn't argue with him for once.

As soon as she was out of earshot, Chad filled him in on the night's events, including Mara sleepwalking. William listened as he now knew that he would need to go to Block Island. He kept thinking about his dream and how he'd been warned by Maria to protect Mara. Yet he didn't say anything to Chad knowing that he was headed to work.

"I'm sure everything will be fine today, Chad. Just get to work. I'll call if necessary." William told him, hoping that he wouldn't need to.

"Well, definitely call if you need her to be picked up early. Kris has her hands full with work lately." Chad advised.

"Is everything okay with her?" William was concerned now. He didn't want his daughter to lose her job that she'd loved all these years.

"Oh, yes, it's fine." Chad told him, although it was far from that, but he didn't want to worry William. "Just call me if you need anything regarding Mara, okay?" He said quickly, as he headed out the door. He was now running late. "Either Kris or I will pick Mara up around

3:30 or 4:00!" Chad yelled out the car window as he was backing out of the driveway.

As soon as William came back in the house, Joanna had gotten up and made her way downstairs. "Good morning," she gave him a kiss as she grabbed a coffee cup, then discovered there was no coffee yet and began making some immediately. He loved that she felt comfortable enough in his house to just go about her routine. "Morning, Jo, sorry, I overslept and Chad was dropping off Mara, didn't get the chance to make the coffee yet." He said apologetically.

"Wow! We slept in! Not a problem, Bill," Joanna laughed as she pointed to the clock which read 7:45am. They were usually up by 6:30. She glanced over toward the living room where Mara was lying down. "Is that Mara over there *sleeping*?" Joanna sounded surprised. William was too, it wasn't like her to just go lie down, she usually had so much energy.

"Is she sick? Maybe I should check on her." Joanna offered, her nursing instincts kicking in. William almost agreed, but then shook his head. "Let me check in on her. She's in a mood today." He told Joanna lightly, but she knew what he meant. Joanna went to start the coffee.

William went over to the couch where Mara was curled up with her favorite throw blanket that he'd had bought for her when she was only two years old. It had been white with unicorns and rainbows on it. Now, it was showing its age, more yellow than white and the emblems had faded, but still always available to her. Her eyes were closed and appeared to be sleeping as he put his hand to her forehead to see if she was running a fever. To his surprise, she was actually cold. "Mara? Sweetheart, would you like some breakfast?"

"No, grampa. Tired." Mara murmured as she rolled over away from the TV that was on. William was concerned but remembered Chad had told him she was sleepwalking last night. He tried not to go into overprotective mode and turned the TV off as he put the blanket over her bare feet sticking out. "Ok, get some sleep. I'll make you something when you get up."

"I'm trying, grandpa, but Jamie keeps talking to me. She won't stop." Mara complained, but then seemed to fall back to sleep. This 'Jamie' was starting to concern William. He knew something wasn't right with her, but he wasn't going to press the panic button too soon. "Grampa, can you turn on the TV? I can't hear her as loud when there's noise."

William turned it on. It was on the local news when a headline going across the screen caught his eye; **'Local Providence Woman in Critical Condition After Hit and Run Accident.'** He turned up the volume to hear more. Her name was Nadine Shaffer. The name rang a bell, wasn't that the name of the psychic that Krista had seen right before she questioned him about Karen? He listened as the news mentioned that she was now in a coma and the outcome was not good. "'Oh I wonder if Kris knows about this,' William couldn't help but think of his daughter. If it wasn't for this woman, Krista may have never found out the truth and Maria's whereabouts would still be unknown. Mara seemed to be sound asleep so he turned the volume down so that it was barely audible and went back out to the kitchen, just as Joanna dropped a coffee mug. "Shit!" She looked flustered as she began cleaning up the wet ceramic pieces amongst spilled coffee.

"You okay?" William asked Joanna who turned her glance from the TV back to the shards of broken ceramic scattered on the floor.

"Sure, I'm okay. Just clumsy this morning and sorry for breaking your coffee cup, and making a mess." Joanna made light of it, although her body language was telling him she was upset.

William gave her a hug. "Jo, it's just a coffee cup. Mara is fine with you, don't worry." He assumed that she was on edge about getting along with Mara today. "I can't believe what happened to that young girl on the news." William was still shocked about Nadine's accident. Joanna was quiet for a moment as she scooped up the last of the cup remains and stood up. "I did. That's awful! I hope she'll be okay." She replied. There was something in her voice that told him she didn't want to talk about it.

"So what's on your agenda today, Jo?" William changed the subject. He'd mentioned the situation with Krista and this psychic in the past to her. Maybe that was why she seemed so uncomfortable.

"I've got the 11 to 7 shift today, so I'll need to get showered and get ready." Joanna looked at the clock, seeing that it was already 9:00. "Oh, wow, I should get going." Joanna hadn't brought her scrubs or any change of clothes. She gave William a hug and kiss. "I'll call you later, Bill."

William couldn't help but feel unsettled about their relationship, but knew that at least they weren't in a place where she was upset. "Have a good day, Jo." He told her as she headed out the door. His feelings made him feel too vulnerable, but he also knew that he hadn't been this happy since he had met Maria.

Chad

Chad yawned as he pulled up to the Carson Realty office and ran his hands through his dark hair that seemed to be peppered with more gray lately. It had been a rough night for all of them, but he knew that when Kris was stressed out, she didn't sleep well. He was sure that she bore the brunt of Mara's sleepwalking last night. 'One more day and then she'll have her appointment with the therapist, then back at school,' he thought to himself.

"Good morning, Mr. Burton." The receptionist, Kathy Cartel always had a smile on her face in the morning. Her sunny disposition was the main reason he'd hired her last year; she was only 23 and going to school to finish her marketing degree at Rhode Island College. She was cute and petite; only 5'1" with long blonde hair that was usually up in a ponytail and coffee-colored eyes with a sprinkle of freckles across her nose. Kathy had the ability to make others feel at ease and always seemed in tune as to how clients were feeling. Chad often joked that she should be a psychology major because she could read people and always seemed to say the right things to bring a smile to their face.

"Morning, Kathy, any calls this morning? I'm running a little late." Chad stated the obvious. He hated being late as he always felt a sense of responsibility to set an example at the office. He was usually at his office before Kathy arrived.

"There was a call for you, but Michelle took it since you hadn't arrived yet. I think it was David Ackwell." Kathy told him, with a look of trepidation on her face. She knew that David was an important client and also knew that it was the one account Chad wanted to manage himself.

"When did he call?" Chad was suddenly on alert that Michelle had decided to take Ackwell's call after he'd told her he wanted to deal with David himself from now on.

"Just a few minutes ago, Mr. Burton. She might still be on the phone now." Kathy said. "Mr. Burton, I'm sorry if you didn't want her to take the call, I didn't know." She began apologizing, reading the concern on his face.

"No worries, Kathy. It's not a problem. I just didn't expect him to be calling, especially at this time of day. But from now on if he calls and I'm not available, please tell him I'll get back to him. He's not to work with our other agents." Chad was angry with Michelle, after he'd specifically told her he would be taking over.

He walked toward Michelle's office when he heard her say, "He won't be a problem, David, trust me. I think it'll all work out as we discussed." Chad didn't think it was unreasonable to assume that she was talking about Stanley Ahearn's property.

Chad was fuming as he was tempted to storm into her office demanding to know 'who' was a problem and what would work out, but stopped himself. Maybe it was better to actually play her game and use it to his advantage. He knew one thing; Michelle wasn't the only one who could be devious. His office was right past hers and he chose the opportunity to walk in her line of sight. "Good morning, Michelle." He said to her and stood there for a moment. Long enough to make her uncomfortable. "I'll need to get back to you on that." She said quickly and hung up the phone.

"Good morning, Chad. I was just talking to Patrick Sampson about another property that he wanted to check out in South Kingstown." Michelle recovered quickly, but not fast enough. The brief look of 'oh, shit' and her flushed face gave her away. Did she really think he was that stupid? He enjoyed her moment of despair, as fleeting as it was.

Chad resisted the urge to tell her what a liar she'd proved herself to be. "Great! I hope that you'll be hard at work on that today." He said evenly, as he went to his office and shut the door, harder than usual. 'That lying bitch,' he thought to himself. He knew he needed a plan, but first he needed to know what hers was. He picked up the phone and asked Kathy to start a log of all calls coming in and out and where they were transferred to. "It's just to get an idea of where our clientele is coming from," Chad told her. "We've been getting some spam calls that I want to track." It wasn't a lie, he'd had a couple of them in the past day.

"No problem, Mr. Burton." Kathy agreed. Chad just hoped he could trust her, as clearly he couldn't trust Michelle any longer. As an afterthought, he added "please keep this to yourself. I just think it's easier to track that way." Chad wanted Kathy to understand this was a private request so that Michelle and Greg didn't feel like they were under surveillance. "Thank you, Kathy. I'll check in with you on a daily basis."

Chad felt a little relieved knowing that he was taking steps to figure out whatever Michelle's plan was with Ackwell. He knew his next step was to talk with Stanley Ahearn. Stanley's receptionist picked up and Chad asked for him. "Who may I ask is calling?" The receptionist asked.

"Chad Burton, it's really important." He made sure he wasn't going to be put through to voicemail. A minute later, Stanley was answering. "Chad, what's going on? Daphne said it was urgent." Stanley sounded interested, yet somewhat irritated at the same time. Chad hoped this warranted as urgent.

"I just wanted to let you know that when I came in today, one of my agents took a call from Ackwell after I had specifically asked her not to. I overheard her on the call saying 'he won't be a problem, it will all work out as we discussed.' I know she was talking to David, because she said his name." When Chad said the words, he felt stupid to bother Stanley. Maybe he'd jumped the gun. Maybe David Ackwell *was* looking at other properties and giving up on Block Island.

Stanley was silent for a few moments and Chad was sure he was going to tell him to stop being paranoid. "Chad, I think it's important that you don't say anything to her about this and in the meantime, collect some evidence of the calls, maybe even recording them if you can. I appreciate you letting me know about this, because there's a reason that David wants this property. I'm not sure what that motivation is yet, but clearly there's someone driving this train and I don't think it's David Ackwell." Stanley surprised him.

"I've already got my receptionist tracking calls in and out for everyone at the agency. She's on it now." Chad told him.

"Good thinking, Chad, you're on the ball. I knew there was a reason Bill put you in charge there." Stanley told him. "I think we should do that Block Island trip next week instead of the following. What do you think? What about next weekend? Apparently, I need to be back in town sooner than I thought."

Chad thought quickly, hoping he could make that happen. After all, it would be over a weekend, or would it? "Would that be the second weekend in October, Mr. Ahearn?" He wanted to clarify.

"Yes. I was hoping to talk Bill into coming over too with his new fling, what's her name? Joan? Joanne? We could get together, discuss what's going on and what the future plan is with my Block Island property. Keep an eye on your agent, Chad. I'll be keeping an eye out on Ackwell, and whoever else is involved. Because there *are* others." Stanley was being cryptic at the end, but then again, he knew David Ackwell personally and what might be driving this sudden interest.

"I can make that work, Mr. Ahearn. I can't speak for my father-in-law but I'll be there with my wife and daughter who's excited to visit." Chad assured him.

"I'm looking forward to it Chad. I'll have my secretary email you an itinerary of the dates and have a boat ready to take you over to the island. Please talk to Bill about coming as well." Stanley said.

"Of course." Chad agreed, although he thought that William would be more likely to go if Stanley extended the invitation himself, but he wasn't going to make that suggestion. "Going forward should I contact you if there's any suspicious phone calls?" Chad didn't want to make a habit of calling Stanley.

"Yes. If I'm not available, then leave a message with my assistant that it's important to contact you. I don't want you to give any details though." He replied after a moment to think it over. "Thank you for the information, Chad. We'll be in touch and see in you in about a week." Stanley hung up.

Just as Chad hung up the phone, someone was knocking on his office door. It was closed, which was rare, but necessary in this case. "Yes?" He asked, having a feeling that it was probably Michelle.

He was surprised to see that it was Greg. "Hi, Greg, what's going on?" Chad was glad it wasn't Michelle. He needed a plan before he talked to her about anything at this point. Greg looked nervous which wasn't like him. He was usually easy-going and nothing rattled him, including finicky clients which was what made him so good at selling properties. He was young, only 24 years old. He had thick black rimmed glasses that was the first thing anyone noticed about him aside from being tall and thin. Krista had met him once and thought he was 'nerdy' looking, but it was his personality that drew people in and made him successful.

"Have a seat." Chad invited him as he continued to stand awkwardly in front of his desk. Greg finally sat down which was a relief to both of them.

"Mr. Burton, I don't mean to be a gossip but I think there's something you should know about." Greg began and then looked behind him. Chad's door was still partially open. "Can I close that?" Greg asked. "Of course, please do." Chad said, intrigued.

Once the door was closed, Greg went on to tell him that he'd overheard many conversations Michelle had been having about the Ahearn property. "I'm aware that she's been talking to David Ackwell." Chad acknowledged.

"But I don't think she was really talking to David, unless David was suddenly put in jail. She was talking to someone else, a woman I think." Greg insisted. "Michelle said something about 'it not being fair you're being caged for something that wasn't your fault. You'll get what you deserve in the end, don't worry.' Then she mentioned something about sending money into her account and that she needs to stay quiet until she gets out." Greg told him. "I'm only hearing her side of the conversation, but I'm certain it's not David." He looked worried and relieved at the same time as he sat back, waiting for Chad's reaction.

"Greg, thank you so much for bringing this to my attention. It shows integrity and I appreciate that. This conversation is between us. I think I'd like you to take over the Patrick Sampson account from Michelle. I'll check with him first, but I think that you'll do a great job." Chad told him. As far as Chad was concerned, Greg had just stole the golden ticket from Michelle. He wasn't about to let her continue when her loyalty was obviously not with Carson Realty. He was glad he'd steered clear of her sexual innuendos. "Thank you, Chad! Just let me know what I need to do." Greg was excited to work a celebrity account.

"Please keep this between us until I talk to Michelle tomorrow." Chad advised.

"Of course. Thanks again, Mr. Burton. I won't let you down." Greg was beaming, seemingly excited at this opportunity to take on some high-end clients.

Chad suddenly felt as though he'd been trusting the wrong person for too long; hopefully not long enough to destroy what William had tried to build all these years. Maybe Greg wasn't trust-worthy either, but he was willing to give him a chance. He had a feeling that he was in for the game of his life; the stakes being Carson Realty and his family's well-being. This was a conversation to have with Bill and Stanley together. And it couldn't wait until two weeks from now.

Krista

After a disaster of a morning, Krista managed to get herself together in order to meet with scheduled students. But she knew that she needed to start taking precautions in her own office. Her anxiety was kicking into high gear, knowing that someone was hacking into her computer, compromising anything that was under her name in the system. Edward's promise to check with security didn't make her feel confident so she planned to check with them herself. As she was headed out, her cell rang with an unknown number, but she took a chance.

"Hi, Krista. This is Marcy Perrell's office reminding you of Mara's appointment tomorrow at 3pm." It was Marcy's receptionist.

"Thank you. We'll be there." Krista told her. There was no way she was missing this appointment; not that she thought it would be helpful to Mara, but it was the only way to get her back in school, where she needed to be during the day. She had an alarm put on her phone to remind her ahead of time tomorrow. She could probably come in early and leave a little early to get Mara there so that Chad didn't have to take time off. Besides, she wanted to be there, and make sure that Marcy understood what Mara's behaviors were.

Just as she was picking up the phone to call the school security office, Edward Childers knocked on her partly closed door. "Hi, Krista are you busy?" The serious look on his face gave him away.

"Uh oh, what happened now?" Krista threw up her hands, trying to make light of what was a shitty situation. "Please tell me they found someone getting into my office on camera." Krista pleaded.

"Well unfortunately not in your office, specifically. But they did see someone going through papers in desks around the classrooms as well as the administrative offices. I was told there are no security cameras in the counseling services offices. But, that's going to change as of today!" Edward nodded looking very determined. "As far as I'm concerned, I'm going to assume that if this person is going through desks, they're likely to be hacking into computers. Although, I was wondering Kris, did you sign out of your computer before you left your office"

"I always do, Edward. Besides, it wouldn't matter. The system automatically signs you out after an hour or so if you're not using it.

"Well, the police have been contacted and will be coming to take statements from everyone that was a 'victim' of this. Several teachers reported items missing from their desks, and one of the administrative assistants for the superintendent had left her Rolex watch that her husband had bought her for her birthday in her desk. It's gone now." Edward looked disgusted, almost embarrassed as if it were his fault. "I'm sorry that this happened, Kris, but security cameras will be installed over the weekend in every office in this department."

"Thank god. I appreciate it, Edward." Krista was relieved. This had taken a weight off at least from a 'not getting fired' standpoint. But she had a feeling she was specifically targeted, but why? "Can you make out who the person is in the security footage? Did you see it?" Krista was hoping she would get an idea if her past 'ghosts' were trying to catch up with her.

"I didn't see it, but if you think it'll be helpful, I'll take you over now. The police will be here soon to take them, so we'd better go. Do you have time now?"

Krista glanced at the clock. She had about 20 minutes before her next appointment. "I can now, but I only have a few minutes." The principal led her down to the security office that was chaotic. Apparently because of the police on their way. "Hey Willard, is there any way for one of the counselors here to view some of the video footage? There were some questionable emails sent from her computer." Willard was an older man, short and stocky with thinning grey hair. His security uniform didn't do much to make him look intimidating. Krista guessed him to be at least in his 60s and on his way to retirement, and this was probably the most excitement he'd seen in his 20 years overseeing security.

"We don't have much time, but there is some footage of the person in the writing lab." He started the recording which was very grainy and dark, but Krista could make out a person that looked like a woman going through desks. There was a janitor cart nearby, and she had on a baggy pair of overalls and a hat, but there was something about the way she moved that was familiar. The overalls covered her up, but there was something about the way she walked, and the way she was checking out different items triggered a memory that she'd forgotten. Until now. "No, it couldn't be!" Krista said out loud without realizing it.

"What? Do you know who this is?" Willard asked. "We assumed it must be the janitor, but our janitor is an older man. This isn't him."

"No, it's not. It's obviously a woman. But it can't be who I think it is. She's in prison." Krista said, still trying to remind herself of that fact.

"Who's in prison?" Edward and Willard asked at the same time.

"Amanda Ahearn. She's been in prison for the past 7 years for kidnapping and attempted murder." Krista said quietly. Neither of them knew that she'd been the victim in the case and because she was Stanley's daughter, he'd made sure that it wasn't publicized to protect his own reputation in Hollywood. "But it can't be her. Who's the janitor here?" Krista asked Willard.

"His name is Jim Eldridge. He's worked for the school for years. It doesn't show him doing anything in the videos except what he's supposed to be doing-cleaning. It appears that he doesn't know that someone else is with him. The police will be talking to him later. We've already talked with him at length and he wasn't aware that anyone else was in the building at the time." Willard said. "Thank you for the information though. The police will be taking your information when they arrive."

Just as he'd finished his sentence, two detectives from Johnston Police arrived. "I'm Detective Shaun Masterson, and this is Detective Mike Murphy" said a tall dark-haired man with striking blue eyes introducing himself and his partner. After Edward and Willard updated them on what had been going on, Krista talked with Detective Masterson about this week, including the email that was marked read and the email sent to a students' parent that had caused problems. She also told him her suspicions about the woman in the security video that reminded her of Amanda Ahearn.

"I hope that she's still in prison, but there's something familiar about her. She's not trying to hide what she's doing. That was just like her; always using her father as a way to get out of things." Krista told him. She didn't care if she sounded like a lunatic; she was tired of the constant crisis at school. It just compounded the drama at home with Mara talking to her 'imaginary friend'. Krista knew there had been a reason Nadine needed to contact her and why she wanted to talk to her despite her injuries after the accident.

"We'll be talking with the janitor and asking questions, as well as the rest of the faculty here." Detective Masterson assured her. "In the meantime, make sure to shut down your computer and change your password, as well as making sure your office door is locked when you leave." He advised.

Krista thought she'd already done what she'd needed to do before this happened, but didn't bother arguing with him. "Are you going to be checking to make sure that Amanda Ahearn hasn't been released yet?" Krista added as an afterthought.

"Of course, we will. But for your peace of mind, you can check to see if that Ahearn woman is still incarcerated on the Rhode Island Department of Corrections website. It's public knowledge." Detective Masterson's tone was suddenly patronizing now. But he was right! Why hadn't she thought of that? She suddenly felt stupid about even mentioning her name.

"Thank you. I plan to do that!" Krista told him in a polite voice although she hated his arrogant tone as she headed back to her office.

It was a long afternoon of student appointments and she felt completely exhausted by the end of the day, but she'd been itching to check on Amanda's prison status all afternoon and immediately typed Amanda's name into the RIDOC website. She held her breath as the computer was searching for the name, and then there it was: Amanda Ahearn, DOB: 11/17/1986, Status: Inmate-medium security. She was still in prison. Krista wasn't sure how to feel now. She was glad that it *couldn't* have been Amanda on the security video. But then who was it? The unknown wasn't a pleasant answer either. Now there was someone trying to ruin her career, and she had no idea who it could be.

When she looked at the clock, it was after 4:30 and she was late to pick up Mara. She quickly changed her password and made sure her computer was shut down before she locked her office door and left the building. She had reached her car when Chad was calling her. "Where *are* you? You were supposed to pick up Mara an hour ago!"

"I'm on my way! It's been a long day." Now that she was out of the school, the stress was beginning to take its toll on her and she suddenly felt exhausted.

"Mine too. I'll talk to you when I get home. I'm finishing up with a client and I'll meet you at home. You okay?" Chad asked her. It was as if those two words unleashed a flood of tears and Krista had to pull over on the side of the road.

"No, I'm not." Krista admitted as she told him what had happened today at school. Chad listened to her and finally she was able to start driving again to pick up Mara. "When will this end, Chad?"

"Mara has her appointment tomorrow. We'll start there, okay? I'm leaving the office now. Do you want me to pick her up?" Chad asked, worried about her.

"No, thanks for letting me vent. I'm fine now and I'll be there in a few minutes." Krista told him. "Love you, see you soon." She hung up, hoping that Mara and her father had a better day than she did. She was headed back out on the road again when the phone rang again. The number looked familiar for some reason so she decided to answer it. "This is Krista."

"Hi Krista, it's Sadie Mercotte." Krista knew the minute she heard her voice that it was not good news. Her voice sounded as though she'd been crying. "Nadine died a few hours ago. She….she tried so hard to fight…." Sadie's voice trailed off. Krista immediately pulled back off the road into a strip-mall parking lot, shocked that this young woman that had helped her was suddenly gone.

"Sadie, I'm so sorry to hear that." Krista felt a lump in her throat as she spoke. "Is there anything I can do?" Krista found herself fumbling for something to say in the situation. With all the chaos going on in the past 24 hours, Nadine's condition had slipped her mind.

"Her services will be next Wednesday at 11:00am, if you're able to attend. I understand if you have prior obligations, but I really need to meet with you. Before she passed away, Nadine made me promise that

I would meet with you. She was very afraid for you and your family, Krista." Sadie told her.

Krista felt a chill come over her. "Afraid? Did she say why?" The last thing they needed was more drama!

"She wasn't able to speak in her condition. Nadine managed to write it down for me before she died." Sadie began choking up just then. Listening to her brought tears to Krista's eyes

"I'll do my best to be there on Wednesday, Sadie. Nadine helped our family out so much just by insisting that I meet with her." Krista assured her, as she brushed tears from her eyes. She suddenly felt partly responsible since she'd texted Nadine the night before the accident. Was it possible that someone had run her over on purpose? She refused to consider the possibilities right now. There was enough to deal with in the moment.

"I appreciate it, Krista." Sadie gave her the address of the funeral home in Providence and Krista promised to be there. "Nadine told me that you need to be careful; watch out for your little girl. She's the one that's most vulnerable." Her words reminded Krista that she was late to pick up Mara.

"I will, Sadie. I'm so sad to hear about Nadine. I'll see you on Wednesday." Krista said, as she pulled out of the school parking lot. After hanging up, she felt as though she was driving on autopilot to her father's house; her thoughts scattered from the news of Nadine's death, to Sadie's message that Mara was in danger. Just then, her father was calling. Krista picked up, knowing he was probably upset that she was half an hour late. "I know, dad, I'm on my way," she said, so tired already. It sounded as if he hadn't had a great day with Mara. Thank god her appointment with Marcy was tomorrow.

William

William had been hoping that Mara would get up from her nap in the morning and become her usual mischievous self. But at noon she was still sleeping on the couch, except for the occasional rolling around as if she were dreaming. He felt her forehead from time to time and checked on her constantly, but she didn't have a fever or have any cold symptoms. Mara didn't actually wake up until after 1:30 that afternoon. William was in the kitchen making some lunch when she wandered out from her long sleep. "Hi, grandpa." There was something different about her eyes that he couldn't put his finger on. Ever since Mara was born, William noticed that he could read her mood from her eyes; when she was content, they were cerulean blue like Krista's, they turned a blue-green when she was angry, but now they seemed dull, almost vacant. Usually she would be insisting on watching one of her shows on TV or playing a game on her computer.

"Hi, sweetheart, are you feeling better? You've been asleep for the whole morning! I was starting to worry about you!" William went to scoop her up and give her a hug, but Mara hung back, with her arms to her sides. He was confused.

"Does your tummy hurt Mara? Did it hurt you when I picked you up?" He was trying to figure out what was going on with his granddaughter. He'd never seen her act like this. She suddenly smiled, but it wasn't one of her cute smiles. More of a malicious smile. As if she was amused by what he was saying, but was waiting......for what? William wasn't sure.

"You didn't hurt me, grandpa. I'm just hungry." Mara told him, her voice sounding as unemotional as the empty look in her eyes. "I really want a bologna sandwich." William was shocked at her request. Mara hated bologna or any other deli meat for that matter. He always had his fridge packed with cheese and he always had bread on hand because she loved grilled cheese sandwiches.

"No, I don't have that. Since when do you eat bologna, Mara? I was going to make you a grilled cheese and some chips for lunch." William told her. He felt a cold chill come over him. This wasn't the Mara that he knew. She looked like her, but something had happened over the past couple of hours and it scared him.

"I'm not hungry then. I want bologna, not grilled cheese." Mara insisted, her voice taking on a whiney tone that William, along with most people hated. He thought about running to the store, but Joanna's words came back to him; 'you're always rewarding her' and he decided against it.

"Then I guess you'll be hungry, until there's something I do have that you want to eat, Mara. This isn't a restaurant." William told her in a firm tone. Mara pouted and went back to the couch fuming for a few minutes. He expected that she'd be asking for grilled cheese soon, but she only became angrier, threw the TV remote across the room and began yelling. "I'm gonna tell daddy! I'm gonna tell mommy! I'm gonna tell Jamie, and she'll get you for this!"

William felt himself losing control over his temper and decided to go outside on the deck for a few moments. What was going on? Was this something that a therapist could help with because he knew that his daughter and son-in-law didn't allow this kind of behavior, or maybe they did? Besides he'd never seen her act this way. He really wanted a drink right now, but he knew better than to allow that, especially with Mara here. 'What would Maria do right now?' he thought to himself and immediately envisioned her going to Mara and giving her a hug while telling her to stop being disrespectful. Mara opened the sliding door to the deck, glared at him and then slammed it shut so hard that he was surprised it didn't shatter the glass!

William had enough of this and immediately opened the door. "That's ENOUGH, MARA!" William had never yelled at her before. Mara seemed to come to her senses and appeared shocked at him losing his temper with her. "Go to your room! Now!" William lowered his tone slightly, but she knew he meant business. She went back to the door and began opening it and slamming it shut once again, which didn't help William's nerves. Mara stood inside so he could see her, as if she were taunting him, daring him to open the door and chase her. Her eyes were narrowed like little blue slits, and her mouth was contorted in a spiteful grin that seemed to be taunting him, as if to say 'what are you gonna do now?'

He knew better than to approach her right now; he was too angry. He could hear Maria's words in his head now, 'Something is wrong. Wait it out.' It was almost as if Maria was with him. He nodded as if she were right next to him. "You're right, as always. I miss you so very much." He said out loud. Just as he said the words, he felt a slight breeze across his face. There was a warmth that spread over his body as her presence came over him and he could hear her soft voice that stopped him in his tracks.

"I'm still with you always. Be careful. She's been talking to an evil presence that's drawing her in. Remember the necklace." Maria's voice was as clear as it could be and William had to wipe his tears away. He was beginning to wonder if he was starting to lose his mind, but he could feel her strength encouraging him to remain calm.

He turned and looked inside. Mara had disappeared from sight, so he took a couple of deep breaths and remembered Maria's comforting words. He slowly opened the sliding door and peered inside. "Mara? Where are you? "Mara?"

A shattering of glass that came from upstairs startled him for a moment. "Mara, are you okay?" He ran upstairs looking for her. She was in the guest room, which he'd dubbed 'Mara's room', sitting on the black and green comforter that she'd chosen. She was sitting on the edge of the bed, her back stiff and her hands folded in her lap. "Mara? Are you okay?" He picked up her hands that felt ice-cold. Her eyes were wide open but staring off as if she couldn't see him. "MARA!" He shouted at her and shook her gently. "Honey, it's grandpa!"

Mara's eyes blinked finally and she looked confused. "Grandpa?"

"Yes, Mara, I'm here. Are you okay? Did you hurt yourself? I heard glass breaking." William felt relieved that she was finally responding. She was shivering so he wrapped an afghan from the foot of the bed around her shivering shoulders. He suddenly noticed that it *was* really cold in this room, which was strange, as it was usually the warmest room in the house.

"I'm cold, grandpa." She continued to shake despite the blanket. William was starting to worry as he picked her up and took her downstairs with him and could feel the difference in temperature as soon as he left. He gently laid her on the living room couch and bundled her up with another blanket as he watched her become more alert. "Is that better?" She'd stopped shivering and she seemed more relaxed. The stiffness that he'd noticed was gone.

"Grandpa?" It was as if she hadn't known that he was there. "I'm hungry. Can I have a grilled cheese sandwich?" She asked as if the argument about lunch never happened.

"Of course you can. Just get warmed up while I make it for you." William was glad that she seemed back to herself again, but there was no denying something wasn't right. "Mara, you asked me for bologna a few minutes ago. Do you remember?"

Mara wrinkled up her nose. "Yuk, I hate bologna! No I didn't ask for that!" She insisted. William didn't argue with her. At least she seemed more like herself and ate her lunch as if nothing ever happened.

Later on, while Mara was doing some of her homework, William walked upstairs when he spied a piece of glass near the wall and looked up. A framed picture of Maria, Krista and Karen at Block Island was still on the wall, but the glass was cracked and ready to fall apart, as if someone had taken a hammer to it. 'That explains what the noise was, but doesn't explain how.' William thought. Was this his granddaughter's revenge during her tantrum? William's thoughts were all over the place now. He took the picture down before it fell and carefully pulled the broken glass from the frame, setting the picture down on the kitchen island. He waited until Mara had finished her homework and was watching one of her shows on TV to ask her about it.

"Mara, did you break this picture in the hallway when you were upset?" He showed her the picture that he'd pulled from the broken glass.

She looked over at the picture. "No, grandpa. I didn't. I like that picture. Mommy has the same one in her bedroom. That's my grandma, mommy and Aunt Karen." She seemed sincere and William didn't doubt her. "But Jamie doesn't like mommy or that picture." Her eyes looked frightened now. "I think Jamie might have done it." She said to him in a quiet voice.

"Mara, it's okay to tell me. You don't need to blame it on your imaginary friend. I won't be angry with you. I just want you to be honest with me." William said quietly, hoping that she would admit it.

"Grandpa, I DIDN'T DO IT!" Mara shouted at him. "It was JAMIE, I KNOW IT!" She turned away from him and pulled her blanket closer around her as if to shut him out.

William backed down and decided not to pursue the issue further. "Okay, Mara. I believe you." He responded quietly, while looking at the clock. It was after 5:00. Where the hell was Kris? He was suddenly exhausted from the entire day. Something wasn't right with his granddaughter. He called Krista to find out if she was on her way. She picked up on the second ring, sounding upset. "I'm on my way, dad!"

Chad

Chad had just arrived home, when he got a call from William that Krista still hadn't picked up Mara. "It's been a tough day," was all that William said when Chad asked how the day had gone. "I just talked to her a minute ago. She said she was on her way." Chad assured him.

"Good, because something is going on with Mara! I can't explain over the phone, but it's been a difficult day." His father-in-law sounded stressed and he knew that must mean something was really wrong. Mara was usually on her best behavior at her grandfather's house. Chad had just gotten home and was exhausted but he knew that it might be better to go to resolve whatever was happening now than later. "Sounds like it's been a difficult day. Be there in 10 minutes, Bill." Chad told him. He grabbed his keys and headed out the door.

He tried to call Kris on his way, but it went straight to voicemail. 'What the hell is she doing? Just pick Mara up and come home, how hard is that?' Chad was more than irritated. It had been a long day and now it was going to be even longer. Not only did he have to worry about Michelle, but now he'd had to move any accounts that he was concerned Michelle might be trying to sabotage to Greg with a plausible explanation to Michelle. He didn't want her to find out he was onto her scheming until he had actual proof.

As he pulled up to William's house, Krista's car was already in the driveway. He was relieved that at least she was okay, since she hadn't answered his call. He knocked as he pulled open the door. "Hi, sweetheart, sorry I was late." Krista looked upset as she gave him a hug. As he pulled back, he noticed that she'd been crying.

"What's going on here?" Chad ran his hands through his hair and took a deep breath. It seemed they couldn't catch a break from drama in the past week. Krista told him about the email sent from her computer at school, the discussion with police at the school, and then the phone call from Sadie Mercotte about Nadine's death. "Is that the woman I saw on TV today?" William interjected when Krista mentioned her name. "I'm sorry, Kris. I know that she was helpful to you." He gave Krista a hug.

"Thanks, dad. I wish I hadn't- She suddenly stopped mid-sentence. "You wish what, Kris?" William asked.

"Nothing. I just wish that she had survived this awful accident. She was so young." Krista recovered, but Chad could tell there was something else she wanted to say. Now was not the time.

"Where's Mara?" Chad asked, expecting her to be at least in the kitchen, greeting them, but she was lying on the couch in the living room with her unicorn blanket over her, watching TV. Chad went into the living room and gave Mara a huge hug. "How's my girl been doing today?" He tried not to let the stress show in his voice. Mara hung onto him as if she were drowning and wouldn't let go of him. "Daddy, I'm scared."

"Sweetheart, there's nothing to be scared of; look we're all here, me, mommy and grandpa." Chad looked over to William, hoping he could fill in the blanks. "Mommy and I are talking to grandpa. We'll leave in a few minutes. Just finish watching your show." Chad said, as he wrapped her blanket around her. She seemed content so he went back out to the kitchen.

William stepped in then, "Mara's had a really hard day; I'm glad she's going to the therapist tomorrow." He launched into Mara's behaviors, down to the picture frame that was broken this afternoon. "She just isn't herself. This isn't just about an imaginary friend anymore." William insisted. "What I saw today was a completely different child. I just don't know what we should do."

Krista had been quiet during the discussion, which surprised Chad. Usually, she was always voicing her opinion, but now she just stood there with a look of confusion on her face. "Are you okay, Kris?" Chad squeezed her hand.

"I'm fine. I'm just not sure it's a therapist that can help her." Krista said quietly. "I'll bring her tomorrow, of course, but I think we need to have a plan that might actually help her."

"We aren't bringing her to that psychic woman whose niece died, Kris." Chad had a feeling where his wife was going with this.

"That's not what I'm saying, Chad. But maybe, I can talk to her on Wednesday about what's going on. She told me that Nadine mentioned this situation with Mara. I never met with Nadine, so how would she know that?" Krista was being defensive now and Chad was certain there was something she wasn't telling him. But he wasn't going to talk about it now. He decided to bring up Stanley's offer of going to Block Island next weekend to change the subject.

"I talked to Stanley Ahearn this week. He invited us out for next weekend to the mansion on Block Island. He invited you and Joanna as well, William." Chad made sure to include his father-in-law in the conversation. William looked surprised.

"I don't understand why he'd want *me* there. Especially with Joanna." He sounded guarded about the invite. "Chad, what are your thoughts about his invitation?" William and Stanley had made amends after Maria died and buried the hatchet, but they hadn't spoken in at least 3 years unless it was to discuss some real estate related transaction. But he had thought about going back there when Mara mentioned it.

Chad wasn't really sure himself, but knew that Stanley wanted him there. "He said that he's put up a new memorial for Maria and would like you to see it. Come on, Bill, you patched things up with Stanley awhile back. It would be a chance to see the memorial as well as enjoy the ocean. Besides, Mara will be there; you can show her around and spend some time with her."

"I'd like to go back there. Mara has done her drawings and asked me if we could go there. I think I'd like to do that. I can't speak for Joanna, but I'll go." William surprised both Chad and Krista.

"Well, that's great! Stanley said he'd be giving you a call too." Chad was glad he didn't have to try and convince his father-in-law about the trip. It was one less thing he had to think about!

"Mara's appointment is at 3:00 so I'll pick her up at 2:30, dad. Are you okay watching her tomorrow?" Krista asked her father. She changed the subject so Chad was guessing that she wasn't sure about the trip. He was sure she'd talk to him about it later.

"Of course. She'll be fine." William agreed. "But it's good that she can go back to school next week after her appointment."

"I'm going back to school? When?" Mara was standing outside the kitchen. They all jumped in surprise as they turned around.

"Yes, sweetheart. We're going to talk to a nice lady tomorrow and you'll be going back to school on Monday." Krista told her. "C'mon, let's get your stuff together and we'll go home." She ushered Mara back to the living room and helped her pack up her homework into her backpack.

"There's something you should know about Michelle that I just found out today." Chad told William about the phone call that he'd overheard and how he was having phone calls monitored that were coming in at Carson Realty. "I talked to Stanley about it. I think that's why he wants us to come out to Block Island next weekend, Bill. There's something going on here. I'm on top of it." Chad assured him.

"Maybe it's time for me to start spending more time at the office." William had worked hard for his business to be a success and he agreed with Chad that there was definitely someone that was trying to sabotage it.

Chad nodded. "I didn't want to stress you out, because I know you've been taking a break, Bill. But I think Michelle is working with someone else. My guess is someone that is mad as hell at Stanley and maybe you. If that crazy Amanda Ahearn wasn't still in prison, my money would be on her." Chad didn't want to tell Krista his suspicions, but it had crossed his mind many times throughout the day.

William nodded, "I'm guessing that Stanley is checking into that as well as anyone that would be connected to her. He's many things, but he isn't gullible. I'll give him a call tomorrow, Chad. Thanks for letting me know."

Mara and Krista came into the kitchen with her backpack in tow. "I think it's time to go home and get some dinner. Mara looked tired and unusually quiet. "Say goodbye to grandpa," Krista coached her, as Mara started toward the front door.

"Bye, grandpa. See you tomorrow." Mara said, in a monotone voice. William scooped her up to hug her, and give her a kiss. She seemed distant, but gave him a brief hug. "I know you're tired, go home and get some rest." William told her, although her reaction bothered him. In fact, everything that happened today was bothering him, but there wasn't anything he could do about it.

Krista

By the time Krista got home, it was past 6:00. Mara had napped on the short ride home and it was tough waking her up. "Mara, c'mon we'll go have some dinner" as she finally got her up and out of the car. She realized that her father was right about her; she was never tired during the day. She remembered the days when she was a toddler, hoping she'd nap, but Mara was always awake and ready to go even if she didn't sleep well the night before. Krista was worried, as Mara yawned, walked inside and immediately went to the couch to lie down.

"Are you hungry, Mara?" Krista came and sat next to her, as she felt her forehead. She didn't have a fever. In fact, she was cool.

"Not really, mommy." Mara said as she pulled the throw blanket over her. It was similar to her comforter in her room; green and black in a leopard print. She snuggled her head under the blanket, just as Chad was coming through the door. "Daddy's home, I'll be right back," Krista patted her back as she headed out to the kitchen.

"How's she doing?" Chad asked as Krista shook her head. "The same. She doesn't have a fever, but she's still sleepy."

"Kris, she didn't sleep well last night, so it would make sense for her to be tired today." Chad rationalized. "I grabbed some take out from Luigis, so let's just eat and she'll eat later if she wants to."

"Thanks for picking up something, I really didn't feel like cooking." Krista gave him a hug, thankful that he was being thoughtful and supportive. They sat down to eat and finished and Mara was still sleeping on the couch as Krista put the leftovers in the fridge. She was still refusing to get up and Chad carried her up to her room.

As soon as he put her down on the bed, Mara seemed to wake up. "Daddy?"

"Hi, sleepyhead! You slept through dinner. Are you hungry?"

"No. But I'm scared. Jamie's here again. She won't stop talking to me." Mara sat up in bed, her blue eyes wide and clung to his arms. "How about if I tell her to go away and let you sleep? Do you think that will help?" Chad asked.

Mara looked surprised. "I don't know, but I hope it will! Try it daddy." Chad made a serious face and said "Jamie, Mara needs to sleep tonight. Come back tomorrow, okay?" Mara looked frightened as he said the words.

"Is Jamie still here?" Chad asked.

"No, not right now, daddy." Mara looked relieved. "But she'll be back."

"If she does, remind her that I told her she needs to wait till tomorrow." Chad advised her and gave her a hug and kiss. Krista had been at the door for a minute listening, then decided it was a good time to come in to say good night.

"Mommy, can I sleep with you and daddy again?" Chad was mouthing the word 'no' as Krista went to respond. She knew all too well that they had agreed when she born that they weren't going to allow children to sleep with them regularly.

"Let's make a deal. First, you eat a little dinner, then I'll read you a story, but I think you'll sleep better in your own bed." It was hard for

Krista to be firm with her now, but for once she and Chad were on the same page. She needed firm boundaries that she'd insisted upon earlier this week.

Mara didn't argue with her, and ate a decent portion of the pasta. Mara was sleeping mid-way through a chapter of Alice in Wonderland, and Krista left her nightstand light on in case she woke up. Krista got up quietly, tiptoeing out of the room, almost expecting Mara to wake up. But she seemed to be sleeping soundly. Krista sighed with relief as she closed the door quietly.

Krista breathed a sigh of relief as she headed back downstairs. It was only 7: 30, but felt more like midnight to her. She was finally able to talk about her day in detail with Chad, about the email and her suspicions about Amanda Ahearn. "But I looked her up and she's still in prison, Chad. How could she have anything to do with it?"

"Kris, she probably has connections on the outside; I'm sure of it! I thought of her today after I caught one of the realtors talking to someone that is trying to claim that Stanley wants to sell his Block Island property. He told Krista about Michelle's deception and Greg admitting that she was actually talking to someone else.

"I hope you told my dad about this. Maybe it's a good idea for you to go to Block Island and meet with Stanley and dad next weekend.

"I think it's a good idea that we *all* go as a family. Stanley specifically said us as a family. He even remembered Mara's name." Chad fibbed a little. Stanley *did* remember after he told him. "Your mother's memorial is there now. You've never seen it. It might be good for you to go after all these years." Chad reminded her.

Krista wished that she could feel more comfortable going back there. After all, it had been 7 years and she really did want to see her mother's memorial. "I'll think about it. I just want to get through tomorrow with Mara's appointment and we'll go from there." She still needed to get through that, get Mara back into school and then Nadine's services on Wednesday. She decided to go to bed earlier than usual, hoping she'd get some much needed sleep.

***

Krista was suddenly awakened by a dull thud. She'd felt the vibration of something hitting the floor and sat straight up in bed. 'Am I dreaming?' She looked over at Chad sleeping next to her, so she knew that wasn't the case. But what was that noise? She glanced over at her phone, thinking maybe that had fallen on the floor but it was still there on the nightstand.

There was a shadow that passed through the hallway and her heart began to pound. "Hello?" Krista called out, wondering if she should wake her husband. There was no answer and she struggled with whether she should get up. Fear for Mara's safety won out so she quietly got out of bed and went to Mara's room to check on her. Maybe she was sleepwalking again. But the nightlight that Krista had left on illuminated her daughter's face and she let out a sigh of relief. She checked around Mara's room to make sure everything was in order and that the windows were closed.

'I was probably just imagining it,' she thought to herself, as she went back to her bedroom. Then she noticed something on the floor next to Chad's side of the bed and reached down to retrieve her jewelry box. 'How did this get here?' Krista was certain it had been centered at the back of the dresser, next to the mirror. There wasn't any possible way for it to have fallen off by itself; unless someone had pushed it. Krista debated about waking Chad, but decided against it. He needed his sleep and really, what could he do? She knelt down to see if anything had spilled out. A few pieces of jewelry were strewn on the floor and she checked the box for the most important piece; the one that mattered the most. Karen's necklace. It was gone. She went into panic mode just then, frantically searching underneath the bed and the dresser for the necklace that seemed to have vanished. "Where is it?" Krista said out loud, desperate that of all that could be missing, it would be her sister's necklace.

She felt restless and decided that instead of tearing the room apart or waking her husband, she'd go downstairs, make some tea to help her calm down and hopefully get back to sleep. The stairwell was dark so she turned on the light to head to the kitchen, and filled the tea pot up with water, set it on the stove to boil. Krista felt herself finally calm enough to sleep once finishing her tea, when she noticed a shadow moving from behind a curtain in the living room to the alcove near the stairs. 'Maybe I'm just tired' was her first thought, but panic was setting in again, and her adrenaline was flowing again. Krista forced herself to move toward where she'd seen the shadow near the stairs, grabbing a nearby knickknack of a jade elephant that Chad had bought for her. It was definitely heavy enough to do some damage if anyone was hiding there. She turned on the hall light and crept around the corner, with the elephant held above her head. There was no one there. Feeling ridiculous, Krista set the elephant back down on the side table. 'It's a good thing I'm seeing Dr. Mayfield soon; maybe I need it!' She chastised herself for being silly as she headed upstairs to bed. She checked in on Mara again, still feeling unsettled. Mara was still sleeping soundly, but something caught her eye as she came closer to Mara's bed. Near her bedside lamp was Karen's heart necklace that had been missing from her jewelry box.

Krista was too relieved to find it and immediately put in back where it belonged. It was only after she was lying in bed and dozing off she wondered how that necklace had been moved from the floor to Mara's nightstand. "You need that necklace, Kris. It's the solution." She heard her mother's voice as she fell asleep.

Chad

Chad got up earlier than usual in order to make it to the office to figure out what was really going on with Michelle. He'd been mulling over all the interactions he'd had with her over the past few months and it was clear that he'd glossed over several signs that she was out for herself. Flirting was one of her skills that she'd clearly perfected over the years and practiced on him regularly. He'd never responded, so maybe that was why she was going behind his back and doing business with whoever it was on the phone. He decided to do further research and talk more with David Ackwell. After all, Michelle had taken the call when he'd told her not to. But according to Greg, she'd never really talked to David. He was going to find out.

When he got to the office, the first call was to Stanley. Only after his voicemail picked up, did Chad realize that it was only 5am in California. He left a message about his plan to get more information from David. His next call was to David Ackwell. David picked up right away. "Chad, how're you doing? I was hoping I would hear from you!" David sounded as though he was in his car.

"Just calling to ask if you contactor one of our realtors yesterday. She'd said that she'd been talking to you." Chad threw out the fishing line.

"What are you talking about, Burton? I've never talked to anyone else in your office!" David's response confirmed that Greg was right. Michelle had never been talking to him. Chad was glad that he could trust Greg, but who the hell had she'd been talking to all this time?

"Okay, sorry for the misunderstanding, David. I just know you're really pushing Stanley to sell his property. But glad to know you wouldn't go behind my back." Chad gave his apology, but he was keeping David on his radar. Maybe he wasn't the one contacting Michelle, but someone that knew him was. If Greg was right, Michelle had been talking to a woman for weeks, but yesterday, the caller had been someone claiming to be David Ackwell to his receptionist.

"Speaking of Stanley's property, has he made any mention about selling?" David couldn't help but ask and Chad rolled his eyes.

"David, I talked to him yesterday. As of yesterday, his answer was a firm NO! I'd tell you if he'd changed his mind. I'm curious. Why do you want this property all of a sudden? It's not like it's an easily accessible place to vacation and it's cold here 9 months out of the year. What's the attraction?" Chad asked.

"Well, it's just. … you know. So different, from other locations, I guess." David seemed to be scrambling and it set off warning bells in Chad's head. Did David really want this property, or did someone else put him up to this because they really wanted it?

"Really? I can name at least 5 other properties that have 'different' qualities to them, especially in Newport and Narragansett. I'd be happy to show you any of those." Chad called him out on his reasoning. He knew damn well David wouldn't take him up on that offer.

"I was looking for a location less 'cliché' such as Newport. After all, *everyone* has had a house there at some point." David's celebrity mind-set was rearing its ugly head. Chad loved the realty business, and it had served him well financially. Yet he still had a hard time with the immeasurably rich, entitled celebrity clientele that was common with Carson Realty. "Well, there *are* other properties on Block Island, David." Chad reminded him. His other line was ringing and Chad was grateful for a reason to end this call that wasn't going anywhere. "I've got another call, David. Call me if you want to check out other properties." He hung up, but the other call had already dropped.

Soon after Kathy, Greg and Michelle showed up to the office and Chad immediately asked Greg and Michelle to meet with him in his office. Michelle came into his office, dressed up in a low cut black dress and red heels. Chad suspected she'd dressed that way specifically because she knew that he was onto her and giving her celebrity clients to Greg. He didn't give her the satisfaction of looking at her cleavage as she sat down in front of him and then retrieved something from her purse, her boobs all but falling out of her dress. Greg came into his office, sitting next to her, and Chad caught his saucer-sized eyes as Greg tried to act as though he wasn't looking. His face turned bright red as he looked up at Chad, like a kid caught stealing candy. Chad gave him a reassuring look as if to say 'don't worry, I get it.'

Chad suddenly felt like he was scolding two teenagers (actually only one was getting the bad news) in a principal's office as he launched into what he needed to discuss. "Michelle, I'm going to have Greg work with Patrick Sampson going forward." Her face flushed red and she started picking at her fingernails and looking down probably so Chad couldn't read her expression, but it was obvious that she was furious. Greg had on one of his bowties. Today, it was blue and yellow and he was pulling at it nervously, as Chad dropped the bomb on Michelle that he knew had been coming. Greg was great with clients and had the ability to smooth over any obstacles, but when conflict hit him in the workplace, he was awkward and passive.

"Are you serious? I've devoted countless hours to find Sampson his perfect home! Now you're giving it to *him*?" Michelle's dark eyes were so full of fury that Chad was glad that he had Greg sit in on this conversation. She was a law suit waiting to happen if there wasn't a witness.

Chad had prepared for this, knowing her temperament. "Michelle, I understand you spent a lot of time on this account, but I've got others that I think would work better for you. You won't have time for the Sampson's." He did in fact have others. They didn't have the notoriety of Patrick Sampson, but they were rich and she would still get a substantial commission. He launched into a brief description of the McKenna's who'd been featured on Shark Tank several years ago making some innovative face cream that made them a fortune. They were looking for a summer home in Rhode Island, specifically around the Portsmouth/Newport area. "This would be a slam-dunk for you, Michelle." Chad insisted.

She sat back in her chair for a moment as she crossed and uncrossed her shapely legs several times, making both Chad and Greg distracted, her target audience. She flicked back a long lock of dark hair and bent over towards Chad's desk, giving them both another glance at her cleavage. "I'm not sure what this is about, but if you want farmer Greg here to deliver for Sampson, that's fine with me! Please give me the information about the Mckenna's so I can start looking up properties." She keep her tone low, but her voice could have frozen lava.

"Thank you for understanding, Michelle," Chad ignored her attitude problem and handed her the information. She snatched the file from his hand. "Is that all, *Mr. Burton?*" Chad was starting to lose his patience with the sarcasm now. It was one thing to be upset and another to be a downright bitch. She was lucky he didn't fire her. He was close to telling her the real reason for the switch because she was caught being shady, but he bit his tongue. In order to find out what was going on with Ackwell and her obvious involvement, he needed her to stay.

"Yes, that's it." Chad replied nonchalantly. Her stilettos clicked loudly on the floor as she quickly left, making sure the door slammed shut for effect. Greg let out a deep breath as if he'd been holding it for the entire time.

"I'm glad you had to deal with that. It was brutal just being here!" Greg admitted, rubbing his palms on his pants to dry them off. He'd been sweating it the whole time.

"Please keep an ear out for any other discussions that she might have, Greg. I need your eyes and ears open." Chad ignored his comment about his comfort level. Greg needed to get over it if he was going to be in this business.

"I will. I'll get to work on the Sampson account right away." Greg was full of energy, and ready to go. Chad smiled as Greg left. He knew he was taking a chance all the way around. But he was determined to prove to William that he could run the agency. Michelle might be putting in her resignation this afternoon for all he knew but it was better than having someone he couldn't trust.

William

William spent the night trying to make sense of his life. Chad's comments last night with Carson Realty made him want to walk in tomorrow and straighten everything out. But at the same time, it was the reason that he'd let Chad take the reins. He was tired of the everyday schmoozing and pretending. Stanley had helped him out with clients in abundance, but it was also a constant reminder to him of what it had cost him. His mind began to drift back to memories of Maria and the early days; her beautiful smile, those blue eyes, the few years that they had together. His Keurig machine chimed, interrupting his destructive trip down the rabbit hole and he filled up his cup. It was 7am and Joanna had the day off. She said she'd come by this morning after a late shift. She rarely worked the 11-7 shift, but she was covering for a co-worker, so she'd worked a double shift.

William brewed some extra coffee and decided to make some bacon and eggs for her. It was the least he could do. She was probably exhausted. It was also Mara's last day until she went back to school and he was secretly glad, although he'd never share that thought with anyone, including Joanna or his daughter. This week with Mara had been an eye-opening experience. There was a brief knock at the door and Joanna appeared a few seconds later with some fresh cinnamon buns that smelled amazing.

"Hi there, handsome! Are you hungry?" She set the cinnamon rolls down on the counter. She was dressed in her blue scrubs, her blonde hair up in a ponytail, signs of fatigue around her eyes, yet he never found her more beautiful.

"Hi, gorgeous." William approached her and embraced her in a hug and a long kiss. He'd missed her, missed her presence in the house. "I missed you." He admitted, even though she had just been there the day before.

Joanna looked surprised with his romantic gesture. "I've missed you too," she replied back with minimal enthusiasm as he finally released her from his bear hug. She glanced around at the kitchen. "You made breakfast?" Her tone sounded flat and she didn't seem impressed with his gesture. 'Maybe she's just tired,' he thought to himself and brushed it off. But it made him feel unappreciated.

"I did! I thought you'd be hungry this morning, so I did my best. It's just bacon and scrambled eggs, but they're homemade!" William laughed. Joanna gave him a weak smile, and he felt more confident that she was just tired. In the back of his mind he wondered if Joanna was losing interest, but refused to overthink any longer.

They sat down to eat as Joanna told him about her recent shift at the hospital. William didn't want to talk about Mara or the growing suspicion about someone trying to sabotage his real estate business. He wanted to enjoy his time with her. He'd just gotten up to pour Joanna another cup of coffee when Krista showed up with Mara in tow. William hated feeling that he wished he had another hour uninterrupted with Joanna, but gave them both a hug. He couldn't help but notice how pale and tired Mara looked. Her petite frame was covered by a thick pink fleece jacket that made her look smaller than she was. Usually, she was jumping up to hug him and then taking off into the house. Today, she just stood there, quiet, barely cracking a smile and looked as pale as a miniature-sized stone statue.

"Joanna is here for breakfast. Mara, why don't you go say hello and she can get you some breakfast if you're hungry." William suggested in hopes to have a moment to check in with Kris. As soon as Mara was out of earshot, Krista confirmed that she'd be picking Mara up around 2:30 for her appointment with the therapist. "How was she last night?" William asked, concerned. "She looks sick, Kris."

Krista sighed, and scrubbed her eyes with her fists with tiredness as she nodded in agreement. "I know, dad. But she doesn't have a fever, and hasn't complained about a stomach ache or anything. She's just so tired. She actually went to bed soon after dinner and stayed asleep all night." Krista threw up her hands. "If she isn't better over the weekend, I'll take her to her pediatrician." She didn't mention her night or the jewelry box falling on the floor or the necklace.

William agreed. "Good idea. We'll have a low-key day here. Joanna just stopped by before work, so Mara can lie on the couch where I can keep an eye on her." There was one thing that he hated to bring up, but knew he needed a heads up. "Kris, has she still been talking about this 'friend', Jamie? It was almost obsessive yesterday."

"I know, dad! I know it's a problem." Krista snapped, suddenly sounding irritated and defensive.

William didn't appreciate the tone. "Krista, I asked you a simple question because I'm worried about her just as you are. But please don't take your stress out on me!" His words came out harsher than he meant them to, but he didn't need the attitude at 7:30 in the morning. Especially when he was helping out because of Mara's suspension.

"I'm sorry, dad. You're right. I really do appreciate you helping out. I *am* really stressed about so many things right now and it's getting to me." Krista's eyes filled with tears that spilled over her cheeks as she quickly brushed them away. "I know we're all hoping that this therapist is going to be the 'cure-all' for Mara's behaviors, but there's something more going on with her. This 'Jamie' person is very real to her. I'm worried that….." She cut herself off, not sure if she should talk about it with her father.

"Worried about what Kris?" William put his hand over hers to let her know he would listen.

"Dad, I'm worried that there's something really following Mara. Something evil. Someone that has come back, because they weren't finished here….while they were alive." She whispered the last few words as if she were afraid the entity might hear her.

"Kris after all we went through with your sister reaching out to you and your mother with her experiences when I met her, I believe you. We just need to find out what will help her." William's skepticism about the afterlife and the paranormal had shifted after he married Maria. Tears spilled down Krista's cheeks again, streaking her face with black from her mascara.

"Thank you, dad. I needed to hear that." Krista gave him a hug.

"Of course, Kris. I'm always here." William gave her a kiss on the top of her head and glanced at his watch. "But you'd better be going unless you want to be late!"

Krista looked at the clock. "Oh, no. You're right! I've gotta run." She brushed the leftover wet tears off her face and went to give Mara a hug. "I'll pick you up later sweetheart. Be good for grandpa!"

Mara gave her a stiff hug and didn't respond to her departure at all. She remained lying on the living room couch with her unicorn blanket and staring straight ahead, even though it was the morning news, not one of her shows. William watched as Krista walked away, brushing her tears away. 'I just wish I could help,' he thought to himself. He had a sudden image of Maria, telling him to stay close. 'You need to stay with them, protect them. There's someone here.....' The voice faded off and for a moment, William thought he'd been dreaming. But Joanna was calling his name and he shook off whatever it was that he'd thought he'd seen and responded. He went back into the kitchen, where Joanna began asking him about what his plans were for the weekend. "Bill, are you okay?" Joanna asked him. "You seem as though you're miles away."

"What? No, sorry, I was just talking to Kris, but everything is fine." He told her. It wasn't, but he wasn't going to talk more about the unexplainable events right now. He felt as though he and Joanna's relationship had slipped backwards somehow. He wasn't sure why, but he had the feeling that she wasn't as invested in their relationship as she'd been initially.

"Let's do something fun after you get some sleep. Maybe go to Narragansett, walk the beach and get some dinner at a non-tourist joint? Kris is picking Mara up around 2:30." William suggested. He almost brought up going to visit Stanley's home the following weekend, but decided against it. After all, he hadn't spoken to Stanley himself. He was still skeptical about it.

"Let's do that," Joanna agreed to his Narragansett idea. He loved that she was up for anything and didn't need an itinerary to follow. It was what he liked best about her and she also reminded him of Maria; free-spirited, spontaneous.

Joanna went home to go get some sleep a few minutes later and William was left with his granddaughter on the couch, asleep again. He made sure she was comfortable as his thoughts turned to Stanley's invitation. It seemed strange that Stanley would talk to Chad and extend the invite through him, but then again Stanley Ahearn didn't follow any rules. He glanced at the clock. It was after 11:00 Eastern time and he was going to take the chance that Stanley was at his office early. Stanley was many things, but wasn't lazy and he was known to actually sleep in his office at times.

It had taken the kidnapping of his daughter, the brief reunion with Maria, (also known as Caroline) and her sudden traumatic ending to finally have a 'working' relationship with Stanley. After all, Stanley had been responsible for the accident that caused Karen's death and William had basically made a deal with the devil when he agreed to not speak to police about the details, specifically not naming Stanley. He had let all of that go after Stanley helped him rescue Krista and Chad. The news that Stanley had a new memorial constructed for Maria was bittersweet. It sat on Stanley's property. William didn't have anything except photographs and memories of them that were starting to fade as he aged.

He decided it was time to pick up the phone and talk to Stanley himself. Chad had said he was still in California, so he dialed his office there and asked for Stanley specifically. When the receptionist gave him attitude and told him that he "didn't have an appointment to talk with Mr. Ahearn today", William rolled his eyes. "Tell him that Bill Carson is on the phone." He tried to sound less irritated than he was. After all, she was just the receptionist, but Stanley's narcissism was part of his brand; he was well aware of that. Some things never changed.

The receptionist put him on hold and immediately came back with "I'll transfer you right away, Mr. Carson." Her tone had changed. Suddenly, he was worth talking to with some respect. God how he hated the way the younger generation equated importance with basic courtesy to another human being!

Stanley picked up in a matter of seconds. "Bill! So glad to hear from you! What's going on?" He sounded upbeat for 8:00 in the morning California time.

"I was just talking to my son-in-law, Chad. You know he's been running the business for some time now. He mentioned that you had invited him and some family to your Block Island house for a weekend." William began with the basics so that hopefully Stanley would fill in the blanks.

"Yes, I did. He contacted me about David Ackwell trying to get information about my property and his interest. Chad's a good one, Bill. A wise choice for a predecessor if I do say so myself." Stanley was buttering him up, so William waited for an actual answer. When he didn't comment, Stanley continued on, "So I thought it's been a long time since....well, you know...everything happened." His voice drifted off, clearly not wanting to get into the details. It was very un-Stanley-like for him to be sentimental, but William could tell that it was hard for him to even mention.

"Yes, it has." William agreed, waiting for him to continue.

"Well, Bill, I mentioned to Chad about having everyone come to visit. I had a new memorial for Caroline, uh, Maria put up on the property. I would really love it for all of you to be there." Bill could tell that it was hard for Stanley to be empathic. But there must be something else.

"Well, that's very nice of you, Stan, but what's really going on here? You've never been one to reminisce." William called his bluff.

He could hear Stan sigh on the other end. "You really got me there, Carson. Can't get anything past you!" He said jokingly as he knew he was going to have to be up front.

"I'm not sure what you mean by that, but I'm listening." William was being honest. Because he didn't have any idea what his agenda really was, but was sure it was self-serving.

Stanley was silent for a moment which was rare for him. "Bill, honestly, I don't like being there. At that house. There's some weird shit going on when I visit. I'm not sure what to make of it. I was there about 2 months ago during the summer. I was outside with a few people that I'd invited from my circle in California. There was some girl that was wandering around outside on the cliffs at night. I saw her and called out, even ran down to find out who it was and what she was doing there. But she just vanished as I got to her. It scared the crap outta me, Bill! Some of my guests saw her too, and when she was approached, she disappeared." Stanley admitted. "I'm not sure what is going on here, but I was hoping that since you and Krista have some experience with this kind of thing, you could come here. Maybe bring one of your daughter's psychic friends, I don't know." Stanley sounded unsettled, almost scared.

William was shocked that Stanley would admit to feeling distressed. About anything. Stanley never really seemed rattled, despite his daughter's death and then soon after, his wife. "Well, Stan, I think your evaluation of my family is misguided. It was *your* daughters that held Krista captive 7 years ago. One died and the other is in jail. Or she still in jail? I'm not sure anymore. What exactly is Amanda's status, Stanley?" He really wanted to know. All this shit happening to Krista at work couldn't be coincidental.

Stanley was silent for a moment. "I know that was hard for all of you. I can't apologize enough for what happened with them. I really haven't spoken to Amanda much in all these years. She.....well....her behavior is an embarrassment to me, and all I've tried to achieve. I believe the last time we had a conversation was when she called me two years ago, demanding that I send money to her account in prison. I hung up on her and haven't spoken to her since." Stanley had never shared anything as personal with him. It made William wonder if Stanley just wanted people around that didn't have an ulterior motive for visiting. After all, he was a millionaire many times over, yet he never remarried after Maria died. In fact, he'd never seen Stanley's name linked with anyone on TMZ news. And if Stanley had been out with another woman, even if it was just an assistant of his, the media would've been all over it.

"I'd like to come spend the weekend at your house, Stan. If it's okay, I'd like to bring a woman I've been seeing as well." William knew that despite his reservations about visiting, he needed to. He needed to go back, see Maria's memorial and be able to move forward with his life. He hoped it would be Joanna, despite his gut feeling that something wasn't right.

"Thank you, Bill. I mean it." Stanley sounded genuine. They discussed the details and Stanley insisted on sending a private yacht to pick them up at Point Judith instead of the usual ferry. William didn't argue that; he hated taking the ferry. It had never been a good experience in the past and he was glad not to have to deal with crowds. "Just one last thing, Stan. Please check into Amanda's status at the prison and let me know." William needed to know that she was still there. It would be peace of mind for him and for Krista.

"I'll do that. I'll give you a call later today, Bill." Stanley agreed. "But just remember that because she's behind bars, doesn't mean that she isn't in contact with other people. She's been there long enough to have connections." Warning bells went off in William's head.

Krista

Krista couldn't stop thinking about how that necklace ended up on Mara's nightstand, yet she didn't say anything to Chad or her father. They didn't need the extra stress, especially her father. She arrived at work on time and relieved that the principal wasn't waiting to talk to her today. Erin Brassuer, one of the other counselors, stopped by her office as she was putting down her coffee and work bag.

Erin looked like a blonde supermodel, turned soccer mom. She was 5'8" and had long blonde hair that fell down her back. Although her nose was slightly crooked, it somehow worked on her face. There was a never ending parade of men faculty asking her if she was married when she'd first started working at the school. She would smile and say yes, but yet she would have no deficit of dates if she ever divorced her husband.

"How're you doing Kris?" Erin usually kept to herself and didn't seem to be part of the 'gossip' crowd so Krista didn't mind her asking. Erin and Krista had gone out to lunch a few times, but it never really grew into a friendship outside of office hours. They didn't have enough in common, but Krista liked her because she didn't appear to be an office 'gossip' as most of the women in the guidance office.

"Hey, Erin! I'm great, how're you?" Krista painted on a smile, as she sat down at her desk and booted up her desktop. Erin began chatting on and on about the security on her computer email yesterday as Krista logged onto her computer. "Did you find out what happened with your email?" Erin asked. Krista bristled now, irritated that Erin obviously just wanted to pump her for information.

"I don't know, the police are checking into it." Krista's answer was blunt as she continued working. Krista wasn't listening at this point and after a few 'uh huh and okays', Erin got the hint. "I'll talk to you later, Kris. Have a good day."

"You too." Krista managed to say as she turned her focus back to work, still fuming. She had been completely off about Erin. Erin *was* a gossip-monger, trying to pry for information. Krista was glad that she hadn't shared anything at their previous lunches about anything personal. There had been no word about who had hacked into her computer or any other problems, so by the time Krista was ready to leave to pick Mara up for her appointment, she felt like a weight had lifted. As she was shutting down her computer and logging out, her phone rang. The number came up 'anonymous' so out of curiosity, she picked it up.

"I need to speak to Krista Burton." There was something in the woman's voice that triggered a memory that seemed to take minutes but was only seconds. That voice taunting her, laughing at her as she was tied up…

"Amanda, is that you?" Krista reacted without thinking, but there was something about her voice that convinced her. There was silence on the other end. Krista waited anxiously to hear the response, to confirm that she was right.

"Amanda?" The woman asked, seemingly confused. "I'm not sure who you're referring to. This is Marcy Perrell's office calling to let you know that she needed to reschedule Mara's appointment today due to illness."

"I'm so sorry, I thought you were someone else." Krista apologized, feeing suddenly stupid about her paranoia. Then realized that if Mara didn't see Marcy, she wouldn't be able to get back into school next week. "Is there any possible way Marcy could see her earlier today, even for a few minutes?"

"I'm afraid not. As I said, Ms. Perrell is out sick today. I can reschedule her for Monday morning, as early as 9:00 if that would work for you." Krista couldn't get past her voice. She *knew* that voice! This wasn't just her trauma playing tricks on her. A voice that was so distinct, the underlying tones of sarcasm and hatred that had threatened her life. She'd never forget it.

"I'll call you back to reschedule." Krista decided. She had a better idea.

"Are you sure? Ms. Perrell's schedule fills up quickly?" The husky voice on the other end asked, suddenly seeming concerned.

"I'm sure. Thank you for calling!" Krista hung up without waiting for a response. She immediately looked up Marcy Perrell's office number and called from her office phone. A young woman with a high pitched voice answered. "This is Krista Burton, I was just calling to confirm that Mara still has her appointment with Marcy today."

"Yes, that's right, she's scheduled for 2:30. Do you need to reschedule, Mrs. Burton?"

"No, I just wanted to make sure that was the correct time. Thank you." Krista hung up, feeling relieved that Mara still had the appointment, but now it was obvious that Amanda or one of her clones had called trying to foil Mara's appointment. Krista was filled with paranoia as well as anger. How did this woman know about her appointment? She checked her computer again to make sure she was logged out, looked over her desk to make sure there were no personal notes or anything identifying on her desk. She suddenly realized she couldn't trust anyone anymore as she grabbed her purse and left the office quickly to pick up Mara for her appointment.

***

They were on their way home from Mara's appointment with the therapist, and Krista felt less confident about Mara's mental state than ever. At least she had the note that would allow Mara back into school, which would take the pressure off of her father. She wasn't entirely sure what Marcy had done, except talk with her without Mara present about the incident. Mara had complained that she was tired all the way to the appointment, but seemed to like her. Marcy met with Mara by herself about 45 minutes. What happened when they returned convinced Krista that she was right. Marcy couldn't give a plausible explanation for what was really happening with her daughter.

"Mrs. Burton, I can tell you that Mara is a very perceptive, intelligent little girl. I find it unlikely that she'd push someone down to harm them on purpose." Marcy began. Krista breathed a sigh of relief at this. "But she does have a preoccupation with this imaginary 'friend' that I think is beyond what I've seen. I'd like to refer her to a colleague, Dr.

Evans. I think he might be able to help." Marcy seemed anxious, as if she couldn't wait for her to leave the room.

"So you're saying she's okay to return to school, but that you can't help her?" Krista tried to keep her frustration in check.

"I'm saying that because she is actively hearing voices, acting out, having periods of fatigue and lack of interest and appetite that seeing Dr. Evans would be helpful to evaluate a need for medications. Of course, I will still meet with her for sessions along her with Dr. Evans. " Marcy explained

Krista bit back what she thought about Mara seeing the psychiatrist and the medication evaluation. "Ms. Perrell, I came here because I need to get my daughter back to school. I appreciate your evaluation, and I'll consider scheduling with Dr. Evans, but I need documentation that Mara can return to her school on Monday."

"I will give you the documentation for her return to school, Mrs. Burton. But just know that I will also be recommending that she have a psychiatric follow-up." Marcy advised her. "You can schedule an initial appointment with Dr. Evans with the receptionist. I'd also like to see Mara again next week, just to check in with her." Krista agreed, although she had no intention of giving Mara a bunch of medications at her age. She'd dutifully scheduled an appointment with Dr. Evans and with Marcy on the same day a couple of weeks away. In the meantime, Krista had the letter in hand to get Mara back into school, but she knew there was going to be a conversation tonight with her husband about other options.

"How did you like Marcy?" Krista asked Mara who'd reverted back into her shell and was quiet during the trip home.

"She asked lots of questions, mommy. But she was nice. I drew her a picture." Mara said quietly, as she looked out the window from the back seat. Whatever animation Marcy had elicited from her was gone now.

"Really, what was in the picture?" Krista was guessing that it was probably the same picture she'd drawn for her father.

"It was a big house on an island near the water. Just like the one I drew for Grandpa. Jamie showed it to me." Mara explained. Krista felt the hairs on her neck raise up as Mara described the drawing. There was no denying that Jamie was more than just an 'imaginary friend.'

"What did you talk about with Marcy?" Krista couldn't help but ask, although she was afraid of what she might hear. Mara was quiet for a minute. "I told Marcy that I don't want Jamie to talk to me anymore. Because I don't mommy. I want her to stop talking to me!" Mara started to cry and Krista was thankful that she was almost home.

Once she parked the SUV, she immediately got out and pulled Mara from the back seat. "It's okay, Mara. I'm glad that you told her about Jamie. We're going to figure out how to get her to stop, okay?" Mara's small frame slid out of her booster seat in the back and into Krista's arms. "I didn't want to tell her mommy, but she kept asking questions. I could tell Jamie was getting mad."

Krista hugged her close as she helped Mara out of the back seat. Her small frame seemed as though it would break and her huge blue eyes seemed to look almost through her.

"You did fine, sweetheart. Daddy will be home soon and we'll have dinner together." Mara agreed without argument. Krista noticed that she'd been more affectionate with her more often.   She knew without a doubt that she'd be calling Sadie Mercotte. After all, it was Nadine that had alerted her to what was happening and yet she listened to Chad. She was going to do things *her* way this time! Krista was too distracted to notice the black truck parked down the street from their house on the side of the road.

Chad

After taking Michelle off the VIP accounts and giving them to Greg, Chad knew there was going to be some push-back from Michelle. He actually half-expected her to quit on the spot and was surprised when she didn't. He would have preferred that she had given notice, or maybe he should have just fired her. But tracking her calls to whomever she was talking to was crucial. He sent Michelle all of the information on the Mckenna account and updated Greg on the Sampson account and updated his receptionist Kathy about tracking calls in and out to both of them.

Kathy was always pleasant and easy to work with, but when he approached her with the new protocol, she had questions. "I don't mean to pry Mr. Burton, but it seems as though you don't trust your employees." She looked him in the eye when she was talking, then turned back to her computer. Very passive aggressive of her, but Chad appreciated her honesty.

"I wish that I didn't need to ask this of you, but it's necessary right now. I do trust you. You will also be compensated in your salary for monitoring calls." Chad told her.

"There's already been a call to Michelle's phone just a few minutes ago. It was a woman that called." Kathy informed him, giving him the number that it originated from. Chad was anxious as he took the number from Kathy. Maybe now, he'd be able to figure out what Michelle was up to. It was a 401 Rhode Island area code. Chad just hoped that it wasn't a 'burner phone' that someone had dumped out after they used it.

He went back to his office and called the number, waiting anxiously as it rang several times, then someone picked up. "Yes?" It was a woman's voice that answered. It was hard to tell her age because her voice was raspy, as though she'd smoked several packs of cigarettes on a daily basis.

Chad was caught off guard, but recovered quickly. "Could I speak to Amanda please?" He decided to throw the dice and hopefully get some information that he really needed. He knew that Krista was certain that Amanda was the one behind her trouble at work with the emails that were sent from her account at school.

"Uh, I think you have the wrong number." She told him, but the hesitation was there. He thought he recognized her voice, but couldn't remember where?

Chad decided to push her a little. "Are you sure? She gave me this number to contact her. Who am I speaking with? Do you know her?"

There was a silence for a moment on the other end. "There's no Amanda here. She must have given you the wrong number, mister." But there was a slight hesitation in her voice. Chad decided to try again.

"I'm sure this is the right number! Please, I really need to get hold of her. There's a family member that isn't well, so I wanted to let her know. Are you sure you don't know Amanda?" Chad questioned certain that he heard that voice before.

"Look, I was just told to answer this phone. There's no Amanda here!" The woman was clearly upset now. "I don't want any problems, just don't call this number again!" She hung up on him.

'Oh, well, I gave it a shot,' Chad thought to himself. He headed out of his office to grab a coffee when the phone rang. He was expecting a call from Greg about the Sampson account as he had shown them a property today. "Chad Burton," he answered.

"Mr. Burton, it's Kathy. I've got some woman on the line that claims someone called her from this number. She wouldn't give her name, but can I put her through?"

"Sure. Thanks, Kathy." He knew he picked the right person for a receptionist. "This is Chad, can I help you?" His adrenaline was going, he was positive that it was the woman that he'd just called.

"You just called me from this number. What do you want?" It was that woman calling him back! He was guessing the family member comment got her attention. Suddenly Chad knew where he'd heard her voice. It was when he was going to Block Island to get Krista. It was Estelle! But he knew she'd been sent to prison for several years. She wouldn't be out already. Or would she?

"I believe you just called me back. You know I wanted to speak with Amanda. You're the one who hung up!" Chad threw the ball back her court.

"I can't talk to you now." Her voice sounded suddenly frantic. "Meet me at the corner of Hartford and Atwood Ave in the CVS parking lot in half an hour. I'll be in a red Kia SUV with a paw print sticker on the back window." The line went dead before he could respond.

'Guess I'm heading out to meet her,' Chad decided. He'd taken it this far. Besides, the location was only a couple of miles away, and it was around noon anyway. He had a 1:30 appointment with a client, but he was sure he could make it work if this woman wasn't late. He wasn't even sure what information he was looking for, but he suspected that Michelle was up to something. He checked his emails then headed out telling Kathy he was going to lunch and would be back in an hour.

"Be careful." Kathy advised, winking at him. She knew that he wasn't just going to lunch.

Chad drove to the designated spot with 5 minutes to spare. He kept a close eye on the traffic at the CVS. She'd picked a busy spot, so he needed to pay attention. He played a few games on his phone, but kept an eye out and sure enough, a red Kia pulled up with a paw print on the back a few parking spaces over. He realized she didn't know what he was driving so he got out of his BMW and went up to her vehicle.

Although time in prison had not been kind to her, he recognized her immediately. It was Estelle, the woman that was hired to pretend to be Caroline Ahearn by Amanda and Jane to sell Stanley's property. Estelle had posed as a limo driver and brought Chad to the house where he and Krista had managed to escape the plan the Ahearn sisters had for them. Although she looked older than her years, he still recognized the now gray-streaked dark hair, and glittering brown eyes. She'd gained a significant amount of weight, and looked very tired, unlike the young actress just playing a role 7 years ago. She rolled down her window. "Get in," she said in a low voice, as he heard her unlock her doors. As he opened the door to the passenger seat, it occurred to him that he might be making a terrible mistake. What if she took off? He reached into his pocket to make sure his phone was with him. Not that it would matter if she decided to pull a gun on him.

"Are you getting in, or just going to stand there with the door open?" Estelle snapped at him. "I don't have all day!" He glanced around the vehicle to see if there were any potential weapons in view, then decided to get in. He hoped that this risky move would prove beneficial in some way.

"Okay, Estelle, I'm here. What did you need to tell me?" Chad got right to the point. He noticed she was looking around in her mirrors. "Is someone following you?"

"That's why I'm looking. To make sure that no one is!" Estelle told him. "I was released from prison a few years ago, and things haven't gone too well as you can probably imagine. The only jobs that I can get as a parolee are housekeeper positions. I even tried changing my name, hoping that I could get back into acting which is why I took that job years ago. I regret every minute of it, I just want to tell you that. It's why I'm here now, warning you. Amanda has people working for her and she's out to get you and your wife. She blames your family for everything, including her sister's death."

"But it was the police that killed her sister." Chad brought up reason, but Estelle was already shaking her head.

"Amanda doesn't have a reasonable thought in her head. She doesn't give a crap about anyone, never has including her sister. She just wants her way." Estelle said simply. "Unfortunately, I didn't have a choice but to start working for her again, but after I was told to call you, I

192

remembered your voice and what you went through. I needed to warn you." She continued to look around her as she was talking, as though someone were watching.

"What *is* her plan?" Her anxiety was contagious and Chad found himself looking around, searching, and anticipating an ambush at any moment.

"You already know that I have contact with Michelle. You were smart to figure her out sooner than later. She's been trying to push for David Ackwell to buy that property. David Ackwell had a fling with Amanda before she went to prison and he's been at her beck and call ever since."

Chad was floored. David Ackwell and Amanda? He never would've guessed that. "So that's why David's been so adamant. But what's in it for Michelle?"

"Michelle has been using me to connect with Amanda on the inside and giving her information about what's been going on. If Stanley sells, Amanda promised her several million dollars." Estelle revealed. Chad wasn't surprised by that news; he knew that she was involved somehow in this whole Ahearn property.

"I need to go, but make sure you don't tell David or Michelle any other updates on Stanley's property. Keep a low profile and watch your back." Estelle warned. "Everyone that has a connection to Stanley and that house is in danger."

"What about my wife and my daughter? They have nothing to do with this." Her words were starting to freak him out. But then again, it would explain what had been happening to Kris at work.

"But they do. The Ahearn girls wanted Krista dead, remember? She foiled that plan. Your daughter is just an innocent victim that Amanda sees as a way to hurt you and your wife." Estelle reminded him. "If I were you, I wouldn't even bother taking David's calls. The less involved you are, the less likely they are to come after you."

"How can Amanda come after me while she's in prison?" Chad questioned.

"Like I said, she has connections. Not just with me, but David has her back as well as other former inmates that she's paid off. Besides, she may be getting out on parole soon. At least that's what she's told me." Estelle's eyes grew wide with fear as she spoke about Amanda. It was obvious that Estelle was terrified of her.

She was looking in her rearview mirror now and her brown eyes grew wide with fear. "I've gotta go! Get down lower in your seat! I think someone has followed us here and watching." Chad turned around in his seat to see a short man with a Boston Red Sox baseball hat and a plaid flannel shirt on get out of his older model black Dodge Ram and head towards Estelle's Kia. "Is that guy in the hat who you're worried about?" Chad asked.

"Yes! You need to go!" Estelle was frantic now, putting the Kia into reverse and prepared to step on the gas. The man began walking faster and Chad wasn't sure if he would be safer staying or going. "Estelle, he knows I'm here. If I get out now, it'll look suspicious."

"It looks suspicious anyway. Just get out and go!" Estelle was yelling at him now. Chad took a deep breath, ducked down in case the guy hadn't noticed him, and opened the door just as the Red Sox hat guy arrived at the driver's side window. He snuck around the side of the Kia, hoping that the guy wouldn't see him and managed to make his way towards the CVS, acting as though he was a customer. Just as he was entering the store, he casually glanced back to see what was going on. Luckily, the guy wasn't watching, but he could see what appeared to be a heated conversation with Estelle. While Chad was glad for himself, he was worried about her safety and once inside continued to watch the interaction. He stood at her window for another minute, then went back to his truck. He was relieved when she left the parking lot. Chad quickly moved from the window and darted down one of the pharmaceutical aisles, keeping an eye out for him in case he decided to return. After about 10 minutes went by, he glanced outside and didn't see the truck so he headed back to his car.

Chad drove back to the agency, looking in his rear view mirror the entire time. He was thinking about the conversation with Estelle, when he noticed a black Ram truck close behind him. 'Shit, where'd he come from?' Chad thought and decided to take a right into a nearby Shell station. The truck kept going straight, so Chad took a minute, grabbed a coffee and headed back out. There was no sign of the truck. 'I need to stop worrying about this,' Chad told himself, as he drove back to work. He couldn't help but make sure the truck wasn't behind him. It wasn't.

"How was lunch?" Kathy asked him as he walked past the reception area. Chad pasted a smile on his face. "Good! Chipotle makes a hell of a burrito!"

"By the way, Stanley Ahearn called while you were out. He wants you to call him back as soon as you can." Kathy informed him.

Chad felt his anxiety adrenaline kick in. "Did he say what it was regarding?"

"No. He just wanted a call back. His words were 'sooner than later.'" Kathy advised him. Chad just nodded, trying to appear nonchalant. Yet all he could think about was the conversation he had with Estelle. Did he know about Estelle? It didn't matter because his 1:30 appointment was waiting for him. He had no choice but to call him back later.

***

His new client ended up taking up most of the afternoon and after 4:00, he had several missed calls from Krista about Mara's appointment. He called Kris back but she didn't answer, so he decided to call Stanley back finally, feeling nervous because he'd expected a call back earlier. The phone rang several times then went to voicemail. Chad felt initially relieved, but then realized he'd have to wait to find out what was so urgent. "Mr. Ahearn, its Chad returning your call. I apologize for not getting back to you earlier, but I had clients all afternoon. Feel free to call me on my cell." Chad left the message, hoping that it would suffice.

As he pulled into his driveway, his phone rang and he picked up on his Bluetooth. It was Stanley.

"Chad are you at home?" There was an urgency in his voice that put Chad on edge.

"I just pulled into my driveway, why? What's going on Mr. Ahearn?" All he could think was that Stanley knew that he'd met up with Estelle? But that was ridiculous. Estelle was trying to help him.

"Look around you, on the street. Do you see a black truck parked?" Stanley's voice was commanding now.

Chad looked around and was shocked to see the black Dodge Ram that he'd seen in the parking lot where he'd met Estelle. "Yes, I do. What's going on?"

"Estelle Stevens was released from jail, just a few weeks ago. She was found dead in her car this afternoon." Stanley's statement left Chad speechless for a moment. The woman he'd met in the parking lot to warn him was now dead and the truck that he'd seen with his own eyes was now parked near his house.

"She was found dead? Where?" Chad tried to keep his voice calm. Should he tell Stanley about meeting with her earlier today? He decided that he needed to. That man had seen him there; that's why he was sitting outside his house now and his family was at risk.

" Call the police and give them the description of the vehicle. Turn off your lights and duck down as you're getting out of your vehicle. Don't ask questions now. Just do what I tell you. Get into the house as fast as you can and then lock the door behind you. Make sure all your doors and windows are locked, Chad."

"Stanley, I don't under-" Chad began, but Stanley cut him off.

"Do it now!" Stanley ordered. "Call me back when you're in the house!" The call dropped and Chad went on autopilot. He called the Johnston Police and reported the vehicle sitting outside his house.

"What exactly are they doing, Mr. Burton?" The dispatcher wanted details. He suddenly felt silly as he knew that him telling the police that he'd seen the truck earlier that had been following him. "I'm just concerned. The same vehicle has been following me this afternoon." Chad gave his explanation, but even he knew it sounded lame. Police didn't have time to just show up because someone had parked across his street. The dispatcher told him that police were tied up, but if the truck remained there for a length of time to call back. Still, he felt it necessary to heed Stanley's advice about keeping a low profile. He shut down the vehicle, ducked down and crouched down, heading to the patio in the back yard instead of the front door. Luckily, it was unlocked and he came inside and locked it behind him. Krista was in the kitchen that was near the door and greeted him with a hug.

"Kris, don't ask questions, just go make sure all the doors are locked! Garage, front door, windows! Just do it, then we'll talk, okay?" She took a look at his face and began scurrying around to check the house.

Krista

She'd just gotten home with Mara and was getting dinner ready when Chad came through the sliding glass door in a hurry. "Kris, don't ask questions, just go make sure all the doors are locked! Front door, garage, windows! Just go make sure their locked and then we'll talk!" Krista knew that from the look on his face that this was real. His words put her into panic mode and she jumped into action, rushing around to check all the locks on the doors, make sure the windows were shut.

"Okay, now can you tell me what the hell is going on?" Krista tried to keep her voice down, but after the appointment with Marcy, she was feeling more stressed than ever. Chad pulled out his phone and put his finger to his lips as he whispered, "I'll tell you in a minute. I'm calling Stanley back. He was the one that told me."

"Told you what?" Krista demanded to know. "What the hell is going on, Chad?"

"About the black truck that's parked on the side of the road." Chad said. "Shh, I'm calling Stanley."
Just then Stanley picked up. "Stanley? Chad here. I'm in the house. Everything's locked up. Now, what's going on?" Chad was pacing back and forth as he kept looking outside the front window to see if the truck was still there. It was. Krista wondered just how long that black truck had been parked. She hadn't been paying attention when she got home with Mara and now she was worried.

Krista was shaking as she watched Chad staring out the window at the black truck talking on the phone and felt chilled to the core. What the hell was going on here? She'd had a stressful enough day with Mara's appointment. Luckily, Mara was happy to eat some leftovers and watch a Disney movie so she was distracted. She overheard him saying 'she was found dead' and immediately stood near Chad as he tried to wave her away. "NO! What are you talking about?" She hissed at him between gritted teeth. "I deserve to know what's going on here!"

Chad nodded. "Give me a minute, ok Kris? I promise I'll let you know what's going on." Chad moved away from her and waved her back to the living room. Krista knew that it was pointless right now, so she went into the kitchen and poured herself a glass of pinot noir and tried to sip it slowly as she kept close to the living room to try and overhear the conversation.

"Stanley, I have to admit to you that someone Michelle talked to this morning called and I called back. The person hung up on me, then called me back a few minutes later. I recognized the voice. It was Estelle. She wanted to warn me about what was going on." Chad began.

"Estelle! What? Please tell me you didn't meet her." Stanley sounded horrified.

"Why? She told me some secrets about David and Amanda." Chad was surprised that Stanley was so against Estelle. After all according to Estelle, Amanda was behind all of this. "She told me that Kris and I were in trouble, she said she was trying to warn me about Amanda." Chad insisted.

"Because Amanda has involvement with the person that killed Estelle. They're sitting outside your house right now." Stanley's information wasn't a surprise to Chad at this point, given he'd seen this truck when he met with her. "She has some shady connections, Chad. She's upset that I cut her off from any funds coming into her account. Did you call the police?" He asked.

" I did. However, they're just sitting there. If they aren't breaking any laws, there's not a reason for them to send someone out. I was just trying to find out what was happening with the business. I told you about Michelle. I know she's involved too. Do you have any idea who the driver is? What do I do now?"

Krista heard this conversation and getting more upset by the minute. She was motioning to him to put it on speaker phone. Chad decided to oblige her and put it on speaker phone as long as Mara was out of the room. He advised Stanley that he was doing so. Krista came closer and spoke up. "Mr. Ahearn, are we in danger right now?" She was direct. She'd had a long day and this was just another aggravation for her at this point.

"Krista, go look out the window and see if there's a black truck still there, but make sure your head is down so they won't see you." Stanley advised, his voice over the speaker phone sounding very confident, trustworthy. Krista went to the picture window that overlooked their yard and the street. She didn't see any cars or trucks parked near their house on the street.

"There's no truck parked outside." Krista announced, relieved that maybe it was just a mistake.

"Good. They must have been told that none of you knew about Estelle and what happened after Chad met with her." Stanley sounded sure of his words, but to Krista, it was just a guessing game. At least he was gone and they had an alarm system.

"But you do believe this person was involved with Estelle's death?" Chad still couldn't believe that the woman that seemed to want to help him a few hours ago had been killed. And he'd seen him. And the same truck *had* been parked outside their house for a few minutes.

"I'm not sure about anything Chad, but the police are investigating now. They may come by and ask you questions." Stanley warned.

"Why would they be asking me? No one else knew that I was meeting her except for whoever was driving the black truck!" Chad was starting to feel paranoid, as if he were being watched now. After the news about Estelle, it was obvious why she'd been so fearful when she'd met with him. Then he remembered that he'd already called them about the black truck. Damn, why had he listened to Stanley?

Krista still couldn't believe her husband had met up with this woman. She'd save that discussion for later, but now her mind was on Nadine's 'accident' in broad daylight. "Mr. Ahearn, a holistic young lady that had given me advice in the past and most recently was killed in a pedestrian accident last week. Do you think any of these recent events have to do with her? I mean, do you think Amanda and her cronies might have targeted her as well?" Krista asked him.

"I really don't know." Stanley was quick to answer. A little too quick in Krista's opinion. "I would like to have you all come to my house next weekend though. I'm sure Chad, you've mentioned this? We can talk further about any other concerns you have as well as enjoy what seems to be a warm fall." It was clear that he was conveniently changing the subject.

Krista knew that she wouldn't get any real answers over the phone with Stanley. Besides, she really did want to visit. The house was spectacular from what she remembered and it would be nice to be there under normal circumstances instead of being kidnapped! "Yes, Mr. Ahearn. I think we would enjoy that. Mara would enjoy it as well. Thank you for inviting us." She agreed, as Chad was nodding his head. He seemed to be worried that she wouldn't want to go.

"Great! As I told your father, there will be a private boat to take you there, so no need for the ferry. I'll email you the details, Chad." Stanley assured him. There was no more mention of the black truck or what to do if it showed up again which was concerning to Krista, but she had enough to talk with Chad about once Stanley hung up.

Dinner was minimal superficial conversation because Mara was at the table and none of the day's events were anything that she needed to hear about. Mara ate very little, even though Krista had made her favorite; chicken tenders and tater tots and was happy to leave the table and go back to the couch with her blanket. "Are you feeling okay, Mara?" Krista felt her forehead, which was cool, no fever. Mara looked at her with tired eyes. "I'm tired, mommy. Not really hungry."

"Ok, sweetheart. Why don't you go lie down on the couch? You can put on one of your shows." Krista normally would have her doing schoolwork, but gave her a pass today. Mara just nodded in response and immediately went to the couch and laid down.

Krista wasn't sure what to do anymore especially after the visit with Marcy today. She discussed the visit with Chad who agreed with her that medication should wait for now. "I'm planning to meet Sadie Mercotte on Wednesday before the funeral for Nadine." Krista was anticipating an argument from Chad, who was surprisingly supportive.

"Kris, its fine. You know more about this than I do. We've both been through some things in the past that have no explanation. She does talk about 'Jamie' a lot and she seems scared. Mara never used to be afraid of anything. I think you should talk to Sadie. Maybe she can have some insight into what's going on with my situation at work." Chad tried to make light of it. He went over events that happened today with the initial call and then meeting Estelle, followed by the guy in the truck.

"Wait a minute. You thought that initial call was Amanda?" Krista was reminded of the strange call that she had received from Marcy's office right before her appointment, telling her it was cancelled. She told Chad about it. "How many people knew about that appointment? Did you tell Jen or any coworkers?"

"No, I just said I had an appointment. I don't talk to Jen anymore and I don't trust anyone at work. It makes no sense. What would Mara missing her appointment have to do with anything?" Krista had racked her brain all afternoon about it. Unless whoever called was trying to keep track of her.

Her husband's response was predictable; "don't worry about it Kris. Maybe it was just a misunderstanding with the office." She knew damn well it wasn't, but there were other topics to tackle in their ever evolving world of drama. They discussed the trip to Block Island and were in agreement that it would be a weekend away from home and a visit to Krista's mother's memorial along with William. "It'll be fun. It's beautiful there, and hopefully the weather will cooperate." Chad was sold on the idea.

"Jamie told me I should go." Mara had suddenly appeared from the living room and obviously been eavesdropping on the conversation. She seemed to have more energy now, and gave her mother a hug which was very out of the ordinary. "Mommy, I want to go!" Her voice seemed to have lost her child-like high pitch for a moment and sounded almost adult like. Krista felt a sudden chill go through her for a split-second. Her daughter's voice sounded different.

"Mara, why does Jamie say you should go?" Krista questioned her. Mara looked confused for a moment, looking like the young child that she was, but then the adult-like composure reappeared.

"It'll be nice to leave home and go somewhere." Mara's eyes were like saucers and her voice sounded as though she were reading a script. Krista looked over at Chad who looked as surprised as she did. Mara was still clinging to her and while Krista appreciated the affection, she felt as though her actions weren't genuine. It was as if her daughter was a puppet for an unknown entity that was moving the strings.

"We'll be going, sweetheart. However, maybe it's better to leave Jamie at home while we visit, ok?" Chad asked casually. Krista was surprised at his direct attention to discuss 'Jamie'. Mara released her arms from Krista and walked over to her father.

"Jamie is coming. She has to." Mara's eyes had a dark fury behind them, the beautiful light-blue eyes that had always been so endearing turned to a dark blue, the tone of her voice was harsh, threatening and in that same mature voice that was not her own. Her hands were clenched and she stood defiantly in front of Chad as though she were ready to go to battle with him.

Both Chad and Krista were speechless for a moment. Chad subconsciously stood up and backed away from Mara. The fear on his face reflected the same apprehension that Krista was feeling. "Mara, if Jamie wants to tag along, that's fine." His voice was quavering as he said the words. Krista was hit with the realization that she and her husband had become afraid of their child. He looked to Krista who just nodded, indicating that 'let's play along for now.' Mara seemed satisfied with the answer and didn't say anything else as she ate her dinner. She stood up from the table without a word and started to walk to the living room.

"Mara, please take your plate to the sink." Krista reminded her. Putting her plate in the sink had been a rule in their house since Mara was four. Mara ignored her and sat down on the couch. Krista's tolerance for her behavior was wearing thin and she took some deep breaths as she waited and counted to three before responding. "Mara! I asked you to bring your plate to the sink!" Mara glared at her from the couch in the living room.

"I don't want to." Her voice had that deeper tone along that didn't match her childish mannerisms. "Mara! You heard your mother. Do it now!" Chad took over, his voice taking on a warning tone that he was ready to hand out consequences.

Mara stood up and walked toward the dining room as if they were invisible. Her pupils were so huge that the blue was barely visible and her face became distorted with an angry smile as she approached Chad. "Mara, pick up your …."Chad stopped in mid-sentence as Mara's plate began to move on its own toward the edge of the table. It stopped for a moment, teetering back and forth then the plate slid off, smashing onto the floor. Both Krista and Chad stared at each other in disbelief trying to take in what had just happened. "Oh my god! Chad! What's going on?"

"What the hell just happened?" Chad turned to his daughter. Mara's angry demeanor turned to shock and she looked surprised about the broken shards of ceramic on the floor. As if the sound of the glass hitting the floor had brought her back to being Mara.

"Mommy!" Mara sounded like herself now, as she began to cry. Krista was in shock as she reached for Mara. "Mommy, daddy, I'm sorry."

Krista swallowed hard, trying to keep composed although she was the furthest from it. "Its okay, Mara. You didn't push it off the table." It was true. The plate had slid off to the floor, reminding Krista of a horror movie. Except it was real.

"No, but Jamie did. She was mad. I don't like her anymore, mommy. She scares me!" Mara's tearful blue eyes were filled with tears. "She's not nice anymore, she's mean." Krista hugged her daughter close, grateful that she'd lost the malicious look on her face from moments ago. It was as if a switch had been turned off.

"It's going to be okay, daddy and I will talk to Jamie. We'll figure this out." Krista told her, trying to remain calm for Mara's sake. Maybe Marcy had cleared her to go back to school, but there was only one person she was going to call now. Sadie Mercotte.

William

William and Joanna took off to Narragansett for a drive and a walk on the town beach. The weather was perfect; not too chilly for later September. "It's nice sweatshirt weather," Joanna commented as they strolled along the beach, enjoying the sun and the solitude. It had been years before he could ever set foot on the beach again after Karen was gone, then Maria. But this experience with Joanna was a resurrection for his love for the ocean, and beach walking with a woman he loved.

"How's Mara doing? Any word from Kris about their appointment?" Joanna asked him. He loved that she cared enough to ask. Mara's behaviors had given her enough reason to disappear, yet she seemed to understand. And she was still here. He glanced down at his watch. It was 4:30 and he hadn't heard anything, but he figured Kris was busy.

"I haven't so I'm taking that as a good sign! But thanks for asking and thanks for hanging in there with this situation." William was only half-joking. Mara had been rude to Joanna on several occasions and he was glad that she stuck around anyway. Joanna reached out for his hand. "Bill, I know what you've gone through and I've gone through a lot too. I've got a granddaughter as well and I understand that you need to be there. Especially with the circumstances." Joanna assured him.

They walked back up to the boardwalk and Joanna excused herself to use the restroom inside the pavilion along the boardwalk. William did the same and then waited for her outside, looking out at the ocean.

209

He was enjoying the peacefulness when he realized Joanna had been gone for longer than it took to use the bathroom. He peeked inside the women's room. He was hesitant to call out to her, but then again, what the hell was going on? Finally, fear took over being yelled at by other women in the bathroom. "Jo? Are you in there?"

There was no answer. "Jo! Where are you?" William felt his heart race when there was still no response. He was beyond worried about privacy at this point and walked into the bathroom. "JO!" He was starting to worry, looking frantically around when he heard her voice. He poked his head around the corner and could see Joanna talking on the phone with someone. What the hell was she doing? He almost called her name again, but then decided against it. She had her back to him and was clearly hiding behind a bush. Who the hell was she talking to? He decided to try and find out, staying out of her line of sight.

"I know that you're worried! It's been hard for me too! I want you to come by but we can't be seen together." Joanna's words were like a knife in Williams' heart. "But I'll see you soon. Yes, he told me." She glanced around her and William hid behind the concrete of the pavilion. "I've gotta go. He's waiting for me. Miss you, love you. I'll talk to you soon." She hung up, looked around before she headed towards the restroom area.

William quickly retreated towards the boardwalk facing the ocean, as she made her way back towards him. "Sorry to take so long! There was a line and then I had to take this call from work." Joanna's voice sounded upbeat and normal. As though she were telling him the truth.

William didn't turn around. She didn't even claim it was one of her children. It was 'someone from work.' Really? She told someone from work that she loved and missed them? It was obvious she had no knowledge that he'd overheard her conversation.

He wasn't sure what he wanted to do, but he knew that he didn't trust Joanna any longer. William tried to rationalize that she'd been talking to one of her kids, but the part about 'it's hard being away from you too' struck him as an unlikely mother/child conversation. It seemed clear to him that there was someone else.

Joanna reached out and put her arms around him. He stiffened up, shrugged her arms off his shoulders. "I'm ready to go home. I need to check on how Mara's appointment went." William tried to mask how upset he was about her obvious deception, but it was tough to keep the anger out of his voice. He started walking towards the car.

"I thought we were going to get dinner somewhere. Are you okay?" Joanna turned to face him and he looked away, avoiding eye contact. William was terrible at pretending, he would rather just get home and let her go rather than have a confrontation.

"Joanna, I'm fine. I'm just feeling tired. Besides, it looks like rain." William was already growing weary of the charade that he was playing. He just wanted to get home and then…what? He wasn't sure how to handle this, but he knew he didn't want to spend more time with Joanna tonight than he needed to.

It was an extremely uncomfortable 45 minute drive back to his house. Joanna made several attempts to initiate conversation, but William wasn't interested. He just wanted to go home, check in on how Mara's appointment went and make himself a drink. He felt silly, stupid really for putting himself out there and he could still hear Krista's voice telling him, 'Dad, you just need to keep trying. When it's right, you'll know.'

But he thought it was and it was obvious it was only one-sided. When they pulled up to his house, he got out and headed into the house, while Joanna stood there, looking confused. She'd met him at his house, he remembered that he liked seeing her car parked in his driveway when they left. Now it just made him feel lost. As though he'd given his heart and it had been taken, stomped on, and now there was very little left to give.

"Bill, what's going on? Do you want me to leave?" Joanna asked him as he walked to the front door.

"Yes. I do. I'm sorry, Joanna, but this isn't going to work out. I thought we were in the same place to be together, but clearly we're not." William's plan was to go inside and forget her, without any explanation, but his emotions had taken over now.

"What the hell are you talking about, Bill? I thought we had a good day!" Joanna's eyes were tearing up now as she approached him at the front door.

"I'm not stupid, Joanna. I was looking for you. I overheard your conversation. You weren't talking to a co-worker, unless that co-worker is someone you 'love and miss and see you soon.'" William couldn't help himself. He'd rather have just left things alone so that he could grieve in private, but he felt better as he said the words.

"It's not what you think, Bill! Really!" Joanna was clearly not expecting that he'd overhead her phone conversation. She seemed surprised, but William was sure it was because she was caught, not because she cared.

"Then what is it? Because I don't believe for a minute it was someone from work!" William couldn't help himself. His good sense was telling him to say goodbye and shut the door but that went out the window.

Joanna was silent for a moment and didn't answer. For a split-second, William thought that she might actually have a reasonable explanation, and he had no reason to be suspicious or upset. Hoping, waiting.

"I was talking to my co-worker. She's my friend and lost her husband recently." Joanna told him, as she sniffled, her eyes brimming with tears.

"That's your explanation?" William asked, not buying it for a minute. She really was going to stick to this. He was done. That had nothing to do with what he overheard, 'Yes, he knows. He's waiting for me. I miss being away from you too.' The words kept playing back in his head. No, he hadn't heard the other side of the conversation, but it was enough to keep him from seeing her again. He refused to be hurt again.

"That's what the call was about, Bill! I swear it was! What do you want from me?" Joanna was shouting now and William decided it was time to end this conversation.

"I need to go, Joanna. We'll talk later." William went in the house and slammed the door behind him. He didn't know if he'd made the right decision for good, but it was right for now. If his past relationships had taught him anything, it was to be aware. He immediately wondered if he was being too impulsive, but when he peered out the door a few seconds later to see her reaction, Joanna had seemed unconcerned, gotten into her car and drove away. Likely to whoever she'd been talking to. William pulled out his bottle of whiskey that he'd managed to keep for several months without drinking every night and poured himself a double.

Chad

After all the drama on Friday night, Chad decided to go to the office to do some paperwork the next day and if nothing else get away from it. The black truck that had been parked near their house had never appeared again. He knew, because he'd been worried and checked multiple times during the night as well as checking the cameras that were set up around the house perimeters. He'd just sat down at his desk to go over some potential property for clients when William called him on his cell.

"Bill, good to hear from you. What's going on?" Chad didn't' want to get into the Michelle/Greg issue or Estelle and the black truck. He'd wait until someone brought it up to him. "Do you want to go have breakfast somewhere, Chad?" William surprised him with the request.

"Sure. Where do you want to go? How about the Lighthouse on Hartford Ave?" Chad suggested. It was 11:00 but he was pretty sure they were open until 1:00. He didn't realize how hungry he was until William mentioned food. Now he was starving.

"Great! Meet you there in 15 minutes!" William sounded relieved. Chad knew something was on his mind, and was hoping that it wasn't Stanley or the business. He needed a few hours break from that today.

William was already sitting at a table waiting when Chad arrived. He looked exceptionally tired and although Chad hated to admit it. Old. He'd never thought of his father-in -law as elderly. But today, he looked every minute of 64 years and maybe older. "Bill, how are you?" Chad asked, resisting the urge to ask if he was feeling okay.

"I've been better, let's just leave it at that." William was being cryptic about it, and Chad figured it had to do with Joanna. He felt bad for him; he knew that Bill had been really happy and even Krista had taken to Joanna. "I hope Mara didn't scare her off." After all, Bill had been watching her and Mara hadn't exactly been on her best behavior in the past few weeks.

"Of course not. Nothing like that. It's just…I really wish that women would be honest in a relationship. I really thought Joanna was one of them." William had cracked the door open on the problem, but Chad wouldn't continue unless he talked about it. It was when the difference between men and women really was obvious. Women talk ongoing about their relationships, even playing guessing games, but guys really just kept it to themselves most of the time.   "Sorry to hear that, Bill. Maybe let things cool down for a little while. It's been a stressful time with Mara. The good news is that she can go back to school on Monday, so your babysitting duties are no longer needed, grandpa! Both Kris and I are so appreciative of you taking care of her this past week." Chad expressed his gratitude. There really was no other options if William hadn't stepped in.

Chad decided to dive into the shit that had been happening at Carson Realty and at home. He told him about the call from Estelle and how he met her, the call from Stanley and the black truck parked at their house long enough to make them nervous.

"It's no problem. Mara has nothing to do with this issue with Joanna, Chad. Don't worry" William seemed as though he was ready to talk about it, but then he changed the subject. "You talked to Stanley. Are you all going to come next weekend?" He seemed casual about it, but Chad knew that he wouldn't go if they weren't going.

"We're absolutely going, Bill." Chad told him and William seemed relieved. "I know that Kris wants to go and see the memorial." He didn't comment on Mara's pictures and descriptions, but Bill did.

"Mara knew about that memorial before any of us, Chad. She did that drawing for me this week. I thought she was making it up, but then I talked to Stan and he'd told me about it. She has it, you know." William took a sip of his coffee. The waitress came to take their order just then and they ordered blueberry pancakes with a side of bacon and eggs. He waited for her to leave and he noticed that Chad waited until she left to ask what he meant.

"Has what, Bill?" Chad was confused.

"Mara has that ability to see spirits, those that have passed. Her grandmother did too, as did Karen. But I'm worried that she's been talking to this Jamie. Jamie isn't just an imaginary friend to her, Chad. Maybe this sounds crazy to you, but I just know what I've seen from her this past week." Bill shook his head, not knowing how Chad would feel about his observations.

"Bill, I don't think it's crazy. Especially after last night." He told Bill about Mara getting upset and the plate flying off the table, then blaming 'Jamie' for it. He felt better talking about it with Bill, because he'd brought it up, and he seemed to understand. "Kris said something about calling Nadine's aunt today, which I'm not opposed to." William agreed with him. It was a subject that neither of them were comfortable with, so Bill changed the subject.

"How did Michelle take being 'demoted' from the Sampson account?" William wanted to know.

"She was upset of course. I'm actually hoping that she'll quit. I'd fire her, except that I think it's better to keep her around; that way I can keep an eye on what she's up to. I did learn quite a bit from Estelle during our 10 minute conversation though. Including that David and Amanda were having an affair and that David pushing for Stanley to sell is coming from his imprisoned daughter. Stanley told me that Estelle was recently released from prison and that Amanda likely had something to do with what happened." Chad was just now putting it all together, now that he'd had the time to think about it. He'd always had a sense that Michelle was trouble and Amanda was a complete sociopath. It didn't surprise him that David and Amanda had been scheming, especially since David was trying to work his way up in Hollywood as a director.

William remembered the conversation that he'd had with Stanley a few days ago. "I talked to Stanley. He says he hasn't had any contact with Amanda for several years after she kept asking him for money. He did tell me that over the past year, he's had guests over and they saw a girl walking along the cliffs around the house, then just vanished. He seems scared, Chad. He even wanted me to bring Nadine, that psychic girl over. Then he said something that really got me unnerved; that just because Amanda is in prison doesn't mean that someone isn't acting on her behalf on the outside."

Chad nodded. "Estelle warned me of the same thing. She said that Kris and I were in danger and then that black truck showed up and she suddenly had to leave. A couple hours later, Stanley called me to warn me that Estelle had been killed and the truck was outside. We locked the doors, but really, whoever was in the truck could've come after us last night. But they left shortly after Stanley told me." Chad suddenly realized what he'd said and his mind was racing. How did Stanley know where they were there?

"How did Stanley know the truck was there?" William seemed to be reading his mind. "Did you ask him?"

Chad suddenly felt gullible. "No I didn't," he admitted. Stanley just warned me, said that Amanda had connections." William nodded. "I think we should go. It *would* be a nice break to get away from all of this. I honestly think that Stanley is just as afraid of Amanda's wrath as the rest of us! Both you and Kris could use a getaway. I'll watch after Mara to give you all some time off while we're there." He offered.

"What about Joanna coming, Bill?" Chad asked. He didn't want to pry but at the same time he wanted to make sure he was okay. After the closure of his wife's death, Bill had been alone for so long and when he'd met Joanna, he really seemed happy.

"No. I think she's seeing someone else, Chad." His voice was choked up as he said the words. Chad was surprised, given that Joanna seemed very committed to their relationship, even pitching in to help with Mara.

"What makes you think that?" Chad was curious. Maybe they'd had an argument about Mara. He hoped not.

" I overheard her talking to someone while we were out at the beach yesterday. It wasn't just a casual conversation. She said 'He knows, he waiting for me. Miss you, love you.' " His eyes had tears in them as he spoke about it.

"Did you give her chance to explain, Bill? I mean, you've been seeing her for quite a while." Chad was surprised that Bill was willing to let this relationship go given that he'd given his all and he'd seemed so sure about it.

William nodded. "I did, but she kept claiming that it was a co-worker that was having a hard time. I even gave her a chance to give me a better explanation, but I wasn't buying it. It just didn't make sense to me, Chad."

Chad wasn't sure what advice to give at this point, because he kind of agreed that it wasn't what he would say if he was just talking to a co-worker or friend for that matter. "It does sound strange, Bill. Maybe having some space would be better." He felt bad for him but he wasn't going to encourage him to pursue a relationship that was already stressful.

"You're absolutely right, Chad. I'll wait for her to contact me. If she doesn't, then it wasn't worth me worrying about. If she does, I'll go from there. But that explanation doesn't work for me." William suddenly seemed more determined to move forward, instead of worrying about what 'could have been.' Chad had watched his father-in-law go through this already after his wife's reappearance, followed by her death.

The rest of day flew by as Chad went back to the office and went through all the clients' records in Carson's database. He had an accountant on staff that did the day to day, but wanted to check it out for himself. He also checked the record of Michelle's calls coming in and out as Kathy had recorded them on a spreadsheet for him. None seemed out of the ordinary, except for one that happened yesterday around 3:46pm. There was something about the call that stood out to him but it wasn't the time of day. It was the number that was dialed out. He knew he'd seen it before. But it wasn't a number that Michelle had called before, at least from this office.

After half an hour of combing through Michelle's phone records, he was feeling like he was getting nowhere. But he knew he'd seen that number before and it wasn't a client. He decided to look the number up online and found the number belonged to someone named Kaden Marcelli. Chad decided to do some digging for information on Kaden and found him on several social media platforms.

Kaden didn't like to share many personal stats, but Chad was able to learn that he was 25 years old, lived in Rhode Island and according to one of Kaden's quotes; 'getting by as only I can.' Chad was surprised there were no photos of Kaden himself, so he continued to search for photos on his Facebook page. His profile had a picture of a dragon, but as Chad scrolled through the previous posts, he found one. It was a picture of a tall and thin gangly looking guy dressed in a leather jacket and ill-fitting jeans with a Patriots baseball hat.

"Oh my god! That's him! That's the guy in the parking lot at CVS!" Chad shouted out loud. Although he hadn't seen his face in the parking lot, he knew it was him. It wasn't just his height, it was the way he stood and looked into the camera. Completely void of emotion and focused on a task. The leather jacket looked the same; an older black color with a zipper and side pockets with his hands shoved in them. The baseball hat was a different color, but it didn't matter. In the background was a black truck. Chad felt his heart racing as he continued to scroll through pictures to find out more. Some more pictures of the truck appeared. It was definitely a Dodge Ram, with him in it. The next picture was of him with a woman that he recognized. She had blonde hair and was standing next to him and he had his around her. He enlarged the picture. It could only be one person. Joanna. Bill's Joanna. Kaden had captioned the picture 'Love my mom!' in the post.

Chad quickly took a screenshot of the picture, as well as some of the other pictures of Kaden and the truck. This was something that he needed to save. Clearly, Joanna had some secrets, and it involved another man. Her son. No wonder Joanna had been hiding this from Bill. She was covering for her son. The fact that he was talking to Michelle was a red flag. It was amazing how nothing made sense, until suddenly, it did.

He knew he was onto something and continued to check into the court records for Kaden Macelli. There were none, but he also didn't have his date of birth, or Kaden had just never been caught. Yet, something told him this wasn't Kaden's first experience engaging in criminal activity. He picked up the phone and dialed the Johnston Police. "I just want to give some information about the woman that was found deceased in her car yesterday. He gave them a description of Kaden as well as the make and model of his vehicle along with his name. "Kaden Marcelli." Chad told the detective who happened to be the officer that had been investigating the break-in at the high school, Shawn Masterson. When Masterson asked him for *his* name, Chad was hesitant. After all, he really didn't want to get more involved than he was, but because of the truck parked near their house the night before, he decided it would make sense, in case the guy decided to return.

"Chad Burton. I called and reported the truck outside my house last night. I didn't see who was in the vehicle, but noticed that it was parked on the street with someone in it for about an hour last night." Chad told Masterson. "I thought it was strange." He suddenly realized he was opening himself up for more questions as Masterson asked him what made him think it was Macelli. Chad didn't want to discuss his own investigation into his employee yet or the fact that he'd seen him right after he'd met with Estelle in the parking lot before Kaden had shown up in the truck. It would call attention to Amanda's thugs and he was certain that there were many besides his own suspicions about Michelle, David and Kaden. "I have a friend of mine who knows this guy, the vehicle he drives and the license plate number. So I thought I'd give the police the information." Chad knew it sounded strange, but at least Joanna's kid would be on their radar.

Masterson took down his phone number and address, thanked him for the information. "Mr. Burton, we'll be in touch. Please let us know if this truck shows up again."

Chad called William to let him know what he'd found out. William wasn't surprised given the way Joanna had tried to defend herself about the phone call. "I've never met him, but she said something about her son and daughter-in-law having some 'problems.' I'll keep my eye out for the truck from now on.

Krista

It was Saturday morning and Chad had gone to the office to do paperwork. Mara was still asleep so Krista wasted no time trying to contact Sadie Mercotte. It went straight to voicemail after the first ring and Krista left a message telling her it was important. She knew Sadie was grieving the loss of her niece, Nadine, but she was worried about Mara. Between her erratic behaviors and fatigue, sleeping most of the time, Krista knew that it was the presence of this 'Jamie' that was the root of all of these behaviors. She was making some coffee and waiting for Mara to get up when Sadie called her back.

"Thank you so much for calling back, Sadie." Krista said as she picked up.

"Krista, Mara is in trouble. There's no time to waste. Bring her to my house as soon as you can." Sadie told her.

"You can see her today?" Krista was both relieved and surprised. But the urgency in her voice concerned her.

"It's important that I see her sooner than later. I got your voicemail. She's in danger from this spirit. This is not just an imaginary friend, or a poltergeist that plays tricks. I'll explain more when you get here. Can you come in at 1:00?" Sadie asked her.

"Of course." Krista thanked her again for calling as she ran up the stairs to check on Mara. She noticed a light glowing underneath her bedroom door. "Where is this light coming from, there's no sun." Krista said out loud, forgetting that she was still on the phone with Sadie.

"Krista! What's going on? Are you at Mara's room? You said something about a light!" Sadie was shouting now. "Krista, be careful! Don't open the door!" But Krista couldn't hear her words as she had the phone at her side. She opened the door and was immediately hit by a wind that almost knocked her over as Mara sat on the edge of her bed staring out her open window. There was an orb of light just outside the window that lit up the room; glowing vibrantly as it were a living being.

"Mara!" Krista ran to her and closed the window and grabbed her daughter's hands that were ice-cold. "KRISTA! Are you inside the room?" Sadie was yelling on the phone as Krista finally remembered she still had Sadie on the line and put it on speaker-phone. "YES! What's going on Sadie?" Krista was in panic mode as she tried to get Mara to respond to her.

"Listen to me! Pick her up, get her out of that room, and run a warm bath for her. That will take off the chill. The spirit is very close to her now, trying to take over. Do it now!" Sadie ordered. "I'll stay on the phone, but get her out of there!"

Krista did as Sadie had instructed. She picked up Mara from the bed, despite her daughter struggling to get out of her arms, and ran out of the room to the bathroom closest to her. As soon as Krista began running the water in the tub, Mara relaxed a little and finally spoke to her. "Mommy, what are you doing? Why am I in the bathroom?"

"Sadie? Can you hear what's going on?" Krista asked, making sure she was still there.

"I'm here! It sounds as though she's safe. For now anyway." Sadie assured her. "But I think it's better if I come to you."

"Please come as soon as you can." Krista was overwhelmed as she watched Mara finally coming out of the chilling 'trance' she'd been in. There was no other way to describe it. Krista gave Sadie her address as she helped Mara into the tub. "Mommy, it's chilly." Mara began to complain, letting her know that she was herself again. After 10 minutes in the warm water, Krista helped Mara into some warm clothes just as the doorbell rang.

Krista still couldn't get over how young Sadie appeared. She was wearing a flannel red and black shirt with skinny jeans and boots, which she could pull off even though she was in her early 50s. Her long dark hair was pulled up in a stylish ponytail that made her look even more youthful. "Thank you so much for coming over." Krista told her, but Sadie wasn't paying attention. She was focused on looking around the house, going into the kitchen and the living room before she spoke. "I could feel the negative energy as soon as I walked in. It's important that I try to find out who they are and why they're after Mara." Sadie tried to make it sound less serious that it really was, but Krista could read the concern in her face as her expression changed from a smile at the door to a furrowed brow as she came inside. "Where is Mara?"

"She's upstairs. I'll go get her," Krista offered, but Sadie suggested that they both go upstairs. "I'd like to see her room if that would be okay with you." Krista nodded and led the way. Sadie took her time, looking at the different photos that were framed on the walls along the stairs; pictures of Mara at various ages, and especially the picture at the top of the stairs where she stopped for a moment. "This must be you, your sister and your mother." Sadie observed as she touched the frame, tracing the images in the photo with her finger lightly. "They're still watching out for you."

Krista was stunned that Sadie could tell just from that picture. "Did Nadine tell you about my family? How can you tell who they are?" She assumed that if her mother and sister were watching out for them, this wouldn't be happening to Mara now.

Sadie shook her head. "They are in a place where it's difficult for them to interfere with the evil spirit that's affecting Mara, but I can feel them watching and doing what they can to protect you. I remember them from the first day when you walked into the shop, then again when you contacted Nadine last week..." Sadie stopped, as sudden sadness crossed her face. Krista knew what she meant and put a hand on Sadie's shoulder. "I'm so sorry, Sadie."

"Thank you. I appreciate you coming to see Nadine. It really meant a great deal to her." She acknowledged but immediately reverted back to the reason for her visit and continued towards Mara's room. Without Krista telling her she stopped in front of Mara's door. "This is it." Sadie said without any question in her voice. Krista just nodded, amazed that she just seemed to *know*.

"It is. Mara is in my room. You had said to take her out of the room, so I didn't want to bring her back in here." Krista had only gone back into the room to grab some clothes from Mara's dresser and shut the door again. It still felt chilly and unwelcoming, with an unpleasant rotten smell that reminded her of decaying animals that Krista had never noticed before. She was actually surprised that Mara hadn't come down after she finished dressing.

Sadie didn't open the door right away, and instead took a step closer and put her ear up to the door as if she could hear something. She immediately backed away. "The evil energy is still present in there. Leave the door closed." Krista felt a chill go down her spine.

"How....how can we get rid of it?" Krista was physically shaking, in panic mode and ready to run from this house and not return. But she needed to make sure Mara was safe and that whatever it was didn't follow them. Sadie didn't answer and went toward the master bedroom. She knocked lightly on the door. "Mara? My name is Sadie, your mom's friend," as she opened the door.

"Go ahead of me, I'll come in after you," she whispered as Krista nodded. Mara was sitting in a chair near the window looking outside. "Mara, honey, there's someone that wants to meet you," she realized that she was shaking, worried that Mara had somehow become controlled by this 'Jamie'. Just a few days ago, a seemingly 'harmless' imaginary friend, now a potential evil spirit wreaking havoc with their lives. As if they needed more drama.

Mara turned toward her with her still-damp blonde curls, her cerulean blue eyes looked terrified. Krista could tell that she was herself, not the catatonic little girl that she'd been in her room less than an hour ago. "Mara, this is my friend, Sadie." Sadie came over and knelt down in front of her daughter. "It's nice to meet you Mara. Is it okay if I touch your hand?"

Mara nodded as Sadie reached out to touch her. Sadie suddenly jumped back as if she'd been electrocuted. "There's a lot of energy here!" Krista looked frightened, "Are you alright?"

"It's fine, Krista. Just a little jolt." Sadie seemed unconcerned. She pulled out a cloth bag from her pocket, extracting a long chain with a chunky pink stalagmite crystal on the end, and placed it around Mara's neck. Mara's expression changed from a frightened little girl to an outraged tyrant as she lunged at Sadie. Luckily, Sadie had been ready for this kind of reaction and grasped her wrists, holding her while whispering in a soft voice, "Stay here with us Mara. Is there someone with you now? You're safe, you can me." Mara's angry face softened a little.

"She's here. Jamie's here. She doesn't like you or my mom. She wants you to leave." Mara's eyes were wide with fear. "Please make her go away. I don't want her to follow me anymore."

Krista went to reach out to Mara, but Sadie stopped her. "Please, just let me talk to her. You're too close to Mara, it will be dangerous for you to be involved right now. Just remain calm and stay where you are." Krista felt the urge to grab her daughter and order Sadie out of the house, but she knew that there was nowhere else to turn at this point.

"Mara I need you to be brave. Can you share what Jamie has been saying?" Sadie encouraged her. Mara shook her head and whispered, "I can't. She'll hear me." She looked terrified and Krista had to stop herself from stopping Sadie from whatever 'ritual' she was doing.

"Mara the necklace you have on will protect you from her so that you can tell me. She won't be able to stop you with that necklace on." Sadie promised, trying to pacify Krista as well as her daughter.

"Mara, who is Jamie?" Sadie began to ask questions.

"She lives on an island. It's cold there sometimes and she wants to leave. But she can't." Mara looked close to tears as she spoke.

"Mara, I want you to close your eyes and just take a deep breath. Can you do that for me?" Sadie sat directly in front of her. Mara nodded. Krista watched as Sadie and Mara sat facing each other, Mara with her eyes closed and Sadie holding her hands while she looked straight ahead, not necessarily at Mara but almost through her as if she was trying to see something in the far distance. "Jamie, I want you to reach out to me and tell me why you're here with Mara." Sadie said in a quiet voice. Krista waited for a verbal response, but instead Sadie was nodding as if she were hearing a voice, which had Krista more confused. She was tempted to ask but terrified that it might interrupt what Sadie was trying to accomplish.

"You can't continue to stay with Mara. She has her own life here." Sadie said firmly. Krista was just starting to relax when suddenly the windows opened by themselves and there was a wind that blew through the room that caused them to cover their faces. Mara screamed and Krista reached toward her as the wind suddenly stopped as if on cue. Sadie signaled to Krista with her hand up to wait a few minutes. "It's okay right now, but let's wait a moment," Sadie whispered.

What were they waiting for? That was the question that Krista didn't say out loud. She waited for what seemed an hour, but in reality was only a minute. "Do you hear Jamie now, Mara"? Sadie asked her.

Mara's golden curls were dried by now as she shook her head. "No! I don't hear her! Thank you, Ms. Sadie!" She jumped off the chair and ran into Krista's arms. "Mommy!"   Krista was engulfed with a sense of maternal connection that she'd been missing since Mara was born. She could finally feel that bond reciprocated from her daughter.

As they headed downstairs, Krista talked to Sadie about the dream from a few weeks ago had been ingrained in her memory. The fear had worn off, but now she could remember. She'd been looking for Mara and couldn't find her. And there was a voice that was taunting her, knew her weaknesses. It was that loud, bitchy voice that didn't care about anyone or anything. 'Don't think you got away with anything, princess.' She could hear it in her head now and see her face as clear as the day she died. The voice of Jane Ahearn. "She blames me for everything. I remember her holding the gun and aiming toward me, but I survived. She didn't. I think she blames me and now she wants to take Mara." Krista felt relieved being able to piece together what she'd experienced and sharing with someone who seemed to understand.

Sadie nodded in agreement. "I think you're right. Everything that I felt and what I heard from Jamie was anger, directed at you and taking it out on Mara. Mara is a child. Children are much easier for spirits to gain their trust because they're susceptible to suggestion. They trust everyone until they have a reason not to."

Krista suddenly remembered several nights ago when Karen's necklace had been lost and then reappeared on Mara's nightstand. She mentioned it to Sadie, describing the events that happened prior to her finding it. "Why do you think it was on her nightstand?"

Sadie didn't think twice before answering. "It was Karen's way of trying to protect her. It's a physical object that's tied you together and will continue. Don't ever lose it, Krista."

William

After having breakfast with Chad, William headed home trying to distract himself from thinking about Joanna. Chad's advice to wait for her to contact him was probably the way to go, but he also knew that he wouldn't be able to relax until they'd at least talked. He tried to watch some TV but still felt unsettled, and tried to talk himself out of being the one to break down and call. But in the end, he *was* the one who'd refused to listen to Joanna and disregarded her explanation. He picked up his phone and was ready to hit call on Joanna's number when Chad called. "Bill, I just found something as I was going through phone records at work. What do you know about Joanna's kids?"

"Not much. They're grown kids, but I've never met them." William was confused. "Why?"

"I think I know who was on the phone with Joanna yesterday when you were with her. And why she seems to be so secretive." He went on to tell William about the phone calls he'd found that were to Michelle, researched the number and found out it was Kaden who he'd recognized as the driver of the black truck at CVS. "He's involved, Bill. She was likely talking to him, trying to keep it from you because she's protecting him. She has to know something's going on with him. I'll even bet that he was the one that broke into Krista's office at school, trying to get her in trouble at work deleting and sending bogus emails to parents!"

"Are you serious, Chad? I mean, I don't know much about her kids but I find it hard to believe that either of them would be criminals!"

William was hesitant. But then again it did fit along with the phone call and the fact that she'd been trying to talk in private. He was caught between being glad that it wasn't another man, but now her kid was likely involved in criminal activity.

"Bill, I'm positive that it was Kaden in that truck!" Chad insisted.

"How do you even know what he looks like?" William was confused.

"I looked him up on social media. There's a picture of him with Joanna online, Bill. If that wasn't enough, the black Dodge Ram truck was in the background! I already told police about Kaden and the truck, and left out the fact that I met with Estelle. I just talked to them about the truck being parked near our house and I'm sure they're going to be checking on it." Chad was getting frustrated with his father-in-law now.

"Actually, I was going to just as you called. I really don't want to leave things this way, it's been hard. Do you think I should bring up what I know about her son?" It was obvious Joanna was hiding her son's phone calls but did she know what was really going on? William wanted Chad's opinion before he called Joanna so he could be prepared.

"Bill, it's important that you find out any information that you can from her. The police will probably be contacting her soon because I called and let them know. Maybe she is seeing someone else, but this might be a way for the police to have evidence. Set up a time to meet up, talk to her about it, but don't bring up what I've told you. You were right that something was going on, whether she's seeing someone else, or involved in some kind of scheme that reeks of something that Stanley's daughter would do. Even from prison."

William agreed and hung up. It was only 1:00 in the afternoon but he poured himself a whiskey and ginger ale as he tried to rehearse some kind of apology to Joanna before calling. The fact that this woman had dragged him along as some pawn to get what she wanted was bringing out the anger in him that he hadn't felt since Maria had left him. He drank several swigs of his drink and then just picked up the phone and called Joanna's number, and as the phone rang several times, he was both relieved and disappointed that she might not pick up. What then, should he leave a message?' All of these was going through his mind when she surprised him by answering right before the voicemail picked up. "Hi, Bill. What do you want?"

William was startled that she'd answered. "Joanna, hi, I um, wanted to…talk. That is if you still want to." As soon as the words came out of his mouth, he wished he'd at least been a little more prepared. He knew he sounded like an immature school kid calling a girl after an argument.

There were seconds of silence on the other end and William actually thought about just ending the call when she said, "Okay, Bill. Let's talk. That is, if you're going to listen to me instead of just assuming that I'm seeing someone else." Her tone wasn't bitchy, it was more as if she'd moved on which made William feel even more desperate to say what was on his mind.

"That's fair. I'm sorry that I didn't listen." William managed. But he didn't want to do this over the phone. "Can I meet you somewhere? I'd rather talk in person. Maybe I could come over?"

"I'd rather come to your house if that's okay." Joanna countered. Maybe she did have some issues that she was keeping from him. After all, why wouldn't she want him to come to her place? He was already making assumptions and refused to entertain them now. He needed to hear what she had to say, then make a decision.

"Okay, how about 2:30?" William said. It was only an hour from now, but he wanted to talk to her before he had more time to think and lose his nerve.

Joanna agreed and said she'd come. He called Chad back to tell him about it. "She's coming over in an hour. I'm not sure what to do now. Should I ask her questions? Record her with my phone?" William was feeling overwhelmed. He still had strong feelings for her, despite the latest information about her potential involvement with criminal activities that involved a murder and breaking into his daughter's computer at the school.

"Just get an idea of what's going on. I have a feeling there's a lot more going on with her than just her son's activities. I think you should record it, just in case. But forget that it's there. Just act natural and listen." Chad coached him.

William was just straightening up the living room when she arrived, knocking lightly on the door. Joanna had once told him early on she hated ringing the doorbell; "it just seems too disruptive, too loud. I think a knock is more personal,' she'd told him. He'd laughed at her idiosyncrasies at the time, but the memory made him realize how much he missed her. Now, he wished Chad had never told him about his suspicions. But still, he followed Chad's advice and hit record on his phone that was sitting discreetly on the fireplace mantle, partially hidden by a framed photo of Krista and Karen.

She looked beautiful even though she was casually dressed in tight-fitting yoga pants and a sweatshirt with sneakers and her dark hair was pulled up in a ponytail, but it was clear that she'd been upset. There were bags under her eyes, and they were rimmed with red as though she'd been crying. "Joanna, I've missed you," William told her, forgetting anything else that he wanted to say at that moment as he gave her a hug. He was already emotional making it much more difficult to believe what Chad had told him about her.

Joanna hugged him back and began to cry as they embraced. "I'm sorry, Bill. I didn't want to break down in front of you, but…it's been hard for me." She accepted a tissue from him after the long hug.

"Let's just relax for a few minutes, Jo." He poured her a glass of her favorite pinot grigio and they sat in the living room while he continued to nurse his whiskey drink. They made some small talk about the weather, until he finally felt some liquid courage to bring up the phone incident from the other day. He was hoping for the best; that he could believe her explanation, but he could almost hear Maria's voice telling him to be careful. 'You're too trusting sometimes,' Maria had always reminded him. Maria had always been right. He *was* too trusting.

"Jo, I should've heard you out about that phone call. I really wasn't eavesdropping, just looking for you. I know my brain went a little crazy from hearing your end of the conversation, but it wasn't fair. I'm listening now, if you want to tell me."

Joanna nodded. "Bill this isn't easy for me to talk about. My son has been struggling lately. He's been staying with me the past couple of weeks, because his fiancé kicked him out." She began and reached for another tissue. "Apparently, he's developed a drug problem that I wasn't aware of and ....it's just been a mess." She pulled out a Kleenex, and wiped her eyes, but William noticed there weren't any tears.

"I'm sorry, Jo." He offered his sympathy although he was starting to suspect that Chad might have been right. Yet it was hard not to care. They'd spent so much time together; it was hard to see her as someone that was out to get him. He started to reach for her hand but pulled back.

"So that call that you overheard was Kaden's fiancé, Lacey. She was calling to tell me that she was worried about him. The police have come by their apartment and asking questions. She warned me to stay away because she was worried that if they knew he was staying with me that they would think I was involved. That's what you heard. Kaden was really upset when he found out I was still talking to Lacey. She wanted to come by and see me, but I'm worried about Kaden finding out. He's not himself and I'm worried that he's got himself into trouble. So what you heard was me telling Lacey that I wish she could come over. She's like a daughter to me and I just want to protect her. Then there was a reported break in at the high school where someone was hacking into the school computers." Joanna finished as she dabbed at her eyes. "I should have told you this at the time, but I was worried......I didn't want to tell you about my son's ....problems. I feel like somehow....it's my fault... " Her voice choked up then. William couldn't help but feel sorry for her and the urge to pull her into his arms and forget about all he knew was overwhelming.

"Jo, I'm sorry that I didn't hear you out about your explanation. You said something about the police coming by? Did Lacey tell you what it was about?" William tried to sound casual, but his heart was pounding because of what Chad had told him.

"She said they were asking where he was at a specific time last week. There was a hit and run in Providence and they were investigating based on witnesses and cameras in the area. I guess they had video of a vehicle that looked like his." Joanna told him as William winced. He knew it was Krista's psychic friend that they'd mentioned on TV.

"Yeah, I've seen that on the news." William said. "She was a friend of Krista's. She's having a hard time with it." He waited for Joanna's reaction, but she was still talking about Kaden. 'If she was involved, she must really trust me. Maybe she really doesn't know, she's not involved.'

"I mean, they haven't arrested him. But today they came by and asked me questions about where he was last night because of a report of a woman that was found dead in her car yesterday." Joanna disclosed, as she shook her head. "They told me that someone called in about a truck that was similar to Kaden's and wanted to know where he'd been." She looked at him pointedly as she said the words and he couldn't help but feel paranoid. He wished Chad hadn't told him that he'd called the police. William had been sipping on his drink and almost choked on it. "Are you okay, Bill?" Joanna stopped, looking concerned.

William tried to pull himself together. "Yes, I'm fine, just swallowed the wrong way." He managed as he coughed a few more times.

"I told them I didn't know. I was out and when I left my son was still in the house." Joanna said. "I told them I went out to lunch."

William suddenly realized that he might have walked into something that he didn't want to deal with, but he had to ask. "Were you specific about where you went to lunch?"

"I told them I was in Narragansett, with you." Joanna didn't seem to flinch as she said the words, but now William was feeling nauseous. And not from the drinks that he'd consumed.

"You told them you were with me? So should I expect a knock on my door from police to corroborate that?" William asked her as he suddenly realized she'd potentially involved him in a murder investigation.

Joanna stared at him for a moment, tears in her eyes. "Yes. I'm sorry Bill, but I had to tell them where I was."

William didn't know what to say now, and excused himself to the bathroom. He splashed some cool water on his face as he tried to regroup and process what Joanna had just told him. Something didn't sit right with him. Nadine's hit and run accident had been on the news. But Krista's school email breech had not been. How did *she* know about it? He knew he'd never said anything. Everything Chad had told him came back to him now. She knew about her son's involvement, and never said anything. He really didn't know this woman after all. Joanna had just told him what he needed to know.

He headed back to the living room, his irritation building. Resentment was his friend now because it temporarily replaced the sadness that had led him to call her. "You need to leave."

"Are you serious? Bill, what's going on?" Joanna had gotten comfortable on the couch and now looked surprised at his words. As she'd never believed he would do that.

"I'm sorry, Jo, this isn't going to work out. You just need to go." William tried to be strong, as it was one of the hardest things he'd had to do in a long time.

Joanna stood up and grabbed her purse that she'd left on the arm of the couch. "I hope you know that if I walk out of here, I'm not coming back!" The look in her eyes scared him just then. There was no fear or sadness because of their relationship crumbling. Just anger because he wasn't buying her explanation or the fact that he wouldn't go along with hiding the fact that her son was involved.

Suddenly, everything became easier because she'd always put moving forward with their relationship on hold, especially moving in with him. Now he was seeing a different side. The incident when she'd been upset with Mara and stormed off instead of talking about it now came back to him and he knew that he wouldn't have regrets. "I hope that you won't. Goodbye, Joanna." William said coldly and slammed the door as she left.

He watched from the front picture window as she hurried to her car and began talking on her phone as she was opening the door. He waited for her to back out of the driveway, but Joanna continued to sit and talk. 'What the hell is she doing? Just go!' William thought it was strange, especially since they'd just ended their relationship. Suddenly, he was worried that she might be calling the police, telling them god knows what! He opened the front door to let her know he was watching and she finally backed out of the driveway. William just hoped that whatever her involvement was in her son's criminal activities that she'd keep him out of it.

Krista

Sadie had been a godsend to help her out with Mara this morning which was the only reason she wasn't blowing up her husband's phone. Sadie had advised her to keep Karen's necklace under lock and key. "It's important; it protects Mara. For now anyway. The only way to make sure the spirit is at rest is to go to the source of the energy. Usually where they died, unless there's another source that's continuing on for them."

"Thank you so much for coming, Sadie. Really, I don't know what I would've done if you hadn't helped out today. I still plan on going to Nadine's services on Wednesday. What do I owe you?" After all, Sadie was running a business and Krista appreciated her time.

"Fifty," Sadie told her, but Krista gave her $100. She'd gone above and beyond, especially allowing her to keep the necklace that Sadie had put around Mara's neck to ward off the spirit.

"You didn't need to do that, but thank you." Sadie said as she hugged Krista before she left. Just then Mara came downstairs and ran to Sadie. "Jamie isn't talking to me right now, Ms. Sadie." Sadie smiled and reached down to hug Mara. "I'm glad. She might return, but I gave your mom something to help you along the way. You make sure that you listen to her, Mara." She bent down to her level. "It's very important, okay?"

Mara nodded as she made eye contact with Sadie. "I will," she promised and gave her a hug which surprised both Sadie and Krista.

"She doesn't do that with anyone, Sadie. She has a good connection with you." Krista told her as Sadie was leaving.

"I'm glad. She loves you and your husband. She's just been struggling for a very long time with this negative spirit. It's been following her probably since birth." Sadie admitted. "Text or call if you need anything. "Remember what I said about Karen's necklace. Use if only if absolutely necessary, but make sure to have it with you if you make that visit to Block Island." Sadie warned her.

"I will, Sadie. Thanks again." Krista waved as Sadie pulled out of the driveway, just as Chad was calling her. As she looked at the clock she couldn't believe it was already 2:00 in the afternoon. Where had the day gone?

"Kris, I just found out some things about Joanna's son." Chad immediately told his wife what he'd found out about Kaden. "Did you tell my dad about it?" Krista asked. She still hadn't told him about her day with Mara yet, which she felt took precedence over whatever Joanna's son was doing.

"I did. He was planning on talking to her today." Chad told her. "What's the matter? You sound upset." He recognized that something else was going on.

"You wouldn't believe what a day I've had. Krista didn't realize how stressed out she was until now. Just when Mara was cleared to go back to school, this morning scared her. Especially after Sadie's advice that the spirit was in constant communication with her. "I called Sadie this morning," Krista began and she could hear Chad's annoyed groan on the other end. "Just listen to me, please! It worked out in the best way possible." Krista went on to tell him everything about the light in Mara's room, Sadie coming over and helping to get rid of the spirit that had been with Mara. "Not for just a few months, but *years,* Chad!

"Are you kidding me? I'm glad that hopefully this Jamie thing is gone for good." He sounded genuinely happy that their daughter was finally going to go back to school and they could get back into a normal routine.

"What time are you coming home? I want to get out of the house, maybe take Mara to the park." It was a beautiful 72 degree day and the sun was shining. Krista felt that a weight had lifted, that the disconnection between them wasn't her fault and she wanted to spend some quality time with Mara outside.

"Go have some fun with Mara! I'll be home around 4:00. Maybe we can go to dinner later." Chad sounded happy. Probably happy that she wasn't being annoying, Krista thought to herself, but then again she'd been stressed out the past couple of weeks.

Krista took Mara over to Johnston Memorial Park to play; she enjoyed watching her swing and play on the slide at the jungle gym area. There were several other kids there and Krista found herself suddenly worried about Mara and her interaction with the other kids, especially on the slide. She could see her behind another little girl about her age at the top of the slide and felt a wave of anxiety as she stepped closer to the bottom of the slide. "Mara, be careful please!" She told her as the little girl in front of her got ready to slide down.

"I'm fine, Mommy!" Mara said with a genuine smile as she watched the girl in front of her go down the slide and steadied herself at the top for her turn. Krista didn't realize she'd been holding her breath until Mara slid down and she found herself exhaling finally she landed at the bottom of slide without incident. She watched as the next little girl slid down and fell off the slide onto the ground and Mara helped her to her feet, asking if she was okay. Tears came to Krista's eyes as she realized that her daughter had turned a corner; maybe she would be the empathic little person that she'd imagined her to be the day she was born.

That evening they went out to dinner at Casarinos on Federal Hill as a family. Krista was feeling positive about Mara's change in attitude and character. She could feel that Mara was different just by being with her. Chad could sense the change in her as well and happy that Krista could finally focus on more than just Mara. Chad was almost to their house when he noticed William's car in their driveway. "Did you expect your dad to come by tonight, Kris?"

"No, he didn't call." Krista told him.

"Uh oh. I'll bet things didn't go well with Joanna today." Chad remembered that William was going to talk to her.

"I hope he's okay." Krista had always worried that if things didn't work out with Joanna that her dad would be heartbroken. "Dad! Are you alright?" He'd gotten out of his car as they pulled up. He looked a little unsteady on his feet. She came closer and realized he'd been drinking. A lot. She could smell his breath from 3 feet away. He swayed back and forth, then steadied himself with one hand on the roof of his car. "Oh, no dad."

"Sorrrryy, Krissssy," William was slurring his words as he wobbled trying to stand up straight. Krista grabbed one of his arms to keep him from falling and was thankful that he'd managed the two miles to their house without getting in an accident or being pulled over. He was completely drunk. In fact, she'd never seen him in this shape before. She turned to call for Chad, but he was right behind her. "I've got him, Kris. Just go get Mara into the house."

Krista helped Mara out of her car seat and tried to distract her from Chad holding her obliterated father upright. "What's wrong with grandpa?" Mara inquired and waved at him. "Hi, grandpa!" before Krista could stop her.

William began waving his hands and calling out to Mara in his slurred speech as Krista made a beeline for the front door. "What's wrong with grandpa?" She asked.

"He just a little tired. Daddy's going to help him." Krista told her and kept her busy upstairs getting ready for bed. She tried to concentrate on reading Mara a bedtime story while she heard the commotion downstairs; her father stumbling and mumbling incoherent sentences as Chad did his best to reason with him. Thankfully, Mara fell asleep and she closed her door, grateful that they'd resolved the 'Jamie' issue with Sadie today. She sighed as she headed downstairs to deal with her inebriated father.

Chad had put on a pot of coffee while her father was lying on the couch with his eyes closed and mumbling something about Joanna. "He's in bad shape, Kris. I should've checked in on him earlier. I knew he was going to talk to Joanna but then I came home and we went to dinner. I should've checked in." He repeated himself as he brought his father-in-law a steaming cup of black coffee in hopes that it would help.

"Jusssst don't want the police to come here." William slurred groggily as he tried to sit up and sip some of the coffee. "Joanna knew aboutttt Kris's officcccce break in. SSShe knew." Krista was suddenly paying attention to what he was saying. "Dad! You're saying that Joanna's son is the one that broke into the school?"

"Joannaaaa," William was beside himself now. "She's gonnnnnne. We're done!" He fell back over onto the couch and Chad put a blanket over him. "Kris, let's let him sleep it off. He's done for the night."

Krista watched him for a few more minutes just to make sure he was okay. "What the hell happened, Chad? He's a mess! He broke up with her so it must have been something significant! He really cared about her." She realized she'd been so caught up with her own and Mara's problems that she'd missed what was going on.

"Kris, I can see that face. Stop beating yourself up. I found out that Kaden, Joanna's son, was the person in the truck at CVS yesterday and parked in front of our house last night."

"What? You're just now telling me this?" Krista felt blindsided with this new information.

"Krista, stop it! I tried to call you this morning, but you were dealing with Mara and Sadie came over! Give me a break, I tried to call you but you didn't answer." Chad told her and she realized he had a point. "I couldn't talk about it at dinner with Mara there, could I? She's 6 years old, but she listens. I didn't want to talk about it in front of her."

"You're right. I'm sorry." Krista realized. She had been in the midst of Mara's crisis and it was definitely not something she wanted Mara to overhear. Chad went on to explain that he'd found out the driver of the black truck was likely Kaden, Joanna's son. "I went on Facebook and found him. There was a picture of him with Joanna and the truck in the background, Kris! I called your dad to tell him and the police as well. He's probably the one that broke into your office! He's definitely involved, Kris. I hope they find him and lock him up. I'm sure that Joanna knew about some of his criminal activities and she was talking to him or someone involved while she was out with your dad yesterday. He planned on talking to her about it today and I'm guessing it didn't go well."

"No wonder dad's such a mess." Krista sat next to her father's head on the couch. He was finally resting comfortably and sleeping off his binge. "Why can't he get a break?" She was sad for him, but the anger she felt toward Joanna made her vengeful.

"I'd like to drive over to her house right now and give her a piece of my mind!" Krista was seeing red now and Chad had to talk her out of it.

"Kris, I know it sucks, but we need to steer clear of her. I don't trust her and clearly, your dad doesn't either. We're lucky that police haven't been coming to us wanting information." Chad knew she was just upset and she wouldn't do anything, but he needed to be the voice of reason now.

"You're right. Maybe you should talk to Stanley Ahearn. Do you think he knows about any of this? After all, he was the one that knew the truck was there in the first place and told you about it." Krista remembered. And it stuck with her. How would he know that unless he knew something about this kid and Joanna?

He glanced at the clock and saw it was almost 10:30. "I'll give him call in the morning, Kris. It's been a long day." Mara was finally in bed and they were finally able to relax before bed. Chad went up to watch a sports channel while Krista went to check on her father before she went upstairs. She knew that he'd been so invested in the relationship; it had been so hard after all the years for him to finally trust someone again. He was sleeping soundly and she was able to relax. A little.

"Mom, you're hard act to follow. We miss you." She touched the picture hanging of the three of them on the beach on Block Island. "We'll be there soon."

Chad

Chad had been sleeping soundly until a noise that could only sound like a gunshot, or a car backfiring jerked him awake. He jumped out of bed and glanced out the window facing the street. There was the same black truck that had been there the previous night. "What the hell? Are you kidding me?" It was 2:03 am and still disoriented as he went to the closet and pulled a locked box out of the closet. Krista didn't know that he'd bought a pistol last year. He kept it in the back of the closet, hidden under a pile of his sweatshirts. Although it had been seven years since Krista had been kidnapped, he couldn't forget how desperate he'd felt and last year, one of his friends had invited him out to the gun range and talked him into buying a Smith and Wesson 9mm pistol. He'd gone to the range several times a year, but never told Kris about it. She'd probably freak out and worry about it being in the house. Now he was glad it was available to him because he was certain this Kaden kid, or someone was out to get them.

Grabbing a cartridge of bullets, he snapped it into the magazine of the gun, waking his wife. "What are you doing?" Krista's voice startled him. Chad quickly dropped his arm with the pistol to his side so she couldn't see it. He tried to sound calm although he wasn't as he looked out the window again and saw the truck still sitting there. He was torn between going outside with his gun and threatening him or doing the logical thing; call the police. "Kris that truck is back out in front of our house. I'm going to call the police." He wished he could just take care of this on his own, but it would just turn into a mess and decided to put the gun away.

"What? Are you kidding?" Krista was wide awake now and got out of bed to look. "Call them now, Chad! What are you waiting for?"

Chad was unloading the gun as she turned to him. "What the hell? Chad? What are you doing with that?" Her eyes were as wide as saucers when she saw him taking the magazine out of the pistol.

"Don't worry about it, Kris, I'm putting it away and calling the police now." Chad didn't need this discussion now and he was chastising himself for even pulling it out of the closet. Another lengthy explanation that didn't need to happen now. He grabbed his phone and called 911 for the police. Krista continued to stand at the window to see what was going on in her t shirt and underwear. "Kris, get the hell away from the window!" He got in front of her as the dispatch from Johnston Police picked up.

"This is Chad Burton. I live on 4556 Atwood Ave. There's a black truck that's parked outside my house that I believe is stalking me and my family. License plate number is RI TU 455. I spoke to Detective Masterson about this truck just earlier today and he asked me to call if the truck showed up again." Chad made sure to specify Masterson so that the police wouldn't tell him that sitting outside his house wasn't a crime. It wasn't except that Kaden was a suspect in many crimes. He was glad he'd informed police earlier today.

"Yes, Mr. Burton. We'll send an officer out immediately. Has the driver attempted to make contact with you?"

"No, but I'm watching. Thank you." Chad didn't want to spend an hour on the phone with the dispatcher. He had his pistol if he needed it.

"Police are in route, Mr. Burton." Chad hung up yet his wife wasn't in the bedroom. "Kris! Where are you?" He checked in Mara's room and then downstairs. He found her sitting in the recliner next to the couch where William was snoring away. "I just wanted to check the alarm system and make sure the door was locked." Krista said quietly. Chad was glad that she at least had put on her robe.

"The police are on their way, so I'll watch for them. I'll try to meet them outside so they don't wake up your dad or Mara." Chad told her although the way William was sawing logs with his snoring, he doubted anything short of an atomic blast would wake him. He could hear sirens in the distance and kept an eye out the window. Suddenly, the truck's headlights came on and Kaden was on the move again. "Are you kidding me? That little shit! He's not getting away with this again!" Chad was infuriated as called the Johnston PD dispatch again. "This is Chad Burton again. That truck that was parked just moved, probably because they heard the sirens. Please let the officers know. I don't want him returning again."

"Thank you for letting me know." Before he hung up he could hear her giving the update on the truck's location.

"Geez, now what? We wait around for the cops to show up?" Krista yawned and leaned her head back on the recliner, with her eyes closed. It *was* 2:30 in the morning. Thank god they didn't have to work in the morning, but Chad wouldn't be able to sleep until that little shit was caught.

"Kris, go to bed. I'll stay down here and wait around in case the police show up to ask questions." Chad yawned just then, but he was determined to get rid of this nuisance kid of Joanna's. He was going to be on the phone with Stanley first thing in the morning. He had a feeling that maybe it would be in their best interest to go there sooner than next weekend. Krista agreed and headed back upstairs while Chad sat waiting. He didn't want to let them know that he had seen Kaden in the parking lot at CVS yesterday when he met Estelle at her request, but at the same time, it was probably all caught on video. He decided to wait and sat down in the recliner as William snored away. 'He sure did dodge a bullet with that Joanna woman,' he thought to himself as he dozed off, only to be wakened by a sharp knock at the door.

He immediately jumped up to answer the door, hoping that his drunk father-in-law didn't wake up too. There were two Johnston officers at the door and he stepped outside, rather than invite them in because of William.

"Did you find the truck?" He asked, hoping this was going to be quick conversation. It was cold and he'd forgotten his jacket and realized he was standing there on the front stairs in his pajamas. And he'd complained about Kris and her appearance? He suddenly felt self-conscious.

"We did find the truck. However, there was a woman driving the vehicle, not the person you'd said. Some woman named Joanna Larsen. She claims that she doesn't know anyone by the name of Kaden."

"Are you kidding me? Joanna Larsen is Kaden's mother!" Chad became enraged but tried to keep his composure. He didn't want to look like the crazy one here. Maybe it was time to tell them what he witnessed in the CVS parking lot, but he was still hesitant. What if they accused him of having something to do with Estelle's murder? And they would be questioning William who was passed out on their couch, not a good look right now. No, he needed to just focus on what he knew about Joanna. That lying bitch. He was glad that William had ditched her for good!

"Really? How do you know that Mr. Burton? Do you know Ms. Larsen?" Suddenly Chad realized he'd walked into an obstacle of questions that he wasn't prepared to answer. Really, the only proof he had was Joanna mentioning Kaden to William a few times and that Facebook post that Kaden had put up. Wait. Maybe he could try that without giving away too much.

"One of my friends went on a few dates with Joanna and wanted me to check out her Facebook page. I did and then went on her friend's page where Kaden was listed as her son. I saw a picture of him with her stating that was his mother. The picture of the same truck with the license plate was in the picture." Somehow Chad had managed to recoup his 2:30 am brain to function. It wasn't really a lie, just different context, Chad figured. He didn't want William's name involved if he could avoid it.

Both officers seemed to accept the answer, although now it wasn't resolving Chad's problem of being stalked whether it was Joanna or Kaden. "Well, the truck is registered to Ms. Larsen and although we do have your report to Detective Masterson about Kaden and your concerns, there's still an investigation going on that we can't discuss. Are you sure there isn't anything else you want to tell us about Kaden Macelli?

Chad knew it was either tell about the CVS incident or shut it down. "No, that's all I know. But I really wish I didn't need to have someone sitting in the same truck parked in front of my house. Doesn't that strike you as strange?"

"If you see it parked there again, you can give us a call, Mr. Burton. But again, unless they make a direct threat to you, we can't really do anything." Chad nodded, he'd made his decision and now he couldn't retract it without looking like someone under suspicion.

"Thank you for coming out and checking on it." He said calmly, but realizing he'd accomplished nothing with another call to the police! Great. 'Now that little shit and his mother are on the prowl', he muttered to himself. He glanced down at William, still comatose on the couch. Chad locked the door and made sure the alarm was set before lying back in the recliner in case Joanna or her son decided to return. He'd be waiting for them. He thought about going back upstairs to get his gun, but he was tired and instead went to the hallway closet for the baseball bat that he kept in there just for such circumstances. He laid the bat next to him just in case and grabbed the throw blanket that hung over the recliner, putting it over him.

"I'll be ready if they come back." He said out loud as his father-in-law was snoring away on the couch. "I'm glad you got rid of her. She's trouble!" Chad didn't drink very often, but now he drank a shot of whiskey that he'd found in an upper cabinet in the kitchen, hoping he could calm down enough to get some sleep.

* * *

Chad was apparently the last to go to sleep and first to wake up. His neck was twisted in knots as he fell asleep with his neck in an awkward position in the recliner. The clock on the wall above the TV which read 7:05. "Oh god, really?" He wished he could crawl upstairs to his bed and sleep for another 2 hours, but once he was up, he knew he wouldn't be able to get back to sleep. Especially with everything that was going through his head now. The first order of business was contacting the Johnston Police and then Stanley.

He headed to the kitchen to make coffee and when he came back to turn on the TV, William was sitting up on the couch, looking hungover and disoriented. "Chad? What happened? I remember driving here, but not much after that." He admitted. William usually looked much younger than his 63 years but today he looked like an older homeless man that hadn't showered or shaved in days.

"I'll get you a cup of coffee, Bill. Looks like you could use one." Chad didn't answer his immediate question. "One milk and one sugar?"

"Yes! Thank you and an aspirin for this headache if you have one!" William requested as he winced, putting his hand on his head. "Make it two aspirin! I feel like someone's tap dancing in my head right now!"

Chad laughed as he grabbed a bottle of ibuprofen and shuffled a few into his hand along with Bill's coffee, and handed it to him. "Here you go. This is why you don't day drink, Bill!"

William grabbed the pills and swallowed them down with a swig of coffee as he groaned. "I get it now. No more drinking or women! I'm done with both!" He laid his head back for a moment, waiting for the headache to subside. "How much damage did I do?"

"*You* didn't do anything with the exception of driving over here when you shouldn't have. It was what happened next that didn't involve you. Well, not directly anyway. Finish your coffee, then we'll talk." Chad advised him. He wasn't sure if he wanted to tell William about the truck and the police telling him Joanna was the driver. Better to leave that one alone for now.

William nodded, as he took another swig of coffee and sat back with his eyes closed. He was definitely hurting from all the whiskey yesterday. "Letting Joanna go was the best thing for you, Bill. Trust me." Chad hoped that his father-in-law's riddance of Joanna would prevent further visits from her son. He grabbed his coffee and went to his home office to call Stanley until he realized it was really early if he was still in California. 'Screw it, I'm calling anyway.' He dialed Stanley's cell and it rang once before Stanley picked up. "Yes? Who is this?" Stanley didn't sound as though he'd been woken up which made Chad feel better, but he sounded irritated which put him on edge.

Chad took a deep breath and launched into the new developments about Joanna and Kaden, the truck parked in front of their house and the police finding out that Joanna had been the one behind the wheel this time. "I did talk to one detective but didn't tell him that I'd met with Estelle before she was killed. I was worried about being a suspect myself."

After Stanley heard what was going on, he sounded concerned and less aggravated which made Chad feel better. "It sounds like Amanda has more connections than I thought. Is it possible that you can meet me at my house on Block Island earlier? Can you come tomorrow? I can make arrangements with the yacht to get you there tomorrow evening. It doesn't sound like your family is safe right now, Chad." Stanley's offer was tempting especially since he didn't feel safe pulling out his pistol in the middle of the night, the threat to Krista at school and Mara's precarious mental state. She seemed fine now, but he was worried that the police wouldn't be able to protect them after last night. They couldn't arrest Kaden or Joanna and Chad had no doubt that the black truck would return tonight.

"I'll have to check with Kris because she works at the school. Mara was supposed to go back to school, but I'm worried about their safety now. And William......." Chad trailed off trying to think of a way to describe his state of mind. "William is not in a good place mentally."

"Sorry to hear that, Chad. I won't be able to get to Block Island until the following day, but your family is welcome to go tomorrow. Let me know and I'll have the yacht ready as well as some staff to open up the house for you. The bar and kitchen won't be as fully stocked but I'll get the house staff to pick up some necessities." Stanley's offer was appealing. He really wanted to get away from Johnston for a few days. "I'll need to check with Krista first. Can I let you know later today?" Chad suddenly longed for some time away and the more he thought about it, the better it sounded.

"No problem. Just let me know by 3:00 Eastern time. That'll give me enough time to arrange everything and I'll see you the following day." Stanley assured him.

Chad's next call to Detective Masterson didn't go as smoothly. "Mr. Burton, I see you called again about this black truck that you insist is driven by Kaden Macelli. But last night, Joanna Larsen was driving it. According to statements from Ms. Larsen, she claims that she was in a relationship with William Carson and he ended their relationship yesterday. She says she was concerned about him because she knew he'd been drinking and came to your house which is why she stopped by your house. All I can tell you is that Macelli is still being investigated in the hit and run in Providence. We're keeping all eyes on him."

"Yes, I remember you telling me that before, detective. I just have one question for you. Has anyone checked the call logs for Amanda Ahearn at the prison?"

"No, why? Is there a reason we should be?" Masterson threw the question back at him and Chad thought carefully about his response. He didn't want to let him know what Estelle had told him, but there had to be a way. He decided to mention Michelle's phone calls with Kaden and had proof through the phone logs that Kathy had kept for him for the past week. "I know for a fact that Michelle has been communicating with Kaden and Amanda Ahearn." Chad told him.

"Does Michelle still work for you?" Masterson asked.

"She does. I have proof of phone calls between her and this Kaden Macelli." Chad felt confident that they would be able to trace that phone log without a problem.

"What does that have to do with Amanda Ahearn?" Masterson kept probing, making it more difficult for Chad to keep the meeting with Estelle out of it. He decided to rely on Stanley's own words, "She's got connections. You should check out the call logs at the prison." He repeated.

Masterson seemed to get his point and agreed. "I'll definitely do that. Do you have a problem with me checking out the phone logs at Carson Realty as well?" He asked as though he was expecting him to have a problem with it "No problem at all. My receptionist, Kathy has them at her desk. Do what you need to do." Chad agreed immediately, hoping that would suffice and maybe they would catch this kid before it was too late. As soon as he said that, he remembered the tentative plan to go to Block Island tomorrow, but he hadn't confirmed with Stanley. They could go the following day. Masterson he would be in touch and Chad was glad that he was done with these calls. He felt like a weight had been lifted.

William seemed to be recovering; he'd showered and although he had on the same clothes from yesterday, he appeared more like himself. Polished, his salt and pepper hair combed back and cognizant of what needed to happen going forward. It was 8:30 by now and Chad was surprised that Mara and Kris weren't up yet. "Hey Bill, you look much better than you did an hour ago!" Chad kidded with his father-in-law.

"Thanks. I feel somewhat human again." William agreed. "But I'm obviously not 25 anymore; can't handle the booz like I used to!" He laughed but Chad could tell he was still hungover and not up for much activity today unless it involved a nap.

"Did either one of the girls show some sign of existence while you were up there?" Chad asked.

"No, they must still be sleeping, I didn't hear anything." William said as he started to get a bad feeling when he saw the apprehensive look on Chad's face. "I'll go see if they're awake," he told Chad. He was looking forward to waking Mara up. "Mara, you awake?" He knocked lightly before walking in, expecting her to be hiding behind the door and surprising him as she'd done at his house in the past.

But she wasn't there. Her bed was empty, with the sheets and comforter thrown to the side. Maybe she was hiding? "Mara, are you hiding from grandpa to scare me? He went to her walk-in closet expecting her to jump out at him at any moment. He was preparing himself, but when he quickly looked behind the door, Mara wasn't there.

'Maybe she was in the master bedroom with Krista he reasoned, but when he knocked quickly there was no response. William felt his heart pounding as he opened the door to an empty unmade bed which was very unlike Krista and the bathroom door was shut. He couldn't hear any water running so he knocked lightly. "Kris are you in there?" No answer. He was starting to panic as he called out to Chad. "Hey, Chad! Are Kris or Mara downstairs anywhere?" He ran back downstairs, hoping that Krista and Mara would be in the kitchen getting ready to eat breakfast. But it was just Chad sitting by himself.

"Why? No they aren't, that's why you went up to see if they were up." Chad sounded slightly annoyed.

"Chad, they aren't upstairs! Mara isn't in her room and Kris isn't in her bed or the bathroom!" William was frantic now.

"What? Are you kidding?" Chad began to panic, running around the house calling their names. "This isn't possible. We were both in the living room all night! They were upstairs!" Yet there was no sign of Kris in the bedroom and as he opened the door to their master bathroom he was dazed to find it empty except for words written on the mirror in bright red, "PRINCESSES ARE WAITING FOR THEIR RESCUE." He felt cold as the shock hit him. "Amanda, you fucking bitch!!" He yelled at the top of his lungs.

Chad didn't want to believe that they were gone as he ran down the hall to Mara's room, somehow thinking that she'd hidden herself away from whomever had snuck in here last night without him and William hearing them. But there was no trace of her, except for her unicorn blanket that he found beside her bed. Mara would never have left that behind. He began to shake uncontrollably as he imagined his daughter taken away with Krista. She was doing so much better too. "NO! This can't be happening!" Chad was beside himself now as he realized that someone had come in and taken them right under his nose while he and William had been sleeping in the living room.

William came running after hearing Chad yelling, then saw the mirror "I'm calling the police now, Chad! Let's go!" Chad felt as though he couldn't breathe for a moment suddenly realized he was going to be sick, and raced to the bathroom, throwing up until he was dry heaving. He knelt down on the floor for a moment, dizzy from the nausea then managed to get up and splash some cold water on his face.

He managed to compose himself before leaving the bathroom, while William was on the phone, explaining that his daughter and granddaughter were kidnapped from their home. He gave the address and their descriptions while Chad tried to pull himself together.

Chad was still in a state of shock as the police arrived, feeling hopeless and guilty. Starting with falling asleep on the recliner next to William. Maybe if he'd been in bed with his wife, she would still be here now. He could have stopped whoever came in and took them. Why hadn't he checked on Kris and Mara when he got up? As he went through the morning events leading up to discovering that his wife and child were missing, he realized that he'd fallen into a routine. And now several hours had gone by because he was busy on the phone instead of wondering why Kris and Mara weren't up. Kris was usually up by 7:00 on weekends as was his daughter.

As the police were doing their investigation, one of them found a necklace near the bed. The chain was broken but it was the half-heart necklace that Krista always wore. "Is this familiar to you?" One detective asked him as he held it up. Chad could only nod slightly as he felt a barrage of tears from behind his eyes. "It's my wife's. She never takes it off. For god's sake, find her! Where's Detective Masterson? I just talked to him a few hours ago!" Chad insisted on speaking with him as soon as possible.

"Mr. Burton, he's on his way." One of the younger officers told him. Chad could tell that he was as alarmed as he was about this situation and wished that Masterson would be there to make everything seem to make sense. Everything about this was a reminder of 7 years ago to Chad. But now it wasn't just his wife. Mara was gone too and that made it a thousand times worse. As he tried to think clearly, he knew that there was only one person that knew their way around their house well enough to capture two people without their knowledge in the middle of the night. Joanna Larsen.

"Let him know that he'd better be looking for Joanna Larsen and her son, Kaden! I know they're behind this!" Chad was suddenly furious with the police and their inability to do anything about that fucking black truck last night! He didn't trust anyone now and was starting to wonder if Stanley was in on it too! His father in law was doing his best to keep him calm despite his own desperation to find his daughter and granddaughter. He led Chad into his office which was the only room at the moment the police weren't picking apart for any clues. "Chad, you need to stop badgering the officers and take a break." William insisted.

"Maybe Stanley knew something was going to happen. I talked to him right before you went upstairs and noticed that Kris and Mara weren't there!" Chad's mind was reeling with the possibilities and no one was beyond suspicion as far as he was concerned now!

"Let me give him a call. I've known Stanley a long time. I get why you don't trust anyone now, but I'm sure he's willing to help if he can." William assured him.

"He said we could come tomorrow because he knew I was concerned about safety! I was going to go." Chad admitted. "I was supposed to talk to Kris and get back to him today by 3:00 this afternoon."

"No better time than the present. It's pretty close now." William pointed at the time; 2:46pm. Time was flying by. Chad began to panic as he realized Krista and Mara had been missing for over 8 hours now. William went to the phone and dialed Stanley's number. "Let me tell him what's going on. You can just listen."

Chad was emotionally exhausted and agreed as he sat back on the small love seat that had been left over from Krista and his early days. In fact it'd been one of the first pieces of furniture they'd bought together. She'd found it at a local second hand shop on Thames in Newport. It was a vintage; which was hideous to Chad but she'd loved it. It was a royal blue with gold roses printed all over it. "I love it!" Krista had been excited when she found it. It reminded her of her parent's furniture growing up. He'd hated it upon sight, but in the end it was a fixture in their little apartment in the early days. Once they'd bought a house and other furniture, the loveseat had been relegated to his office. And now he sank down on it, praying that he'd see his wife and daughter again.

William had Stanley on the phone now and was telling him what was going on. "Stan, I'm going to put you on speaker phone now. Chad's in the room with me."

"Chad, hang in there, okay? You're welcome to come to my place anytime if you need to. In the meantime, I haven't heard anything from Amanda, but I've asked some people that are in the area to check out what you and Bill have told me about Joanna, Michelle, and Kaden. I already know that Dave Ackwell is a pain in the ass and can't be trusted.

"What people exactly? I mean, if you knew that your daughter was scheming all along, why wouldn't you let us know?" Chad was suddenly angry with him. He wasn't trusting anyone now.

"I did warn you about the truck being there the other night. I'd heard something from one of Amanda's high school friends. Believe me, I want to help." Stanley surprisingly didn't take offense to his tone. William put his fingers up to his lips to get Chad to stop talking.

Chad nodded. It was true; Stanley had warned them. "I'm sorry. I just don't know what to do or who to believe anymore. Too bad I'm not a psychic." He was being sarcastic now, but why hadn't he thought to call someone who was a psychic? Sadie! He knew that Krista trusted her and she'd really seemed to help Mara.

"Stan, Bill, I need to go check something out!" He rushed out of the room and upstairs, hoping that he could find Sadie's number somewhere. Krista's phone was gone, but he remembered that her purse was still downstairs. He did something he'd never dare do before; go through her purse, praying that she'd saved Sadie Mercotte's number instead of just putting it in her phone and throwing it away.

Krista

She was only half-asleep when she heard her bedroom door open slowly. Assuming it was Chad coming back to bed Krista didn't bother opening her eyes, and waited for him to lie down next to her and settle into bed. When a few seconds went by and she didn't feel his body settling into bed, she rubbed her eyes and sat up just as a person dressed in black with a ski mask on reached for her and clapped a rag filled with a foul-smelling chemical over her nose and mouth. She tried to rip the cloth off, but the intruder managed to keep it there long enough for the effects of the chloroform took over quickly and now she felt nothing but numbness taking over. "Chad, help!" Krista tried to yell as loud as she could through the rag, but she felt herself feeling faint and just before everything went black, she heard what sounded like a woman say, "her daughter's room is down the hall." Her last thought before losing consciousness was 'oh no, Mara!'

* * *

It seemed as though only minutes had passed when she woke up to almost complete darkness with one small dirty window to let in enough light to see what was right in front of her. There was a musty smell that was indigenous to basements. Krista began to panic; it was freezing causing her to shiver uncontrollably, her head ached and her brain felt foggy, as though she were hungover. Her hands were tied in front of her and it was so dark that she could barely see them in front

269

of her face. It smelled damp and moldy wherever she was, along with the strong smell of marijuana that made her gag.

"Let me outta here!" Krista yelled as she instinctively tried to free herself. She was now glad she'd fallen asleep with her sweatshirt and long fitted yoga pants instead of a t-shirt and shorts or she'd probably be hypothermic by now. She continued to struggle when she heard a voice that was familiar to her

"Someone is awake. The fun begins." It only took a few moments to realize that it was Joanna, her father's girlfriend. What the hell was she doing here?

"Joanna? Is that you? It's me, Krista! I need help!"

"Really? You do?" She could hear someone's footsteps coming forward and a flashlight suddenly blinded her. Krista's eyes squinted, trying to make out who was there. As the figure came into focus, Krista could see that she was right. It was Joanna; she was dressed in all black and any resemblance to the woman that she'd gotten to know over the past year was gone. The menacing glare in Joanna's eyes made it clear to Krista that she was no longer a friend, and Krista knew she had an uphill battle trying to play the mother sympathy card with her.

"Joanna. You don't need to do this. I understand you're upset with my dad, but I can talk to him for you, help you work things out." Krista tried to keep her voice calm instead of whining like a weakling. She had something that Joanna didn't with this situation; experience! This was exactly what she'd gone through 7 years ago but had luckily learned a few things that might help her. She tried to move from side to side to feel if she'd left her phone in one of her side pockets of her yoga pants which she did all too often.

"Are you looking for this?" Joanna pulled a phone with a leopard print case out of her pocket and knelt down as she held it in front of her. Krista's hopes that she had it on the phone being useful to her died, along with the chance that somehow she could reason with Joanna. She was just like one of the Ahearn sisters; a sociopath. Maybe this is why Mara never really warmed up to her.

"So here's the thing, Krista. You did leave your phone in your pocket of your yoga pants. I've watched you do that while I was dating your father so it was the first place we looked. But here's where there's a problem. You were smart enough to have a security code password to get in. I need you to give me that password and fingerprint. Smart thinking by the way! It works really well!" Joanna's compliments were reaching their end. And Krista felt her heart racing, knowing what was coming next.

She was right. Joanna had pulled out her phone, but Krista wasn't planning on giving in to her demands. "You expect me to do that? What's in it for me? Don't you plan to kill me, dig a shallow grave in a remote area so they can put out a search team so my father can find my body weeks later? Would that make you feel better?" There was no way she would give this bitch access to her phone. She wasn't going to make it easy on her, them, whoever was involved, but she was sure that there were others.

Joanna's face came close to hers, so close that she could smell the alcohol and pot on her breath and see the frown lines and pores on her face. "I'll show you what's in it for you, Krista!" She pulled out another phone. "You didn't leave by yourself." She pulled up a video on the phone and hit play.

"Watch it!" She pushed the phone in Krista's face. It was Mara in her bedroom! There was a person dressed in black that nudged her awake and immediately put a cloth over her mouth muffling her screams. Mara stopped fighting as the chloroform took effect, then carried her small limp figure out of the room. Krista's ability to stay composed evaporated. "NO!!!!! What have you done with her? Where is my daughter?" She began to struggle against the ruthless zip ties around her wrists, so much that the ties were cutting into her wrists, beads of blood seeping out of the cuts.

The video continued with the person with Mara lying limp over their shoulder and making their way down the stairs. The camera continued to roll as they continued downstairs, where Chad in the recliner and her father on the couch were sound asleep. Krista was crying as Joanna forced her to face the video that showed the person bringing Mara to a black truck and placing her in the vehicle.

"I'm going to fucking kill you and anyone else involved if you hurt my daughter!" Krista hissed at her and knew that she had to find a way out of this. She had never hated anyone as much as she hated Joanna at this moment. If she'd had Chad's gun, she'd have shot her on the spot, without hesitation!

Joanna laughed in her face as Krista lunged at her, spitting in her face. "Fuck you, bitch! " Joanna wiped her face off and without warning swung at her face, hitting her nose which began to bleed. Krista was dazed and everything was spinning, then went dark. When she came to minutes later, her vison was blurred but she could see someone else in the room next to Joanna. "What the hell? I told you to show her the video, not knock her out! We need her passcode!" It was a deep male voice, one she didn't recognize.

"She spit in my face, David! I reacted, give me a break!" Joanna was still furious, as she began grabbing small items that were in her way, tossing them to the side.

"Well we can't have her looking all beat up! That wasn't the plan! She needs to look as though she hasn't been harmed. That's gonna look bad in a few hours, get a grip, Joanna. Did you think she was going to thank you for the video of her daughter being kidnapped?" David was sarcastic and clearly focused. Deranged in the head, but at least focused.

Krista remembered a David that was one of Chad's client's; what was his last name? Ackerberg, Ack-something. Ackwell! That was it! She remembered Chad saying the he kept bugging Stanley about selling his property. It didn't matter what his name was at this point. She knew they were going to hold Mara's safety over her until she gave them the password to her phone. Krista could feel the blood trickling from her nose but tried to distract herself to remember if she had her phone locator set to 'share'. It would be the only thing in her favor of them having access. She was just glad that she'd never put her bank account on an app on her phone like many of her friends and co-workers had. But they could send her husband and friends messages as if they were from her; make her seem as though she left on her own.

The assault on her nose was taking its toll and she was feeling dizzy, almost nauseous now but she knew she needed to do what she could to keep Mara safe. Surely Joanna wouldn't allow them to hurt her daughter, but then again, she remembered that Joanna had never been a fan of Mara, especially lately. It was the first time she wished that Mara would somehow have this Jamie to rely on, no matter how evil the spirit was. Krista remembered the necklace that Sadie had given Mara to wear to keep the spirit away, but she'd taken it off Mara at bedtime.

Joanna and David had stopped their bickering and focused their attention back on Krista now that her eyes were open. "I see you're back with us again, Krista. I hope you've learned that you being a spoiled bitch won't change your circumstances right now."

Krista refused to answer. She decided she'd give as little information as possible unless it would be useful to someone finding her and Mara. She had no idea what time it was but it must be morning and her husband and father must know that she and Mara weren't there by now. Tears were running down her face despite her resolve to be strong, but she could hear her mother's voice in her head. 'Krista, I'm here. Just trust in your instincts and remember those who love you are looking. They'll find you if you can hang on.' Krista tried to keep her tears in check, but a few escaped that did not go unnoticed by Joanna.

"Aww, I can see you're sad right now. But you can help your daughter right now. Give me the passcode to your phone and we'll let Mara go." Joanna was trying to play nice now that even her co-conspirators had called her out on her actions. Krista could see David behind her, although he was dressed in dark clothes, she could still make out his face; he was handsome, and with his designer clothing and Rolex watch he obviously had money. What the hell was he doing getting mixed up with this crazy woman that might land him in prison?

"David is it? Are you the same David that was my husband's client?" Krista ignored Joanna and addressed him directly.

David didn't answer right away, as if he didn't know how he should answer. Joanna was not at loss for words. "Stop talking to him. You don't know him."

"Actually, I do." Krista wanted to one up on this stupid woman that had manipulated her father into falling in love with her. At least her father was smart enough to break it off with her after finding out she was a lying piece of shit just like her son. "You're the guy that kept trying to get Stanley Ahearn to sell his property. Why? What's in it for you?"

David was silent as Joanna sat by stewing, waiting for him to pounce on Krista to give out the password to her phone. Krista could tell he was thinking and she wanted to use every advantage that she could right now by talking common sense. After all, David didn't become wealthy by listening to dipshits like Joanna. Or have someone commanding them from prison, like Amanda.

"David, listen to me. You're not this person that is involved with kidnapping; especially a young child! You're successful because obviously you came to my husband to find the perfect home. I don't know how you got involved with these people, but Amanda Ahearn is in prison for a reason! She tried to kill me in the past as well as other people involved. All for money and an inheritance that she doesn't deserve anyway!" Krista didn't know if any of her words were reaching him, but he *had* intervened when Joanna hit her in the face. It was worth a try.

David hadn't moved yet, sending Joanna into a frantic rage. She ran upstairs, only to return with a pistol a few seconds later as she handed it to David. Krista worried that she'd poked the bear too much. She'd hoped that David could talk some reason into this lunatic, but he only stood there like a deer in headlights. "David, you need to get the password to her phone! Shoot her if she doesn't!" Joanna commanded. He shook his head and handed it back to Joanna. "I'm not going to do that." Joanna's face turned red with anger as she turned to Krista, wielding the pistol.

"I'll give my passcode to my phone. When I get to see my daughter in person, not on video." Krista knew she wasn't in a position to negotiate, but she wasn't giving up. Giving her the password would mean suicide for her, but she was willing to take a chance if it meant letting her daughter go.

Joanna pointed the pistol at Krista's head. "Give me the passcode or I'll pull the trigger!" David looked shocked. "Hey, I never signed up for this. I'm not going to be involved in killing people!" He turned to leave and walk up the stairs when Joanna fired a shot towards his feet, missing him by only a few feet.

"What the hell?" David came back down the stairs. "Put it down, Joanna." Joanna refused and pointed the gun at him. "If you're not going to help me, then get upstairs before I fire this again. I won't miss the next time!" Krista realized this woman was becoming completely unhinged. David ran back up the stairs, away from her craziness. So much for him helping her! Krista knew once they had the passcode, they could send endless messages from her phone and they'd kill her anyway.

"Go ahead. Then you won't have it and you'll have to figure out how you're gonna cover your tracks." Krista was calling her bluff, but she was shaking with anxiety not knowing if this woman was crazy enough to pull the trigger, and waited while Joanna seemed to ponder her options. She sprinted up the basement stairs without another word; Krista guessed she was going to consult with the 'mastermind' of this whole scheme, the illustrious Amanda Ahearn or one of her other looney friends that had dreamed this up.

Now she was left alone and checked her surroundings to see if there was anything she could use to cut her bound wrists. The basement was clearly a storage space for random items. There were boxes stacked up with labels written in a black sharpie; *Eldridge-photos, Eldridge-books, Amanda's stuff.* Eldridge? Where had she heard that name before? It wasn't one of her students at school, but it seemed familiar to her. And how was Amanda's stuff in this house when the other boxes were listed as Eldridge? Was she in Amanda's house? Was she in Joanna's house? She had no idea where Joanna lived. Her father had told her, but he was very rarely at her home.

Was Joanna living in Amanda's house? Shit! She'd gotten sidetracked and realized that they'd forgotten to tie her feet together. There were no windows, but she thought she could hear the ocean in the distance. She scrambled around looking for anything sharp to cut through the zip ties that bound her wrists. Spying a pair of small pliers that might work if she could get them around the zip ties without cutting herself, she managed to pick them up with her hands together and work them around so that the cutting edge was aligned underneath the zip ties on her wrists. It was risky; one wrong move and she might cut a major vein in her wrists but there was no time to lose. It was either risk cutting herself or being forced to give up information on her phone that would render her useless and then Mara would be at their mercy. Krista was willing to take her chances. It was tough maneuvering around with her hands tied, but managed to get the pliers underneath the zip ties on the top side of her hands and squeezed as hard as she could and the plastic ties came apart to her relief. Krista decided she'd keep them on her for safekeeping. After tucking them into her sweatshirt pocket, she made a beeline for one of the 'Eldridge boxes' marked 'photos' and ripped the duct tape off, and began quickly searching for photos of anything or anyone that would give a clue to where she was and who were the Eldridge's.

She grabbed a handful of photos that had faded with age, all depicting a handsome young man with his wife and a little girl no older than three years old in front of a yellow house. There was something familiar about the little girl, and a chronology to the pictures; every year the same people in front of the same yellow house. The final picture had the same couple and girl, except there was another girl alongside her. On the back read '*1985'- Jim, June, Joanna and Amanda'*. She recognized the name and the man's face although he was much older now. Eldridge! Jim Eldridge! He was the janitor at Johnston High School where she worked! He was Joanna's father and it was Joanna in these pictures as a young girl, standing next who must be Amanda. She looked closer and realized it was Amanda Ahearn!

Krista thought back to the deleted emails, and the email that was sent to a parent to get her in the hot seat. It started to make sense to her now; Joanna had known Amanda from childhood and Jim went along with it. She was certain Jim knew nothing about technology and hacking into computers, but he held the key to get someone who did in the door. Amanda might be in prison, but she still had everyone in the palm of her hand.

Krista could hear the door open at the top of stairs and shuffled the pictures back into the box quickly and scurried back to her chair, pretending to have her wrists tied with the opening to the zip ties hidden toward her body. Feeling the weight of the pliers hidden in her sweatshirt front pocket gave her a sense of security; a weapon to rely upon and Krista was certain it would be necessary.

 She braced herself for what Joanna might try to do to her and plan what *she* might have to do to *her* in order to avoid being gunned down. But all of that went out of her mind when Mara appeared. "Mommy!" Mara was excited to see her and ran toward her. Krista almost gave away the fact that her hands were no longer tied, but when she saw Joanna coming down the stairs, she managed to pull herself back into her 'role' of being tied up.

"Mara! Are you okay? Come here and give me a hug sweetheart!" Krista remained in her chair to continue the illusion of her hands being tied under Joanna's watchful eye. Mara ran to her, grabbing onto her as if she were drowning. "Mommy, Jamie told me that we're in trouble." Mara whispered in her ear as Joanna came closer.

"The necklace that Sadie gave you, do you have it?" Krista whispered, as Mara shook her head. Now Mara was in danger of Jamie taking hold. Suddenly, she had a plan that might work if Joanna came at Mara. After all, Jamie wanted to control Mara and if there was a threat to Mara, Jamie would take action as she obviously had yesterday. It was risky and Sadie had warned her that Jamie could eventually take over Mara's body if the spirit remained there. "Maybe Jamie could help you in this situation. Maybe you can ask her to help you." Krista whispered to Mara who shook her head.

"Jamie's gone now. She won't help me. She went somewhere else, mommy. I'm scared." Her blue eyes were filled with tears that spilled down her cheeks. Krista had never felt so helpless, but she smoothed the baby fine blonde curls that were free of her messy ponytail. "We'll be fine sweetheart. I promise. Daddy and grandpa will be looking for us. Just do what they tell you and we will be home soon." Krista mustered all the confidence she could so that she could believe it as much as Mara. "Ok, mommy." Mara whispered as her grip on Krista's neck tightened.

"Sorry to interrupt this reunion, but now you've seen that your daughter is alive and well, it's your turn to hold up your end of the bargain! I want your passcode and fingerprint to your phone, Krista." Joanna's face was twisted in an ugly frown that made it impossible for Krista to believe that her father had ever found this woman attractive.

She was truly evil; inside and out. Joanna pulled out her pistol again and kept it to her side. Perhaps because she had some respect that her 6-year-old daughter was there, but not enough to not bring it with her. "You can deal with me when Mara isn't here!" Krista refused. She drew the line at having her daughter witness any more than she had already. Joanna had some common sense after all and she called for David to come down and take Mara back upstairs.

David came downstairs and came over to Mara. Krista was shaking that he might harm her daughter, but he was surprisingly friendly, and went out of his way to make her feel comfortable. "Mara, let's go upstairs and watch some TV okay?" He glanced at Krista and gave her a wink, and a slight grin. Krista knew that Mara would be safe with him, for now anyway.

Mara's lower lip was starting to tremble and she threw her arms around Krista. "No! I don't want to leave my mommy!" Her tears made Krista feel more determined than ever to get them out of here. But she needed to bide her time so they could both get out alive. Joanna had made it clear that she had no problem using the gun on her own conspirators. And Joanna's face reflected her irritation that Mara was stalling. Krista knew she needed to get Mara upstairs and out of harm's way.

"Mara, I need you to listen to David, okay? He'll take care of you." She looked pointedly at him. "Won't he?" David nodded. "Of course I will. I promise." He winked at Krista, and she took that as him being trustworthy. There was no other choice as she faced the reckless, insufferable bitch of a woman in front of her. The time of reckoning with her had come and the only weapon she had was a pair of pliers. If only she could remember if she had turned on the location on her phone. If it was, it wouldn't matter if the phone was secured with the passcode, the phone could still tell Chad where she was if he was looking for it!

Chad

He realized that Krista's purse was still hanging on the kitchen chair where it'd always been. He'd never dreamed of looking through it before; he knew better. He remembered his father always telling him when he was younger; "whatever you do, don't go through a woman's purse!" His father had never said why, but the message was clear early on. But now the brick red Coach purse that he'd bought her for her last birthday was staring him in the face and he needed the number to contact Sadie Mercotte. He only hoped that the number was somewhere in there instead of just stored in her phone which was a lost cause now. Her phone was gone along with her and he was certain whoever had taken her, the phone was the first thing to hold hostage.

He picked out her small black wallet that was worn and old. Seeing it reminded him of Kris telling him she needed a new one, but she couldn't find one just like it. Now he wished he'd put in the time to find her one. 'Stop it and find the number,' he thought and tried to focus as he went through all the endless cards in her wallet. He was starting to wonder if she'd thrown it away after storing it in her phone as he went through her entire purse which consisted of make-up, tampons, old lipsticks, pens covered in make-up dust, old receipts, but there wasn't any business cards or numbers. He sat down at the kitchen table with Krista's purse emptied, trying to figure out what to do next when his phone rang showing a 401 Rhode Island area code. He picked up immediately, expecting it to be the police.

"Hi, is Krista there, please?" It was a woman's voice that he didn't recognize as one of Krista's friends, but sounded somewhat familiar. He immediately felt irritated that this was probably a spam call and was getting ready to hang up, but curiosity won out.

"I'm sorry, she isn't here right now. Who's calling?" Chad asked tersely, prepared to hang up at the mention of a selling car warranties.

"This is Sadie Mercotte. I was just calling to see how Mara was doing since I was there the other day."

"Oh, hello, Ms. Mercotte." Chad 's irritation dissipated, replaced by relief. Hopefully she could help! "This is her husband, Chad. I wish I could say that they are doing well, but I don't know where Krista or Mara are right now. They're missing, I think they were taken in the middle of the night." Chad felt himself choking up as he spoke.

"I'm so sorry to hear that, Chad. Krista and Mara are very special to you, I know. They are special to me as Krista's well- being was important to my niece. I can come by in an hour if that works for you." Sadie offered, and Chad agreed immediately, knowing that finding them in time was important.

"That would be fantastic, Sadie. Thank you so much! Whatever your fee is won't be a problem." Chad was grateful and would spend whatever it cost to get some help. Detective Masterson seemed to be taking his time as with the rest of the department.

"I'll see you soon." Sadie told him. For the first time since he'd discovered they were missing, Chad had some hope. He confided in William about the call and that Sadie would be coming over. He expected William to think it was a ridiculous idea to have her come, but he was happy to hear the news. "She was able to help Mara. I do believe she can help, Chad. There's something else I need to make sure to keep with us. Krista still has Karen's necklace with her, right?" William asked him.

"I'm sure she does. She kept it in her jewelry box. I'll go get it." Chad ran upstairs to look through his wife's jewelry box, praying that the necklace was there. He had to search for it, but he figured Kris had put it in a special place and he was right. It was in one of the small compartments behind the lid as it opened up. "I've got it." He showed it to William and gave it him for safekeeping. It didn't occur to him at the time why William would even think of the necklace. Before he could ask, Detective Masterson finally called back with updates about the prison phone logs made by Amanda Ahearn. "There have been some calls to numbers that have been identified as calls between people at Carson Realty, but it will take some time to find out who specifically she was talking to."

"I can get you that information now." Chad informed them. He got on the phone with Kathy, his receptionist and asked her to email the spreadsheet phone log she had been keeping for him. "It'll just be a minute." He informed Masterson who suddenly seemed surprised that he was on top of this situation.

"I'll check these out right away." Masterson told him. "In the meantime, the police have checked Joanna Larsen and Kaden Macelli's residence's for any disturbances in those homes."

"What do you mean, 'checked for disturbances'? Does that mean you searched the homes?" Chad knew by now that it took a search warrant to go through homes, so he doubted that they'd bothered with that detail.

"We've checked with neighbors and knocked on the doors of both residences. No one was at home at Ms. Larsen's. We're working on getting a search warrant to get access to the property." Masterson told him. Chad rolled his eyes as heard the news. "Thank you." There was no point in stating the obvious; they should've done that earlier, but there was no use in arguing about it. "What about Kaden Macelli? What happened there?"

"He was at home with his girlfriend. They allowed us to search the house and answered questions. He says that his mother owns the black truck and borrowed it a few times. He claims he doesn't have any knowledge about your wife or your daughter."

"Why was his number coming up in my phone log at my agency then? Did you ask him that?" Chad felt as though he was doing all the work here. Really?

"Mr. Burton, it is possible that someone else used Macelli's phone to call your agency. Just like you thought it might be him driving the truck, but we later discovered it was his mother." Masterson was patronizing him now and it was pissing him off.

"Of course it is! But..." He realized he couldn't tell him what he knew about Kaden without telling about his meeting with Estelle. And he had been trying to avoid that all along. "Okay." He wanted to wait for Sadie to show up and tell him anything that might lead them to where they needed to be. Obviously Joanna wasn't at home, so it was doubtful Kris and Mara were being held hostage there. But

Masterson's questions were concerning to him; he thought Chad was lying. Chad felt as if he was on Masterson's radar and knew he needed to keep his meeting with Estelle to himself.

"What were you going to say, Mr. Burton?" He asked. Chad felt a rush of panic hit him. The guy actually was listening, probably recording him now. "I meant that since it was from his phone, he might have knowledge about what was going on." Chad recovered, confident that his explanation would smooth things over. It suddenly dawned on him that the cameras from the CVS likely caught him on camera with Estelle. Masterson was trying to draw him in. Maybe it was time to tell him about his meeting with Estelle. His mind was spinning with possibilities but his focus needed to be on finding Krista and Mara. Someone knocking at the door saved him from any further explanation. He was praying it was Sadie Mercotte. "I need to go, but call if you have anything else." Chad told Masterson.

"I'll be in touch." Masterson told him. Chad was glad to hang up, anxious to meet with Sadie who hopefully had more answers.

William had already answered the door when he walked into the living room. He was expecting a woman that was older, perhaps in her 60s, Sadie looked maybe in her late thirties, especially with her trendy ripped jeans and combat-style boots. Her long dark hair was pulled back in a ponytail and pulled through a pink baseball hat that made her look even more youthful.

"Hello, Sadie, I'm Chad Burton. This is Krista's father, William Carson. Thank you so much for coming." Chad wasn't sure what to do now. Did she just start giving him ideas, pull out some cards, or sit at a table with candles?   "What do you need from me?" Chad asked. He was out of his comfort zone and had no idea what to expect. But Krista trusted her, as she'd trusted her niece so he gave her the benefit of the doubt.

"It's nice to meet you, Chad, William. I just want to get a sense of the space that Krista and Mara rest. I can already feel some of their energy that they left, as I've been here before." Sadie was already headed toward the stairs. Chad liked the way she took charge and raised his arm up as he followed her up the stairs with William behind him. Sadie stopped at the master bedroom and closed her eyes for a moment. "Krista didn't leave on her own. Someone took her; they drugged her and she was unconscious when she left." Sadie told them. "It wasn't one person, it was two people that took her. Her necklace fell off when they picked her up." Chad nodded to William. The detectives had given him the necklace. He was glad he'd found her number, and that she was here. "Do you know who they are?"

"A blond woman and a dark-haired woman. I can feel some conflict that was happening when they were here." Sadie said, her eyes closed as though she were concentrating. All Chad could think about was Joanna and Michelle. Blond and dark hair, they fit what Chad had in mind anyway. Now he needed to know where they were!

Chad wasn't sure if he could ask or if Sadie would tell him, but she continued on. "They brought her down the stairs and out the front door. They did the same with Mara."

"Where are they? Can you see them?" Chad asked anxiously. Sadie shook her head, very focused and put her finger up to her lips, giving him the 'be quiet' sign. He had the urge to apologize, then realized he'd be talking and interrupt her concentration.

She seemed to be in a trance as she walked to Mara's room and stood still at the entrance. 'What is going on? Why isn't she going in there?' Chad was beside himself without talking to her. William was behind him and kept poking him and whispering to him. "What's she doing now?" Chad turned around and shushed him the same way Sadie did. "Oh, sorry," William whispered back.

Sadie began walking through the room slowly with her eyes closed. Chad realized he'd been holding his breath as William was standing behind him, gripping his arm. He saw his daughter's bed with her green and black comforter off to the side, seeing where his daughter had been sleeping hours before and imagining her being taken away. It was too much for him. He began to panic, hyperventilating and felt nauseous, running past William to the master bathroom. "Chad, you okay?" William called after him.

"I'm okay," He managed, as he began splashing cold water on his face. The nausea had passed, but he had to sit down for a moment to catch his breath. He realized this is how Kris must feel when she was having a panic attack and how difficult it was to explain until it happens. He remembered instructing Krista to take deep breaths and now he tried to follow that advice himself. He closed his eyes and concentrated on his breathing for a few minutes when William knocked on the door. "Chad, you okay?"

Chad took a last deep breath. "I'm okay, I just needed a minute. Be right out." Chad splashed some more water on his face and dried off.

"I'm fine. We'll find them." He muttered to his reflection in the mirror. The light in the bathroom began to flicker on and off for a moment. "What the hell, I know I changed that bulb just last week." Chad said out loud as the light finally stayed on. Just as he looked back in the mirror an image of a little girl appeared behind him out of nowhere. He brushed his hand over his eyes to make sure he wasn't seeing things, but she was still there. He felt surprisingly calm despite her sudden appearance. It was Mara! He was sure of it, but how was that possible? He was starting to wonder if he was losing his mind and closed his eyes again.

"Daddy! Help me!" It was definitely Mara's voice! He opened his eyes, but the image was gone. "Mara! Are you there? Come back!" Chad's voice was loud enough that William was knocking on the door.

"Chad, are you okay? Who are you talking to?" Chad opened the bathroom door to his father-in-law looking confused.

"It was Mara, I heard her! I saw her in the mirror, Bill!" Chad was frantic. He needed to find her!

William grabbed Chad by the shoulders. "Chad, you really need to get a grip right now. Mara's not here. Are you on something? Did you take some of Krista's anti-anxiety meds that you aren't used to?"

" Of course not! I saw Mara!" Chad insisted, irritated that his father-in-law didn't believe him. "Where's Sadie, Bill? William nodded down toward Mara's room. Chad found her in Mara's room sitting on the bed with her eyes closed and nodding slowly. "Sadie! I just saw Mara! She needs our help! Where do we go?" He'd never felt as helpless as did now. The sight of his daughter screaming for help had put him over the edge.

Sadie opened her eyes and seemed troubled as she spoke. "Krista and Mara are in trouble." Chad nodded, "We need to hurry! She was crying out for help! What do we do?   She told me you would know where to go." Chad wasn't sure if Sadie would even believe him, but Mara had told him she needed to know.

"I know. She told me where to go. She showed me a house that's further away from the cliff. It's a small yellow house with a wraparound porch. There's a two person seated swing in the front near a gravel driveway. The mailbox says the name "Eldridge" on it." Sadie began describing the house, although I can't seem to make out the name of the street." She seemed very insistent and William nodded. "I'll contact Stanley right away. Maybe he can get us there. Chad, call the Shoreham police on Block Island."

"Block Island is small enough, and you have a name. How many people with the name Eldridge can live on the island?" William had to imagine it was small enough that the police probably knew everyone that owned property there. Chad was frantic and was getting ready to dial the Shoreham police, when he noticed there was a notification on his phone at the top that he didn't recognize. He slid his finger down and there was a dot with a location on it. He suddenly remembered that he and Kris had decided to share their locations on their phones when Mara began school just a few weeks ago. "Bill, Sadie, look! There's a location on my phone!" It was in fact Krista's phone or at least that was the number that was coming up as located on Block

Island. The location was right where Sadie had said it was, a little ways away from the cliffs and the Ahearn estate. It didn't give an exact address, but it was better than telling police that he was going by what a psychic told him! He contacted the Shoreham police and gave them the information, forgetting that Shoreham had only two police officers in the town. Officer Blaylock who'd answered the call informed him that he had several other calls that evening that were ahead of his call.

"Are you kidding? This is an emergency! My wife and daughter have been reported missing since this morning! Don't you watch the news out there?" Whatever patience Chad had was gone at that point. William took over as he could tell that his son-in-law was ready to lose it. William motioned for him to stop talking and put his phone on speaker.

"Officer, this is William Carson." He began in a clipped even voice. It was the voice he used very rarely, but William had a knack for getting his point across without threatening, though by the time he was done, the person on the receiving end seemed to respond immediately to whatever he told them. "My daughter and granddaughter have been missing since probably 3:00am this morning. We also just got a notification from my daughter's phone that she is located near the Ahearn property on the bluffs, somewhere near the Eldridge residence. I'm notifying the State Police now, but perhaps you could get a jump on it and head that way, considering they were kidnapped!"

"Of course, Mr. Carson! I'll speak to the State Police myself right now and head out there. It's just myself here tonight, so I may need to have some back up." Blaylock's tone changed in an instant. The name

'Ahearn' was well-known on the island and any mention of Stanley's name warranted immediate attention.

"Please do that! I'll be notifying the Johnston Police as well. This is my number so you can contact me, do you have it?" William insisted that he recite it back to him. "We're on our way out to Block Island and help is on the way, but please go there now!" William hung up and turned to Chad who'd sat down against the wall.

"Bill I can't do this! I can't go through this again. I can't lose Kris or Mara!" He was starting to panic again, but William knew what he needed; a swift kick in the ass. "Chad, stop it! Kris and Mara need you now! Let's go!" William snapped him out of his moment of paralyzing anxiety that was preventing him from being effective. Chad knew he needed to get himself together and immediately got up to call Detective Masterson, while William contacted Stanley to see about the use of his boat to get them over to Block Island within an hour or two. Masterson wasn't there, but the officer that answered was responsive and said they would be contacting the State Police to assist Shoreham PD, as well as contact Masterson about the new developments of the case. "We'll notify him immediately, Mr. Burton." He assured him.

In the midst of the drama of the phone calls to police and calling Stanley to get expedited transportation, Chad realized that Sadie was still sitting in the living room. She had been sitting quietly on the light-blue sofa looking at a framed family photo of Chad, Krista and Mara. "Sadie, I'm so sorry to keep you waiting. How much do I owe you?" Chad was prepared to pay whatever it cost especially on short notice. She didn't respond immediately, so he touched her shoulder. She turned and looked at him. "Why, Chad, not a problem at all," she cooed. Her voice was different, sultry, enticing and very un-like the person he'd met an hour ago. Her entire persona had changed. "I'm not charging a fee today. I'm glad to help, but I'd like to stay until you all get things figured out here." She began to fan herself in a flirtatious manner. "It's kind of warm in here."

Chad's initial gut feeling was to say 'no thanks' and send her on her way. Clearly, Sadie was not only looking for spirits, but some male attention. Something about her wasn't right, but he chalked it up to being under so much stress today. Besides, she had been right about the location, after Krista's phone confirmed it.

"No problem, thank you. I appreciate your help, Sadie." Chad agreed. "Let me check with William about the transportation." He used the excuse to get away from her as she came closer to him. He was already regretting agreeing to have her come with them as her dark eyes met with his. Her eyes appeared vacant, instead of focused and friendly when she'd first arrived. "Are you okay, Sadie?" Chad asked. "You seem....tired." He wanted to say 'different' or 'strange' but she hadn't done or said anything wrong. It was just his interpretation.

"Oh, I'm fine, Chad. I'm happy to help out. I can't wait until we're reunited with Krista and Mara." Sadie smiled.

"Right, I can't either." Chad agreed. It was just as he headed to his home office where William had gone to call Stanley that he realized what Sadie had said; 'until *we're* reunited with Krista and Mara'. He realized something wasn't right with Sadie's demeanor.

Krista

Seeing Mara fueled her resolve to get them both out of here in one piece. It was one of the most difficult moments of her life having Mara taken back upstairs as she had to watch. But now she had to face Joanna standing over her as she tried to pretend that her hands were still tied together; waiting for a moment to take her down by surprise, but it needed to be timed just right. Krista had the pair of pliers in her pocket and it made her feel more confident, as if she might have a chance out of here. If carefully placed, the pliers could incapacitate her and buy her some time. Her only saving grace was that David Ackwell appeared to be human and seemed to care about Mara. But Joanna cared only about herself. She also had a loaded gun that clearly she wasn't afraid to use, as she'd already made that clear at nearly missing David when he disagreed with her.

"Now that you've seen Mara, I need your passcode to your phone, Krista. I'm done playing games." Joanna came closer and Krista could smell the alcohol on her breath. Apparently, Joanna needed a little boost of confidence to go through with what she was saying. Krista waited, trying to think of something to distract her, buy some time. The problem was that if Joanna got close enough and fired the gun, she'd never have time to grab it in time before Joanna pulled the trigger.

"Well? What's it going to be?" Joanna was within an arms' length of her now. The pistol was at her side, but Krista knew it probably wouldn't remain there for long.

"How long had you been planning this with Amanda? What has she done for you that you would risk your life's work to become a felon on the run?" Krista decided to put her clinical tools to work. Joanna was a mentally unstable person and if she had to guess, probably in the midst of a manic episode. She was hoping to distract her with a reality check about what she was doing. If only she could get Joanna to put the gun down, she could grab her phone that Joanna was waving around in her other hand and run out of here!

"Don't you talk to me about Amanda as if you know her, Krista! You don't know what she's gone through! I was with her when she was brought in bleeding to death and clinging to life in the emergency room 7 years ago after she was shot! I was with her when she was recovering and suicidal after she was told her sister had died and her father had practically deserted her! I was her nurse that whole time, held her hand and watched her cry. You only know what you've been told, so you weren't there! I *need* to help her! Her family sure as hell won't!" Tears were streaming down Joanna's face as she recalled the trauma aspect of Amanda's rescue back to life at the emergency room that fateful night.

Krista knew she had that one moment to create some kind of supportive rapport with Joanna, and chose her words carefully. She resisted the urge to bring up what she'd discovered from looking at the pictures. Clearly, they'd been close as young girls too. It made even more sense now why Joanna was determined to take the deviant path to get revenge.

"I had no idea. You're right that must have been hard, Joanna." Krista said in a quiet voice, trying to buy some time with her empathy.

If she could just get Joanna to put down the pistol, she'd be able to have the upper hand. Her heart was pounding as Joanna was within inches from her face.

"You're damn right it was hard! I helped save her life! All she wanted was for her father to give a shit, but he ignored her! But he'd still take your father's calls wouldn't' he? Her father wouldn't visit her for weeks, but when he did, I remember him answering calls from William! It was heartbreaking for me to stand by and watch her wither away, knowing she was going to jail." Joanna continued on, revealing the true reason she'd approached Krista's father, pretending to care, but manipulating.

The more the woman talked, the more Krista cringed inside. Joanna was a mentally ill woman with a traumatic background. She was a dangerous person who finagled her way into her father's life to turn it upside down. Krista was more determined than ever to get away, and make sure that Joanna would never be able to hurt anyone else again. She'd sought out her revenge and involved innocent people, especially William. All he wanted was to love again. Joanna had ruined that for him.

"I can't change what happened, Joanna. Neither can you. But you did help her live." Krista said softly, using every ounce of compassion she could muster for this woman. At least she'd managed to avoid giving her access to her phone which might end any chance that Krista would have to get out of here. All Joanna had to do was send a text as though she were Krista and then any search that might be underway would be delayed, if not cancelled. She only hoped that she had her location sharing on her phone. She had talked to Chad about it weeks ago, but couldn't remember if she'd actually switched it 'on.'

"I did help her live. But now, she's stuck in prison. Because of you!" Joanna inched closer to her and glanced down at Krista's hands that were superficially zip-tied. Krista's heart began to pound as she came closer, hoping that she wouldn't notice the slack in the tightness of the ties, and preparing to grab the pliers out of her sweatshirt pocket. She didn't want to hurt Joanna, but she wouldn't hesitate to if it was necessary. If she didn't make it out of here, it was unlikely that Mara would be found. "So now, I need you to give me your password and your prints, so that I can carry on with our plan."

"Who else is involved with *your* plan?" Krista was stalling, but she was also livid and never had a filter, especially when she was angry.

"It doesn't concern you, bitch! I let you see Mara, now you need to keep your end of the bargain!" Joanna's face took on an evil leer that made Krista want to knock her out cold right then and there. But she needed to wait. Joanna still had the gun in her hand and she'd risk being shot at close range. "Now, give me the passcode and put your thumb on it!" Joanna held out her phone, her voice was filled with anger and Krista knew that negotiation wasn't an option for her at this point.

"What are you going to do with it?" Krista decided to try and keep her talking as long as she could, preparing to reach into her pocket and grab the pliers.

"Exactly what you think I'm going to do, 'princess.' I'm going to let your family know you're fine and that you just decided to take Mara on vacation to get away." The anger and desire for revenge in her voice was clear as she raised the gun to Krista's head. "You have to the count of three, before I'll have to find a new mother for Mara." Joanna laughed at her own words and looked down at the gun to make sure the safety was off.

It was that moment that Krista had waited for; that split-second that Joanna had lowered the gun away from her head. It felt as though everything was moving in slow motion, as she reached into her pocket, grabbed the pliers and thrust them toward Joanna's ribcage. She cringed in horror as she could feel the metal of the pliers penetrate the skin and stop at rock-hard bone. Tears sprung to her eyes in horror as she watched Joanna's blue shirt turn crimson from blood that was pouring out.

Joanna's scowling face quickly changed to grimacing in pain, as she dropped the pistol to the floor to grasp at her ribcage. She fell to her knees and screamed so loud that the neighbor's miles away could have heard her. David came running down the stairs, "Hey, what's going - -?" He stopped in mid-sentence as he saw Joanna lying on the floor. "JOANNA!" He froze as he saw Krista standing near her, the bloody pliers dropped next to her feet.

Krista's hands were shaking as she managed to grab her phone and the pistol. 'Wow, this is really heavy', she thought to herself. Such a strange thought to have after having stabbed someone, then recognized that she was in shock as well. Krista felt as though she was watching someone else as she pointed the gun directly at David while attempting to put her password into her phone. But in the midst of the chaos, she kept typing in the wrong one. Then the silence ended and she realized this was real. She needed to act, get out, put the passcode into her phone and get help!

"WHAT DID YOU DO?" David yelled at her as he took off his sweatshirt and wrapped it around Joanna's ribcage to try and stop the bleeding. Her emotions were going in different directions as she realized what she'd done, but her instinct was to find her daughter. Krista wasn't trusting him or anyone else now, this was about survival. She managed to put in the right code finally. The 911 dispatcher answered and Krista began talking as fast as she could. "I need help! My name is Krista Burton, my daughter's name is Mara! We were kidnapped last night! Their names are Joanna Larsen and David Ackwell!"

There was no response from the dispatcher and as Krista looked down at the phone, it had been disconnected! Shit! She hit send again and it connected, but then lost service again. Apparently, her captors weren't aware of this as they were trying to get her password all this time! She needed to get to Mara as well as get cell service somewhere on this godforsaken island! She desperately tried Chad's number, hoping that it would go through, but that call wouldn't connect! She needed to get to Mara and leave!

"Where is my daughter?" Krista came closer to him, pointing the gun at his head and trying not to look at Joanna. She needed to focus on finding Mara. She'd never meant to cause Joanna harm, but there had been no choice; she had to keep reminding herself. Finding Mara and bringing to safety was her focus now. Joanna had made her bed, and she was suffering the consequences.

"Mara is upstairs in the only bedroom on the first floor. You can't miss it when you get to the top of the stairs! Please hurry!" He was focused on Joanna's wound, as she continued to writhe on the floor in pain .Krista didn't trust any of them and wasn't about to be tackled at the top of the stairs.

"I've tried calling 911 for help, but thanks to your shitty cell service here it won't stay connected! Maybe you should've thought of that before you decided to pick the location!" Krista yelled as she ran up the creaking stairs backwards with the gun still aimed toward David. He got up from tending to Joanna with a malicious look on his face as if he were going to try to come after her.

"You try and stop me and you'll ruin any chance for her to get medical help." Krista warned him as she made it up to the top and shut the rickety door behind her. Luckily it had a latch lock from the outside, so David would have to work hard to get it open. She managed the old-fashioned latch door and glanced around at the kitchen area. Clearly, no one had ever updated this house! The kitchen had one large sink that was probably dated back to the 1940s, along with an old cook stove that was wood burning. The cabinets were painted white although it was clear that neglect along with time had settled in and now appeared a dingy tan color, with simple U-shaped metal handles that were from the same era as the single large porcelain sink that had red-yellow rust spots from decades of use.

It was a dismal existence that maybe had once been somewhat clean, but years of neglect had taken its toll. It was obvious why Joanna had turned out to be mentally unstable; her father clearly was unhinged as well! It made her only more intent on finding Mara as she called out her name, "Mara! It's mommy! Where are you?" She could hear muffled screams from the next room over and quickly ran to the nearby bedroom to find her daughter who had some kind of harness on her like an animal around her body. Mara was trying to scream but her small mouth had a rag stuffed in it and Krista immediately yanked it out and hugged her.

"Mommy, mommy, I don't like it here!" Mara was crying as Krista undid the makeshift harness holding her captive, then hugged her tightly to her, then looked at the service bars on her phone and attempted another call, this time to Chad. "Ssshhh, it's okay, Mara! I'm calling daddy, I'm going to get us out of here!" Krista crossed her fingers as the phone was actually ringing and prayed that her husband would answer. It rang three times and Krista was ready to hang up when Chad's voice was yelling her name. "Kris! Is that you? Talk to me!"

"Chad, it's me! I'm here with Mara! We're okay!" Krista began to cry in relief that she'd been able to get through. "We're on Block Island at some house that belongs to someone named Eldridge. It's Joanna's father's home!" She wasn't even sure he could hear what she was saying.

"You're okay? Are you safe? We're on our way to get to you, Kris!" Chad was firing questions at her.

Krista had him on speaker phone as she grabbed Mara's hand, and went out the front door. The wind was ice-cold and both she and Mara were shivering, still wearing pajama bottoms and light sweatshirts. "Mommy, I'm cold!" Mara hugged her arms around her. Krista struggled with the phone as she put an arm around Mara to try and keep her warm. "I know, sweetie, but we need to get out of here."

"Can you hear me?" Chad was yelling now.

"I can hear you! Mara and I just got outside. I have no idea where we are though and it's getting dark, it's freezing out! I'm going to go in and find us some coats. Call 911 and tell them that someone's been hurt, she needs an ambulance!" Krista was yelling into the phone and had no idea how much Chad could hear.

"You're hurt? You need an ambulance? Hang on Kris! We're coming! I know where you are!" Chad was shouting into the phone.

"We are okay! Hurry!" Krista handed the phone to Mara. "Honey, talk to daddy, I'm going to go in and find us something warm to wear. Stay right here until I get back, okay?" Krista hated to leave her for even a moment, but the wind was brutal and the sun that might have warmed them was beyond the horizon, as dusk began to take over.

Mara was scared but managed to nod okay as Krista handed her the phone and ran back into the house to find some jackets. She opened a closet next to the front door only to find another gun, a rifle this time! 'What the hell? This guy doesn't have any jackets, but guns for days!' Krista thought to herself. 'Why not? Just in case we need it.' She decided to hang onto the pistol that she'd taken from Joanna and went to the living area, finding another closet that had a couple of men's camouflage hunting jackets, all of which wouldn't even begin to fit either one of them, but it was better than nothing.

Grabbing two of them, she turned around to find a figure blocking her way. It was dark in the house, but Krista could tell that it was a woman; "Going somewhere, princess?" The voice could only belong to one person. It couldn't be, but as the figure came closer, she recognized her immediately. It was Amanda Ahearn, wielding a silver revolver pointed directly at her.

William

He'd been on the phone with Stanley who was concerned and had promised to help them out with transportation but he also had more news that made him realize how dire the situation was now. He'd just found out that Amanda had escaped from prison a few hours ago. "I don't have to guess where she's headed, Stan."

"They're looking for her, Bill. But she's got a few hours ahead of them. She's angry and good at disguises. It wouldn't surprise me if she was already headed toward Block Island now. She doesn't have any access to my accounts, but she has connections. Head down to the dock at Point Judith and I'll have a boat waiting to take you over there. Go right now!" Stanley insisted. "I'll be on my way there as soon as I can."

"What? How the hell did she escape? I know Chad and Krista have both talked to the police about concerns about her!" William was furious now. He remembered how many times Krista had called the police and Chad had just talked to that Detective Masterson. Just how did this woman escape from prison? Likely with some help from the outside!

"I don't know, Bill. Just get to Point Judith as soon as you can. I'm going to get a flight in as soon as possible. I'll meet you there." Stanley told him. "Call the Shoreham Police out on Block Island and give them the name of the house! They'll know where to go even if you don't have an exact address!"

"Thanks, Stan, I appreciate it." William hung up, just as Chad's phone began to ring. "Chad! Your phone is ringing, hurry up!" He yelled to his son-in-law who was scrambling to get it from the bathroom. Sadie was still sitting and waiting for him. Her sudden coquettish, flirty routine was getting on his nerves and he knew something wasn't right. "Chad, I should go with you two!" Chad ignored her, focusing on the phone now.

"It's Kris!" Chad grabbed the phone, almost hitting ignore as he fumbled to answer. William ran to his side. "Kris! Are you there?"

"Chad, it's me! I'm here with Mara! We're okay!" He was shaking as he heard her voice. He could tell she was crying. "We're on Block Island at some house that belongs to someone named Eldridge. It's Joanna's father's home!" It was what Sadie had told them. Sadie nodded as she stood by, overhearing the conversation.

"You're okay? Are you safe? We're on our way to get to you, Kris!" Chad assured her while he motioned for William to get something to write with.

"Chad, put her on speaker phone!" William was frantic to hear his daughter's voice. Chad hit speaker phone, it was somewhat easier to hear but her voice kept breaking up.

"I can hear you! Mara and I just got outside. I have no idea where we are though and it's getting dark, it's freezing out! I'm going to go in and find us some coats. Call 911 and tell them that someone's been hurt, she needs an ambulance!" Krista's voice continued to fade in and out. There was suddenly a lot of background noise. "It sounds like wind!" William told him. "They're outside, I can still hear Kris talking and I hear Mara." Chad was starting to panic when he heard 'hurt, needs an ambulance', just hoping that it wasn't Kris or Mara.

"You're hurt? You need an ambulance? Hang on Kris! We're coming! I know where you are!" Chad tried to assure her, as William pointed to his phone. "I'm going to call the Shoreham police and hopefully they can get there as soon as possible

"Mara and I are okay, but hurry!" Krista's voice was difficult to hear with the sound of the wind. He grabbed his jacket and keys as he continued to listen. "Kris? Are you there?" Sadie was following them out the door and jumped into the back seat as soon as the door unlocked. William was wondering what the hell was going on, but Chad was focused on the phone call and nodded. "She could be helpful and insisted on coming," He whispered to William. Sadie was quiet as the phone call continued and buckled her seatbelt.

"Daddy, daddy! I can hear you!" It was Mara's voice!

"Hi, sweetheart, daddy's here! Where's mommy?" Chad wished he could see what was going on. William had just come in from the other room. "I just got off the phone with the police." Chad was frantically pointing at the phone. "It's Mara! I don't know where Kris went!" He whispered.

"Mara, honey, it's grandpa! Where is mommy?" William tried to sound calm, but now he was desperate.

"She's inside….it's cold grandpa! She went to get us coats. I wanna come home!" Mara was crying into the phone and it broke his heart. William motioned to Chad to head to the car and continued to talk to her as Chad got behind the wheel and headed out to Point Judith.

"Are you outside the house? Can you see her?" William kept talking to her. The phone connected to blue tooth in the car. Chad had an idea and couldn't believe he didn't think of it a few minutes ago! She could be on the camera as long as there was a cell signal!

"Bill, see if you can get her to touch the video icon on the phone while she's talking, that way we can see her!" It just occurred to him that if Mara could hit the camera button on the phone, they'd be able to face time. William wasn't up to speed on the whole explanation but when he told Mara to touch the video on the phone, she seemed to understand. "Ok, grandpa. I see it!"

"Bill, now you need to touch the same icon. It looks like a video camera, right there at the top of the screen." Chad told him. 'That's what that's for', William thought as he touched it and suddenly he could see his face in the corner of the phone and Mara on full screen. She was barely visible in the dark, but William could make out her small face with her eyes wide with fear as she was staring back at him. Her blond hair was whipping around her face and he could tell she was shivering in her thin long-sleeved shirt.

"Mara, can you see me?" William waved at her on the phone, hoping to keep her distracted until Krista came back.

"I can see you grandpa! Are you coming to get me and mommy?" Mara pleaded. It was awful seeing his granddaughter frightened, freezing in the cold wind while Krista wasn't there with her! "Chad, please get us there quickly!" If he could arrange to fly there, he would pay any amount of money to be there sooner! But that was impossible! Or was it? He had an idea, but it would mean he'd have to get off FaceTime with Mara for a few minutes in order to make it happen.

"She should go back in the house and get warm," Sadie finally spoke after a few minutes.

"I don't think so, Sadie. There's a reason she shouldn't be going back in there. Kris is there, she didn't want to keep inside." Chad replied from the driver's seat. William could tell that he wasn't happy that Sadie had tagged along, but wasn't sure why. After all, she'd been helpful so far. Maybe she could have some psychic insight into what was going on inside the house.

"I was just thinking that she's so cold. She's shivering." Sadie told him, but it wasn't enough to convince William. He glanced around at Sadie who was staring blankly out the window, as if she weren't even paying attention. Chad was right. Something was definitely wrong with Sadie, but his focus was on Mara right now. They'd have to deal with her later. One thing he was certain about is that Mara wasn't going back into that house when they didn't know what was going on.

"We're on our way, sweetheart! I'm going to have to turn the camera off for a few minutes, so I can talk on my phone, but you can still talk to your daddy. He's driving us to get to you right now!" William assured her. He turned to Chad, "I'm going to call Stan. Maybe he's got access to a helicopter, something faster than the boat; it's still going to take at least an hour from now!"

"Great idea, Bill! Call him!" Chad thanked his lucky stars that they knew someone that had enough clout and the funds to t get them a flight over to Block Island! William contacted Stanley about the situation. Stanley was working on chartering a helicopter from somewhere near Point Judith. "Thanks, Stan. I feel helpless just waiting to get there." Stanley knew that there was not time to waste; Amanda was out now and he knew exactly where she would go, if she wasn't there already. "I'll do my best and call you back in a few minutes!" Stan advised.

"Is mommy back with you yet, Mara?" Chad couldn't see what was happening, but he felt like Krista should've been back in the few minutes that he'd been talking to her. Sadie had been quiet in the back seat during this discussion, so William decided to ask for her input. When he turned to talk to her, she was still staring out the window with a blank look on her face. "Sadie? You okay?" William was starting to wonder about her, as Chad had before they left. Her outgoing, friendly disposition was replaced by a quiet careless attitude that was disturbing. Sadie immediately turned to William with a slight grin on her face that gave him chills. Her eyes were no longer friendly and resembled someone he'd seen in a horror movie. "Mara will be fine. She just needs to go in and get warm. Krista is just getting clothing for them." She repeated what she'd said before about going into the house, but William disagreed.

"Sadie, that doesn't sound safe at all! Can you try and figure out what's going on with Krista? Why hasn't she come out yet?" William asked. Sadie was proving to be almost detrimental at this point. It was as if she were a different person.

"Bill, Krista is fine. I can see her rummaging around finding something for them to wear now." Sadie shut her eyes for a moment, but it looked as though she were making it up, unlike her previous prediction at Chad's home. And she'd called him 'Bill.' Only people closest to him called him Bill. She'd referred to him as William earlier, another red flag.

William nudged Chad in the arm as he was driving and whispered, "Something isn't right with her at all! It's almost as if she's trying to put Mara in harm's way! What do we do?"

Chad nodded in agreement. "Stop asking her questions. Something *is* going on with her, but we don't have time for this! I'm focusing on Mara. Let's just get through this and keep Mara calm!" William just nodded.

"Nnnooo, daddy. She's not. I'm cold, daddy!" Mara was crying as William picked the phone back up while waiting for Stanley to call back. The camera was still on and he could see the tears streaming down her face. The wind blowing was making it difficult to hear her.

"Mara, your daddy and I are trying to get there faster, but you need to get out of the wind. Go to the side of the house where you don't feel the wind blowing so hard, okay? Tell me when you're there." William's fingernails were digging into his palms with anxiety. And where the hell was Krista? He only hoped that Amanda hadn't made it over to the island, but he wouldn't let himself think about that scenario. It was too much.

Mara went to the other side of the house that prevented some of the wind blowing directly on her, but she was still shivering. But where was Krista? "Mommy said she'd be back in a minute," Mara told William. But that was almost 15 minutes ago, according to the phone. He knew something must have happened. Krista wouldn't have left Mara outside unless she intended to come back out with warm clothing. Someone had stopped her!

Stanley called back to tell him that the helicopter was set to pick them up at Point Judith in about 20 minutes. "Great! Thank you so much! We'll be there shortly!" William assured him, hoping that there was no traffic to contend with. It was about 5:00 now and they were passed the red lights on Route 4 through North Kingstown. They still might have some traffic, but usually it was going in the opposite direction.

William focused on Mara again after getting off his own phone with Stanley. "Mara, tell me what's going on now." He could hear the wind blowing and see a faint image of her in the camera, but the daylight was fading to dusk.

"There are cccarrrs cccoming, I see some people getting out of the ccarrs. They look scary and they hhhave guns." Mara's teeth were chattering in the cold. For a moment, William was beside himself. What was going on?

"Bill, you called the police! That's probably what's going on!" Chad reminded him.

" That's right! The police must be there!" William took a deep breath, trying to get a grip. "Mara, turn the phone around so that I can see who's there." Mara turned the phone so that the camera pointed toward the persons that had just gotten out of the car. William could tell that they were police. "Mara, I want you to let them know that you're there, and stay on the phone with me, okay?"

"Okkayyyy." Mara sounded frightened. "Are you sure they're not gggonna hurt me or mmmommy , grandpa?" She was still hesitant.

"I'm on the phone with you. Point the phone toward them when you're going toward them, then I'll talk to them." William was nervous as he watched her point of view walking toward the cars. There were no flashing lights or sirens and he was glad that they'd listened about the situation. Any indication that they were at the residence would put Krista and Mara at risk. One of the officers saw Mara and came toward her and Mara stopped. "Grandpa, he's coming! Wwwwhat should I do?"

"It's okay, honey. He's there to help you. Just stay there, let him come to you. Point the phone back toward them." William could tell he was wearing SWAT gear as he neared Mara and called out to her. "Hi, there. I'm Officer Sloan. Are you Mara?" The man asked her as he bent down to her level.

"Mara, it's going to be okay. Give him the phone so he can talk to me." William reassured her. Mara was shaking with fear and cold as she did as her grandpa instructed

Krista

Krista had just been grabbing some camouflage hunting jackets out of the closet and was ready to run out the door to meet Mara when she heard the voice that had haunted her for the past 7 years, "Going somewhere, princess?" There was enough light coming through despite it becoming dusk to make out her shadow standing between her and the front door. There was no ignoring the revolver that was pointed straight at her as she gasped and dropped the coats in surprise to see her standing there. Instinctively, she reached into her sweatshirt pocket to make sure the pistol hadn't fallen out. It was there, she just hoped she wouldn't have to use it.

Krista pretended that Amanda's sudden appearance hadn't thrown her off her mission to get out of here. She knew that this woman fed off of entitlement and enjoyed creating fear, surprise and harboring hate because somehow the world didn't bend to her needs as she would want them to. She was the epitome of evil, just like her sister had been that had been invading her life from the grave through her daughter for god knows how long! She had no idea how this woman had finagled her way out of prison where it was documented just days ago, but she had a pretty good idea that Joanna and her cohorts had something to do with it.

"Hello, Amanda. Must be nice to be out and about." Krista did her best to sound casual, keep her voice from shaking, because her best weapon against her right now was to remain calm, unruffled and in control of her anxiety.

Amanda's face showed her confusion for a moment and Krista knew that she was on the right track to beating her at her own game; at least long enough to get the upper hand and disarm her, which didn't look too difficult. Amanda was waif-thin after years in prison. Her face showed wrinkles that hadn't been there before, since she couldn't get her botox or go get her daily facials. Her light brown hair looked mousy without any highlights, and there were multiple tattoos visible on her wrists and even on her fingers that hadn't been there before. She looked like a low-end stripper that was looking for her next heroin fix.

"My sister is dead because of you! I've spent the past 7 years in prison because of you and now you get to pay for it, princess!" Amanda had recovered from the brief shock of Krista not running away screaming and reverted back to her scare tactics as she motioned the hand holding the revolver that was still pointed at Krista.

Her words were infuriating to Krista. She had to call her bluff and continue the nonchalant attitude for now and could tell it had a conflictual effect on Amanda because this time, she wasn't able to have Krista running scared. Krista did her best to tamp down her anxiety and remember her daughter that was outside, counting on her. If she didn't make it out, what would happen to Mara? She didn't even want to think about it.

"Your sister is dead because she didn't appreciate what she had! You could have stayed out of it, but you didn't. And as far as being in prison, Amanda, you've been imprisoned your entire life. The only difference is the location. Your recent stay hasn't been as luxurious." Krista surprised even herself at how unruffled she'd become in this situation. She suddenly felt more at peace than ever, and noticed that a small orb of light was near her. 'This is my mother with me right now,' she believed it to be true. Her presence was felt, and it strengthened her resolve to get away from this woman that deserved to pay consequences.

Krista watched Amanda's actions carefully as she put one hand casually into her sweatshirt pocket, feeling the steel of the pistol in her hand to remind her that at least she was armed now. Amanda scowled and tightened her grip on the gun.

"I'd watch what you say, princess. As you can see, I have the upper hand here." She raised the revolver in her hand. "Especially after what you just did to Joanna." Krista was beginning to realize that she'd actually have to use the gun in her pocket and was feeling panic setting in. She'd need to distract Amanda though, get her to drop her gun for even a split second.

"I can see that, I'm not blind." Krista retorted. She was tired of this game with Amanda and with whatever Jane tried to accomplish from the grave with Mara. "Joanna took her own risks when she decided to play along with your kidnapping scheme, Amanda. I'd say that you might as well have stabbed her yourself. By the way, how *is* Joanna doing? Last I saw, she was bleeding pretty badly. Did you bother to call someone to help her or are you just gonna let her bleed to death downstairs?" Krista reminded her. She needed to figure this out soon, Mara was still outside; scared and freezing!

Krista was thankful as David Ackwell became the distraction by running up the stairs yelling for Amanda. He didn't even flinch as he made his way to Amanda, standing directly in the line of fire. He was so frazzled he didn't seem to notice the gun that had been aimed at Krista and now at him. "David! What the hell is going on? Geez, I could've shot you!" Amanda hissed at him, as she tried to push him to the side with one hand, while continuing to hold the gun in the other.

"We need to call someone! I can't stop the bleeding!!" David was freaking out on her and Amanda was getting annoyed. "Michelle left so she can't help me!"

"David, Joanna is a nurse! Surely she can guide you through what you need to do to stop the bleeding, at least until I can take care of this one here." She nodded toward Krista, moving her head slightly in order to keep her in sight. Krista was starting to wonder if there was any way to distract this woman who had made it her mission to kill her no matter who else had to suffer.

David was shaking his head, "That's kind of hard for her to do, when she's unconscious! She just passed out, probably from blood loss! We need to do something!" He moved over the living room, grabbing a throw blanket from the couch and going toward the basement

"What would you like me to do? Call an ambulance so that we can all be arrested? As you can see, the princess has managed to escape, no thanks to the two of you! And in case you haven't forgotten, I'm an escaped convict! Amanda scoffed. She really was a heartless sociopath!

Krista was increasingly concerned about Mara, tired of biding her time and ready to pull out the gun the next time Amanda looked away for even a second, when she noticed a light that was moving toward the door from the window. Luckily, Amanda and David were still arguing about Joanna when she could see that it was not one, but several police officers that were dressed in full protective gear. Krista tried to maintain a stoic facial expression, hope was renewed and she hoped they could get her out of here. The officer noticed that Krista had seen him and put a finger to his mouth telling her to not alert them to the situation, then motioned to her to move away. She began to slide to the right toward the living area slowly, as David continued to argue with Amanda. Amanda was so angry with David, she looked as though she were going to point the gun at him.

"Don't be stupid now, David! We're almost there! I just need to take care of the princess Krista here and we'll be done!" She spun around to aim at Krista who was frozen in place, instinctively closing her eyes. There was nowhere to go now. She only hoped that the police would find Mara and bring her back to her father. "I'm afraid your time is up, Krista. Now you'll be dealing with my sister, in the grave!"

Krista's survival instinct kicked in as she quickly took cover however inadequate. She ducked behind the arm of the loveseat in the living room, making herself as small as possible but knowing that if the officers didn't intervene soon, she'd have a bullet through her head. She heard the click of the round being chambered just as the door burst open, almost knocking Amanda down in the process. Four officers dressed in SWAT gear, complete with bullet-proof vests on the outside, helmets and AR-15 rifles took over. Amanda managed to squeeze out a round toward one of the officers which luckily hit his bullet-proof vest. Another officer immediately fired at Amanda, which seemed to just graze her lower left calf. He clearly knew how to aim to minimize any lasting damage. Yet, it served the purpose, as Amanda screamed and fell to the floor, dropping the gun that was intended to end Krista's life. Krista felt as though she'd been holding her breath for an hour and finally was able to breathe again as relief set in.

"Amanda Ahearn, you're under arrest for attempted murder on a police officer as well as escaping from a prison facility." The officer handcuffed Amanda, as she was taken out to a waiting ambulance, still screaming and yelling at the officers.

Krista was hovering nearby, trying to keep calm behind the arm of the living room couch, as one of the other officers found her. "I'm Krista Burton, my daughter Mara is outside and needs help! Please go find her!" Krista pleaded.

"Mrs. Burton, Mara is fine. We found her outside as we arrived and she's comfortable in one of our cars. Can you tell us how many other people are in the house?" There were other officers arriving now and doing a sweep of the entire residence. "There's at least two other people! Joanna Larsen is in the basement and I'm not sure where David Ackwell went. There might be at least one other person here, Michelle, but I overheard David saying that she'd left." Krista informed him as he helped her outside. She could see Mara waving to her in one of the police cars and ran to her. The other officers and two of the EMT staff ran down the stairs to check on Joanna.

"Mommy!" Mara threw her warming blanket off as Krista reached her to hug her.

"Mara, sweetheart, are you okay?" Krista looked her over, but there wasn't a scratch on her, aside from being very cold. She was still shivering and Krista retrieved the blanket that had been wrapped around her as they were approached by EMT staff to check them over. Krista's nose was beginning to show signs of bruising from Joanna's assault on her earlier and Mara was still very cold, but they were lucky.

"We're gonna be okay, sweetheart. I'm so sorry you had to wait for me in the cold." Krista hugged Mara to her, trying to warm her up as she saw David Ackwell in hand cuffs being led out by police. He was sobbing like a baby as he was put in the police car. Krista couldn't help but feel sorry for him as he glanced toward her and Mara. He'd been the one to help Mara and insist on helping Joanna. He smiled at them just then and said something that Krista couldn't hear, but looked apologetic for his actions. David disappeared into the car and Krista wondered if he'd regretted getting involved with Amanda, Joanna and Michelle. He'd spent so much time building his fortune only to throw it away. She realized Chad and her father must be sick with worry and remembered her phone that Mara had with her. Immediately following was Joanna on a stretcher.

Krista tried not to feel guilty for causing her injury, but she couldn't help but look at her pale face that appeared lifeless as she was lifted into the ambulance. She'd overheard that there was a life flight helicopter that was meeting the ambulance due to the severity of Joanna's injuries, but she needed to focus on Mara right now. After all, she was the one that was kidnapped and being held against her will and forced herself to look away.

"Mara, do you still have my phone with you? We need to call daddy and grandpa." Krista looked over at her daughter as Mara held the phone out to her. "Daddy and grandpa were here with me the whole time!" She smiled as Krista found herself looking at her husband's face. "Kris! Thank god!" Chad was crying with relief as he passed the phone over to her father who also had tears in his eyes. "We're on our way to you two. Sit tight!" There was a loud noise in the background and it was difficult for Krista to hear anything now. "What is that noise?" Krista was yelling into the phone.

"We're getting on a helicopter!" Chad was yelling back now. "Courtesy of Stanley Ahearn! We'll be there in about 15 minutes according to the pilot. I have to go, but I love you two and see you soon!" Chad's face disappeared and the call was dropped.

"Daddy and grandpa will be here soon, Mara!" Krista had never felt so relieved in her life. She was suddenly exhausted and felt faint. Officer Sloan noticed Krista swaying as she stood and grabbed her arm just in time as she was ready to fall to the ground. "Let's get you checked out by the medics just to be sure, Ms. Burton." Krista began to protest, but the ground beneath her felt as though it was spinning and she was dizzy. "Mommy!" Mara grabbed her hand as Officer Sloan made sure she could walk, took Mara's hand and brought her over to the EMT staff to get checked out when Krista blacked out.

Chad

They'd made it to the helicopter that had landed near Galilee near Judith Point in an empty beach parking lot. Sadie followed them, exhibiting the same strange behavior including saying that 'her sister needed to be free.' When Chad asked her what she was talking about, she just looked at him with a blank expression. "Oh, nothing. I was just thinking about something else." While Chad and William were ecstatic that Kris and Mara were safe, Sadie was sitting in the back looking out the window with a cryptic look on her face, as if she were somewhere else.

"I don't think she should go with us, Bill." Chad was skeptical and wished that she'd never come along. Her positive energy and helpful abilities that were spot on about where Krista and Mara were located had turned into a babysitting expedition and Chad was beginning to wonder if she was affected by the same spirit that had plagued Mara.

William nodded, "I know, she's acting really weird. But what are we supposed to do, leave her here? She doesn't have a way back to her car which is at your house." Chad thought about paying for a Rideshare to take her back to her car, but then realized that wasn't a good plan. What if she decided to hang out at *his* house instead of going home? No, they were going to have to bring her. Chad wasn't comfortable with this woman being around his home at this point. At least if she came with them, they could keep an eye on her.

They climbed into the helicopter and were handed headphones that allowed the pilot who introduced himself as Jack Sheffield to talk to them as well as providing noise reduction. The sound of the propellers was deafening and all three of them had been putting their hands over their ears, so the headphones were a welcome reprieve. Jack Sheffield had been given instructions to keep them updated about Krista and Mara. "Kris and Mara sounded okay, they'll be fine." William assured Chad. As they took off, Chad closed his eyes and prayed that they'd get there safely. He never liked flying and the helicopter ride was bumpy and making him nervous.

"We'll be there shortly, everyone! The weather is clear sailing to Block Island." Jack announced through the headphones.

"Thank god." Chad said out loud, then realized that the Jack could hear him as well. He gave him a nod. "Sorry, just not a good flier, no offense."

Jack just laughed, "No worries, Mr. Burton. I understand. But just to put your mind at ease, I've done this trip at least 20 times for Mr. Ahearn so I know my way." He joked which made Chad feel better. "Do you know anything about a family named 'Eldridge' on Block Island?" Chad asked Jack. He found himself yelling in the headphones.

"No need to shout, Mr. Burton. Remember, I can hear you through the mouthpiece," Jack reminded him. "But, yes, I've met Jim Eldridge before. He keeps to himself, especially after his wife died several years ago. I heard he works on the mainland at a school during the year as a janitor. Then comes back to his house on the island for the summer months. He keeps to himself." Jack answered his question. "Especially since his daughter moved away."

"Oh, that's too bad. Does she still live in Rhode Island?" Chad kept talking, mostly because he needed to be distracted from his growing anxiety of being on the helicopter.

"I think so. Joanna got married and had a son many years ago. He must be an adult now. His name was Kyle, or maybe it was Kaden something like that." Jack said. William's eyes were like saucers as he said the words. "You said her name was 'Joanna'?" He jumped into the conversation. "Do you know anything about her?"

"I never met her myself. I went to school on the mainland, but I heard through others that she was quite the wild one in high school. She used to hang around the main beach which is now Ballards in the summer and party with the tourists. She kind of had a reputation." Jack left it at that.

"Really? Interesting." William tried to stay calm, but knew without a doubt that he was talking about *his* Joanna. He didn't want to hear any more about her, so he deliberately didn't make any other comments in hopes that it would shut down the topic.

But then Jack continued on. "Come to think of it, there was one incident the summer I came here for a few days when I was in college. She was good friends with some hotshot director's kid that was only here for a few weeks. There was some guy that went to a party with her, then disappeared. No one knew what happened to him, but he was found washed up on the shore of the beach a few day later. The sheriff here kept it quiet, and there was some kind of 'investigation' but nothing ever came of it. I wonder what ever happened to her." Jack's voice drifted off as William and Chad looked at each other, knowing that they were thinking the same thing. Joanna and Amanda were friends. It was all starting to make sense now. Chad didn't say anything, but he didn't need to.

*   *   *

Sadie had been quiet so far, but as the bluffs of Block Island were visible, she seemed excited. "I'm finally back," Her eerie statement was in a low voice but they could all hear her because she was speaking directly into the mouthpiece connected to the headphones.

"Did you vacation here in the past?" Jack asked casually. "Sounds like you've been here before."

"I have. A long time ago." Sadie told him, then glanced over at Chad. "It was just a day visit to the beach, but I really liked it." Chad wasn't fooled. She'd been here, not just on a visit. He watched her as she gazed down at the scenery as if she was remembering an old friend. Sadie had never once mentioned the island despite all the conversations that they'd had between Krista, William and himself. He could tell that this wasn't Sadie. He nudged William and moved his head from the mouthpiece of the headset, "Something is wrong. Don't talk to her anymore," whispering so that Sadie couldn't possibly overhear him. William nodded his agreement. Jack seemed to sense the tension and stopped talking to Sadie. "We're about to land soon, guys. We'll be at the Ahearn estate in about 5 minutes."

"How far is that from where Jim Eldridge lives?" Chad asked. He knew that was where Krista and Mara had been.

"Probably about a 15 minute walk. Everything's close on Block Island." Jack told them. "I was told to bring you to Mr. Ahearn's house. Do you want to go there instead?"

Chad was about to say no, but he wanted to make sure that Kris and Mara had been brought to Stanley's house before they were dropped off. "Do you mind checking to see if there's any people still there?" The perk of having a helicopter was to be able to hover and see before landing. Chad figured it was worth the trip considering he'd made it this far!

"Of course, Mr. Burton. We'll be there in a few minutes." Jack agreed and true to his word they were there. As Chad looked down he could see an ambulance with lights flashing and a group of police still there. "We need to check this out." Chad told William who agreed. Sadie didn't say a word as Jack began to bring the helicopter down to land. Chad wasn't sure what to do about Sadie, but he knew he would be keeping her far away from Krista and Mara. The scowl on her face as they began their descent scared him. "This is not where we're supposed to be! Why are we stopping here?" Sadie snapped at Jack, as if she hadn't heard the previous conversation.

"Ma'am, Mr. Burton has asked to stop here." Jack replied in a polite but sharp tone. Enough to keep her quiet. Sadie stopped talking, but sat back in the seat pouting like a spoiled child. Chad couldn't wait to unload this woman and send her back on the next ferry. Whatever help she'd given previously was forgotten and he wished he'd never answered the phone, let alone come to his home.

They landed in the parking lot a few minutes later and the emergency lights from police and ambulance were still flashing. "That's the Eldridge place," Jack motioned toward the commotion that hadn't wrapped up yet. Chad felt numb as he realized that Kris and Mara were still in the area. He and William took off their headphones and immediately took off to the scene that was less than a quarter of a mile away. Chad realized after they'd walked a few hundred feet that they'd left Sadie. "We should go back and get her!" Chad was yelling to William.

"Why? She's giving me the creeps!" William yelled back.

"We can't leave her here. What if something happens to her?" Chad knew he didn't want that responsibility weighing on him on top of everything else. He ran back to where Sadie who looked confused. "Oh, there you are! When are we going home?" She stared blankly at him.

"We'll take you home soon." Chad promised. Anything to get her moving. He wasn't even sure if she was talking about going back to Providence now. "We've gotta go, let's go!" He insisted and she finally followed him and William to the Eldridge house. As they got closer, he could see a life flight helicopter taking off and his first thought was Krista. "Oh, no! What if that's Kris and Mara?" He began running toward the house as fast as he could. He couldn't think about anything else. They could catch up as far as he was concerned.

Krista

The lights were blinding as she opened her eyes with what felt like 10 people staring back at her. "Krista, my name is Scott. I'm an EMT and you're in an ambulance here on Block Island. You passed out a few minutes ago. Can you tell me what your name is?" Krista felt groggy, but she thought the request was ridiculous, considering he'd already called her 'Krista.' It was a dead giveaway for someone that had amnesia.

"I'm Krista Burton. My husband is Chad Burton and my daughter is Mara Burton." Krista recited, giving the extra information just so he wouldn't ask more. Scott nodded in response. "Can you tell me why you're here?" He asked her and she wanted to roll her eyes, but managed to refrain from making a smart-ass comment which might delay this.

"I was kidnapped with my daughter." Krista responded immediately. She was trying not be frustrated with this whole process and knew why he was doing it but it was getting annoying. "Look, Scott. I'm fine, I probably just passed out because I've been through a lot in the past 24 hours. I just want to go meet my husband who's on his way." Krista insisted, as she sat up on the gurney inside the ambulance. Mara had been standing outside with Officer Sloan when she suddenly ran off and was yelling "Daddy!" Krista began sobbing with relief; her husband was here! "Chad! I'm over here!" She called to him through her tears.

Scott smiled. "I think he's arrived, Krista. You have your own personal alert system there!" Krista was able to stand up without getting dizzy.

"I'm think I'm fine. Thank you though. Am I cleared to go see my husband?" She tried to joke through her tears as she pulled one of the blankets that the ambulance had over her shoulders. Now that the sun had gone down, the temperature had dropped and she couldn't seem to get warm.

"Absolutely! Nothing better than a happy ending." Scott smiled as he helped Krista out of the ambulance. Chad was running toward her with Mara on piggyback. He was tearing up as he saw her, his face looked exhausted, dark bags under his eyes and wearing a pair of old worn out jeans and that stinky Patriots sweatshirt that she could never get him to take off long enough to wash and he never looked better to her than he did just now. With their daughter on his back, he ran to her and hugged her so hard she was breathless.

"Oh my god Kris! I was so worried when I saw the ambulance that I started running. Your dad is behind me. Along with Sadie." Chad was still trying to catch his breath as he finally set Mara back on the ground.

Krista was so relieved to see him that it took her a minute to realize what he'd just said. "Along with who? Sadie? You mean Sadie as in the psychic woman; Nadine's aunt?" Krista was confused now.

Chad launched into his explanation of how Sadie became involved. "She called me and asked how Mara was doing. She seemed as though she really cared about her. I told her what had happened and she came over immediately. She *was* helpful at first; she was able to see the Eldridge place and give us the location. But she started acting really strange when we were leaving to come here." Chad began to explain her behavior, just as Sadie came up behind him. "Hi, Chad, I've been looking for you!" She said in a pouty voice, not even acknowledging Krista who was standing in front of him. Krista had a sense that whatever effect 'Jamie' had on Mara, had moved on to Sadie. "Hi, Sadie, remember me?" Krista asked pointedly as she put her arm protectively around Chad's waist. A frown flickered over Sadie's face for a moment as if the sun had just slipped under the clouds ruining her day. "Of course, good to see you again, Krista!" Sadie managed to recover quickly, although it was clear that she was not happy to see her. Gone was the helpful Sadie from a day ago. Krista wondered just what had happened between the time she'd gotten to the house to help Chad and her father until now. Was Jamie's presence that strong that she was able to infiltrate someone like Sadie?

"Thank you for your assistance with finding us," Krista continued in an even tone, as she watched Sadie closely. The lack of empathy and warmth in her eyes was obvious especially when she looked down at Mara who was still hanging onto Chad's leg as if she were drowning. It had been a traumatic experience for her, yet Sadie was only focused on Chad. As if she were a different person. There something different about the way she looked; the eyes were different and she'd remembered Sadie being shorter, more petite. The rapport she'd had with Sadie a few days ago had disappeared.

"Anytime." Sadie replied casually as she continued to stand closer to Chad than necessary. Chad moved a few inches away on instinct and Krista pulled him closer toward her. William came up to Krista next to hug her and Mara. "Thank god you two are okay!" He was trying to keep from crying as she'd seen him do hundreds of times in her life with her father. He'd been by her side through the loss of her mother, her sister and then finding her mother again.

Krista was grateful when Chad announced that they would be heading to Stanley's house for the night and needed to leave as he continued to feel as though Sadie was crowding him. "Sadie, head back toward the helicopter. He's been instructed to take you back to the mainland." He pointed toward the helicopter that was probably costing Stanley thousands as it sat waiting.

When Sadie hesitated, Chad nodded at one of the officers that were standing nearby to get a statement from Krista. "Do you mind giving Ms. Mercotte a ride back to the helicopter down the road?" Krista immediately felt relieved as her husband began making sure that this woman that had once been helpful was now proving to be as scary as what she and Mara had just gone through. She didn't want to spend another minute with her. One of the other officers offered them a ride to the Ahearn estate and Krista gratefully accepted even though it was probably only a 5 minute walk.

"But I could go over with you, help out, make sure that there's no danger for Mara." Sadie tried to spark some interest that she might join them. Krista opened her mouth to object, but Chad beat her to it.

331

"No, thanks. You've been a great help Sadie, but I think we'll be fine now. Mr. Ahearn will be arriving in the morning and he was specific about who is allowed in his home. I'd rather not push his hospitality." He chose his words carefully, kind but firm. He nudged Krista to get in the car with the officer with Mara and William.

Sadie wasn't finished. "There's also the matter of my fee, Chad." Her voice took on a sharp tone, knowing that she wasn't being invited along. Krista stood outside the car, while Mara sat in the back and William took the front seat next to the officer. This woman definitely wasn't Sadie. She recalled how she'd had to pretty much insist on paying her the other day for her help with Mara! But when Chad handed over $250 in cash, Sadie had no more excuses.

She thanked him, although she was visibly irritated as she finally got into the police car with the officer that was going to drive her back to the helicopter. Chad watched as the car left with her finally and joined them in the other car. "Wow! That was very strange and can't say that I want her back at our house anytime soon, Kris!"

Krista agreed wholeheartedly. "Trust me, Chad. That wasn't her. Either whatever happened to 'Jamie' when she helped affected her or she's not Sadie. Honestly, I don't think she *is* Sadie." She was talking in a low voice in hopes that Mara couldn't hear her, but Mara seemed to have that selective 'child-hearing' where she paid attention when she wanted to.

"Mommy, that wasn't Sadie." Mara said in a small frightened voice as the car drove them the short distance to Stanley's home. It had been over 16 hours since she and Krista had been taken from their home and they were both emotionally and physically exhausted.

"She definitely was acting different, but she's gone now." Krista agreed with her daughter, but wanted to forget about her and made an excuse. "We're all pretty tired. Let's get something to eat and relax!" She changed the subject as the officer pulled up to the Ahearn estate which required a passcode to get through the massive iron gates that Stanley had added several years ago for security. Chad quickly gave him the code that he put into the keypad and the heavy gates opened slowly, creaking as the view of Stanley's mansion came into view.

Krista gasped as she saw it again, as if for the first time. Actually it was the first time she'd seen it in seven years and it was barely recognizable. Stanley had completely redone the exterior of the home as well as the landscaping. The huge bushy vegetation that had lined the entrance were gone and replaced by beautiful purple and pink hydrangeas that created a soft, almost romantic ambiance of the massive house that stood before them. The house itself had been given a facelift; the wrap-around porch had been updated by taking down the railings, freshly painted an eggshell color and grey Adirondack chairs set strategically in their place. The shingles on the house had been replaced by yellow siding that was more likely to stand up to the Block Island winters and more pleasing than the gray paint that had made it look dreary, almost mausoleum-like before.

"Wow! It doesn't look like the same house, Chad! It looks beautiful! I mean, it was amazing before, but now it looks....almost like I would want to live here, if that makes sense!" Krista laughed, still unable to take her eyes off the house. She looked over at Mara who looked as if she'd just arrived at Disney, her cerulean blue eyes were wide and she was smiling despite how exhausted she was from the past 16 hours. "What do you think, sweetheart? We'll be staying here tonight!" Krista scooped her up and hugged her.

"Jamie showed me this, but it looks much nicer now. The dark is gone." Mara commented in her unfiltered 6-year-old way. Yet, it reminded them of what a dark place Mara had been in before Sadie had helped her with Jamie. Krista tried to put Sadie out of her mind at least for tonight. Luckily she was on her way back to the mainland and they could rest easy. Krista couldn't think past tonight, let alone tomorrow. She just wanted this nightmare to end. She had to admit that she wasn't crazy about staying in this mansion that was reminiscent of her own trauma 7 years ago, as well as the grave of Jane Ahearn that was on the property near the cliff where she'd almost lost her life. But Sadie or whoever was pretending to be her, was probably well on her way back to the mainland. They were all hoping for a quiet drama-free night finally.

William

William tried to keep his mind on Krista and Mara and their safety after their escape from the kidnapping that involved Joanna. He was quiet with the exception of calling Stanley to let him know that they'd arrived at his home and everyone was safe. "Thank you so much for your help, Stan. I appreciate it." William told him.

"Not a problem, Bill. I'm glad Mara and Krista are safe. I'm sorry what happened with Joanna." Stanley seemed to have softened as he grew older. He was still the shrew of Hollywood, but William knew he'd gone above and beyond for them tonight.

'She's a monster, she kidnapped your daughter, your granddaughter. She deserves what happened,' he had to keep reminding himself. Yet it was all still a nightmare that he was living and couldn't begin to wrap his head around the past 48 hours. William was doing his best to block out what Joanna had done to his family, how she'd obviously manipulated and planned out her attack on his family because breaking it off with her was still so fresh. There was no band aid for this except for time and he knew he needed to focus on his family now more than ever. Thank god Krista had been able to keep her wits about her and escape.

He'd just walked into the house and almost didn't recognize it from 7 years ago when he come there to rescue Krista and Chad. The beautiful staircase was still there, but instead of the outdated carpeting off-white carpeting it had been updated with wood flooring and a tasteful stair runner in pastel shades of rose, beige and light blue. The entire foyer had been repainted in the palest yellow that was a huge change from the darker brown that he remembered. He expected to see a portrait of Caroline hanging up somewhere around the hall or in the living room, but to his surprise there was only a simple photo of her settled on the mantle on the fireplace. As he came closer, he recognized the photo; it was one that he'd taken of her and the girls on the trip when they were married. Before the accident. His eyes filled with tears then as he realized he'd still been fighting a ghost for a long time. It wasn't Stanley that had taken his wife from him; it was the life circumstances and what had happened that had led her to Stanley. He suddenly felt as though a weight had lifted; after all these years he was able to really accept what had happened to their family.

Mara interrupted his thoughts as she excitedly grabbed his hand with renewed energy that only a 6-year-old could muster at 8:00 at night after a 16 hour fiasco. "Grandpa, look! There's a huge fish tank in the living room! It's ginormous!" Her blue eyes were lit up as she spread her arms as wide as she could to show him. Her energy was infectious and he couldn't help but smile and follow her to the one of three spacious 'living rooms' in the house. As he walked into the space, the enormity of the built-in fish tank into the wall took him by surprise. It was at least 5 feet long and took up the entire wall; filled with exotic fish and even what appeared to be a Moray eel swimming amongst them. "Wow! Mr. Ahearn sure has an amazing house! How cool is that!" He commented as he put his arm around her small shoulder. He loved watching the look on her face as she watched the fish swim around and the eel dart for cover under the many rocks that had been planted.

"I love it! I want to live here, grandpa!" Mara was fascinated by the fish and he took a minute to look around the rest of the spacious living area with an inviting buttery brown leather couch that he decided to check out while he watched Mara. He sunk down into the lush comfort and closed his eyes for a moment. An image of his Maria came to him and he smiled as he swore he could hear her voice. "Look at our granddaughter, she's so special. But keep your eyes open, Bill. She isn't done yet. You need the necklace. The evil is still here." He knew he must dreaming as she came closer to him, her bright blue eyes filled with love for him and her blonde hair like a halo around her. He could smell the scent of her rose scented perfume that she'd always worn. He reached out to hug her, but she disappeared, and hearing a familiar voice.

"Dad! Are you okay?" It was Krista tapping him on the shoulder. "Dad!" He sat up straight as she jumped back, startled for a moment.

"I'm awake! Sorry, I must have dozed off for a minute. How're you doing, Kris? Come sit." He sat up and patted the seat on the couch next to him.

"I'm okay. Just exhausted and trying to take a break from everything." Krista burst into tears as she finally was able to sit and talk. Just being here with her father, husband and daughter was surreal after a few hours ago when she wasn't sure if she would see any of them again. "I just wish I'd been more careful, I could have done something so that never would've happened." She sobbed in Williams' arms for several minutes while William just held her. The dream or whatever it was of Maria was in the forefront of his mind and he wanted to share it with his daughter in hopes that it might help her. She'd had so little time with her mother, and seemed to like to talk about her when he brought up the subject.

"I had a dream about your mom just now." He told her and Krista immediately leaned against him, as if she were a little girl and he was going to read her a bedtime story.

"Really? Tell me." Krista closed her eyes as she waited for him to begin. As if somehow it would erase what'd happened today. But she needed to hear more about her mother. The mother that was there when she was young and disappeared. The insight about their early days always made her feel as though her mother was still here with her, giving her emotional security.

"I was dreaming that your mom was talking to me and told me that she loved watching Mara. She's so proud of you, Mara and Chad. But there's something that is still out there. I believe she was talking about Sadie. She told me about Karen's necklace. That we needed it." William said gently, as he reached into his pocket. He'd grabbed Karen's necklace from the special place in Krista's jewelry box before they'd left to find them.

"But we don't have the necklace, dad. It was in my jewelry box at home!" Krista opened her eyes and sat up, frightened. He held out the necklace with the tiny half-heart that belonged to Karen so long ago.

"But we do. I didn't forget it, Kris." William smiled. "I knew when you had mentioned it before when Sadie had come to the house. "It's time to give it to Mara, Krista. I know you've been waiting for whatever reason, but it's time." William nodded.

"You're right dad. I'll give it to her in the morning." Krista took it from him and wiped the tears from her eyes as Mara had grown tired of watching the fish. "Mommy, I'm hungry." Krista suddenly realized that neither one of them had eaten today, unless Joanna or David had fed Mara earlier. "Let's go see what Mr. Ahearn has in his pantry!" She knew that Stanley wasn't here most of the time, but considering the fact the house was immaculate she anticipated that he probably kept the pantry stocked. When she opened the fridge, she was shocked to see it was fully stocked with cold cuts, a crudité platter, steaks, water, soda, beer and anything else they could possible want.

"Stan knew we were planning to come here so he had it stocked!" William shrugged. "He's a pretty good guy for a millionaire!" He was joking, knowing how eccentric and selfish Stanley had appeared in the past.

"He really is a nice man, dad. I'm looking forward to seeing him tomorrow so I can thank him myself." Krista was grateful as they managed to put together a late night dinner of sandwiches, crudité with dip and chips. William had gone into the wine cellar and brought out a bottle of pinot noir. "I thought this was warranted for us given our day." Krista and Chad agreed and soon the bottle was empty.

After their meal, Mara had been in bed for a couple of hours in a beautiful room with light pink walls and a view of the well-manicured lawn that she'd claimed as hers, despite the fact that it was pink, not green and black. It was also was right next to Krista and Chad, which

Krista had insisted on. She was having a hard time leaving Mara alone for any amount of time, until Chad gently reminded her that she needed to relax. "She's fine, Kris. We're all here and those responsible are in police custody. In fact, I just got an update about Joanna. She's going to be okay, but after she heals, she'll be arraigned on kidnapping charges and likely have some jail time. We won't need to worry about her." Chad assured her.

William didn't say a word as Joanna's name was mentioned. It still hurt the way she'd deceived and manipulated him in order to help Amanda Ahearn. Even after he'd broken things off, he'd never expected that she would've been as vindictive as to assist in kidnapping his family. Chad gave him a hug before they went up to bed. "Bill, you're the best father, grandfather and friend. We're always here for you."

William couldn't help but tear up as Chad hugged him and spoke the words that meant the most to him. Above all, he wanted to make sure that Krista and Mara were happy before it was his time to leave this world and join Maria. Maybe it wasn't in the cards for him to have a new relationship now. His focus really was about his family.

"Thanks, Chad, I'm proud to call you my son-in-law. You've really done a fantastic job with the business and you've been there for the girls." William knew that Chad's brief affair with Jane were just that. In the past. "Stanley is arriving first thing in the morning, so hopefully tomorrow we'll all be too distracted to think about the past 24 hours." He was hoping for a more subdued stay at the Ahearn estate this time around.

Yet as he finally went to bed after Chad and Krista had headed to their room, he found it difficult to sleep. He poured himself a whiskey and ginger ale from Stanley's bar and went to visit the memorial for his Maria that he'd never seen. Her gravestone remained, but this was special and he could see it as he walked toward the edge of the bluffs, hearing the ocean more clearly. The spotlights that had been installed to illuminate the garden-like structured area led him to the memorial that had been dedicated to the woman that they'd both loved. His Maria. Stanley's Caroline. There were all of Maria's favorite things there; pictures of her, Karen and Krista that had been set in stone, as well as one of her and William and the girls. There were several pottery versions of sparrows that were sitting on branches of a tree that overhung the garden. Maria had always believed that sparrows were carriers of a spirit rather than the usual cardinal.

She once told him that 'the sparrows are very ordinary, but extraordinary at the same time. When I hear them chirping, it's almost as if they're singing to me." It was the one thing that stood out to him at her funeral; the two sparrows that had been sitting on a tree branch and then flew away right after the ceremony.

There were several old style rod-iron benches around the garden and he sat down to relax for a moment with his drink. He thought he saw someone walking close by on the cliffs but didn't think anything of it as he decided he was tired and finally got up and started walking back to the house. It was silent with the exception of the sound of crickets all around him and he thought he heard footsteps behind him and turned around, but there was no one in sight. Still, he felt as though someone were watching him and he walked faster, feeling relieved when he closed and locked the door behind him. He glanced out the window again before he walked upstairs. There was no one in sight.

"I must be hearing things, either that or I had one drink too many." He said out loud and laughed at himself. Except that he hadn't. He'd only had the one drink. 'I'm really tired. That's it. There's no one there, just not enough sleep and a drink. Besides, Stanley had one of the best security systems on the planet.' He thought to himself as he finally fell asleep after an exhausting day. Within a few minutes, William was sound asleep and didn't notice the shadow in the darkness of his bedroom.

Krista

Although exhausted from the past hours of drama, sleep wasn't coming easily. It was enviable that Chad had the ability to fall asleep sitting up if necessary. It was a gift that he had really; anytime they had flown anywhere, he would be asleep before they even took off, unlike herself who was riddled with anxiety from start to finish and that was before Mara was born. Tonight she was exceptionally on edge and knew she needed to distract herself; she turned on the TV and found an episode of Three's Company that was nostalgic and funny. It helped to relieve some of her anxiety and she fell asleep halfway through the episode.

It was around 3:00 am that Krista woke up and felt as though someone were watching her. She didn't recall any bad dream, but kept her eyes shut, afraid to open them. There was no sound, so someone had either turned the TV off or it was on a timer. She rolled over toward Chad, his body heat warming her up and hugged him closer to her in hopes that this feeling would go away. But it didn't and she finally forced herself to open her eyes halfway to ensure that she was just being paranoid.

Despite the darkness, the crescent-moon gave enough light. She didn't see anyone there and let out a sigh of relief, 'it's just my imagination, there's no one there,' she told herself. She was just drifting off back to sleep when she felt the pressure of someone sitting down on the bed. 'I'm not imagining this!' she told herself and opened her eyes. There on the edge of the bed was the silhouette of a woman.

Krista sat up, frozen for a moment as her heart raced. The woman turned toward her and Krista immediately shook her husband to wake him up. "Chad! Chad! Wake up! Someone's in our room!"

Chad responded by blindly scrambling to get out of bed and trying to get his bearings. "What? Where?" Krista was too afraid to move. "Chad can you see someone sitting on the end of the bed?" She kept her eyes closed and pulled the blanket over her head as if that would somehow make her invisible.

"Kris, there's no one here. You must have been dreaming." Chad said sleepily. "Go back to bed, sweetheart. I'm right here." He was still half-asleep, tumbling back into the bed as he spoke.

"Are you sure? I *felt* them sit down, Chad. I swear I wasn't dreaming!" Krista trusted that Chad didn't see anyone and finally came out from underneath the covers. Chad shook his head. "Krista! There's no one here!" He reached over and switched on the bedside lamp to prove it. Krista shook her head.

"I know there aren't there now, but I felt someone sit down! Right there!" She pointed to the bottom of the bed, between her and Chad. "Feel it!"

"What do you mean, 'feel it?' Chad shook his head, confused.

"Feel it. See if it's warm. If it's not, I'll let it go and won't say another word!" Krista promised, although she wasn't sure she'd be able to keep it.

"Seriously? Okay, Kris." Chad sighed. He had an amused smile on his face until he felt the bedspread. Then he stopped for a moment and felt the other areas outside where Krista had told him.

"You're right. It's not just a slight difference. It's like night and day." Chad got out of bed, putting on his slippers and began to investigate closer. "Stay here, I'm going to go check out the rest of the house."

"Be careful!" Krista's anxiety heightened now that her husband had confirmed that it seemed as though someone had just been there. She kept the blanket up to her chin, while doing the deep breathing exercises that her therapist had her practice so many times. After what seemed like an eternity, Chad came back to report he didn't see anyone. "Kris, the alarm would have gone off if someone had broken in. We couldn't be in a more secure location right now, considering its Stanley's house." He reassured her.

"Did you check on Mara?" Krista hadn't heard anything from the next door bedroom, but now she was becoming paranoid.

"I did, Kris. She's sleeping just fine. Let's go back to bed, okay? You've had a horrible experience, so I get why you're anxious, but I'm here. I promise we're fine." Chad got back into bed, enveloped her in a hug. She'd needed that.

"You're right. We are okay now. Thank you for getting up and checking. I'm sorry if I'm being a little dramatic." Krista suddenly felt silly. Of course they were in the most secure place possible. She instinctively knew that Chad would do what he could to protect her and Mara. The other night had been....well, out of the ordinary. But Sadie had helped Mara. Mara was fine. Just as she started drifting off to sleep again, an image of her mother's face was in front of her. "Your instincts are right. Someone was here, but you're safe for now. I'm with you." Her mother's voice comforted her and she was able to fall back to sleep.

*   *   *

Krista woke up to the bright sun shining directly through the window as she yawned, still feeling tired. She looked over and saw that her husband had already left and glanced at the clock. 10:00am! She couldn't ever remember sleeping that late with the exception of being a teenager on a Saturday morning! The middle of the nights' events came rushing back and she wondered if she'd dreamt the whole thing about the person in the room and sitting on the bed. It was tempting to go back to bed, but she knew that Chad, Mara and her father had been up for at least a couple of hours. Besides, she could never go back to sleep once she was fully awake. It was only after starting the shower, Krista realized she had none of her belongings with her. The way she ended up here at Stanley's house came back to her and triggered a memory of her stabbing Joanna and running away, and she could hear someone screaming. Then she realized it was herself. Within seconds, Chad was at her side.

"Kris! Are you okay? I heard you screaming!" Chad checked in as she'd slid down to sit on the granite tiles of the floor under the warm spray of the luxurious shower. "Kris! Answer me!" Chad didn't bother undressing as he stepped into the shower.

"Look at me, Kris! You're safe, I'm here." He knew just what to do. She managed to nod, hear what he was saying and take deep breaths to manage her panic attack. It was what he'd dealt with 7 years ago.

Posttraumatic Stress Disorder, the psychiatrist had called it years ago. She could almost hear Dr. Mayfield's voice now. "You're just remembering what you went through. You need to learn the triggers and coping, you can't just take medications." She'd been right and Chad was here. She could hear him and he led her out of the shower and wrapped a towel around her.

"I don't have any clothes here, Chad." Krista could feel the tears running down her face, mixing with the water from the shower.

"But you do. I brought a small bag with some of your things here with me. It's not much, but you'll have some clean underwear at least!" He joked with her, hoping to get her out of the moment, bring a smile to her face. While she stood wrapped in a giant towel, he went into the bedroom and pulled out an overnight bag that had a pair of her favorite jeans, sweatshirt and sneakers as well as her make-up bag and other facial products that he knew she used daily.

Krista began crying tears of gratitude as she hugged this man she'd been lucky enough to have by her side all these years. "Oh my god, you're the best! Thank you! You just made my morning."

Chad hugged her and gave her a kiss on the forehead. "Go get your cute ass dressed. Breakfast has been waiting for you. Sorry if I grabbed the wrong outfit, but I was in a bind." He joked.

"Everything you chose is perfect. You know me too well." Krista laughed through her tears. "Okay, I'm getting ready now. How long have you been up?"

"Oh, since about 7:30. Your dad was up at 6 and Mara was up at 6:30. We all ate already, but we saved you some. Hurry up or we'll

347

eat the rest before you get downstairs!" He smacked her on her butt and then left her to get dressed.

She couldn't help feeling ridiculous after her episode in the shower, but it was to be expected given the circumstances. Chad always had her back and understood. Luckily, Mara had been downstairs, which made her feel better. Krista hurried to finish getting ready and arrived in the kitchen that was easily bigger than their entire house. There was a sliding glass door adjacent to the kitchen, bright with sunlight and Mara was sitting at the dining room table. She looked cute in her little jeans, her pink hoodie and sneakers. 'Chad thought of everything', she thought to herself, knowing that he must have packed a little overnight bag for Mara. Krista ran up to greet her with a hug, initially chasing away the black cloud that she'd felt over her since she'd awakened this morning. Mara whispered something in her ear that she couldn't understand. "Honey, I can't hear you. What did you say?"

"Mommy, I'm scared. Something bad is back. Can you make it go away?" Mara looked at her with wide blue eyes that were clearly frightened. Yet, she wasn't willing to talk about it out loud with her husband or grandfather.

"Why do you think that? Did you sleep okay?" Krista was surprised considering how Mara had been so excited to be here last night. "Did something happen during the night?" Her night had certainly been interrupted, and she hoped that Mara hadn't had the same experience.

"It feels different now, mommy. Like someone is watching me." Mara continued to whisper, which was making Krista feel more on edge. Now she knew that Mara was sensitive to the spiritual world just like her mother and her sister. Mara was probably not off track given what happened to her last night. "We've had a tough few days, sweetheart. We're safe here." She reassured Mara the best she could. Just then her father walked in and Krista gave her daughter a kiss on the cheek.

"Hi, dad. You're looking well rested." Krista gave him a quick hug. Mara gave him a quick greeting but was suddenly more interested in the pancakes that were waiting for her.

"Kris! Good morning, sweetheart!" William set down his coffee cup and gave her a hug. "How'd you sleep?"

She gave her father a hug and resisted the urge to tell him the truth about what she'd seen in their bedroom. "I slept great! Stanley really did a great job with the updates on this house. Our bedroom was straight out of a magazine! Do you know when he's coming?" Krista quickly changed the subject to Stanley's arrival today.

"He said he'd be here around noon or so." William looked at his watch. "Oh, wow, that's only an hour from now. I'm gonna give him a quick call and see if he's on schedule." Chad handed her a cup of coffee as she sat down at the breakfast bar with a window overlooking the front lawn. Krista thanked him just as William poked her and whispered in her ear, "I need to talk to you, come with me." He nodded his head toward the other room. Krista nodded, confused as to what this apparent secret conversation was about. Maybe he was planning a surprise? But for who? She grabbed her coffee mug, while she followed her father down the hall into what appeared to be a formal office that Stanley used and shut the door.

Krista was confused about this sudden private conversation. "What's going on dad? Is there some kind of surprise I should know about?" She laughed nervously, as the expression on his face read otherwise.

"Kris, I couldn't tell the others about what I saw last night. But you need to know, and I don't want to scare Mara." William began as he sat down in one of Stanley's expensive wing-backed chairs that were upholstered in black and a deep gold color. "How about these chairs? You think I should get some for my living room?" He changed the subject, trying to lighten the mood.

"That comfortable, huh? Guess I'll try one." Krista sat in the chair across from him. It was actually more comfortable that it appeared. "Still doesn't compare to our living room recliner, but I'll give it a 5 out of 10." She kept the joke going but she was ready to hear whatever her father was being so secretive about.

William got up first, locked the door and came back to his chair. "Geez, dad. What's going on?" Krista was getting more worried by the moment.

William

He knew he needed to talk to Krista about what he'd seen and how he'd felt last night. The necklace, Karen's necklace, was in his pocket. He was sure whomever he'd seen last night wasn't a ghost, nor a figment of his imagination. But he did know that he had always trusted Maria. And he hadn't dreamt about Maria in so long that yesterday had been a surprise to him. So when he did, he truly believed that she was trying to reach him.

Krista had had a rough morning. He'd overheard her screams upstairs and kept Mara occupied. He'd also heard her in the middle of the night, claiming that she'd seen someone in their room and she was probably right. It wasn't the ideal setting to discuss this, but time was running out. He had a feeling that whoever had been skulking around the grounds and potentially in their room last night was still there. It was almost as if Maria had given him the ability to sense a potential storm and prepare for it.

"Geez dad, what's going on?" Krista gave him that look that he'd only seen on a few occasions; when her mother left and when he'd found her again years later. William took the necklace that belonged to Karen out of his pocket. "We talked about giving this to Mara this morning and now I know it's more important than ever. I was outside last night just sitting in the new garden that Stanley made in tribute to your mom and I saw someone walking along the cliffs in the distance. Then when I was walking back to the house, I felt as though someone was following me. I got in the house and locked the door, but I don't think I set the security system. You know how I am with technology, Kris. Then I overheard you talking with Chad in the middle of the night about someone being in your room."

Krista nodded. "Sorry that I woke you. I don't know what's going on, dad! It's as if something followed us. Mara was just telling me that 'the darkness is back.' She can feel it; she said that she feels as though someone is watching her."

"Unless there's some other person that was connected with your kidnapping, I'd bet money that Sadie didn't go home. Remember how weird she was behaving yesterday?" William didn't need to remind her. Krista was already nodding her head.

"Yeah, it was pretty obvious that wasn't the person that helped Mara a few days ago." Krista readily agreed. "But why would she stick around here?"

"Didn't she give Mara something and told her not to take it off after she got rid of whatever 'spirit' was following her?"

"Yes, I remember that." Krista's memory wasn't great considering the past 36 hours.

"Mara wasn't wearing it. She must have taken it off, or it got lost when she was taken from her room. Maybe it affected Sadie. Maybe that's why she started acting so weird." William hypothesized.

"I would think it would. Especially since she's been vulnerable. Her niece died recently and she's been stressed. I remember her telling me when I saw her that spirits can take advantage if you're emotionally drained." Krista felt like her father was making sense, although she was surprised that he was this in touch with the supernatural. "Wow, dad, been researching the psychic world lately?" They both laughed, but it was partially true. She tried to remember if Mara had the necklace on, then knew for sure she didn't. She would definitely remember; it was kind of clunky and Mara probably took it off because it was bothering her.

"Laugh at me all you want, Kris, but I did learn a few things from your mother as well as our past experiences. Although I learned, sometimes you need to see people for who they really are." William turned away from her for a moment. Krista could tell he was struggling emotionally as she got up. "I love that you seem so in touch with mom now." She gave him a hug just as his phone rang. It was Stanley to let him know that he was in route by boat and be arriving in about an hour. "He'll be here in an hour."

"Who's coming with him?" Krista wanted to prepare herself for any entourage that Stanley might bring along. Stanley had always done a good job at keeping his private life away from the media, but last year he was seen and photographed with an up-and-coming young actress, Gwen Stafford, which led to paparazzi to follow them wherever they went. William doubted that he'd be bringing anyone with him that would encourage the media to hunt down his whereabouts.

"As far as I know, no one, except for his assistant and agent. Don't worry, Kris, you know how Stanley likes to keep his visits to the island low-key." William assured her. He could understand her worries though. Especially after the kidnapping that was nearly next door to Stanley's home, it was cause for worry that there would be an entourage. None of them wanted to deal with that.

"Well, let's go get ready then. Although I hope this is informal! I don't have anything else to wear." Krista joked, but William could tell she needed to relax.

"It's a family thing, Kris. Stop worrying. This isn't formal at all! How about we just give Mara her necklace at the memorial? There isn't much time and it'll be almost ceremonial in a way." William hugged her before they left the room. Krista was glad to have some extra time to prepare, so she agreed.

William agreed to ride in the chauffeured car to pick up Stanley from the dock. During the ride he began to worry about Sadie's location and whether she'd actually gotten on the helicopter and gone back to the mainland was bothering him. With no idea who Stanley booked the helicopter through, he decided to call Shoreham police who gave Sadie a ride to the helicopter to make sure she actually got on and left. Officer Sloan was on duty and remembered him. "Mr. Burton, I saw her get on the helicopter and then watched it take off. What she did after it landed, I couldn't tell you, but I did see her leave. Did something happen?"

"No, I didn't see her if that's what you mean. I just thought I saw someone hanging around the Ahearn estate last night when I was outside." William was glad to know Sadie had definitely left and not run off and hid somewhere.

"We'll be doing extra security detail today because Mr. Ahearn will be in town. Please let us know if there are any other concerns." Officer Sloan seemed to be on top of his game.

"Thank you so much for your help, especially last night. I appreciate it!" William said, grateful for his assistance.

Just as William hung up, the chauffeured Bentley Bellinger that Stanley had parked at his house arrived just in time to meet his illustrious host. The 100 foot yacht with triple decks and enclosed space was easily the most luxurious docked at Ballard's marina, and William wasn't surprised to see some off-season tourists standing by and taking pictures with their phones as it docked. William stayed inside the car while he waited for Stanley. He definitely didn't want any extra attention from the 'touristy paparazzi'. Stanley came down the dock by himself with only a small suitcase dressed in casual khaki's and a green North Face fleece with sunglasses. His salt and pepper hair looked elegantly styled in a short military-type cut and his deep tan set him apart from native Block Island residents. He could try to blend in, but at the end of the day, Stanley Ahearn looked every bit the part of the elite celebrity. He walked quietly to the car, while the tourists gathered around, whispering to each other as if trying to guess who he was. Of course, he wasn't recognizable as an actor, but it was clear that he had money that was quintessential Hollywood.

"Bill! Great to see you!" Stan greeted him as William got out of the car. "You're looking well! Sorry to hear about everything that happened over the last day. How are Krista and your granddaughter doing?" Stanley asked a barrage of questions, as if he were a reporter. William had to take a deep breath before answering. He didn't want to bother Stan with his worry about the potential 'intruder' last night, so he thanked him again for chartering the transport to the island last night and the basic details of what had happened, including Amanda's arrest and how Kris and Mara had managed to get away from Joanna who's condition was still critical as far as he knew. He hadn't checked but then again as long as she was no longer at risk of coming back to finish the job, he didn't want to know.

"I'm sorry that I didn't know about Amanda's escape. I don't keep in touch with her, Bill." Stanley seemed sincere about his relationship with his daughter after she and Jane had attempted to kill Krista 7 years ago. William decided to bring up Sadie and the question of where the helicopter dropped her off. "The psychic woman that accompanied Chad and I was supposed to be transported back to the mainland. I want to make sure that she made it back safely. Do you have the number so I can call and check?" William asked casually.

Stanley pulled out his phone, pulled up a number and dialed. "Hi, Daphne, would you please get that helicopter charter company that I asked for last night? Let me know when I can talk to them. Thank you!"

William was speechless at how quickly Stanley got things done. "Wow! Easy enough, huh? Glad I asked!" He tried to sound less impressed than he was. He and Stanley had a decent relationship considering the circumstances. Stan's arrogance had dissipated over the years, especially after Caroline's death, but William couldn't help but feel subservient in Stan's presence.

Stanley shrugged it off. "Daphne is a good assistant. She always gets the job done. She'll get back to me soon. So let's talk about what the afternoon is going to look like." Stanley began to talk about the memorial dedication this afternoon. "It won't be anything formal, just having a few of Caroline's...." He paused for moment. "Do you mind if I refer to her as Caroline, Bill?" Stanley paused to ask and William appreciated it. It still bugged him, but he understood.

"I don't mind, Stan. It's what you called her. I know you didn't know her as 'Maria'." William agreed. He did appreciate everything that he did for them last night. He wasn't going to nit-pick about *their* wife's name.

"I appreciate that, Bill." Stanley thanked him, then went on about the small 'event' that sounded more like a Hollywood event as he went on about the catering company coming and the bartender that he'd hired. "They should be arriving soon." His phone rang and he excused himself for a minute. "It's Daphne." He whispered to William. William was curious and glad that Stanley had her on speaker phone. "What did you find out, Daphne?"

"The charter company told me they dropped her off at Point Judith on the mainland." William gave him the thumbs up with that news.

"Well, that's good news." Stan smiled. "Thanks for checking."

"Mr. Ahearn, there's more. Apparently, after she was dropped off, she was seen immediately hopping on a Block Island ferry to come back." Daphne advised him.

"Are they sure that it was her?" Stanley made a circular motion around his temple, as if he were mocking the charter company and their accuracy. William wasn't paying attention to him; he just hoped that she was mistaken that Sadie had hopped a ferry back over.

"I asked them that specifically. They saw her run for the ferry as soon as she got out of the helicopter. They had landed almost directly across from the dock, Mr. Ahearn." Daphne's words made William's heart sink as now it was almost certain that she was somewhere on the island. Possibly hiding in Stanley's house somewhere? He hoped not.

Stan hung up with Daphne and turned to William. "It seems there's a little situation here, but we can manage it. I did hire police detail while I'm here, so I'm sure we'll be fine, Bill. Don't worry. Besides, I have the new security system that has cameras and everything."

"You have cameras? Where? Can you look at the footage?" William was hopeful that if there was someone in the house last night it would be on the security footage.

"Sure. It's in one of the rooms on the lower level. I can ask the security detail to check it out."

"We need to. And now this person, Sadie, is probably here. So please let your security staff know to be on the lookout." William knew from the way she behaved last evening that she was not in her right mind.

"Don't worry, Bill. You're all safe here. Calm down. Try and relax." He reached over to the cooler in the Bentley and pulled out a couple of Crown Royale nips. "Here. This will take the edge off." William hesitated for only a moment, then screwed off the cover and downed it. Stanley did the same. "Better now?"

"It's not going to make anything better, but at least it takes the edge off." William admitted. They'd arrived at Stanley's house and William was eager to look at any footage that the cameras might have caught.

Stanley was more focused on the catering company that started their arrival. The security detail from surrounding police departments had arrived as well. There were five officers, with Sergeant Scott in charge that evening. Rather than explain the details himself, Stan introduced them to William. William felt put on the spot, but Stan did give instructions about the camera location. "I only have them turned on if people are staying here." That was when William knew that the officers reviewing it would be useless. He did emphasize that there might be someone here that they need to watch out for and asked that they pay attention to anyone that seems to be out of place.

William was fuming as he waited for him to finish instructing the security, but pulled him off to the side. "Stan, I thought you said that the cameras would show if anyone was here last night. I guess I assumed that meant they were *on*!"

"When I suggested that, I'd forgotten that they usually aren't on, Bill. I'm sorry, the house is usually empty so we started turning them off unless people are here. But as you heard me tell the officers they will be looking out for anyone suspicious. In fact, give them a description of that psychic person, what's her name? Shelly, Shirley?"

"Her name is Sadie." William reminded him, trying not to lose his patience.

"Right, Sadie. Give them a picture and/or description and they can be on the lookout." Stanley told him. William could tell that he was preoccupied now that the caterers from Georges from Galilee had arrived. He knew there was no use in asking more questions about the cameras not being on, so he just agreed. And he wasted no time, making sure the security officers had a detailed description.

Chad

As soon as Stan arrived, there was suddenly a flood of activity that he could tell was causing stress for Krista and his father-in-law. Especially Bill, who seemed suddenly upset about something. He had been standing in the kitchen watching Stan talking to the police who would be doing security and then Bill's exchange with Stan afterwards. After Stanley left to talk to the caterers and left the area, Chad went outside to talk to him.

"What's going on, Bill? You seem upset. Everything go okay with Stan?" Chad could tell something was up. William gave him the run-down about seeing someone on the property and then Krista's experience in the middle of the night, the cameras being there and then finding out that the cameras hadn't been turned on. Stan had also found out that Sadie had apparently gotten on a ferry headed back to Block Island after she was dropped off on the mainland. He could tell that Bill had really wanted to see if there was camera footage and now there wasn't any. And now he was worried that Sadie could be here.

"Bill, it'll be fine. Security is here now and you gave them a description, right?" Chad didn't feel certain about the situation either, but he wasn't going to tell Bill that.

"I did. I just wish someone had gotten a picture of this woman. I'm guessing she'd be in a disguise unless she was really out of it or stupid. She's none of those, so we'll need to be on the lookout as well. Do you think we should mention this to Kris?" William was undecided. He knew she was stressed enough and would rather have her relaxed than looking over her shoulder the whole afternoon.

"I think it's best to just keep our eyes out for anyone that looks suspicious and not mention it to Kris. Between us looking out, keeping Kris and Mara within eyeshot and security, I think we should be fine." Chad agreed.

"I'll be watching her and Mara the whole time." William agreed.

"Hey, Bill, what if we were to lure Sadie in if she's here? Then we could find her before she catches us off guard?" Chad suddenly had an idea. It was risky and it would involve Krista and Mara. "What if we have Krista and Mara take a walk by themselves away from the gathering so that Sadie thinks they're alone. But we'll be watching the whole time." Chad began to suggest, but William was already shaking his head.

"No, we can't take a risk like that, Chad! She was out of her mind last night; who knows what she's like today? Whatever is going on with her, possessed by that spirit of Jane or whatever, I don't want to put Kris or Mara into danger like that!" He was adamant about it.

Chad knew he was right; it was too much of a risk. But there had to be a way to get this woman out in the open without putting Krista and Mara at risk. Then he remembered Karen's necklace and its significance to protecting Mara. "Did you give Karen's necklace to Mara yet, Bill?"

"No. Krista wanted to wait until the ceremony today to do it. I have it with me right now." William pulled the half-heart necklace that had belonged to Karen out of his pants pocket. The half-heart pendant gleamed as the sunlight hit the gold. William could still remember the day he'd given Krista and her twin these necklaces.

" That's it! Sadie knows about this necklace and we can use it as decoy! We'll plant the necklace on a random object, maybe on a tree branch in sight." Chad was just brainstorming ideas. William was nodding in agreement.

"I think that's a good idea, Chad. You're right! She did go on about the importance of the necklace. So let's think about this; if we leave it on a tree branch or an object, what if she gets to the necklace before we get to *her?*"

"We'll just have to keep an eye for her." Chad already decided. "Let's go get ready for the gathering. We'll wait until everyone is occupied then you'll place it nearby where we can see it. If Sadie show's up we can make sure that security gets to her before she gets to it." Chad knew it was taking a chance; maybe Sadie had wandered off in her demonic state and got lost. But he had a gut feeling that she was there. Watching and waiting for the opportunity to get to Mara.

*   *   *

A couple of hours later, there were at least 30 people that had arrived, most arriving in blacked-out Escalades, Bentleys, Rolls Royce's, and Mercedes parked along the long drive that led up to Stanley's mansion. There wasn't a cloud in the sky, it was a comfortable 70 degrees and Stanley had the caterers from Georges set up buffet style out on the sprawling lawn facing the ocean. Although Stanley had insisted this was a casual event, most of the guests were more formal than a backyard picnic; the women were wearing dresses, the men were dressed in dress pants and a shirt with a tie. "I guess this is Stan's idea of 'informal'." William's sarcasm made Chad laugh. Neither of them had been thinking about this event when they'd ended up here. Now they were committed to their jeans and button-down shirts. Krista was already freaking out about her jeans when she saw the guests arrive.

"Now, I'm going to look awful!" He could see that she was close to the breaking point and told her to just wait; "Kris, take a breath, I'll take care of it." It was then that Chad approached Stanley to ask if there were any dresses left that her mother had in her closet.

Stan shook his head. "I'm sorry, Chad. It took me two years, but I finally had to clean out her closet with her belongings."

"I understand that, Mr. Ahearn. It's just that Krista didn't pack for herself. As you know the situation, I ended up throwing things into a bag for her at the last minute. She's just really stressed out about everything." Chad did his best to explain, but Stanley was already smiling as if he had idea.

"Let me see if I can fix this. I'll be right back." Stan winked at him and strode toward the guests, with one woman in mind; Claire Abascal. She was the wife of one of his friends from Hollywood, Sean. Sean had always told him that Claire never went anywhere without other "possible clothes" that she would reject at the last minute.

He came back in ten minutes and said "Krista will have a dress and shoes in 5 minutes. Meet me in the living area with Krista." Chad was shocked. He always knew how to fix a situation. Except for the one with his daughters and now Sadie. He knew that the ceremony would be starting soon, so he was considering his options for planting the necklace in case Sadie was there. Krista was in her room stewing when Chad came up and ordered her downstairs. "Don't ask questions, Kris, just go downstairs."

When she reached the living room, Stanley was standing there with a simple but beautiful lilac-colored knee -length dress that was casual with a tie on the side. "I believe these might be your size, Krista." He also held a pair of nude casual low-heeled sandals. Chad could see her eyes light up and she immediately headed to the nearest bathroom to try them on. A few minutes later, she emerged smiling like Chad hadn't seen in weeks. Maybe even months. She looked beautiful. It reminded him of how he was glad he'd never given in to temptation again with Michelle; it just wasn't worth it.

"Thank you so much, Mr. Ahearn." Krista told him and gave him a short hug.

"I'm glad that you're here today. I know that you went through so much last night, but I wanted you to be happy with your mother's new memorial and feel comfortable." Stanley returned her hug, and Chad was glad that he'd approached him with this what seemed like a ridiculous request. "You do look stunning! Claire will be jealous of you!" Stan kidded with her.

She blushed as Chad held his arm out to her. "Let's go out to the party, you look amazing." Krista agreed, but then realized Mara wasn't with them. "Where's Mara?"

Chad pointed to William and Mara over getting some crab cakes from the lavish catered buffet. Stanley had spared no expense with the catering. "Let's go over and get some of this food! It looks amazing!" He and Krista joined William and Mara to get some food. None of them had eaten much in the past couple of days, and the food was delicious. Krista had an additional glass of champagne and Chad could tell that she was getting a little buzz so he wanted to keep an eye on her. He was already on edge with the knowledge that Sadie might be somewhere close. His phone rang and the number came up as a Rhode Island number so he answered in case it was the police with information. "This is Chad Burton."

There was a moment of silence. "Hello? Is anyone there?" Chad was ready to hang up when someone answered.

"Hi, Chad. This is Sadie Mercotte. I'm sorry to bother you but I've been trying to get hold of your wife to let her know that the funeral services for Nadine have changed to next weekend. She gave me your number in case I couldn't get in touch with her. " Chad almost dropped the phone.

"Sadie?" Chad was confused. Why wouldn't she have just said that last night while she was with them?

"Yes, this is Nadine's aunt. I met with Krista and Mara a few days ago. I thought your wife told you I'd come by." She sounded confused.

"Ms. Mercotte, you called me yesterday and came to help us find Krista and Mara." Chad told her, but a chill came over him as he realized what this meant. After all, he'd never met her before. And it would explain why she didn't seem to recognize Krista or Mara.

"Chad, I couldn't have been there. I've been in Boston for the past two days." Sadie sounded upset now. "Whoever came to your house was pretending to be me for some reason, although I'm not sure why."

"I'm not sure why either, but I intend to find out!" Chad's initial shock turned to anger, frustrated that between Mara's 'possession', the kidnapping and now being duped he was wondering what would be next.

"I'm sorry this happened." Sadie sounded genuinely concerned and proceeded to ask about Mara and Krista's well-being. Chad gave her the short version of what happened, that they were on Block Island now at a memorial ceremony and Mara had begun talking about 'Jamie' again.

"I'm surprised that Krista didn't realize it wasn't me." Sadie commented. "Whoever this is must have had some experience."

"She apparently disguised herself, although Kris noticed that her demeanor seemed much different." Chad observed.

"You brought Karen's necklace, right?" Sadie asked.

"Yes, we have it. What do we do now?" Chad felt his adrenaline going as Sadie instructed him to put it around her neck as soon as possible. "It will protect her. She's very vulnerable because she's close to where the spirit originated. I'll be back in town the day after tomorrow. Please call me if you need anything at all." Sadie was sincere and Chad realized that Krista never would've put up with that 'imposter' from yesterday; their personalities were completely opposite. Chad thanked her and hung up, then hurried back over to the party. He pulled William aside to let him know what had just happened.

"We should let Stanley know and call the police as well so they can be on the lookout for anyone with her description in case whoever that was decides to show up here!"

Chad agreed. "I'll contact Officer Sloan and have him notify the security officers, while you talk to Stanley. William went to go find Stanley while Chad contacted Officer Sloan "It seems that our 'Sadie' from last night was not the real Sadie Mercotte after all."

"Do you know why anyone would want to pretend they were her?" Officer Sloan asked the ultimate question.

"Unfortunately, there's been so much going on, that it's hard to narrow down," Chad admitted, "But I have to think that they must all be connected in some way." Officer Sloan let him know that he would come out to the Ahearn property and radioed the security detail officers at the party as well.

Chad thanked him, then tried to decide if he wanted to let Krista know what was going on. She was so emotionally fragile right now that he was afraid this might send her over the edge. He found William talking to Stanley about the situation. "Hey Bill, Stan did he brief you on the latest on this 'Sadie' revelation?"

Stan nodded, looking very irritable with the whole situation. "I can't understand why someone would bother impersonating a psychic woman!"

"Obviously someone who thinks she's going to gain something from it. Money. You have a lot of it and she obviously didn't want to leave here. Now we know it wasn't the psychic, so it must be someone who knows you." Chad threw out a potential motive.

"Do you think we should tell Krista about the imposter and more importantly, that she might be back on the island?" William was unsure and wanted to Chad to make the final decision.

"I'll tell her about Sadie potentially being back on the island, but I think we don't need to tell her about the imposter part yet. Maybe she won't resurface." Chad tried to put a positive spin on the situation. William agreed. "We'll go with that for now and cross our fingers that she doesn't."

"Let's hope so. I've got a houseful of people here and I don't want any lawsuits in my future." Stanley was showing his selfish side now. Chad bristled at the statement, but William gave him a look that made him bite back a sarcastic comment. Chad looked around for Krista in an effort to avoid giving up his poker face. "I see Krista headed our way. I'm going to go talk to her now." William followed him for back up.

"Just vague details, Chad." He warned.

Krista

When she'd seen what the other women were wearing at this event, Krista's first thought was to claim she didn't feel well and stay inside. After all, they'd buy it because of what she'd gone through the night before. But she wanted to be there for her mother's new gravesite ceremony. Even though she'd only reconnected hours before she died, she respected what she'd given her in explanation at her end and understood why things had turned out the way that they had.

So when Stanley approached her with the beautiful dress and shoes, she was excited and ready to head out to join the gathering. At least she felt as though she belonged, even though she knew these people had more money than she could ever dream about. To her, it was more about feeling as though she fit in with them. As Chad led her out, she accepted a glass of champagne from one of the servers making their rounds. Mara was with her father getting some food from the buffet, so she decided to join them. Krista wasn't a huge fan of seafood, but she did love crab cakes and some of the other appetizers offered; there was bruschetta and Roma tomatoes stuffed with sausage and cheese that were delicious. She'd already downed the first glass of champagne and reached for another when Chad's phone rang and he excused himself.

Krista figured it was probably a wrong number or maybe the agency, so she sat with her father and Mara at one of the small tables that were assembled in a café style outside. Her father seemed to be looking around for Chad. "Dad, is everything alright? You keep looking around for someone, maybe Chad? He got a call from someone, I'm sure he'll be right back."

"Oh, I'm sure he will. These crab cakes are delicious, how about I get some more? Would you like one more, Mara?" He was quick to answer. Too quick in her opinion.

"Dad, what's wrong? Is something going on?" Krista could tell something was wrong, knowing that her father would sugar-coat the truth.

"No, everything's fine, Kris." Her father replied, as he kept glancing over his shoulder. He could see Chad walking back from the call and excused himself. "I'm going to go find Chad, see if everything's okay. It's probably just the office." William assured his daughter. She was starting to feel a little buzzed from the second glass of champagne and decided to enjoy the rest of her wine and food. Watching Mara smile while being at a social event was rare. Besides, the wine had her more relaxed than she'd felt in months.

*   *   *

An hour later, Krista had finished her glass of champagne and Mara was beginning to get cranky, "Where's daddy?" She wanted to know.

"Good question, Mara. Let's look around for him." She grabbed Mara's hand and waded through the small crowd of people that kept stopping her to ask how old Mara was and commenting on how adorable she looked. "You do that dress justice, Krista!" Claire Abascal complimented her, and kept her talking for longer than Krista wanted about fashion and 'how do you stay so fit?' questions. All the while she

371

scoured the crowd, looking for her husband. Finally she noticed him walking with her father and Stanley.

"What was that about? That took a while," She tried her best not to sound like a nagging wife, but the higher pitch in her voice gave away her anxiety. Her father was few feet away, still talking to Stanley, but she could tell that he was privy to whatever was going on.

"Just a call from the office." Chad said casually, but Krista knew her husband. He had a nervous look in his eyes, glancing around as if he were looking for someone.

"Chad, please. I know you, I can tell something's wrong. What's going on?" Krista didn't want to nag at him, but it was just making her more on edge. William overheard his daughter. He knew she wasn't going to let this go and he'd be right.

"Kris, we found out that Sadie didn't stay on the mainland; there's video and witnesses that she grabbed another ferry back over to Block Island, so we're watching out for her." William told her quietly, glancing quickly at Chad before moving closer to her as if he were waiting for her to start flipping out.

Krista could feel her palms start to sweat as they always did when she was anxious. She took some deep breaths as she remembered Dr. Mayfield instructing her. "Does Mr. Ahearn know about a potential party crasher?" she decided to joke about it. As she looked around, there were many security personnel here, and she was trying to be rational about this. What could she possibly do with all the security here? The chances were slim, she needed to remind herself.

Chad was quick to respond. He knew she was upset. "Of course he does. He assured us that there is enough security; especially looking out for anyone with Sadie's description. We were just being cautious and didn't want to worry you."

Krista took a deep breath and decided she needed a minute to herself. "I'm fine. I'm going to take a short walk by myself." She restrained herself from saying anything else as she stood up. "Please keep an eye on Mara. I'll be fine by myself. As you said, the security is here, right?" After everything that had happened yesterday, she wasn't taking any chances.

"Of course. I'll be with you the whole time." Chad reached out to hug her as she was leaving.

"Just keep an eye on Mara, I'll be fine." She repeated as she grabbed her phone off the table and headed off towards the cliffs near her mother's burial place. Feeling surprisingly relaxed, she made her way to the cliffs where she'd clung to the side after the Ahearn sisters kidnapped her. She made her way to the original headstone where her mother was buried. Just as she saw the tombstone, she heard a voice calling her name. It was faint, and for a moment she thought she was just hearing things, but then she heard it again. "Krista. I'm over here."

She recognized her voice. It was one that she'd heard many times when her dream became a nightmare. It sounded just like Jane.

Krista stood up and tried to keep calm as she looked around. "Hello? Who's there?" There was no answer, so Krista started back toward the party when she heard it again.

"I'm right here, Princess. Right here, following you." Now she knew it was Jane and she took her high heels off her feet and ran back toward the crowd of people that were in her sight now. She could hear someone following her, although there was no one in sight. 'Probably hiding in the trees so others don't see her.' Krista felt as though she were reliving her nightmare again, running from that sound. Jane's voice.

Chad saw her and ran toward her, catching her in his arms. "Kris! What's going on? She was shaking as she grabbed her husband's arms, insisting she'd heard a voice. "It was Jane, I know it was!!"

"Did you see anyone? " Chad gently held her face. "Look at me, did you see anyone? " Krista shook her head. "I *heard* someone." She admitted to her husband. "I didn't imagine it, I heard them!"

"Krista, you've had a rough couple of weeks, it's no wonder you're getting upset and hearing things. You'll see Dr. Mayfield when we get back." Chad did his best to rationalize what she'd heard to calm her down. Krista did her best to rationalize with herself. She *had* been traumatized last night and maybe she *was* hearing things. After all, there was no way it was Jane. Jane was dead. Mara was sitting with her father, digging into her second helping of crab cakes. Krista tried to calm down, focusing on Mara.

"That's my favorite too! Can I have a bite?" She sat next to her and gave her a hug as her daughter smiled at her and handed her a forkful that she'd shoveled up with her fingers first. It struck Krista as funny and suddenly she was laughing so hard tears came to her eyes. Mara was staring at her with a funny smile on her face, while Chad and

374

William burst into laughter along with her. She wasn't sure why it was hysterical, but it felt good to laugh again! It distracted her from worrying. At least for now.

*   *   *

It was shortly after her fit of laughter that the DJ that had been playing music all afternoon gave the mic over to Stanley. "Thank you so much for coming to this gathering; it means a lot to me. I worked with one of the best garden designer's in the country, Gabe Spencer to create a space that would be a peaceful place to remember Caroline and her daughter, Karen. Unfortunately, Mr. Spencer couldn't be here today, but I'm grateful that all of you have come to see the masterpiece that was created. It surpassed what I'd imagined it would be and I hope all of you will find it as beautiful as I do. Please join me in walking down to the new Maria Caroline and Karen Carson Memorial garden." There was a huge round of applause, as Krista sat shocked that he'd included her sister in this special memorial. She felt tears in her eyes and looked over at her father who reached for her hand.

"Did you know he was going to include Karen?" She asked him.

"I had no idea!" William was speechless for a moment. "How about that? I think Stan's softened in his older age." He joked, but the tears that shone in his eyes showed his gratitude. Stanley led the way as they all walked the few hundred feet down toward the cliff where the entrance was announced with a 5 foot tall piece of polished marble. On the top of the stone were two brown sparrows entwined. In the middle of the stone was "Maria Caroline and Karen Ann- Forever with us" Below was a an engraving of a photo that depicted their likenesses perfectly. There were hundreds of small tea candles lit that surrounded the moment atop multiple marble slabs that were set several feet apart, separating the garden from the rest of the lawn. A small pebbled outlined path led them to a koi pond with exotic fish swimming around with cobblestone that bordered the water just inside the garden. "Mommy, look at the fish!" Mara pointed to a beautiful rainbow colored fish that swam by close to the surface.

"Aren't they beautiful?" Krista whispered, tears coming to her eyes after the sentimental tribute to her mother and sister. Watching them swim around was so calming that she made a mental note to look into an aquarium for home. As they continued through the garden there were copies of photos of her mother and Karen placed within marble stones around the garden accompanied by a plaque indicating the time and place of the picture, giving a glimpse into the lives that were Maria and Karen.

Krista came across one that was closest to the cliff; a picture of her and her mother which was probably taken the same day as her death. Krista didn't even realize that it was taken, so Chad or her father must have taken it and given it to Stanley. It brought her back to the moment as she looked at the photo; she was hugging her mother who was lying in her hospital bed with a beautiful smile on her face. The caption read *"Reunited after so many years with her daughter, Krista."* She'd just been reunited with her mother after she disappeared for over 20 years.

She felt overwhelmed with emotions as she knelt by the picture. "I'm so glad I got to see you again, mom. I know you're still here with me."

She whispered. Just then a sparrow similar to the clay sparrows that were placed all around the garden came to rest on the marble and chirped. Krista brushed her tears away and smiled. To her, it was her mother letting her know she was still there in spirit.

"Kris!" Chad's voice jolted her back to the present. "Where's Mara?" He and William had been looking around at the different photo-embossed monuments around the area. Krista looked around, but Mara wasn't beside her. "She was just with me! Maybe she went back to the aquarium to look at the fish!" Krista tried to keep herself from panicking, taking deep breaths. After all, it was an enclosed area. Mara couldn't have wandered off far.

"Bill, you go to the left and we'll go the right and circle around. I'm sure she's here." Chad kept his voice calm, knowing that she was probably starting to worry. Krista and Chad started to work their way around the garden which was not a large area, but because of the people that were here, it was difficult to navigate. "Where is she, Chad?" Krista tried to remain calm, but her adrenaline was already going.

"She's here, Kris. Don't worry. She couldn't have gone far." Chad reassured her, but after 15 minutes of searching, and meeting back up with her father, there was still no sign of Mara. "Where could she go, Chad? She was just here!" Krista had the sensation of déjà vu, she'd been through this moment, or dreamed it. But she wasn't dreaming now as she could tell that Chad and her father were also looking for Mara. This was real.

She noticed that Chad went up to the DJ and was talking with him for a few minutes. The DJ stopped playing music for a moment.

"Sorry to interrupt the music folks, but it seems that one of our smaller guests has wandered away. Would Mara Burton please come out from her hiding place and join her parents?" Krista felt some hope, knowing that Mara would hear that if she were anywhere in the vicinity. She looked around to see if Mara appeared anywhere, but after a few minutes there was still no sign of her. The other guests began looking around for her as well. Mara had been very visible during the party and now they were concerned as well. Chad and William continued their search and other guests joined in as Chad's arm encircled her waist. "Let's go find Mara," he whispered in her ear. "Stay calm we'll find her." He knew her too well enough to keep her calm. She just nodded and took his hand. What else could they do?

Chad

He knew he needed to keep composed for his wife. He hadn't told her about the Sadie imposter yet, only that 'Sadie' might have come back to the island, but now he was more worried than ever for Mara.

The other guests had heard the message about Mara missing and the party had broken up in order to help search for her. He, Krista and William stayed together and made their way toward the cliffs. It was a quiet uncertainty that they might find Mara near the cliff after Krista's experience 7 years ago. They were coming to close to the area where Krista had found her mother's jewelry box years ago, close to the edge with only small trees and bushes between them and the drop off to the ocean below. "Mara! Mara!" But there was no answer. Where could she have gone? Unless…Chad looked at the ocean below. "NO. She's somewhere here, we'll find her!" He said out loud more to convince himself than his wife.

They could hear the other party guests calling out her name along with Stanley, joining in the search for Mara. As the dusk slowly turned into night with only stars in the clear sky, Stanley turned on the floodlights that surrounded the outside of the house. The darkness made the landscape around the property seem eerie and ominous, which drove them to hurry and find her before more time went by.

Stanley brought out with some flashlights that security had given out to the search parties. "I have an idea of where she might be. It's a long shot, but I remember when I first bought this place and Jane and Amanda were younger, they found an old tomb-like stone that was

379

carved out under a hill that they called their 'secret cave'. Maybe Mara went looking around and found it."

"An old tomb? What? Why would there be an opening like that here?" Krista didn't like the word 'tomb'.

Stanley shook his head. "It's not really a tomb. More of a structure built underneath a small hill. I think it used to be some kind of mausoleum as it appears to be a small cemetery surrounding it. I remember where it is. There were many times I found the girls there when they were young." Stanley had a frown on his face, reflecting back on their outrageous behaviors even back then. The description struck familiarity with Krista; a flash from a dream, a rock structure, gravestones. "Yes." Krista said with certainty. "She must be there."

"How do you know that Kris?" Her husband questioned her.

"I know because I dreamt it." Krista said quietly. Chad looked shocked for a moment, but didn't want to entertain any further discussion. They needed to find Mara before the temperature went down as it always did at night. There was a strong wind now and a rumble of thunder warning an upcoming thunderstorm. Stanley informed the security crew that he was going to the other side of the property. Two of the security personnel accompanied them, while the other three continued to monitor activity within the immediate area of the house.

They walked for what seemed like at least half a mile through the manicured lawn until they met up with the outer lying area of Stanley's property that probably hadn't seen a lawn mower in the past year. The overgrown grass was almost waist-high and difficult to navigate. "It shouldn't be far now!" Stanley called back to the rest of them as he led the way. The full moon had been out but dark storm clouds had blown in, and leaving them with only man-made lighting. The flashlights were a necessity now. Even then, it was difficult to navigate the deep grass. "Stan, what if Mara isn't there? We can barely see with flashlights! What if---" Chad was starting to worry that they were looking in the wrong place.

"She's here, Chad! I know she is!" Krista was surprisingly calm now, focused as if she'd been here before.

"Okay, Kris." She surprised him with her persistence. She was right. They needed to take one thing at a time. He was ready to ask how much further the site was when Stanley announced that they were there. "This is it," pointing to a bunch of overgrown trees and bushes around a stone opening that was barely visible. Chad was shocked that he'd found it. As they trudged through the taller grass the stone cave opening became noticeable. He could see why it would work as a 'secret cave' and the closer they came to it, the more sinister it appeared.

"Maybe we should have security go in first." Krista's anxiety had returned and Chad was already shaking his head. "No, if she's in there, it'll just cause more drama than we need right now. If she's in there with Sadie or whoever is involved, she'll be more likely to be honest with whatever is really going on." Chad knew that sending security officers into this situation wouldn't help. William agreed. "He's right, Kris. We need to find out who we're dealing with first."

Chad could tell that there were some grave markers amongst the long grass and then looked further. Stanley had been right; there was a stone structure with an opening; as if it were built as a mausoleum back in the 1800's. There were about a dozen old gravestone markers that were so decayed, it was difficult to read the names and the dates on some of them. He could imagine young kids that wanted to explore this cave, make up stories and have fun. He suddenly remembered that he and William had been planning to plant the necklace. "You didn't leave the necklace behind?" Chad asked.

"No, I didn't have time. Good thing, huh?" William said, wiping his brow to signal they'd dodged a huge mistake.

"Exactly. Do you still have it with you?" Chad asked. William nodded as Krista kept turning around to make sure they were with her.

The weather-worn stone was crumbling in some places on the outside with moss helping to camouflage it. It looked as though it might have served as a mausoleum or even a war bunker at one point, but there was no door so it was easily accessible once found. It was the perfect hiding place for kids with an imagination *or* an insane person that kidnapped children.

"Mara! Are you there?" Chad yelled, hoping to hear something as they struggled through the deep grass toward the opening of the cave-like structure. Krista, William and Stanley all joined in calling her name, "Mara! Let us know if you can hear us!" There was no response. They continued walking slowly into the gloomy blackness of the cave, the shadow of their flashlights creating an eerie glow around them. Krista gripped Chad's hand as they moved further into the darkness.

"Mommmyy." The voice was muffled, and faint, but it was definitely a child's voice. "Mara!" Chad and Krista answered in unison. All of them, including the security guards ran forward into the cave opening that was deceivingly longer than it appeared. The inside floor of the cave was surprisingly easy to maneuver with few fallen leaves and stones. "Mara! Where are you?" Chad shouted.

"Daddy! I'm over here!" The voice was louder than before. Chad was shaking and grasped Krista's hand who had a grip on her father's hand as well. Stanley and the security team were behind them. "Daddy, where are you?" Mara's voice sounded clearer, closer.

"I have a light with me. Tell me when you see the light!" Chad told her as he crept forward. The cave narrowed a little, so they were having to bend down so that their heads didn't hit the rock ceiling above them.

"I can see light." Mara's voice guided them until they could make out a small area that indicated the end of the cave. Chad could spot a small figure in a huddled position. "Mara! Are you okay?" He moved toward her as fast as possible to reach her with Krista and William close behind. He shined the light on Mara and then spotted a taller figure, who was standing behind her. As he came closer, Chad noticed her hands together that further infuriated him and he tried to tamp down his anger until Mara was safe.

"Hello, Chad! I'm glad you and the Princess have finally found your way here!" It sounded like Jane, but as Chad raised the flashlight up to where the voice was coming from, he recognized the pink baseball hat, the long dark hair that was like Sadie. But there was something different about her face; she was wearing no make-up, and suddenly it was obvious to him, the 'imposter'. It was Michelle! He almost lost his balance and fell backwards, but Krista was behind him and caught him.

"So Sadie was right. I knew it had to be someone conniving and crazy, so I guess I shouldn't be surprised it's you, Michelle. Just how long have you been trying to pass yourself off as Sadie?" Chad was seeing red and wanted to drag her out of the cave and throw her off the cliff just then.

" I thought I did a good job impersonating Sadie, you have to admit! You bought it! I spent a few weeks watching her and getting her silly 'readings' from her and that niece of hers. What was her name? Nadine? That's too bad about her accident." Michelle smirked. "I even got to watch her interaction with Krista and Mara when she did her whole 'voodoo' spell thing at your house. She's pretty good at it, I'll give her that!" She looked pleased with herself. "I was following her, and was able to sneak in since Princess here left the door open. I was impressed! But it was easy to replicate." Michelle spoke as though she were up for an Oscar at an awards ceremony.

Chad couldn't believe he'd been tricked into thinking she was Sadie at this point. "I did have to up my game with the make-up. I went to the best make-up artist in town and you bought it!" Michelle was enjoying his moment of humiliation to the fullest.

He just wanted Mara back and was sick of this crazy woman's psychotic rantings. "Just let Mara go. There's no reason for her to be involved in your nutty scheme."

"Not so fast, Chad. It's not just that Jane was my friend and told me about you and Princess Krista here, but she was killed because of you.

I've followed you two since the day she died and knew I'd have a chance at getting what Jane deserved; this house that she loved. And our secret cave that we used to play in when we were kids." She turned to Krista who was standing beside Chad and moving in closer to her. "You know, Princess, watching you and then Mara sleep last night gave me the inspiration I needed to see just how much this little girl means to you and this family." Michelle pulled out a small pocket knife.

Krista lunged toward Michelle trying to grab her arm, but Michelle dodged out of her reach. "Don't bother, Princess. If you haven't noticed, I have a knife. It might be small but trust me, it can do some damage. I don't want to use it, but I will if I need to." Michelle threatened as she turned to Stanley. "Mr. Ahearn, I see you joined the party tonight! How nice! I'll bet Jane would've loved for you to pay attention to her when she was alive!"

Stanley moved forward, standing protectively in front of Chad and Krista. "Let Mara go. They have nothing to do with Jane or her sister!"

"I'm willing to negotiate, Mr. Ahearn. You seem to have unlimited resources when it comes to the rest of the family, or should I say those that aren't *really* your family." Michelle seemed to grow angrier by the minute and Chad was afraid of what she might do to Mara.

"What are you suggesting, Michelle?" Stanley seemed to wear his business hat at all times, although Chad knew he had no intention of giving her anything, at least he hoped not. This woman that had worked for his agency, then pretended to be some psychic woman just to find out more information and hold his daughter for ransom made him want to strangle her. He was impressed at how calmly Stan was handling the situation.

"What I want is to have my friend, your daughter back. But since that can't happen, although this little girl seems to believe that she can see her, I want $2 million. I'll walk out of here and you'll never see or hear from me again." Michelle named her price.

Chad winced as he knew that Stanley wasn't the type to give up that kind of money. It was why he still had it! Stanley's face remained stoic, unreadable. Chad knew that if he hadn't been a director, Stanley would've made an excellent poker player. "Is that just for you, or the rest of your criminal friends promised you a share of the money?"St anley questioned her as if he were making a business deal with a production company in Hollywood.

Michelle looked confused, almost blindsided by the unexpected response. "There are no others. It's just for myself." She managed, but it was obvious she was struggling with what her next move would be.

"And why do you think you deserve two million dollars? Have you earned it? Don't try to tell me you earned it by being my daughter's childhood friend; let's not insult my intelligence with that, young lady! Money and greed go together; Money, greed and death equals more greed. Even from the other side" " Stanley's voice was stern now. Chad looked over to see one of the security guards sneaking into the cave entrance and put his finger to his lips when he made eye contact with Chad. Chad winked to let him know that he got the message that help would be on the way. Stanley was stalling.

Michelle seemed to know that she was no match for Stanley with conversation about why she was holding Mara for ransom, so she went back to her threats. "Don't tell me what I deserve and don't deserve! You don't know me! All I know is you have 1 minute to agree to the money or this little girl is headed over the cliff just like her grandmother!"

Chad's fists began to clench at the mention of Caroline and he looked at his wife who looked ready to jump over and pummel the woman. "Kris, stay calm. She still has Mara." He whispered in her ear. Stanley lost his poker face at the moment. He didn't appreciate the words about Caroline either as he moved closer toward Michelle. "Don't you dare---"

There was a sudden deafening scream that filled the cave that startled all of them, including Michelle who almost dropped her knife. Chad initially thought it was Krista who had been unstable in the past few weeks and finally came to her breaking point. But then he realized it was Mara. It became louder and the tone changed from that of a 6-year-old girl to a voice that belonged to an adult woman. The voice was much lower than Mara's child voice. She began to fight her hands being tied together, as Michelle laughed at her efforts, "Go ahead, little girl. Those are zip ties, you're fighting a losing battle."

Mara looked at her in the face and in the same strange voice said, "I don't think so bitch! It's you that's gonna lose!" She pulled her wrists apart with force as the zip ties broke. Michelle was stunned as were Chad, Krista and William. Chad realized then that "Jamie" must have returned; there was no other explanation for the voice or the superhuman strength to break those ties.

"Mara! Is that you?" Chad asked quietly, as Michelle tried to regain control over the situation by grabbling Mara's wrists, but in the process had dropped the knife that had been her only weapon. Michelle realized it seconds too late as Mara grabbed the knife and held it to Michelle's neck. "I think it's time for you to beg for something other than the money that you didn't earn, Michelle!" Michelle was suddenly shaking, her face going from a human monster to a confused victim in a matter of seconds. "What's going on? How did you....." She was unable to get out the words, as Mara pressed the small pocket knife into her neck.

"One more word and I'll cut your throat! You sure picked the lamest weapon ever! And I'm *not* Mara. I've been watching since the *real* Sadie tried to get rid of me. All because of you!" She pointed at Krista. "But I'm back! That silly necklace that Sadie used didn't last very long!. I'm back to save Mara and take back the life I deserve before *you* took it away!" She pointed at Krista.

"Is that you Jamie?" Krista asked quietly.

"You do pay attention once in a while, Krista! Yes, I'm Jamie. Also known as Jane Ahearn, but you've probably known that all along. I've been with Mara since she was born and now I have control so that no one will ever hurt her again!" The woman's voice was venomous now and Krista backed away, gripping Chad's arm. It was hard to imagine that voice coming from her daughter's little body.

"We're not trying to hurt Mara, we love her." Chad managed, although it was completely bizarre that he was speaking to his 6-year-old daughter who was yelling at him like a maniac.

"If you did, she wouldn't be in this situation now." Jamie retorted back. Chad knew there was no talking to this demon, spirit or whatever it was that had taken over Mara's body. She turned back to Michelle who was trembling by now with a knife to her neck. "It's time to get out of this cave that you think I enjoyed playing in with you when we were kids. I hated it! Get up!" Jamie's voice yelled at her. As Michelle did as she was told, Chad and the others stood aside to follow her. The security officers were on the outside of the cave, awaiting instructions, but Stanley shook his head at them and motioned for them to follow. They had no choice now. They had gone in to save Mara from who they thought was Sadie. Coming out, they had to save Mara from Jamie.

William

William followed along with the rest of the group, trying to figure out what to do to save Mara. This wasn't her! He remembered the necklace that had belonged to Karen that he was supposed to plant for 'Sadie' earlier, which was still in his jacket pocket. He nudged Chad, showing him the necklace as they walked out of the cave into the darkness that had enveloped them.

"We've got to get to her before she either kills all of us, or gets arrested or both! This isn't Mara!" William whispered. Chad nodded, as he gripped Krista's hand. "Give it to me, Bill. I'll work my way over closer to her. When I talked to Sadie earlier, she said we need to put it around her neck." William handed him the necklace, as Krista looked at her husband. "What are you going to do?" She looked at him with eyes filled with tears of despair.

" I'm going to save our daughter, Kris." He told her quietly and squeezed her hand while the other hand gripped Karen's necklace that he needed to put around her neck and hoped that it would bring Mara back. Stanley was the closest to Mara and Michelle, with the security guards near him. They were looking for a way to grab Mara before she could continue on, but she kept the knife held to Michelle's neck. Stanley began trying to talk to Mara as if he were talking to his daughter, Jane. "Jamie, I know you don't want to do this. It won't help anyone, especially this little girl. She still has a life to live. I'm sorry your life had to end as it did."

Mara's small body stopped and she whirled around with a scowl on her face. "Really? Because I don't see any memorial for my death here. All you care about is your precious Caroline and some little girl that you never even met!" Her grip on the knife near Michelle's neck became even tighter to where it was leaving blood marks from the blade.

"That's not true, Jane! You know I always tried to show you how much I cared, but you wouldn't let me. You just took off, then did some terrible things that led to your death. You were going to kill someone, so the police had no choice." Stanley wouldn't back down, as everyone else cringed feeling as though he was pushing her further. They were getting closer to the cliffs, the sound of the ocean was close as lightening lit up the sky with claps of thunder announcing the impending storm. Mara didn't say another word until they reached the top of the cliffs. She looked over at a headstone that read *"Jane Marie Ahearn: Gone but not forgotten."*

"Don't call me Jane, dad! My name is Jamie now! And this is my memorial? Are you kidding me? I was forgotten a long time ago, but I'm back and I'm here to stay!" Jamie's voice was menacing as she came closer to the cliff. "Now I can get rid of this supposed friend that said she'd help me. This is what happens when friends don't follow through." Mara's body showed the superhuman strength that had helped her break the zip ties as she managed to drag Michelle toward the cliff's edge, despite Michelle's effort to dig her heels into the ground.

"Jane! It's me! Why are you doing this?" Michelle was pleading now. She had been quietly struggling the whole walk, maybe hoping someone would be able to stop her or that it was a joke on her. Now she was realizing that Jane was really here and she was scared.

Jane turned to Michelle with a look of disgust on her face. "First of all, it's Jamie now, don't ever call me Jane again! " She retorted. "You just kidnapped someone in order to get money for yourself! How does that relate to 'remembering me?" She scoffed at Michelle. "You've used me as a platform for your own gain and trying to harm a child in the process. I think it's time for you to understand what it means to be gone." The sound of the waves crashing against the rock near the cliff combined with the thunder was terrifying. Mara's body continued to shove Michelle closer to the edge of the cliff that was only a few feet away. Michelle began to scream for help, as William had an idea that might distract Mara until Chad could get to her with the necklace.

"You do know that if you do this, if you take Mara's place, you'll be Krista's child? The person you refer to as 'Princess?' Remember, Mara's only 6 years old, so you've got a long time to be raised by a woman that you hate, **Jane**!" William had to yell over the thunder and the torrential rain that had begun to pour down.

"Then Krista and Chad will have to follow my lead won't they?" Jane's spirit was relentless, careless. Stanley nodded to the security guards to stand by near the cliff. They had been following them, undetected at Stanley's request. Now they ran toward Mara and Michelle, armed with tasers to diffuse the situation. "Don't use the taser yet! Give Chad a moment with her!" Stanley yelled out to the officers, as William nodded to Chad who had the necklace in his hand and ran forward to fasten it around Mara's neck.

"You need to come back to us Mara!" Chad yelled as she gave out a scream that was earth-shattering in Jane's adult voice.

She let go of Michelle as she grasped at her own throat, gasping and falling to the ground, Mara's body was seizing and writhing. Chad remained by Mara's side as a misty fog of light seemed to hover above her body.

Michelle tried to catch herself but she lost her footing and screamed as she began falling backwards off the edge of the cliff. She managed to grab a tree branch, and tried to get her grip with her feet. One of the officers rushed to grab her hand and pull her to safety. Michelle could only lie on the ground traumatized by the turn of events. Security radioed for back up to arrest her for kidnapping Mara, and informed them of the situation, knowing that it might take time due to the storm. The EMTs were on their way in the ambulance but there was only an urgent care center on Block Island.

"You can't do this...I want to come....back...," Jane's voice began to trail off, as Mara lay on the ground, silent, motionless. Chad was frantic and felt for a pulse on her neck, and Krista knelt down next to him, panicking, tears rolling down her face as she locked eyes with her husband. "She's still here, Kris." Chad told her softly as she grasped her small hand. "Mara, stay with us. Mommy and daddy love you," She whispered. Mara was still alive, but her eyes were closed and he kept waiting for Jane to reappear. Krista reached down and held onto the half heart necklace that had belonged to her twin sister, praying out loud that Karen could hear her; "Karen please help Mara through this. I need you to help her now." She whispered as she watched Mara's face for any sign that she could hear her. After several minutes, Mara still didn't open her eyes, although her pulse was still strong.

The Block Island rescue ambulance had arrived; one of the EMTs checked on Michelle who was not injured, and the other, who introduced himself as Scott Mercotte rushed to Mara to check on her vitals. "Her heart is nice and strong; BP is normal and oxygen is at 99%, so no worries there. Did she hit her head on anything?" He was concerned about a possible concussion because she was unconscious. Krista just shook her head, unable to speak as she sat next to Mara. Chad and William did their best to explain the situation; that Michelle had lured Mara away from the party and had held her hostage.

"That doesn't explain what happened with your daughter. Why is she lying here now? What happened?" Scott kept asking questions. Chad had hoped to avoid discussion about Jane and the involvement she'd had with Mara in the past few weeks that led to her possession of Mara this evening, but he started to explain. He expected Scott to look at him as if he was delusional, but he kept nodding his head. "My mom is a psychic, so I grew up with more knowledge of the paranormal world than most people."

Surprised and glad to hear this news, Chad asked, "What's your mom's name?"

"Sadie Mercotte. She has had a spiritual shop in Providence for years. Do you know her?" Chad's jaw dropped as he realized this was Sadie's son. No wonder the name 'Mercotte' sounded familiar.

"I do. My wife had just met with her last week and also knew your cousin." Chad told him. "I'm sorry to hear about your loss." He felt the need to express that despite Scott's focus on Mara. "Do you think you can help her? Have you seen this before?"

"I can tell that someone is there to help her, a relative that has passed." Scott closed his eyes for a moment as he held Mara's hand. "It's my sister, Karen," Krista said quietly as she continued to grasp Mara's other hand. "And my mother. I'm hoping that she's helping her too."

Chad showed him the necklace and told Scott about how Jane had left her body after he put it around her neck, and now Mara appeared to be in some kind of a coma. "Your mother had mentioned that when she came to the house last week to meet Mara. She was great help to us, told us that we needed to keep this necklace that belonged to her aunt."

"She does know what she's talking about." Scott agreed. "If you don't mind, I just want to hold the necklace for a moment. I won't take it off, but I have an idea."

"Please help her!" Krista pleaded with Scott as she put her hand on Mara's forehead. "She's so cold. That can't be a good sign." She began to panic again and Scott put his hand on hers. "Krista, I'm going to do everything I can for her." He was sincere and genuinely concerned. He turned to Chad. "Can you take her away from here for a few minutes? I need to concentrate." Chad nodded, "Of course." He went over to Krista and managed to get her over to William despite her protests about needing to stay with Mara. "He's Sadie's son, Kris. He's the best chance we have right now, so give him some space." Chad hugged her. "I trust him. We'll stand right here and watch, ok?" Krista just nodded, praying he could bring Mara back.

*   *   *   *   *

They watched as Scott closed his eyes for several minutes while holding onto the necklace and whispering words that they couldn't hear. He began running his hands above her body from head to toe and Krista suddenly noticed that several sparrows came to rest near Mara. Krista watched as they remained for several minutes, while Scott continued holding his hands an inch above her body, this time concentrating on her head. Mara's eyelids began to flutter as if they were trying to open. Chad had to remind himself to remain quiet, as he wanted to run over and talk to her. Scott fastened the necklace around Mara's neck again and sat next to her with his eyes closed. The sparrows that had been sitting near her took flight and her eyes opened. Scott looked relieved as he grasped her hand.

"Hi, Mara, welcome back." He said quietly.

"Hi. Where's my mommy and daddy?" Mara seemed confused and immediately tried to sit up, clearly having no recollection of what had happened. Chad and Krista were by her side in a second.

"We're right here, sweetheart." Krista tried not to cry, but tears of relief were pouring down her face and onto Mara as she hugged her.

"Mommy, I saw Aunt Karen. She showed me pictures of you and her when you were little and then grandma came to visit too. They told me Jamie wasn't my friend and suddenly she was gone. She's not coming back." Mara told her with certainty.

"No, she's not," Scott agreed with Mara. "I can't say that she's at peace, but she's crossed over to another place separate from this life now. She's been stuck for years, lying dormant and waiting to take full advantage of Mara's abilities, and openness to spirits. Mara just sent her back with the necklace and protection from your sister and your mother. "

Krista nodded as another sparrow came to rest on her shoulder. Tears came to her eyes as she reached out to the bird, its eyes looking directly at hers as if it was waiting for something. "You always come through for me, Karen. Thank you for being my other half." Krista said softly as she softly stroked the brown silky feathers. The sparrow chirped loudly in response and paused a few seconds before taking flight again up over the bluffs and out toward the ocean.

Epilogue

Several months had passed since that 'memorial' weekend and life had finally gotten back on track finally. Mara went back to school without any other problems, although Krista brought her to Marcy for a few more sessions to help her cope with nightmares that occurred several weeks following. Mara had very little recollection of when Jane had taken over with the exception of seeing 'Karen and Grandma', which she described as "seeing a pretty girl and lady that floated on clouds in the blue sky. I felt happy then." Mara had drawn a picture of her experience during therapy and shared it with Krista afterwards. The drawing was as she'd described, but Krista noticed a small yellow object that was on the green grass drawn on the bottom of the page. "What's that, Mara?"

"That's the heart necklace. She told me it's mine, and it will keep me safe." Mara said without blinking an eye. Krista nodded and gave a hug as they left the office. "I believe that's true, sweetheart."

William had begun to heal from Joanna's deception and finally started going out on a few dates. Joanna had recovered from her injuries, and was held at the prison without bail on kidnapping charges with intent to commit murder. She was also being charged with two counts of first degree murder after evidence led police to believe that she'd been the driver that had hit and killed Nadine as well as Estelle. Kaden had been eliminated as a suspect after police could verify that he had been at work at the time of both incidents. Joanna had called William a few times from the prison but William had refused the calls. She wrote him several letters, but he simply put them aside unopened. He wasn't ready to read them now and maybe he never would. Krista was surprised that he saved them and when asked he said "Maybe someday I'll want to read what she had to say. If I throw them away, I won't be able to."

Police caught up with Jim Eldridge, who admitted to breaking into Krista's office and allowing access to her computer, although it had been Joanna and Michelle that had done the dirty work. He plead guilty to breaking and entering as well as forgery. He was fired from the high school and is currently on probation. Krista was present at his hearing and he apologized to her. "My daughter Joanna had convinced me that your family was out to get us. Clearly I should have listened to my own intuition. I'm very sorry."

David Ackwell was also charged with kidnapping but cooperated with prosecutors to testify against Joanna. His sentencing was still pending, but he'd likely only serve a year in jail with the rest of the sentence being on probation for several years. He is currently out on bail while awaiting sentencing with a no contact order with the Burtons and Stanley Ahearn.

Michelle was charged with conspiracy to the first kidnapping of Krista and Mara as she assisted in helping to move both of them after they were knocked out with chloroform as well as transporting them to the Eldridge house on Block Island. Michelle taking Mara away against her will during the Ahearn party and holding her hostage led to another charge of kidnapping with intent to murder. She is currently still waiting her trial as she tried to claim that she was 'possessed by Jane' and had no knowledge of what she was doing. She somehow managed to make her $50,000 bail. There has a been a no contact order between Michelle and all parties involved including Krista, Chad, Mara, William and Stanley. She recently missed one of her bail hearings and now has a bench warrant for her arrest for failing to appear in court.

Amanda Ahearn was returned to prison and put in solitary confinement with 24/7 security due to her escape. After some investigation, it was discovered that Amanda had seduced one of the correctional officers to assist with her escape. Stanley called Krista a few days before Christmas to tell her that Amanda had committed suicide in prison. "She does things her way, always." Stanley told her in his usual stoic tone. "I wish things could have been different, that she'd take some responsibility for her behavior and serve the time. But admitting she was wrong was never Amanda's style." Stan had never really talked about either of his daughters with Krista before.

"I'm very sorry for your loss, Stanley. Is there anything we can do?" Krista felt awkward offering condolences, especially after everything Amanda had done. But through the drama-filled years, Stanley had always been protective of her family; emotionally and financially. She genuinely liked Stanley and considered him 'family' as did Chad and her father.

"Thank you, Krista. But no, she's at rest and its better this way. I did want to let you know that I added your family into my will. The Block Island mansion and land will be yours and starting now, you can visit anytime you like. As you know, I'm not there most of the time, so whenever you want to get away from the mainland, let me know and I'll arrange it. Start considering it your home."

Krista was shocked at his generosity. "Thank you so much, Stan. Is there going to be a service for Amanda?"

"No. She's been cremated, along with Jane's remains. I wanted them both to be together and not on the same ground as your mother. I don't want them to be part of what will be your home someday." Stan sounded melancholy now.

"You didn't need to do that, Stan. After all, Jane's grave has been there for the last 7 years. It didn't stop her from finding Mara." Krista reminded him.

"Yes, I did," Stanley insisted. "Amanda left a note." His voice wavered with unexpected emotion as he read it to Krista.

'Jane is waiting for me. Let us both go. Throw us off into the ocean beyond the bluffs.'- Amanda